The Unsired: Vampire Hunter

by Lee Duke

DORRANCE PUBLISHING CO., INC.
PITTSBURGH, PENNSYLVANIA 15222

Dorrance Publishing Co., Inc.
701 Smithfield Street
Pittsburgh, PA 15222
Visit our website at *www.dorrancebookstore.com*

ISBN: 978-1-4809-0169-8
eISBN: 978-1-4809-0439-2

This book is dedicated to my father, Patrick Hansen Duke (1944-2011), a retired police sergeant who died peacefully in his sleep in May 2011, after a nine-year battle with progressive supranuclear palsy (PSP). Though he was technically my stepfather, the close bond and long-suffering support of West Bromwich Albion Football Club we shared together meant the word "step" was never applied to our relationship. He taught me right from wrong, and how to choose the correct path, even when it wasn't the easy one. His love of reading was an inspiration to me as, first, a reader, and now as a writer. I will always regret that he missed out on this, my first novel, and like so many other people whose life he was a part of, he was my friend and I miss him.

Contents

Introduction

ampires exist, not the angst-ridden teenagers currently tugging at young girls' heartstrings as they glow in sunlight on our movie screens. Not the suave, dark-suited, European-accented men in capes, who could become mist or turn into bats or wolves, and certainly not the sex-mad schemers whose fangs click down in place of their second incisor teeth on television.

Real vampires have existed for hundreds of years, and they are more than happy to stay hidden behind this public perception. They laugh at all the Chinese whispers that over the years have developed into the legends and the myths that surround them. You see, each and every one of these false rumors keeps us ignorant of what a vampire can and can't do, what can and can't hurt them, and worst of all, these rumors allow them to walk around among us undetected.

Vampires don't fear the crucifix, they don't have a problem with garlic, apart from it having a particularly strong scent, that can interfere with them tracking their prey, and while they don't particularly like a lot of sunlight, they don't glow, explode, or burst into flames upon exposure to it. Vampires do need human blood to survive, and they do fear the stake in the heart, which immobilizes them. To kill a vampire, you need to decapitate them and or incinerate them. Just be careful in trying to kill a suspected vampire, though, as they are faster and stronger, with far keener senses than we normal humans have.

So why haven't they taken over the world then? Well, actually, they tried that way back in the 1200s. Large clans of vampires started to gather and younger vampires were sired (created) to swell the ranks of the various clans as they fought for control of the mid-European lands around Russia, and what was then a much larger Lithuania. Once the war was over, the clan leaders realized that there were too many vampires and not enough humans to feed on. With hundreds of years of experience came a certain amount of wisdom, and the vampire elders selectively culled their own victorious army. By controlling their own numbers, they could effectively allow the human population to flourish once more, and they could once again become the secret hunters who lived only in myths and legends.

The vampire clan wars decimated the human population, and the vampires almost starved themselves out of existence. However, some of the remaining humans became aware of the vampires, and they sought ways to destroy them. Most died in their attempts to fight back, but gradually, more and more people were recruited to the cause and they quickly became organized and were even quicker to learn (if they survived) from their mistakes. Soon, hunter groups were formed and villagers banded together against the threat of the vampire. The vampire elders became aware of these hunters, but, after careful consideration, chose to ignore them. After all, humans only lived around forty to fifty years, so within three generations, the vampires would once again be forgotten about, if they returned to their old, secretive ways. The vampire elders were correct, and the old tales that were passed down became greatly exaggerated and eventually bore no real truth in them; this caused the general population to foolishly consider the vampire merely a thing of fantasy.

Lucky for us, those early hunters kept journals and secretly passed their information around between them. More people have continued to learn these horrible facts for themselves by somehow surviving vampire attacks or exposure to the truth, and over the years, they too, have joined these secret organizations of hunters. Now, with global communications and munitions being as advanced as they are, the hunters are starting to have an increasing effect on the balance of power. Their one and only aim is to wipe out the vampires among us, and anyone who helps them. The hunters are not hampered by laws, lawyers, courts, and the ineffective justice systems. Their only motivation is that most powerful and destructive of human needs: the need for vengeance.

The vampires, themselves, have become lazy and comfortable in their own secrecy. They have set up their own clubs, where selected humans can become their all-too-willing companions and allow the vampires to feed on them, hoping to eventually be sired into the vampire ranks themselves. The growing problem of international people smuggling no longer just supplies sex slaves and prostitutes to the shady gangsters of the underworld, but it also unknowingly supplies victims to be fed on in vampire clubs around the world. The vampires have unlimited funds available to them, from years of investment strategies and careful manipulation of the humans around them, and they have humans aligned with them in positions of power. They are now suddenly being made aware of the extent to which the hunter organizations have grown, and they are preparing to fight back once more, in order to tip the balance in their favor.

Caught in between these two warring parties is one man. He is also driven by the need to avenge the murder of his own family and the circumstances that led him, to his own cursed existence. He is alone, he is different, he is the "unsired," one who should not exist, but does, and this is the beginning of his story…

Chapter One

Infiltration

The full moon hung low in the early morning sky, as if it were waiting for the sun to rise and send it on its way. The faint outline of some high-up clouds could be seen as they were being sped along by the steady northerly wind. The silhouette of the nearby industrial park was outlined by the lights of the main downtown area farther to the east. The view was one the tall man standing on the rooftop was now familiar with, for he'd occupied this spot for the last three nights running. How different to the views he'd seen in his early life, he thought. He remembered how the hills around his simple village and the nearby small town were untouched by man's industrial might. Then he wondered how much of the future changes he would get to see.

This morning, he would not simply be disappearing into the shadows when the sun came up; he would be making his carefully planned move. He knew that as the morning sun crept lazily past the smog and the factory smoke, he would either have taken another step toward his long sought-after revenge or, alternatively, he'd lie crumpled on the floor, finally knowing death, as did those many souls he'd sent to the reaper before him.

The chill wind swept past his neck, ruffling his shoulder-length black hair. He hardly seemed to notice the cold, despite the icy patches that lay on the ground and against the side of the exposed fire escape stairwell. His breath was not showing the same mist trail as the two security guards standing at either side of the heavily reinforced door on the street below. From his vantage point some ten floors above, he could hear their conversation quite clearly. No other traffic sounds interrupted the steady stream of chatter between them. Nor were any pedestrians braving the early hours of this cold and frosty morning, not around here anyway. Though most of the city was now cleaned up, few people ventured into this area at night unless they really needed to. Even the hobos and the junkies kept clear of this place. Tales of demons and such were spread around the brazier fires of the homeless and the dropouts, and with no one to sell their product to, the pushers had no reason to come here either.

"Man, I'll be glad when this shit detail is over…fuckin' waste of time… standin' here, freezing my ass off…I could be home, drillin' some sweet little ass of my own, just like them pale-faced motherfuckers upstairs," said the heavyset African-American man on the right side of the doorway. In between each sentence, he puffed blasts of warm breath into his hands. He then vigorously rubbed them together to try to keep the cold and numbness at bay. He wore tight, thin, patent leather gloves, with the forefinger and thumbs missing on the right hand. A line of padding was stitched across the knuckles of the gloves, and stitched onto the top of this were several layers of coarse wire.

From his rooftop vantage point, the tall man caught sight of the wire as it glinted in reflection from the nearby streetlights. He knew the glove was designed to keep his trigger finger and thumb free for both shooting and quick reloading. The knuckles were designed to maximize the damage caused by a punch targeting the eyes. The coarse wire would rip the skin and cause maximum pain and injury to the target area. The blood from the injury would then flow into the eyes and help to blind the victim to any further violence being meted out.

"You still seeing that little rich bitch Cassie?" asked his equally heavyset Caucasian accomplice, situated on the left side of the door.

"I sure am, my man. Sweet little thing can't get enough of me," the black man replied, chuckling.

"Jeez! Marlon, you are one lucky son of a bitch. I sure would like to get me someone hot and loaded like her."

Marlon turned to face his friend to gloat further. "Well, that ain't ever gonna happen with her, my friend, 'cause now she's had black, she ain't never going back, and with your tiny little needle dick, you'd need to be loaded to get any half-decent lookin' broad interested in you."

Above them, he'd held his vigil now for twenty minutes or so, waiting for them to lower their guard enough to allow him to make his move swiftly, precisely, and silently. Killing them would not be a problem, but to do so and not to raise the alarm to those inside would take something special. He sensed their relaxation as they teased each other over the size of their respective manhood. They had moved slightly closer together, jostling each other, their minds fully occupied by their banter, their guards down. In that fleeting moment, their fates were sealed.

He drew in a large breath and simply stepped off the building, falling toward them. At the halfway point of his fall, he drew his legs up into a crouching position.

His eyes were fixed on the two heads looming larger into his view as he rapidly descended. As he reached the level above them, he initiated the move he'd planned so carefully, extending his legs from their crouched position and sharply locking his knee joints at the moment of impact. His heels struck each of their heads with the force of the fall plus his stomping kick, and had a devastating effect on each of his targets. Marlon's skull was instantly shattered by the blow, which also forced the upper two vertebra of his neck in through the base of his skull. His partner fared a little better, as the kick fully tilted his head back, hyperextending his neck and shattering the upper four cervical vertebrae. Both bodies crumpled almost silently to the floor, their thick coats softening the sound, even of their hidden armaments crudely holstered beneath them. They'd had no time to realize they were under attack, let alone draw either of the large-caliber handguns or the sawn-off shotguns they each carried.

A rat scavenging through the overturned bin by the adjacent alleyway merely looked up for a second at the muffled sounds. It assessed that there was no threat to him with nothing moving by the doorway, and simply continued with his scavenging. The drop and the double stomping kicks had been executed perfectly, as had his landing. The tall man quickly scanned around for any sign of alert and noticed none; he heard the rat stop its sorting to look up for a moment then continue about its business. He allowed himself a smile; his attack had been just as he'd planned it to be. Then he steeled himself once more, ready to continue his appointed task. Rising from his crouched landing position, he took a step to the crumpled body that had been Marlon.

"No more hot and loaded young ladies for you, my friend," he said under his breath as he effortlessly lifted the limp carcass with one hand and dragged it over to the right side of the doorway again. Once there, he placed him into a sitting position, making it look as if he were merely sleeping, with his coat collar pulled up and his woolen cap holding the mush that was now the top of his head in place. Only a small trickle of blood ran from his left nostril, and the clear fluid coming out of his right ear had ceased to flow. Not enough for anyone to notice at a quick glance from the side, he judged.

Next, he returned to the other body and stripped it of its coat and baseball cap. Then he dragged the body over to the other side of the road, to the large industrial garbage bin situated on the corner of the next block. With the use of only one hand, he righted the bin and tossed the limp body into it. He threw it like a child would when discarding a rag doll it had become bored with.

The rat, now trapped inside the bin, and having a large mass of dead human dumped on him, squealed in fright and rapidly scampered up the rubbish piled at one end of the bin. Its intention was to run up and leap away to freedom, escaping from whatever had disturbed its nightly sauntering. However, as it left the edge of the bin and leapt into flight, it came to a sudden halt in midair. Its escape had been halted by a rapidly moving hand that shot out to grab it in mid-flight. The fingers of a second hand quickly snapped its mouth closed to silence the squeal.

"Sssssh! My friend, it's not you I'm after this evening," the tall man spoke with a calming voice as he gently stroked the rat's abdomen. He heard and felt the rat's heartbeat pounding, but as he stood there looking into its widened eyes and calming it with his stroking, the rat's pulse began to slow. The rat kept a fixed, wary eye on him, as the tall man scanned up and down the street and alleyway, and strained to hear any sound of an alarm being raised. "Now, away with you to somewhere else, my friend. There will be nothing here for you but ash by the morning," he added as he crouched to release the rat onto the sidewalk.

Once released, the rat instantly ran off away from its captor and squealed wildly as it went.

"Rats! Dumb little rodents," he "tut-tutted" under his breath and shook his head at the escaping animal. Next, he returned to the left side of the door and put on the coat and cap, carefully tucking his long hair beneath the cap and pulling the collar up as if to ward off the chill night air.

After no more than ten minutes, he heard them inside as they approached along the long, bare concrete floor. Their boots and weight made a silent approach impossible to one such as him. He quickly pulled out the half cigarette and lit it. As they opened the door from the inside, he bent over, faking a coughing fit, and proceeded to stub out the cigarette, bending down to dispose of the filter end in the open sewer grate at the road's edge.

"Ted! That shit is gonna be the death of you one day. You should give it up," the first man said as he exited the door and walked forward. Turning to his left, the guard commander spotted Marlon's body, apparently crouched down and sleeping. The commander frowned deeply as he walked over and kicked Marlon's outstretched leg. "And as for you, ya' lazy motherfucker, you ain't paid to sleep on the job. Get the fuck up!"

The ruse had worked perfectly, as the commander had gone over toward Marlon to discipline him, the same way he had two nights earlier. The second man had half stepped out of the doorway to get a better view of the scene, another fatal mistake.

From his crouched position over the sewer grate, the tall man spun around one hundred and eighty degrees anticlockwise, rising as he did so, and extended his left arm. The karate chop caught the man in the doorway in the middle of his exposed throat, instantly shattering his hyoid bone, crushing his larynx and severing his spinal cord. He slumped to the ground, blocking the entrance and holding the door open exactly as had been planned.

Next, the tall man took a single step forward and grabbed both sides of the guard commander's head, just as he was starting to turn to his left to see what was happening. The two hands sharply turned the head to the right, and the tall man heard the snap of the commander's neck breaking. The body went limp beneath his grip and he let it fall to the ground. He caught sight of the man's eyes, now wide and the mouth moving as if to scream and shout, but no sound was being issued and all facial movement stopped within a few seconds.

He turned again and proceeded to drag the body of the man at the door a little further inside but still kept it leaning against the door to prop it open. Then he went back outside and grabbed the other two bodies by their respective collars. Both heads rolled from side to side lifelessly as he dragged them inside the building entrance. Stepping back outside once more, he produced a large piece of red chalk and inscribed the letter "H" on the front of the door. The letter "H" was a sign to those he sought revenge on and meant that "hunters" had been here. He'd written such symbols around all routes leading to the club before he'd taken up his vantage point. The tall man knew that the signs would deter anyone else from approaching the area. There would be no others visiting the club this night. His task complete, he walked back in the open doorway and closed the door behind him.

He piled the three dead bodies against the door, and then produced a hand grenade from inside his left jacket pocket. He lifted the arm of the body on the top of the pile and placed the grenade into the armpit. Lowering the arm again, the grenade was both held in position and hidden from view. He then attached a wire to the exposed pin in the grenade and finally attached the ring at the other end of the wire to one of Marlon's fingers.

"I now pronounce all three of you married and dead. I hope you'll all be very happy together."

From the other side of his jacket, he pulled out a resealable plastic freezer bag full of brown fluid, which he carefully placed over the arm with the grenade under it. He then took off and gently placed Ted's jacket over the scene to hide his handiwork. If anyone should escape his attention in the main room above, he figured this would slow their escape through the door a little. The brown fluid was a concoction of chemicals that made up something similar to napalm. The grenade, if triggered, would spread the burning chemicals all around the entrance and make it impossible to leave that way; he planned to do the same to the basement as he left, in order to set fire to and destroy the building.

His task completed, he stood up once more and removed his black leather gloves before he brushed his suit jacket and trousers down with his hands. Straightening his tie and smoothing his hair as he looked into the cracked hallway mirror, he was satisfied that he looked how he wanted and allowed himself another smile. *So far so good*, he thought as he paused for a moment to consider his plan. Now was his last chance to turn back. Once he continued, he was in their lair, and things were going to get dangerous, a lot more dangerous. He took in a large breath, and then slowly exhaled. He nodded at his own reflection, then turned sharply and began to walk down the corridor. Whatever happened now was up to fate, and he was as ready to meet his as he would ever be.

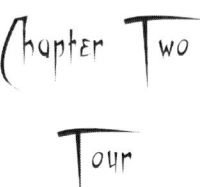

Chapter Two

Tour

He walked briskly down the corridor and turned right, to begin his ascension up the old, creaking stairwell. As he climbed, he became aware of a faint burning smell emanating from the cellar below. The smell was something familiar to him—burning human flesh had a very particular aroma that he recognized instantly. Listening carefully and smelling the various scents of the building, he proceeded to climb the stairway. As he moved up the stairs, he sprinkled a fine dust like powder behind him on the stairs; it would be most beneficial on his way out to know if someone else was still walking around in the building. As long as on his return the powder was not disturbed, he'd know he was safe; if it were disturbed, he would know by how many with their footprints revealing those details to him. At the eighth floor, he paused for a moment to walk along the corridor a short distance. He sprinkled a little more of the dust across the whole corridor, then returned to the stairs and continued up to the ninth floor.

Here were two more heavyset guards, sitting down on opposite sides of a large, wooden dining table. They were playing cards and were more wrapped up in their game than in keeping a watchful eye on the stairwell. Neither wore a jacket and their shoulder holsters were clearly visible. Each holster contained a nine millimeter automatic pistol, and on the opposite side, attached to the straps, were three additional magazines. By the side of each man, lying on the floor, was a pump-action shotgun with the shoulder brace folded away and the barrel professionally shortened rather than crudely sawn off. The effect was to make each gun a short-barreled weapon more suitable for use in the confined spaces inside a building. A bandolier full of shotgun shells lay across each of the weapons, too. As he came closer into view, the tall man, clapped his hands to remove the last of the powder from his palms. The two men took a pause from their game for a moment to give him a wary glance. He smiled back at them and one man returned to continue viewing and sorting his cards, while the other pointed down the corridor to the left.

"Head down that way, Buddy. The guy at the end will sort you out." That said, the guard returned to his hand of cards and the game once more.

The tall man gave a curt nod in the card player's direction to acknowledge him, carefully noting which side both men's holsters were on, and at which side the shotguns lay. Both, it seemed, were right handed, with holsters to the left side and both shotguns were against the wall, on one man's left and the other's right. The man on the right was a smoker; the one on the left had probably recently given up, as he was chewing on a toothpick, and empty gum wrappers littered the ashtray on his side of the table. Both smelled of coffee, but he couldn't pick up any trace of alcohol from either man.

He walked down the corridor toward a pale-looking older man, who was sitting behind an antique desk. Fooling the guards had been easy; this next customer would be something totally different. The tall man knew he could not afford a single slip up from now on, but tried to appear relaxed and confident in his walk. As he closed in on him, he noticed the pale, old man carefully watching his every move, as well as looking him up and down as if to judge him.

"Good evening, Sir. Good of you to join us this fine night. I'm afraid I don't recognize you, though. May I ask your name?" The voice of the old man was sickly smooth and patronizing, yet still carried an air of authority.

"My name is Gnislehnav, Rotciv Gnislehnav," the tall man with long, dark hair said rather arrogantly, staring down at his pale inquisitor.

For a moment, the old man at the desk froze; he was taken aback. His pale expression hardened a little as he regarded the man in front of him studiously. One of the two guards down the corridor picked up the mood change immediately and both then moved their hands almost silently to their pistols and clicked off the safety catches, ready to spring into action at the hint of any problem. The tall man's face then broke into wide smile; he almost chuckled, it seemed. Instantly, the old man's face beamed into an equally broad and knowing smile, and he did allow himself a chuckle.

"Excellent, excellent, and can we expect your old friend, Alucard, to be joining you this evening, too?" the old man cackled.

"No, I believe he lost a high-stakes game with the hunters some time ago, so it will just be me tonight," the tall man replied.

"It's been a while since my old grey matter has been so subtly tested, and while I've obviously heard of Dracula backward before, Van Helsing backward was indeed a new and original name to come up with," added the old man.

The mood broken, the two guards reapplied their safety catches and returned to their cards. Once again, the tall man had gleaned valuable information about how alert and ready for trouble they were. While they had appeared consumed by their game, not a single nuance of the theatre played out by the two men at the end of the corridor had been missed. They had both been ready to act had this small, pale, old man not signaled them with the slightest wave of his right hand as he'd started to laugh.

This vampire doorkeeper was also far sharper than any the tall man had met before. He had picked up his wordplay almost immediately and was also very subtle in his commands to his guard dogs. He would have to be careful not to tip this wily fox as to his real intentions.

"Forgive my suspicious nature, Excellency. I am head of security of my Lord Dimitri's house, and I personally check all entrants into this establishment. I also take responsibility for the behavior of the many younglings we have over here in the Americas. With your more modern dress and mannerisms, I thought for a moment you were one of them, trying to rise above his station," the pale old man explained before he stood and gave a slight bow of respect.

"Yes, I've heard these American *'vampir'* are keen to rise in our ranks, well before their time," the tall man said using the old word for vampire from his native country.

"Indeed they are, Excellency. But one can tell after a short time if they have the required breeding or not. For instance, even the younglings from your home no longer speak with the same accent as you. Your years and breeding set you apart by far," the old man stated, warming to his task of greeting someone who he thought was one of the ancient vampires of the old Eastern European countries.

"Tut! Tut! Such flattery, you embarrass me with your knowledge of my background and language, when I know so little of you," the tall man replied, beginning to probe, seeking confirmation of what he had been seeking for many years.

"I am but a humble servant, Excellency. I am called Roberto. I have served my Lord Dimitri now for some six hundred and forty-six years, and I'm glad to say, unlike some others, I did not rot in my coffin for too long before turning. My body may have been taken when I was old and failing in my human life, but my mind was ever sharp. There is not a lot that gets past me, and many a youngling has tried over the years, believe me."

The old man's guard was lowering as he continued to try to impress this visiting member of vampire royalty.

"I don't doubt it, Roberto, and by all accounts, you have served your master well over those many years. I believe the hunters have long considered you the fox that guides the wolf packs to the sheep. I have also heard tales that they have put a sizable bounty on your head, too," the tall man said. He was probing for more information, knowing that this creature was indeed a wily fox and had engineered most of Lord Dimitri's current security operations as well as the whole of the model now being used throughout North and South America. Anything he could glean from this wise old man would possibly be of use in the future. That was, of course, provided things went as planned, and he was still alive at daybreak.

"Now it is you who flatter me, my lord, and though I could spend all of darkness chatting about these matters, I would be remiss in my duties if I did not take care of your needs first. May I extend to you my master's hospitality and offer you a guided tour of the premises, Sire?" The old man stretched out his arm to indicate the way forward.

"Certainly. Well met, Roberto. And for your records, I am called Pieter, and I look forward to chatting more with you over the coming days during my stay in America."

"Nothing would please me more, my lord. I look forward to any such discussions your Excellency would care to engage in with this most humble servant." Roberto bowed once more as he led his guest forward.

Another stage complete, Pieter thought. *Here I go into the wolf's cave, led by the very fox that designed and built it. Have I really fooled him, or he I? And what awaits me in the cave?* "Long have I been waiting to explore the delights you have to offer," Pieter stated aloud to his host.

Roberto led the way to the large double doors, which slid apart as he touched a green, illuminated button mounted on the wall to the left-hand side. Once they had walked inside the small room, the panels slid silently closed behind them, blocking any chance of retreat for Pieter. After a short pause, another pair of plain, metallic panels then slid apart in front of them, opening the way into the main room. As soon as these doors opened, the sound of music and the smell of incense assaulted Pieter's ears and nose. All at once, he heard both screams of pleasure and one of obvious pain. The smell of fresh blood, even though covered by the incense, made him stagger back in sudden shock. His eyes glazed over red as if he were about to make a killing, and his fangs involuntarily extended down into place from the roof of his mouth.

The old vampire's arm suddenly shot out to support him at the shoulder. The hold was strong and firm, as well as fast. This Roberto was everything he'd feared, smart and cunning, yet also as fast and strong as any vampire Pieter had met before. He may look old and withered, but he was by far one of the most dangerous adversaries Pieter had yet faced. He knew he would need to quickly control his bloodlust and gather his wits about him if he wanted to succeed in his task.

"Intoxicating, is it not, my lord?" The older-looking man spoke proudly as he led his guest through the open doorway and into the room.

Over the next fifteen minutes or so, the old man led him around and explained the workings of the premises. He chatted about how the whole of the ninth floor had been converted into one large room with a single side room. This main area now had only the marble columns he'd installed and outer walls to support the upper floor. To separate the different areas, they had made use of drapes and soft furnishings. In so doing, they had created many small niches at the periphery of the room. The guests could then enjoy a little privacy as they played and ate their fill if they so wished. He went into great detail on the workings of the club and its various rules and etiquette.

In the center of the room, there were four girls, naked except for a blue dye splashed across their shoulders. They were chained loosely by one wrist to the center-most column. All were huddled together and their body language was that of frightened, trapped prey, awaiting the inevitable slaughter that they knew was coming. None were crying, although all showed the puffy marks of red, tear-stained eyes. They were silent, as if hoping to remain unnoticed, yet their eyes noticed everything around them and had doubtless seen many horrors since their arrival.

Another single female was chained far more uncomfortably to a column at the far end of the room. She was naked and had been daubed with red dye, splashed haphazardly over the front of her upper body. A set of leg and wrist shackles as well as an iron collar around her neck held her firmly upright against the marble. The chains at her wrists were looped around the back of the column and secured there, restricting her movements to a few inches. A high-placed hook in the column kept the metal collar she wore on a taut leash that would strangle her if she fell unconscious, and her feet only just reached the floor. The shackles at her ankles were also attached to the back of the column, giving her little more than six inches or so to move her feet, and no room to kick.

Her one eye was blackened and her lower lip split in the middle; a scab of dried blood showed the injury to be a day or two old. Her body was covered in bruises; her blonde hair, though short, was matted with dried blood and dirt. Many small incisions had been made over her arms, legs, and torso. The cuts were just deep enough to bleed, but not enough to cause too much blood loss. There were signs around each incision that a vampire had been drinking the blood as it trickled down the flesh. No vampire saliva had infected the wounds, though, so they had clotted naturally. Had a vampire licked or sucked at one of those wounds, then the anticoagulant it contained would have ensured that this poor girl would have bled to death.

Although shackled, beaten, and in a hopeless situation, the girl's look as Pieter passed her was one of both loathing and open defiance. Her spirit was not broken, not yet anyway. As he walked around the column, he noticed several short, sharp spikes were mounted into it and were pressing at the girl's back. Some of the spikes had pierced the flesh, no doubt as the poor girl had succumbed to fatigue or had been shoved back by one of her tormentors.

Elsewhere, two other naked women walked freely around the room, talking, smiling, and drinking from large goblets of red wine. His host explained how the girls were color-coded; those with blue dye on their arms and chained to the column at the center of the room were merely food to be drained and disposed of in the basement furnace. Five or six per day were brought in by various agencies and affiliated organizations. Most of their suppliers had presumed that they were being sold into slavery somewhere or forced into prostitution. No questions were ever asked and none of these girls were ever locally sourced. They were made up of mostly runaways or prostitutes or girls stupid enough to go out walking alone late at night.

The girl shackled on her own was different; sometimes specially ordered kidnap victims were brought here to be dealt with. In that case, the victim would be covered in red dye and be the sole property of the one who had paid for the kidnapping. That girl was a captured "hunter," which explained her rebellious nature and the hate rather than fear in her eyes. A youngling vampire and his clan had surprised a group of hunters and slaughtered all but this one, who had been unlucky enough to be taken alive. The youngling had advanced in stature and rank for this act, and had presented her to Lord Dimitri as a tribute.

Those without dye freely roaming were the companions, women who remained human, but were willing to have a vampire feed from them in the hope that they would one day be turned and sired by a vampire. While it was a club rule that no companions would be fed on to exsanguination, that rule only applied to the younglings and middle-order coven leaders. Any elder vampire was free to feed as he wished and also punish those he felt had insulted him, in any way he felt was appropriate.

In the north corner of the room was a young man of about twenty human years. He had no blue dye on his shoulders or arms and two female vampires were enjoying teasing him and playing with him in a mostly sexual way. Unfortunately for him, the drapes had kept him from viewing a lot of what was going on in the room around him, and his dilated pupils showed he was doped up enough to think that he was in some kind of sexual orgy with some pretty gothic girls. That would change very soon, when the vampires began to feed on him. A vampire in a blood-lust was not known for his or her gentility, and a frightened prey had plenty of adrenalin to make the blood in the deeper vessels flow faster and stronger. Where the young man felt the trappings of bondage ropes being applied and started to get excited, his obvious erection and blood flow was going to force a very quick reaction on the part of his two playmates.

Elsewhere in the room, he counted only three more male vampires, all were younglings and not adept at the slow kill favored by most of the older and senior vampires. Two were viciously chomping and slavering at the neck of a girl with blue dye across her shoulders. It was her screams that Pieter had heard when he first entered the room. While the only other vampire was happily feeding at the wrist of a companion who was willingly indulging his sexual appetite as she straddled his naked torso, the only other companion sat close to them, openly playing with herself as she watched her friend and the vampire's rising sexual frenzy.

The two companions walking around drinking wine had gone through a doorway to the left, which Roberto had explained was where the toilets and lounge rooms for the human companions were located. Since it was also their drugstore and shooting-up room, Pieter thought it unlikely that these girls would return in time to interrupt him. He had gathered all the information he required for his next move, and to delay that move much longer would likely be his undoing. It was now time to act.

Chapter Three

Immobilization

At the conclusion of the tour, the two men now stood close to the entrance door, the soft furnishings keeping them hidden from all but the naked girls chained to the central column.

"So, Lord Dimitri is away at present... Such a pity. I would very much have liked to renew our acquaintance. It has been some... How long did you say you had been in his service, Roberto?" Pieter asked thoughtfully.

"Six hundred and forty-six years, my lord," replied Roberto, his interest piqued at this coincidental revelation.

"Yes, that's it, six hundred and forty-six years. How time flies," Pieter added wistfully.

"Then you were with my lord at the time of the betrayal and the attack of the cursed hunters," the pale old man asked, surprised at such a revelation.

"Indeed I was, Roberto. It was where, like you, I became what I am." This last sentence was delivered with wild-eyed venom as Pieter's right hand struck out with incredible speed and force, driving a sharp, steel stake deep into Roberto's chest. The pale old man barely had time to register shock on his face before he slumped paralyzed to the floor. Quickly, Pieter looked around for any sign of alarm. Two of the girls in the center of the room continued to look at him with wild-eyed terror, but they remained silent. He put his finger to his lips to signal them to remain that way. One of the girls nodded, scarcely believing that she may be being rescued; the other remained still in dumb shock.

Pieter turned to the door and quickly located the master switch and key. He turned off the power and removed the key, which he then slipped into the inside pocket of his jacket before he began removing it. One of the girls at the center of the room gasped slightly as she saw what was lying beneath his outer layer, as he wore only the body of the dress shirt. The arms had been removed with the cuffs having been stitched into the jacket itself to lend the appearance he'd sought. She saw the row of wooden spikes holstered in the rear of his cummerbund and saw him start to assemble the contraption holstered beneath each armpit. Pieter continued about his task without looking at his hands. Instead, his eyes were scanning the room for any sign that his actions had been noticed. The assembly of his small crossbow was something he'd practiced regularly in both pitch blackness and in blindingly bright light. It was something he'd repeated until he felt he could do it in his sleep and, most of all, without making a mistake. Once assembled, he drew back the string and applied the safety catch. He then lifted his foot onto the chair he'd draped his jacket over and pulled up his trouser leg to reveal a number of grey-colored bolts strapped to his calf. He removed one and slotted it into position on the crossbow before laying it down on the chair. He then unfastened the strap around his ankle and reapplied the quiver of crossbow bolts to his right forearm. Once that was done, he removed the shoulder holster he'd used to hide and carry the parts of his crossbow beneath his jacket and picked up the crossbow once again. Reaching behind his back with his left hand, he withdrew one of the wooden stakes from his cummerbund. Now he was ready.

He quickly walked across to the two youngling vampires, who were still greedily sucking out the last dregs of blood from the now pale and lifeless corpse. He struck out with his left hand, catching the first vampire through the back of the chest with the wooden spike he held. Then instantly raising his right arm, he fired the crossbow bolt into the second youngling's chest, just as he raised his head in alarm at his friend's sudden slumping to the floor. He rolled back with the force of the blow and lay immobile on his back. The crossbow bolt had pierced him in the lower chest, slightly off center to his left.

Once again, Pieter paused to reload the crossbow, and scanned the room as he did so. He was meticulous in his work and kept checking for any sight or sound of alarm as he decided on the next best place to attack. Luckily, the gothic metal music favored by the vampires in the club that night was the perfect cover for what he was doing. With all the heavy drumbeats, it wasn't a problem to time his crossbow firing to coincide, so the twang was covered by the music. No alarm had been raised so far, so it was time to carefully move on. Next, he lifted his other trouser leg and removed a slim-bladed throwing knife, and walked into the area occupied by the two companions and the vampire. He calmly walked in with his hands clasped behind his back. The girl watching the couple on the couch noticed him first.

"Hey, handsome, see anything you'd like a taste of?" the girl said seductively as she pulled both her hands up to cup and offer her breasts forward to Pieter.

He noticed the bite marks on both breasts, as well as on her arms and legs. Strangely, nothing around the neck, though. He smiled and nodded at her as he stepped forward, entering further into their little alcove. The vampire and the girl on top of him both paused momentarily to check him out as he stopped and leaned against one of the columns, as if to watch their performance. They both smiled at him and then continued with their intercourse. Pieter watched them for a few minutes as the girl became more aroused, being both watched as she was being pleasured and fed on at the same time. Then when he judged the moment was right, and without a word, Pieter swiftly raised the crossbow and shot a bolt into the vampire's chest. The vampire's head slumped back, his body immobilized, while the girl, still humping up and down on him in the throes of an orgasm, failed to notice anything amiss.

The girl draped across the chair was about to scream, but Pieter swiftly cast the throwing knife at her. The blade pierced her throat, instantly stifling any cry of alarm. Her hands reached to her own throat to stifle the flow of blood mixing with the gurgling of her gasps for air. Her face showed the look of shocked alarm and confusion. Her dying thoughts were of not understanding how this could possibly happen to her; after all, she was such a good friend to the vampires.

Pieter paused for a moment to let his eyesight adjust as his eyes turned red. The smell of blood had made his nostrils flare and his teeth were once more extending, ready to feed. He shook slightly as he struggled to maintain his composure and control the bloodlust threatening to overtake him.

The girl atop the motionless vampire came out of her bliss-filled moment and saw the arrow sticking out of her vampire lover's chest. She quickly turned to see her friend as she clutched at the wound at her throat, then she screamed. It was a loud, shocking, terrified scream that echoed throughout the whole room. Pieter recovered from his bloodlust and laughed loudly, a hearty yet cruel laugh. He then stepped closer and covered her mouth with his hands, stifling her cries. She looked into his eyes, which still burned crimson in bloodlust. She had seen that look before, and in that instant, she knew that she was doomed. As she gazed into those terrible red orbs, unable to look away, she saw them widen for an instant as she felt a sudden sharp tug at her neck. After that, she felt no more as the twisting force he applied severed her spinal cord, and she slumped onto her motionless, undead lover's chest. Slowly, her sight dimmed and the lights went out. Paralyzed and unable to breathe or move, her brain starved of oxygen, she simply died. Probably a far kinder death than the many she had been witness to over the past few months, Pieter thought.

The two female vampires, on hearing the scream, both looked up from what they were doing. One had been lapping at the young man's earlobe, where she had torn out his earring; the other was fellating the man's blood-engorged penis. She was slurping on the trickle of blood escaping the small tear she'd made at his foreskin on the underside of his penis. They looked at each other and then smiled, a wicked, knowing smile. Some poor girl had just become dinner, they thought, then they laughed and their eyes glazed over in bloodlust as their fangs slid down into place once more.

They both turned to the human they had trussed up between them, and both fell on to either side of his neck. They were like wild animals now, tearing the flesh and gorging themselves on his blood. The man awoke from his dreamlike fog with the pain of the two-pronged attack; both girls paused to sit up and look him in the eye. He quickly looked from one blood-drenched maw to the other, and the horror of his situation finally dawned on him. He screamed as he saw the teeth and those terrible red eyes. His scream, though, was short lived, as the two vampires once again descended upon the streams of blood escaping from either side of his neck, and one of their hands closed his mouth in order to get a better tilt on his jaw and, with it, better access to the rich, red fluid escaping from his wound.

Pieter silently swept the net curtains away with his left hand as he entered their little alcove. His right hand was leading, the crossbow poised and ready to fire. They were so intent on their prey that neither heard him enter. The one on the left was the closest, so he shot her first, through the back and slightly to the left of the spine, a couple of inches below the level of her shoulder blade. She dropped motionless at her feeding position. The other vampire still continued to feed, oblivious to her friend's situation. Pieter slowly reloaded the crossbow, not taking his eyes off the still slavering vampire. She was now in full ravenous, uncontrolled bloodlust and feeding hungrily.

After fifteen more seconds or so, the remaining vampire stopped her feeding; the young man lay dead and motionless, the blood no longer pumping from his torn arteries and veins.

"Mmmmmh! What a high, eh? Honey? He had just enough of Mr. Brownstone to give his blood that buzz I love. Hey you! You fallen asleep?" She quizzed her friend, seeing her now motionless form. Just as she spoke, she noticed the arrow protruding from the rear of her friend's chest. In shocked awareness, she tried to turn and rise quickly. The narcotic that they had fed to their victim was now at its most potent. She fell back onto the floor in a heap of uncoordinated, flailing limbs.

Pieter slowly walked around the side of the bed to look at her, lying there struggling with the drugs in her system, trying to raise herself up. He straightened his right arm out and aimed the shaft just to the right of midline.

She saw him now for the first time; her eyes widened in total confusion at what she saw. "B-but you're one of us…why are you doing this?" There was fear and confusion in her voice.

"Oh, but I'm not one of you. I'm *unsired*, and you… You're dead." As he said his last words to her, he pulled the trigger and sent the bolt to its resting place in her cold, black heart. She slumped back onto the floor, immobile. There was an eerie silence all around now, the music having ended just after he'd fired his last bolt. He could hear the breathing and the heartbeats of the girls in the center of the room, and the one shackled to the column. All else remained quiet.

Not knowing what was going on, but fearing any noise they made would bring them to this stranger's attention, the blue-daubed girls had remained mute throughout.

Pieter walked toward the door he'd been told was the entrance to the toilets, and just as Roberto had told him, there was a lock to secure it from the outside. During certain rituals and during siring, it was necessary to herd the companions up and lock them away, Roberto had said. The toilets were far more than just that. The room had been kitted out for the comfort of the companions, as such ceremonies and occasions could last many hours. Pieter listened at the door for a moment, then reached down and flicked the latch locking the door.

As he walked back toward the main entrance, he began to remove the quill of crossbow bolts from his right forearm and took off his cummerbund with the stakes in it. Then finally, he stripped off his shirt and lay all the items carefully and neatly down on the chair with his jacket. He recovered the keys from inside his jacket pocket and then walked over to the doors. He inserted the key once more and pressed the door control button. As the doors opened, he walked through into the small room once more. He turned and looked back to the girls in the center of the room. Three sets of eyes now held his attention.

"I'll be back," he stated.

Chapter Four

Subterfuge

Pieter turned to face the closed doors in front as those to the small room closed behind him. Then as the front doors slid apart, he continued out into the corridor. The guard facing down the corridor saw him first, a tall, pale-skinned figure with long, flowing dark hair; he jealously thought how good the guy looked stripped to the waist, all lean and muscular, his movements supple and catlike. He remembered how he'd used to look something like that. That was back in his younger days in the army, when he'd been working out. Except, of course, the hair, he'd always had short, crew-cut hair, nothing that could be grabbed hold of in a fight. This guy looked like one of the men on the cover of those romantic novels his wife read. He was certainly muscular and had that strong jawline and the piercing eyes, but back in the day, he was sure he would have been able to put this guy down with his superior training and combat technique. Now, in his older years, the vampires he served always made him feel inferior, the way they arrogantly walked about the place. Knowing they would live forever and still look as good as they did today really irked him. He looked down at the coffee by his right hand and decided to take a sip, rather than watch the man approach. The other guard became aware of something catching his partner's eyes and turned to look just as Pieter approached and smiled broadly at them both.

"Hey, guys, any chance I can bum a cigarette off either of you?" he asked politely.

"Sure, here you go," said the guard on the far side of the table, who had first spotted him walking down the corridor. *Anything to get rid of the guy as soon as possible*, he thought to himself. He put the cards he held in his left hand face down on the table and reached across to his right toward the pack of Marlboros and the

Zippo lighter with the Green Beret's crest on it. He was still holding the coffee cup with his right hand when Pieter, in one swift movement, reached forward and removed the nine millimeter Beretta pistol from his now exposed shoulder holster.

Pieter flicked off the safety catch and cocked the weapon before he pulled the trigger twice, sending two bullets into the first man's chest. As he'd correctly figured, the gun was already cocked and ready for use, but rather than find that out after he'd tried to fire it, he'd gone through the motion of cocking and ejecting one cartridge just in case. This had cost him only a second in his surprise attack, and because of his speed, this still gave them no time to react. Pieter swiftly turned toward the other guard and shot him twice in the head. Both men were knocked backward to the floor by the close range and the impact of the nine millimeter bullets. The second guard had managed to get his hand onto his own weapon, but hadn't been granted enough time to remove it from the shoulder holster. Both now laid on the floor, their spilled coffee mixing with the blood flowing from the holes in their chest and head, respectively. The first guard raised his head slightly to look at the tall man and he coughed. His mouth suddenly full of blood, his breath coming in short, sharp rasps, his vision blurred, and he died before he could do anything else.

Pieter quickly recovered one of the shotguns off the floor and checked it. It was fully loaded, as he suspected it would be. He ignored the bandoliers of spare shells; he knew he would not have time to reload. The men he'd killed were all professionals and skilled in the use of their weapons, which were all at the ready. Where they were trained to expect the dreaded vampire-hunting teams, they were not expecting one whom they were protecting to attack them from within. So far, they had all been caught with their guards down and had paid the ultimate price. From now on, Pieter knew things would go differently.

He pulled out the spare magazines of nine millimeter shells each man had in their shoulder holsters and put them in his front and back pockets. He removed the second man's berretta and took out the magazine, then discarded the gun, adding the magazine to his pockets. He placed the gun he had used into the waistband at the back of his trousers, picked up the shotgun, and was about to head off down the stairs to the next level when he turned to look back at the two men he'd just killed.

"Didn't anyone ever tell you guys that coffee and smoking would be the death of you?" he quipped.

The next level was the only one where he'd detected traces of movement and sounds of occupancy, as well as the smell of coffee and sweaty men. If he'd figured it right, then the off-duty guards would be located somewhere there and maybe they were even still asleep. If they were as well trained as he surmised, he figured that they would have heard the gunshots above and would now be ready and prepared for anything that followed. Hopefully, though, they would not be expecting someone who looked like him to come knocking on the door.

Pieter jumped down the last few steps, landing catlike with the shotgun leveled and looking down the corridor to the room he sensed that the guards were accommodated inside. The corridor was empty apart from the black scuff marks on the floor leading up to one of the doors halfway down the corridor. Typical military types with their big black boots and their need to make them all shiny and new, leaving boot polish marks all the way up and down the corridors. On checking the floor around him, Pieter saw that the powder he'd spread across the floor lay undisturbed. No one had either come up or gone down the stairs, and the corridor on this particular floor had not been walked over at all.

He approached the door silently and gave it a quiet knock. After a few seconds, he heard the preparation of men and guns behind the door. He also heard the scraping of something heavy being moved back a short way from the door. The lock clicked and the door opened slightly. The muzzle of another nine millimeter pistol appeared at Pieter's waist height. Behind the pistol, a man with a handlebar moustache looked up at him from his position, crouched behind what appeared to be a large, wooden table lying on its side.

"Hunters…on the top floor," Pieter said in an urgent whisper. "They've taken out the guards at the top and are working on the doors to the club," he added nervously, looking back up at the stairwell as if checking that he'd not been overheard.

"How did you get past them then?" came the suspicious response, as the man with the moustache raised the pistol to aim it at his head.

"I was on my way back from the basement, had a body to dispose of, grabbed this from the table upstairs while they were otherwise occupied with the old guy," Pieter quickly explained, holding the shotgun out in both hands.

The man with the moustache quickly looked past the tall man down the corridor to see if anyone else was about. Satisfied that the corridor was clear and comforted by the fact that the man in front of him appeared to be one of the vampires he was paid to protect, he lowered his pistol and signaled to another guard inside to allow the door to be opened.

Pieter appreciated the technical know-how of the men inside; they had placed the table across the doorway and braced it to prevent a number of occurrences. A standard SWAT (special weapons and tactics) team would likely smash or blow the lock and charge the door in numbers while in body armor. The table braced against it would fortify the door and prevent any quick access. If subterfuge were to be used to get the door open in order to allow someone to throw a grenade or tear gas canister inside, the position of the table would prevent the low throw that was most commonly taught and used in most combat schools. The man with the moustache had positioned himself low so he could view and shoot anyone before they could adapt to his low position. Just as Pieter had surmised, they were all pros, but he still had the advantage of surprise.

Pieter saw the heavy table being slid out of the way by two other guards, and he listened carefully to the four raised heartbeats within that room. As soon as the table was clear of the door, Pieter took a large breath and then kicked the door open forcefully. In so doing, he caught the man behind the heavy wooden panel completely off guard and knocked him out of the way. Pieter fired the shotgun as he stepped into the now open doorway and sent three shells into the three men on the left side of the entrance. The man with the moustache's chest was flailed open and he slid down the back wall of the hallway, leaving a large, red smear on the paintwork. He sat there slumped down and unable to move, with a look of complete surprise on his face. The nearest of the two men had been bent over and was still pushing the table out of the way as he was caught in the left midriff. The force of the blast sent him twisting away to also collide with the back wall and slump down, all twisted limbs and agony. The final man pulling the table back had been given just enough time to look up and start to react. Pieter saw the shocked expression on his face before the shell he fired changed the appearance of his face forever. The blast almost took his head off and snapped the upper part of his body back, leaving him sprawled out on the floor, flat on his back.

The guard hit by the opening door wasn't out of the fight for long, though. The man quickly recovered from the hit that sent him reeling into a side room, and as he hit the floor, he rolled over and peeled off two shots from his pistol in the direction of the front door. They missed Pieter and splintered the heavy table his comrades had been moving out of the way. Pieter, realizing that he'd not incapacitated the man as much as he'd hoped, dived out of the way past the side room doorway and into the main living room of the apartment. As he dived, a third bullet caught him in the upper outer thigh.

Pieter's thigh stung with white heat. He rolled to the side and discarded the shotgun, pulling out the pistol from his rear waistband. He quickly checked his wound, a deep flesh wound, but the bullet had passed through. *That's why it's so painful*, he thought to himself as he pressed his hand against the wound to add pressure and stop the blood flow. He could hear the other man now, breathing heavily on the other side of the wall dividing them. Pieter calmed himself and concentrated. The man on the other side of the wall was holding his position. He was waiting for the attacker and any accomplices he had outside the apartment to make the next move. He remained low on the floor, covering both the main doorway and the entrance to the room Pieter had dived into, his pistol at the ready.

Pieter raised himself and hobbled a few steps back into the middle of the room, still resting against the right wall, using it to support himself so he could keep more weight off his injured side. Once he judged that he was far enough back to be out of immediate danger, he reached across his body and, with his left arm, he pressed his thumb against the internal wall. His nail easily pushed through the ten to twelve millimeters of plasterboard. He smiled to himself as he pointed the pistol at the position he approximated the man to be lying prone in. Pieter took a long, slow breath and then slowly exhaled as he squeezed off a whole clip of ammunition. Adjusting his aim slightly after the recoil of each shot, he peppered the lower part of the wall from close to the entrance to about seven feet back from it. Then he quickly limped to the left-hand side of the room and stayed standing tight against the left wall. He was wary of any return fire that may come through the flimsy protection the wall offered between him and the last remaining guard. No return fire came, and so Pieter concentrated on calming himself and ignoring the still burning pain at his hip. He tuned his senses in to the room and the apartment around him. The man he had shot, still leaning over the table, was no longer screaming in pain or flailing his limbs around as he desperately tried to cling to life. Pieter could no longer hear a heartbeat from any of the guards and the smell of blood was increasing. He ejected and let the empty magazine fall noisily to the floor as he reloaded the pistol once more.

He listened intently for a few more moments and heard only silence—no heavy breathing, no rapidly beating hearts…nothing. He slowly walked back the way he had come and carefully peered around the corner into the room. A young African-American man lay in position, staring at the door lifelessly, his out-stretched arm still held the gun, but his wrist was now limp and his head slumped back against the wall. A pool of blood was rapidly oozing its way around his now stationary body. Gradually, the blood was spreading across the polished wooden floors in a large, expanding pool. Pieter looked at the wall and noticed that he could only see one or two of the bullet holes down at the level of the man's legs. His adversary had been leaning tightly against the wall, so the unexpected attack and the accuracy of Pieter's shots had doubtless given him a quick death.

He put the pistol back into his waistband and winced as he moved, the burning at his hip reminding him of how good these men had been at their jobs. *They had not been good enough, though*, he thought as he began to carefully limp his way back up the stairs.

Chapter Five

Bite

As Pieter re-entered the room, he put the pistol down on the floor by the chair and calmly put his shirt back on. He grabbed the loaded crossbow from its resting place on the chair and then shuffled purposefully over to the toilet door. He flicked the latch across and swung the door open. Gingerly, he walked into the room. Not totally sure that there were only the two companions inside, despite what Roberto had told him, he locked the door from the inside, too. He felt in no shape to chase after anyone getting past him from here.

Roberto had informed Pieter that when his master came down to feed, all the companions were instructed to lock themselves away in here for their own safety; hence, the locks on both sides of the door. Lord Dimitri's raging bloodlust was a spectacle only other vampires were permitted to be present for, and no human, companion or otherwise, was ever allowed to see Lord Dimitri's face and live.

The room was spacious and plush for a toilet, it contained tables and chairs, a couch, wardrobes, a shower, and two toilet cubicles at the far end. Half of the room was expensively carpeted while the far end by the cubicles and washbasins were equally expensively tiled. The two companions lay on the carpeted floor. One was drinking red wine while the other was sucking at her wrist, on the small cut she had just made. The smell of the incense was still strong in the air even in here. Drug paraphernalia was scattered around the room at the basins and on the tables. The girl sucking at the cut had a tourniquet around her left bicep, and a syringe and needle lay close at hand.

"Hey, handsome, you come to turn me?" the one drinking the wine inquired as she saw him approach.

The other girl turned slightly and raised her head to get a look at the person her friend was talking to. As she did so, Pieter fired a crossbow bolt into her chest. She squealed in pain and clutched at the shaft of the bolt. Her eyes searched wildly from her friend's face to that of this tall, handsome intruder who had just shot her. She was looking for an answer as to why she'd been shot. Her breath came in sharp gasps, then her vision blackened and she slumped silently still.

"Oh shit! Oh shit! L-look, I'm sorry, Sir. We were only playin'. We didn't know it wasn't allowed. We were just playin'. We just wanted to be like you so much," the girl said, blurting out her excuses and thinking that she'd been caught doing something she shouldn't have been doing.

Pieter calmly walked around the room, checking the two cubicles, which were large and spacious with a toilet and bidet in each. Both were empty. The girl continued to prattle on her excuses and of how sorry she was for doing something wrong, and that she would never do such a thing again. He walked toward her again and signaled her to be quiet, then motioned for her to come towards him.

"Stand up," he instructed gruffly, when she failed to respond to his hand signal.

She stood before him, now suddenly aware of how naked and vulnerable she was. Her gaze dropped from his and one hand spread instinctively across her crotch as the other arm was placed across her breasts.

"What's your name, sweetie?" he asked.

"A-Annie-May, Sir, Annie-May Redfern," she stuttered.

"How long have you been coming to this club, young lady?" he asked very simply and straightforwardly.

"About seven months now. My friend, Julie, brought me for my birthday last year," the girl answered nervously, nodding in the direction of her slain friend.

"And how many nights have you visited the club?"

"Usually, two or three nights a week, but in all that time, I never—" She was going to start making her excuses again, but Pieter quickly raised his hand to cut her off once more.

"So I take it you've seen what goes on here, and you've seen the people who are brought here to be fed on." His calm demeanor and gentle questioning set her at ease slightly.

"Oh yes, Sir, I've seen it all. I've even stabbed two of the blue girls in the neck myself then helped by holding glasses at the arteries to collect the blood to feed the seniors in their meetings upstairs, and I've offered myself up for feedin' a whole heap of times," she said, warming to his questioning.

"So you think you would be able to feed on someone yourself?" he probed.

Oh yes, Sir. I even have the first ones picked out—my ex-boyfriend back home, he was the point guard in the school basketball team, and then there's my old best girlfriend, too. They done me wrong and deserve it, and I'm gonna pay 'em back big time," she replied rapidly, now warming to his questioning, thinking it may be leading somewhere she wanted to go.

"So what did they do to you?" he asked, intrigued by what horror someone could do that would send someone into such a warped quest for vengeance.

"They dun run off together and eloped on my prom night. They snuck around behind my back together. My boyfriend said in the note that I was dumb and he was only with me 'cause my daddy was the team's head coach, and I had a lot of money and influence, and she said I was really mean and didn't let anyone do anythin' I didn't want 'em to, and my butt was too big to be a cheerleader. Now he's a college player and she's the cheerleading captain, and I'm just the laughingstock of the town," she explained.

"Is that a Southern accent I hear there, darlin'?" he asked her, smiling.

"Yes, Sir, it is. I'm from Alabama, like in the song and the film, *Sweet Home Alabama*." She smiled broadly.

"Well then, little lady, I think it's time we got Annie-May Redfern turned into a sweet, lil' old vengeance machine, don't you?" he exclaimed brightly, putting on his best Southern accent.

"Oh yes, please, Sir. I'd be mighty grateful. Why, I'd do anythin' for you." She came in close, excited, her nakedness and her slain friend all but forgotten. She wrapped her arms around him, hugging him close and offering her neck to him.

"Just one thing, sweetie pie. Have you taken any drugs tonight, any at all, and how much wine have you drunk?" he asked, maintaining the Southern accent.

"I've only had the one glass of wine 'cause I'm the driver tonight, and I never do drugs, Sir, not so much as a puff of grass, not ever, cross my heart." She spoke with genuine conviction and her heart rate, he heard, kept constant, as did her breathing.

"Well then, suga', here we go." He leaned into her and felt her nervously hug him. As he thought about the feeding, his eyes reddened and his fangs slid down into place. He felt her wince at the first touch of his fangs as they punctured her skin. A small gasp escaped her throat, before the anesthetic properties of his saliva numbed the area. The blood began to flow freely at first, then it came in great spurts as his teeth sank deeper and pierced the artery. He sucked on the wound voraciously, his mind fully engulfed in the bloodlust. The pain in his hip spurred him on to feed, so his body could speed up the repair of his damaged flesh.

Once the initial pain wore off, the girl began to thrill at the sound and the feeling of his feasting. It was like the necking she used to do when she first started dating boys. Her hand moved up to cradle his head and hold him tight against her neck, his strong hands reaching down and around her back and effortlessly lifting her off the ground. She became aroused at his feeding and wrapped her legs around him, beginning to thrust herself against him. She started to writhe and shake in his grasp, loving the feeling of him slurping loudly at her neck. She could feel his lust for her through his clothing and she delighted in pressing herself against him, her sexual bliss rising. She began to moan loudly, encouraging his every mouthful, enjoying the sudden cold shiver she experienced. After a few minutes of writhing and moaning, it suddenly dawned on her that she was becoming tired and sleepy, and also starting to get cold.

"S-shouldn't I get some of your blood now, Sir? I'm startin' to feel real cold." A small amount of fear crept into her voice. She knew about being turned, all the companions did. The vampire would feed on them until they felt cold, then the vampire who was to sire them would cut an opening at their own wrists and allow the companion to suck out as much blood as they could. The companion would eventually faint, caused by the blood loss of the vampire continuing to feed on them. The companion would then slowly fall into a deep sleep and peacefully die as they slept, only to reawaken as a newly sired vampire. "Sir! Sir! You're taking too much. I need some of yours now. Sir, I'm getting real cold." Genuine fear now gripped her voice. She knew that some vampires could be cruel, and she had heard stories of companions in the past who had displeased some of the older vampires and had suffered as a consequence; some, she'd heard, had even died. She began to panic and struggle in his grip, but it was no use. He was far too strong and held her tightly as he drank his fill.

As she struggled and brought her hands up to try and push him away, she noticed the blood on her left hand. It was Pieter's blood from the wound at his hip. In her struggles, she'd unwittingly pushed against the bullet graze. Annie-May lifted her hand to her mouth and licked off all the blood she could find and swallowed it down. Then she began to cry and babble, asking for forgiveness and pleading for her life. Pieter was too intent on his feeding to hear what she actually said, but it was annoying, so he reached up with his right arm and brought his hand around to muzzle her as he continued to drink. Then Annie-May started to feel suddenly weak, her arms and legs grew heavy, so much so that she couldn't maintain her struggling any longer. She felt a cold sweat spread across her skin as the room began to spin. Her vision first became covered in little black spots, and then it turned completely black as she passed out.

He continued to drink for a few moments after she'd passed out, but stopped when there was no longer sufficient blood reaching the heart to be pumped around. He staggered back, letting her body flop to the floor in a heap. His bloodlust sated, he walked over to the basin and washed the remnants of her blood away from around his mouth and the small dribble from down his neck. A few small drops of blood had stained the right side of his collar, but otherwise, it had been a clean kill. He walked back to her now pale, lifeless body and kneeled beside her.

"I'm sorry for what your friends did to hurt you, but that doesn't give you the right to come here and butcher people and get turned into a vampire. Not so you can run off and extract some bloody revenge on them. I thank you for the blood, young lady. I needed it to repair myself after being shot downstairs. In twenty minutes or so, this place will be an inferno, and like all the other in here, you'll be dead and just a pile of ash. You won't feel a thing now, so consider yourself lucky. Especially compared to the poor souls you've helped feed to your vampire masters." That said, he stood up and grabbed her and her friend's bodies by an ankle each.

He dragged their bodies along the floor to the end toilet cubicle and stacked them across the seat of the toilet and bidet. He pulled the door, too, then turned and headed out of the restroom and into the main room once more.

Chapter Six

Unchained

Once inside the main room again, Pieter headed directly toward the girl chained to the column on her own. Though wracked with pain and fatigue, she saw him approach, and when he was close enough, she spat on his face.

"Thanks! Nice to meet you, too," he said, wiping the spittle away with the back of his hand.

"Go fuck yourself, you dead piece of shit!" she angrily retorted. Her face twisted into a grimace as her movement caused one of the spikes she had resting at her back to dig into her again.

"You stupid hunters are always jumping to conclusions about the color of someone's skin," he said as if reprimanding a child.

She looked at him, suddenly puzzled by both his manner and what he was saying. Since her arrival, she had not received a kind word from anyone, and most had taken great pleasure in adding to her pain every time she showed any open defiance.

"For your information, young lady, there is nothing dead about me, and I'm actually trying to help you. So unless you plan to free yourself and find your own way out of the building, I'd suggest you change your attitude. Or then again, maybe you'd like to stay here and burn with your vampire friends. Your choice," he finished, looking at her with his palms open and extended, facing toward her.

His words shocked her; she hadn't dared hope for any chance of a reprieve from her grisly fate. Was this just another vampire trick, though, some kind of ruse to help break her spirit before the inevitable, painful end?

"I'll take your sudden silence to be a yes to being freed then," Pieter added indignantly.

She watched silently as he produced a "Leatherman" tool from his pocket and opened it into a pair of pliers. He used the pliers to grip each of the hammer-flattened bolt heads on her shackles and twist them off. Then he gripped both sides of them and forced each of the shackles open using only his bare hands. *If he truly isn't a vampire, then how does he have such strength?* she reasoned silently to herself. *More importantly, if he isn't a vampire, why does he have bloodstains at his collar and that red tinge to his eyes, like only vampires get after they have recently fed on someone?*

She quickly decided to go along with this stranger for a while. She figured that even if it were a trick, she would use it as an opportunity to fight back and hurt as many of them as she could. Better to go down fighting than to be tied up and slowly tortured to death. At least that way, there was a small possibility that she might be able to effect an escape if the situation presented itself.

Once all the shackles had been released and the collar around her neck opened, she collapsed. She hadn't realized how fatigued she really was, and how much her adrenalin had been keeping her going. He caught her effortlessly and gently carried her to the nearby furniture. He laid her upon a soft couch and then tore down an expensive-looking drape, and covered her naked body with it. The warmth was comforting to her after her long ordeal.

"Okay, you rest here for a while. I'm going to go free the other girls and get them to help you while I sort out a few things around here." Pieter's tone was more matter of fact now, which only added to her confusion and suspicion.

"Why are you helping me?" she asked.

"Long story. Maybe for another time and place. Let's get out of here first. You just relax and gather your strength for the walk down the stairs," he said, resting one hand on her shoulder.

She half wanted to believe him, but her training and past experience left her with alarm bells ringing in her head. *Go along with him for the moment, but be prepared to act*, she thought to herself. She nodded her head at him and drew the drapes tighter around herself.

Pieter walked over to the girls at the center of the room. They were still not sure what to make of this pale-skinned stranger and remained frightened and hesitant.

"Where's the key to the cuffs?" he asked impassively, to no reaction. "Where are the keys?" he repeated a little more forcefully and with a tinge of impatience, miming a twisting motion with one hand directed to his other wrist.

"T-The old man was always the one to unlock anyone, when one of them chose from us," said the striking girl with cappuccino skin and blonde streaks in her shoulder-length brown hair. She was the first to come out of the shock and seemed to be gathering her senses faster than the others.

Pieter walked back over to Roberto and began to search through his pockets. After a short search, he located a key ring in one of his waistcoat pockets. He returned and proceeded to unlock each of the remaining girl's cuffs. The small blonde one was last and she recoiled at his touch. She began to struggle in frenzied hysterics, kicking and punching in all directions. Pieter realized that she had been severely traumatized by all that had occurred and was going to become a problem. He ignored her flailing arms and shrieks, and grabbed her and pulled her in close to his chest. He wrapped his arms around her and started talking to her calmly. He stroked her hair and rocked gently backward and forward. After a minute or so, she exhausted her struggles and began to calm down. He released his grip slightly, but kept his voice calm, telling her that she was all right and that the nightmare was over. Eventually, she started crying and hugged him back, though he could still feel her shaking with her head buried against his chest. The older, busty redhead and the oriental girl seemed to have recovered some of their wits about them now, and Pieter gently coerced the blonde girl into the busty redhead's arms.

"What's your name?" he asked the girl who had spoken first, looking directly at her.

"Veronica, but my friends and people who have just rescued me from a night in hell can call me Ronnie," she replied, smiling both nervously and gratefully. She stood and viewed more of the scenery around her for the first time. She was rubbing her wrists where the cuffs had dug into them.

He noticed how beautiful she was as she stood there. She was perhaps five foot seven or eight, with a well-proportioned figure and a lean and athletic physique. She had almost catlike eyes, he thought, and her movements were fluid and graceful.

She caught sight of him looking at her and nervously turned sideways, bringing her arms up to fold across her chest, suddenly aware of her nakedness.

Pieter looked away, a little embarrassed at being caught admiring her in such a way. Taking the time presented by the awkwardness of the moment, he took stock of the situation, and then once he'd settled on a plan, he turned to face her again. "Okay, girls, I'm Pieter, and I'm going to get you all out of here, but we need to get organized first. Ronnie, I need you to take another girl and look around for some clothing for you all. I also need you to get some water for that girl they had trussed up. She's in a bad way with blood loss and dehydration. One of you needs to stay with this young lady, as she's been severely traumatized, and I don't want her left alone, okay?" As he said the last part of his tasking, he gently stroked the blonde girl's head and smiled encouragingly at her.

The blonde girl seemed to relax very slightly at his words, but she was far from coming out of her shocked state. He had seen this kind of thing before and knew how the next few weeks were going to continue to be a nightmare for the poor girl. He also knew he was going to have to take her with him, and see to it that she was looked after and given the kind of care she would require. *So much for jumping in, killing all the vampires and their companions, freeing all the civilians, and getting the hell out of "Dodge,"* he thought.

He knew he shouldn't be collecting more strays, but he also knew and accepted that to do so was part of what made him the way he was. It was something he'd long since come to terms with about his own particular makeup, and he knew it was the major difference that separated him from the vampires. A vampire had no compassion and no thoughts toward anyone but their own survival and advancement. Pieter was far more human than he was vampire, and while he knew this would be seen as a weakness by his enemies, it was a weakness he had long ago come to terms with in himself. Though his own training dictated that he should finish his task and leave these girls for the authorities to assist, he knew that he could never do that, no matter what the cost. He also knew that without his help, the blonde girl would probably end up in some asylum, dosed up on drugs for the rest of her natural life. He was determined to do his best to prevent that outcome, and give her every assistance and opportunity to recover from this ordeal.

"Okay, whatever you say." Ronnie's reply brought his thoughts back to more pressing matters. "However, just one…well, two things actually," she added, trying to think of a way to ask him what was on her mind.

"What's that, Ronnie?" He looked, back giving her a knowing smile as she worked up the courage to ask the question he knew everyone he came across in this kind of situation wanted to ask. He also knew that most people were usually too scared or busy running away to actually get around to asking it. Ronnie, it seemed, was not someone afraid of getting a situation clarified. *Good for her*, he thought.

She took a swallow and held his gaze, slightly more at ease with his smile. "Well, one, are those things really dead? And, two, are you really not one of them?"

"Well, okay, one, yes and no. They're undead to start with. They're vampires, not the late-night movie variety that melt at sunrise, but the real things. Anyway, I've staked them so they are immobilized and can't hurt you anymore. What I have to do now is decapitate them, then we'll burn them as we leave this place. That way, they will be permanently dead and can never come back to bother you again. And, two…no, I'm not one of them. I'm a living, breathing person like you. However, I am slightly different than most people, but that story will have to wait until later, when we have more time. Okay?" He nodded in her direction, awaiting her response.

"Okay by me, not that I understand most of what's going on, but I am kind of glad to be alive right now, so, you know…" she said with a certain amount of relief in her voice.

"I know. Now, I have to step out for a moment. I have to get some more equipment and bring my car around to the back for our getaway. I need you to hold the fort here and keep everyone together. Can you do that for me, Ronnie?"

"Yes, I can do that for you, but if you aren't back in about fifteen minutes, then I think we should all be getting the hell out of here. Fair enough?" she replied, moving her hands to her hips in an assertive stance.

"Okay, Ronnie, fair enough. Fifteen minutes it is, but don't worry, I'll be back to get you all out, I promise." As he spoke, he looked at all the girls and held eye contact with each for a moment.

Ronnie then paused for a moment as she formulated her own plan then swung into action. "Can you stay here and look after blondie for a while?" she asked the older redheaded lady, who nodded in reply. "Then it's you and me to go poke around then," she added, looking at the oriental girl, who was already rising to join her in their search. As she brushed past Pieter, Ronnie caught his eye for a moment and added, "I really don't want to be hanging around this place any longer than I have to."

She spoke with some authority now and Pieter smiled. His instincts had told him she would do well. He couldn't help watching her walking away, her hips swaying in that graceful way. *She is some woman*, he thought.

With the Asian girl in tow, Ronnie headed off in the direction of the toilets. The older redheaded lady then stood up, and he noticed how top-heavy she was. *Someone had spent a lot of money having some serious breast augmentation*, he thought.

She turned and pulled at a nearby drape and began wrapping it around the blonde girl's shoulders, giving her a hug and speaking softly to her as she did so. Then she looked up at Pieter and extended her hand, saying, "I'm Roxanne, and thank you."

Pieter gently held her hand for a moment, then leaned forward in a bow to kiss it as he replied, "You are most welcome."

She coyly pretended to blush, while giving him a knowing smile herself. "My, aren't you a gentleman. It's been a long time since anyone's kissed my hand."

"Come now, Roxanne, I'm sure you get plenty of attention," he stated jokingly, looking wide-eyed at her obvious assets.

"Indeed I do, but not all of them are as sophisticated in their approach as you, honey," she flirtatiously replied.

Momentarily lost for words, he turned away and unintentionally ended up looking in the direction Ronnie and the oriental girl had gone.

"She's a hot one, that Ronnie…maybe too hot for you to handle," Roxanne added, thinking he was looking that way on purpose to catch another glimpse of her graceful walk.

"Really, Roxanne, I don't know what you mean. I'm old enough to be her great-great-great-grandfather," he replied mockingly.

"Yeah, well, I know sparks when I see them. And you two got sparks flying between you," she said knowingly.

She was right, and he knew it, but this was neither the time nor the place to be getting involved in anything like that. He would face up to that situation once they were all safely out of the building and it was a blazing fire in his rearview mirror. He nodded and smiled at her, then turned away and walked over to the limp body of Roberto. Checking once more to make sure he wasn't being watched by the girls, he grabbed the old vampire by the collar and dragged him out of the main room, past the sliding doors, and into the outer corridor with him.

Chapter Seven

Coercion

As the Asian girl approached the half-covered girl lying on the couch, she couldn't help noticing the bruises and the cuts covering her body. This girl had suffered a far tougher experience than she and the other girls had. She placed one hand on the girl's shoulder to gently wake her, while holding a glass of water in the other hand, ready to offer her a drink. The moment her hand touched the injured girl's shoulder, the girl awoke. Startled, she spun around and rolled off the other side of the couch. In a second, she was standing naked in a defensive position, ready to strike out at the person approaching her.

"I-I'm sorry, I didn't mean to startle you. I've brought you some water," the Asian girl said, holding forward the glass, now only half full after she'd jumped back at the shock of the injured girl's reaction.

The injured girl looked around in wild-eyed shock. It took her a couple of seconds to readjust to her current situation and realize where she was again. Once she'd gathered her wits, she relaxed a little and lowered her hands to support herself against the couch. She was still weak and felt faint after her ordeal.

"My name's Grace…I was one of the girls handcuffed to that column over there," the Asian girl said, nodding in the direction of the other two girls, still seated next to the central column. Grace offered the glass of water to the injured girl, which she warily accepted, noticing the brightly painted nails of the girl offering the drink. Her eyes still scanned the room as she drank, looking for any sign of trouble. She took a couple more mouthfuls of the water then looked up at Grace. "I'm Isabelle, but most people call me Izzy… Thank you," she said wearily. The adrenalin rush of her sudden awakening was passing very quickly now, and she struggled to support herself.

"Here, let me help you lie down again," Grace offered. "You are probably very weak from blood loss. You look very pale." She helped Izzy lie down again and covered her nakedness once more with the drape.

Izzy shivered as she pulled the drape up tightly around her shoulders and neck.

"Would you like some more water?" Grace asked.

"Yes, please. My mouth is still very dry," Izzy replied with a half smile.

"Okay. I won't be long. There's a fridge in that other room, so I'll see if I can find you some food while I'm at it." Grace turned and walked away toward the restroom once more.

As she walked across the room, she couldn't help looking around warily. She was still not comfortable in this place. Even though Pieter had said that they were all safe now, she wasn't as confident in that fact as he was. At any moment, she felt one of those silent, still bodies would leap up at her. It would be all teeth and hunger, she feared, and it would drag her back to the nightmare she'd been living for the last few days.

Upon entering the room, Grace noticed that Ronnie had been rifling through the lockers and cupboards. She had collected various items of clothing, which were now scattered on the floor in front of her, or on one of the nearby chairs. She had found and put on a short, black skirt and had a long, white blouse tied up under her breasts, keeping her midriff bare. She had rolled the sleeves up past her elbows and was struggling into a pair of calf-length black leather boots as Grace caught sight of her. Ronnie stopped what she was doing and looked up, startled at the sudden intrusion.

"Sorry, just me. Didn't mean to scare you," Grace said, seeing Ronnie jump at her sudden appearance.

"Phew! I thought you were one of those things again for a moment," Ronnie said with relief in her voice.

"I know what you mean. Just walking around this place still gives me the creeps," Grace replied with a shiver.

"You and me both. I'll be so glad to see the back of this place. I think I'll be buying the biggest crucifix I can find and wear it high on my neck for as long as I live," Ronnie stated, returning to struggling with the boots.

"I don't think that works…the crucifix, I mean," Grace offered.

"Oh! Oh well, whatever it is that you use to keep the fang people away, I'll be getting lots of it—garlic, silver, wooden stakes, and crossbows, and I'll be bathing in holy water from now on. You name it and I'll be buying it, just as soon as I get out of this place," Ronnie replied with determination in her speech.

"You can sign me up for that course, too. I'm Grace by the way."

"Glad to meet you, Grace, although I would have liked it to have been under better circumstances. How's that other girl doing?"

"She's been pretty badly beaten up and is very pale from blood loss. We will need to get her to an emergency room so they can get some fluids into her as soon as possible. Then all those cuts will need cleaning and dressing properly, and she'll need tetanus and antibiotic shots, too, in case of infection from the bites. We'll need to get checked out, too, especially where we all got those weird little cuts on our wrists by that guy earlier."

"Wow, sounds to me like someone has some medical knowledge. You a doctor or something?" Ronnie was taken aback by Grace's knowledge of what medical treatment would be required.

"No, not a doctor. I'm a third-year nursing student at Brookdale University Hospital and Medical Center in Brooklyn, New York."

"A nurse with a fancy set of nails like that?" Ronnie pointed out, noticing the light-blue, silver, and gold painted nails Grace still had on most of her fingers.

"Oh that, that's my cousin's work. She's a nail technician and helped me get ready for a special night out I went on." Grace spoke wistfully of the night all her plans went awry, when she was abducted.

"What happened?" Ronnie asked, suspecting something had gone amiss.

"Well, my boyfriend picked me up in a limo to take me out for our anniversary, and he told me that he owed some people some money and had to go pay them first. When we arrived at the place, he got out and chatted with this pale man, who then got in and…" Grace didn't finish the story. Tears welled up in her eyes and she sniffed.

"Well, no prizes for guessing how that ended, you being here and all," Ronnie stated matter-of-factly.

"Yeah, how about that? I thought he was about to propose, and ended up here instead," Grace added angrily, tears flooding out of her eyes.

"Well, you just remember that payback is a bitch. You and I are both getting out of here and we can go deal with that son of a bitch later."

Grace smiled through her tears and nodded her agreement back to Ronnie, then sat up, took a deep breath, and calmed herself before carrying on looking for clothes to wear. "How about you? What did you do before all this?" she inquired, breaking the silence and trying to get back to having a normal conversation.

"Me? I'm a stress management therapist," replied Ronnie.

"Wow! How interesting. I used to take relaxation classes in between studying for my end-of-year exams. I always wanted to study more of that New Age type of stuff," Grace said with genuine enthusiasm.

"Yeah! Well, I'd stick to your nursing if I were you. All that New Age stuff is interesting, but it doesn't pay the bills. Those busy executive types are all the same. They start with a bit of relaxation therapy and some massage, but then it becomes 'forget the relaxation therapy, just give me a massage with a happy ending,' and if you don't want to lose a client or even a group of clients and the income they generate…" Ronnie let her last sentence trail off incomplete and with a certain amount of world weariness in her voice.

"What do you mean happy ending?" asked Grace.

Ronnie mimed the action of giving a hand job.

"Oh!" exclaimed Grace, letting the conversation trail off into silence, the coin having suddenly dropped into her understanding of the situation.

"Okay, that's me all dressed ready for the party," Ronnie stated, changing the subject as she stood up, having at last struggled into the boots. "I'm going to take this dress out for our young blonde friend. I reckon it's about her size. I'll send the lady with the big boobs in, so she can look for some stuff for herself, too. Not that I think she'll fit into much of what's on offer here. You okay to look after that other girl still?"

"Yes, I'll take care of her till Pieter gets back, then hopefully, we can all get out of here," Grace confirmed with a nod and a smile.

That said, Ronnie headed out the door to the main room, carrying the small, dark-green dress she'd picked out for the blonde girl. As she entered the room, she couldn't help taking a nervous look around, fearful of what she may see. After pausing a moment to check that all was as she had left it, she strode back over toward the two girls at the central column.

Meanwhile, back in the restroom, Grace had found a pair of black pants that were only slightly too big for her, and added a purple polo neck sweater, a pair of white socks, and ankle-length, brown slip-on boots. Neither she nor Ronnie had been tempted to try on any of the dead girl's or vampire's underwear.

As she refilled the glass of water and went over to the fridge to check its contents, she noticed, sitting on top of the fridge, was one of those new palmtop computers. It was plugged into a charger on the wall. She'd seen one or two of the consultants at a hospital she'd worked as a clinical placement with similar "boys' toys." If she was right, it was not only a computer but also had both a phone and a GPS (global positioning system) built into it.

On opening the fridge, she discovered some bottles of alcoholic spirits and white wine, plus some long-life, ultra-heat treated milk, which was still okay, but nothing else that would be of use to her or her patient. She grabbed another glass and filled it with the milk, then took a few quick sips herself. She refilled the glass and headed out the door, and across to her patient with both the water and milk.

"Here we go, got you some more water and some ultra-heat treated milk that doesn't taste the best, but will be good for you," Grace said brightly.

"Thanks, Grace," Izzy said, now fully awake and somewhat more recovered from her ordeal.

"You're welcome," replied Grace with her well-practiced bedside manner.

"Where did that guy who got me down go to?" Izzy asked as nonchalantly as she could.

"Oh Pieter, he's gone to get some more equipment he needs, and to bring his car around for us. He said he'd be back in about fifteen minutes," Grace stated matter-of-factly.

"Okay... How long ago did he leave?" Izzy probed.

"Probably about five minutes or so by now," Grace answered after a moment's thought.

Izzy drank both the water and the milk while she looked around the room, taking stock of the situation. She needed to get a weapon from somewhere and she needed to be prepared for the pale man's return. As she looked slightly behind to her right, between the hanging drapes, she caught sight of the girl in the chair. She was slumped down, head rolled off to the right, and a silver throwing knife handle was visible, protruding from the front of her neck. "Grace, I need to ask you to do something for me," Izzy said seriously, holding eye contact with the Asian girl.

"What do you want me to do?" Grace replied, dread creeping into her voice.

"I need you to go over there and pull that knife out of that dead girl's neck, and bring it to me," Izzy stated, keeping her voice low and even, maintaining eye contact with the now wide-eyed girl.

A look of horror came over Grace's face. She cast a glance over Izzy's right shoulder, in the direction she had indicated. She saw the slumped body with the knife protruding from the neck wound. She looked back at Izzy, and was just about to plead her case for not going over there when Izzy raised her hand to stop her from speaking.

"Look, I know it's not a pretty sight, but I need you to do this for me. That guy will be back soon and there's no telling what he'll do when he does. Look at me, Grace. You have to do this," Izzy insisted.

The Asian girl stood hesitantly looking around, trying to find an excuse not to go into that horror-filled alcove.

"What do you do for a living?" Izzy asked calmly.

"I-I'm a student nurse," Grace replied, glad of the change of topic.

"Good, then there's nothing in there you aren't familiar with. My mother always told me that nursing was nothing but blood, shit, and piss. You can do this, Grace. You just walk over there and pull that knife out. Just like it's a surgical instrument left in a body in the morgue," Izzy stated with as much encouragement as she could.

Grace took a deep breath, looking once more at the body she was to approach. Then she looked back at Izzy, who nodded at her. "Okay, here goes," she whispered under her breath as she turned and took her first step toward the nightmare scene she would be remembering for the rest of her life. She brushed away the drapery and walked forward tentatively into the alcove they had created. Immediately, she caught sight of the two bodies slumped on the bed. The male vampire's eyes were wide in shock and bright red in the arrested state of bloodlust. The look of that face and the eyes made her shiver again. Stepping around the bed and toward the girl slumped in the chair, she noticed the blood on the floor. A small pool of blood had dribbled from the wrist of the girl on top of the vampire. As she'd slumped forward in death, her arm had fallen limply off the side of the bed and continued to bleed due to the anticoagulant in the vampire's saliva.

This blood had joined with a much larger pool of crimson that had escaped the girl in the chair's neck. She had obviously attempted to pull the knife from her throat. *Probably to breathe*, Grace thought, seeing the position of the flat instrument. The poor girl had only succeeded in making a wider cut and had allowed more blood to escape, some of it into her lungs, to choke her. The blood had streamed over her shoulders, down the insides of her arms, and around and between her breasts. It had pooled around the seat of the chair where the weight of her body had compressed the red leather cushion. Then it had gathered and flowed over at either side onto the polished wooden floor. A pool of blood now surrounded the chair and Grace was forced to tiptoe through it to get within arm's reach of the knife.

The blood was both sticky and slippery, and Grace almost tumbled at one point. She steadied herself by holding onto one of the arms of the chair. Reaching forward, she grabbed the knife. It was tacky and had a rough surface where the girl's hands had smeared the now congealed and dried blood on it. She wiggled it from side to side, and as it came free, she almost lost her balance again on the slippery floor. Grace then wasted no time in walking quickly out of the alcove, drawing the curtains across behind her. "I've got it," she said, somewhat relieved, as she approached Izzy again.

"Good girl, Gracie. Well done," Izzy replied, holding her hand out to receive the knife.

Without another word, Grace handed her the knife and began wiping her hands clean on the fabric seat of a nearby chair. She was glad to be rid of the sticky instrument of death.

Izzy examined it for a moment then tested its balance. *Not bad*, she thought. *Enough weight to gather a fair amount of momentum and penetration upon throwing, and perfect midline balance.* The double-sided blades were exceedingly sharp and some telltale scratches along the flat sides showed that the knife had been well used and regularly sharpened. Now Izzy had a weapon, something with which to resist and fight back. She felt better already. No more helplessness and shackles. Now she felt like a hunter again.

Chapter Eight

Basement

Pieter headed along the corridor, dragging the still paralyzed form of Roberto with him. As he reached the two guards he'd dealt with earlier, he paused and released his hold on Roberto, hearing the old vampire's head thump as it hit the floor. Since he was going to have to lead the girls back out this way, he didn't want them confronted by the sight of two more dead bodies. Especially that poor blonde girl, she was going to have enough trouble dealing with what she'd already seen. He grabbed the nearest of the two guards and heaved his body up and over the balustrade to fall to the basement below. The second body fell awkwardly and bounced from side to side between the stairwells, twisting and tumbling wickedly as it fell.

"Ouch! That's gotta hurt. Sorry!" he called down after the flying corpse, chuckling at his own sick sense of humor. Then he grabbed Roberto's collar once more and turned down the stairs, dragging the limp form behind him and bouncing the heels down each flight of stairs.

On reaching the basement, Pieter propped the old vampire against the wall as he dealt with the locks on the door to the outside. Once all the bolts were undone, he used the keys he'd found on Roberto and unlocked the door. He carefully exited the building and quickly scanned the street for any signs or sounds of movement. Detecting nothing amiss, he proceeded quickly down the street and around the corner, then around another corner to where he had left his car. He'd parked the four-wheel drive in an alleyway and covered it with a large tarpaulin, so as not to draw any attention to its shiny, black exterior.

He opened the doors remotely as he approached and quickly removed the tarpaulin, which he rapidly folded and threw into the back of the vehicle. Once inside, he started the engine and used the touch screen to activate his phone and make a call. As he gunned the engine out of the alley, he heard the ringing tones start on his call. At the third ring, the phone clicked and a male voice answered.

"Hello, Pieter. How did it go?" the voice inquired.

"Almost exactly to plan, Jurgen. I expect to be home within a couple of hours, but can you let Mechtild know I'm bringing some guests home with me?" Pieter answered.

"More strays, I take it," came Jurgen's deadpan response.

"Yes, Jurgen, more strays," Pieter replied, smiling at the other voice's expected response.

"Long or short stay, Pieter?"

"One looks like a long stay, the other four are probably short stays, certainly the one who's a hunter will be for a very short stay," Pieter said, chuckling to himself, expecting his last sentence to elicit a less-than-calm response from Jurgen.

"A *hunter, you say*?! Are you quite mad, Pieter?" came Jurgen's predictably loud response.

"Oh, Jurgen, don't be like that. Where's your sense of adventure? Look, she's hurt. She's been tortured and she has no idea where she is. They captured her interstate somewhere and brought her here to kill her. We'll patch her up, drug her, and then drop her off somewhere for her friends to pick her up," replied Pieter, outlining his plan.

"You be careful, don't trust her for a minute, and watch your back. The last thing you need is a hunter getting to know anything about you." Jurgen's voice gave away his concern.

"Hey! Who raised who here?" Pieter asked jokingly.

"Pieter, you may well be six hundred plus years of age, but sometimes, you act like an immature twenty-year-old."

"Okay, okay, I'll be careful. I promise. I'll phone again when I'm a couple of minutes away," Pieter responded more seriously.

"Roger that, we'll be ready," said Jurgen.

With that, Pieter pressed the touch screen to end the conversation just as he pulled up at the rear of the building. Exiting the vehicle, he went around to the rear and swung open the door. He pulled out a large canvas bag from under the tarpaulin and swung the door closed again, before he stepped away and pressed the remote control to lock the doors as he went back inside.

The basement was hot and slightly smoky, mainly due to the old furnace that they kept running there. Not only did it supply heat to the whole building but also came in handy for disposing of the blood-drained bodies. Pieter noticed that it was kept running by a gas supply, but also had some solid fuel available in the form of coal and wooden blocks. As he opened the furnace door, he noticed how large it was inside. One could easily throw in a whole body or even two, and judging by the ash built up inside, more than one body had found its resting place in the embers here recently.

He grabbed Roberto once more and laid him out on the floor, and then opened the large canvas bag he'd brought in from the car. He pulled out a large plastic body bag from the top and placed it beside Roberto. Next, he lifted out two two-liter bottles of water and stood them up next to Roberto's head. Then he pulled out a large, wooden handled torch with a large wad of material wound around its one end. He placed the wadding-covered end of the torch into the edge of the furnace and twisted it as it caught fire. He left it sitting on the edge, ready for when he needed it. Finally, he reached into the bag and removed a large pair of scissors and a saw.

Using the scissors, Pieter proceeded to cut away Roberto's clothing high on his arms and legs, pulling the material out of the way down each of the respective limbs. Then he grabbed some of the blocks of wood to be used in the furnace and placed them beneath Roberto's shoulder and midway down his upper arm. Next, he took the saw and swiftly drew it back and forth on the old vampire's upper arm, just below the neck of the humerus. The saw was razor sharp and swiftly tore apart the flesh, and made short work of the bone within.

Very little blood spilled, considering the extent of the wound, as vampires tended not to bleed, Pieter knew, especially when their hearts were paralyzed by a crossbow bolt or a stake of some kind. Pieter reached up to grab the burning torch and used it to seal the stump on the old vampire. The stench of the burning vampire flesh was distasteful to say the least. It was worse than that of a rotting animal being dumped on an open fire and almost made Pieter sick. He swallowed some of the water and then poured some onto the still smoking flesh to cool it down. He swallowed down his nausea as he continued the grisly task of removing all the old vampire's arms and legs and sealing each wound.

Once the task was completed, he removed his sleeveless shirt and used it to wipe his face and hands before he tossed it into the furnace, along with the torch and the arms and legs that his makeshift surgery had removed from Roberto. Walking back to the stairwell, he grabbed an arm of the body of the second guard he'd tossed over the balustrade. He felt the ends of the broken bones rub against each other as he pulled him off his colleague. He really was in a mess, with his limbs all twisted around and about-face. The first guard was relatively unharmed, except for the small bullet holes in his head and the larger exit wound that had removed the back of his skull. Taking each one by the collar, Pieter dragged them along to the furnace, where he heaved them through the opening. He then closed the furnace door and pushed the latch into position.

Lifting Roberto's torso by the scruff of the neck once more, he inserted it into the plastic body bag and zipped it up. Opening the large canvas bag once more, he slid the body bag inside it, folding up the lower flap of plastic and stuffing it all inside, too. He tossed in the scissors and then sealed up the bag using the large zip. He took one last drink of water from the still half-full second bottle, splashing some on his face, and then tossed it away as he had done the first. Grabbing the bag by the handles, he lifted it up and walked back out to the car. First checking the coast was clear once more, he unlocked the doors with the remote and proceeded to stow the bag away in the back of the car beneath the tarpaulin. He grabbed a pale-grey sweatshirt from the back of the wagon and quickly put it on, rolling the sleeves up past his elbows.

He checked his watch and found that he was at the fourteen-minute mark. *Not bad*, he thought as he grabbed the saw and began to race up the stairs. Now all he had to do was pop in to check on the girls' progress, lop off a few vampire heads, quickly check out the room upstairs for any useful information, and then torch the building. Once he'd completed all that, he would be on his way home. *Piece of cake*, he thought.

Chapter Nine

Contact

"Okay, have you seen a phone anywhere? And are there any more clothes in that room I can put on?" Izzy asked Grace.

"There's one of those palm computer/phone things in that room on charge, and there are some more clothes on the floor in there, too."

"Great. Can you give me a hand? I'm still feeling a bit weak."

"Sure," Grace responded. Anything that didn't involve another weapon-gathering chore was fine by her.

The two girls made their way across to the toilet/lounge, and just as they were about to enter, the door opened and Roxanne emerged. The older woman was wearing a big, black, knee-length fur coat tied up with a belt at the waist and a pair of Dr. Marten's boots. She didn't appear to have found anything else to fit her and she was showing even more cleavage than she probably intended.

"This is some kind of fashion statement we're all making, isn't it?" Roxanne said as she stepped slightly to the side, holding the door open so that the other two could enter unhindered.

"It sure is," Grace replied, joining in on the obvious jest at their current clothing predicament.

Izzy gave her a stern look. She was still in no mood to jest about this situation, and this stupid old woman obviously hadn't got a clue about how serious their current predicament remained.

"I'll leave you two to it then," Roxanne said, making a rapid exit. She had immediately picked up on the barely disguised hostility being aimed at her by the injured girl's look. She'd seen that look too many times before not to recognize it.

Having spent years on the road going from town to town, performing what she called her "burlesque act," she'd had many such glances from the so-called respectable women of each town. So she headed back toward the central column to help Ronnie get the traumatized blonde girl dressed.

Back inside the toilet/lounge room, Grace pointed toward the palm computer as she sat Izzy down on a nearby chair. "See? There it is. I'll grab it for you." She grabbed the device, pulled out the power cord, and quickly returned to Izzy with it.

Izzy almost snatched it out of her hands, then she quickly opened it and got to work on fathoming out how it worked.

"I'll start looking for something for you to wear," Grace said as she began sifting through all the remaining clothes.

It didn't take Izzy long to get into the telephone system. Luckily, it was turned on and hadn't got any security features activated on it to prevent any unauthorized use. She quickly keyed in a number she knew from memory and hit the dial button. After three or four seconds, the phone at the other end began to ring. She nervously tapped her feet between the ringing tones. One ring… Two rings… Three rings… Four rings.

"Come on, come on, answer it. Don't go to message bank," Izzy muttered under her breath, her agitation growing with each unanswered ring. She was rocking backward and forward in her chair now, as well as tapping her feet nervously.

On the eighth ring, the phone clicked, and after an agonizing second of waiting, a groggy voice at the other end answered, "Hello."

"Hello, Martin. It's Izzy. I'm alive," she blurted out, her words in quick succession, almost overcome with emotion, and the tears welling in her eyes.

The voice at the other end was silent for a moment as the man tried to wake himself and grasp what had just been said. "Izzy! Oh my God, is it really you? I… We thought you were…" The voice trailed off, not wanting to say out loud what he had feared.

"I'm okay, Martin. A few bruises and cuts, but I'm alive."

"My God, where are you? What happened—?" Martin started to ask.

Izzy cut him off and started giving him instructions, "No time for that now. I need help and fast. I don't know where I am, but I've got one of those palm computers here and it's got the GPS system on it. I need you to talk me through how to use it."

Over the next few minutes, Martin and Izzy swapped information and instructions. Grace kept busy looking through the clothes for something she could offer to Izzy. Then Izzy stood up and walked over to the window at the end of the room. The window was painted over to prevent any kind of view inside the room; it was also securely padlocked. Izzy opened the fridge and grabbed a bottle of spirits. Holding the neck of the bottle, she swung it against the window and smashed the bottom pane of glass. She then used the bottle to chip away at the sharp edges hanging in the frame, leaving a hole big enough for her to easily put her hand through.

She finished her conversation with Martin and then reconnected the power cord to the palm computer, that done, she reached out through the broken window and placed the computer on the outside window frame. Martin, being the total gizmo nerd that he was, had been able to talk her through the use of the GPS system. Now all she had to do was localize her position and send him the coordinates off the phone; he would then be able to mobilize the nearest hunter unit to aid her. As she had looked out of the broken window, she had seen the distant city lights and the industrial area, so she figured that she was in a major city. Every major city in the United States and Canada had a hunter unit, so she knew it was only a matter of time before help arrived. All she had to do was get her location, and then stay here and stay alive long enough to be rescued.

After a minute or so, Izzy retrieved the palm computer from the ledge and read off the location and street name on the display map. She phoned Martin back again, and this time, the phone was answered on the second ring. She relayed the information, and then ended the conversation and hung up the phone.

That done, she returned to the carpeted end of the room to see what clothing Grace had managed to sort out for her. A pair of skinny leg black jeans and a "Heaven and Hell" tour T-shirt were the only clothing she could use. She used the knife to slit the outside seams on the lower parts of the legs to stop them chafing at her cuts and scabs. She put on a pair of black canvas baseball boots that were too big for her, but with only stiletto heels as an alternative, they were by far the better choice.

"Okay, Grace, we need to have a good look around for anything else we can use," Izzy stated authoritatively.

Grace nodded and set to opening cupboards and searching through them. Where Grace was careful and slow in her searching, Izzy was like a bull in a china shop. She opened doors and heaved any and all contents out onto the floor to be examined.

"What am I looking for, Izzy?" Grace asked as she saw the carnage Izzy was leaving in her wake.

"Anything we can use as a weapon—knives and anything else sharp," Izzy answered, barely stopping in her search to explain.

The two girls continued the rest of the search in silence, finding only a short cheese knife for all their efforts. Then Grace spotted a pool of blood creeping along the floor from the end cubicle.

"Do you think there may be something in there?" she asked worriedly, not wanting to be the one to explore the cubicle.

"Could be…I'll check it out," Izzy replied, sensing Grace's reluctance to do so.

As Izzy pushed the door open, she caught sight of the two bodies slumped over the seat and bidet. She approached them and pulled the top body off the other, letting it fall to the floor with a loud slap into the puddle of blood. She saw that the girl had a bite mark on her neck, and was pale from being drained of blood. She recognized her as the companion who had repeatedly come up to her and punched her in the face and stomach, laughing and teasing her. She was not sorry to see her meet a sticky end like this.

The other girl, Izzy saw, had been shot with a crossbow bolt in the chest. *But why?* she puzzled. This girl was no vampire. She had a tan for a start and the eyes staring blankly at the ceiling were blue. Izzy pondered the scene for a moment, then reached out, gripped the shaft of the crossbow bolt, and pulled it out. As she did so, she heard a gasp from Grace, who had crept up to a nervous viewing position by the open door.

"Won't she come back to life if you pull that out?" Grace asked nervously.

"No. It's all right, Grace. She wasn't a vampire. She was just one of those companion bitches," Izzy stated with barely concealed contempt.

"So how does that work with the stakes and the vampires then? Pieter said he still had to cut off their heads and burn them to stop them from coming back," Grace said, her inquisitive mind getting the better of her fear and revulsion.

Izzy walked across to the basin and began washing the blood from both the crossbow bolt and the throwing knife, then she gave a quick explanation of what she understood about vampire lore. She told Grace how a vampire, once staked through the heart, didn't die, but was incapacitated and unable to move voluntarily. If left that way in a coffin, then the body would eventually decompose and the vampire would die. However, the decomposition would take months or years rather than the hours and weeks a human body takes to rot.

Should the stake be removed after only a short period of time, the vampire could recover, the recovery being dependent upon the amount of time the stake had prevented the vampire's heart from pumping, and if the vampire was able to feed and speed up his or her recovery process. Indeed, if able to feed, a vampire was able to recover from almost all injuries he could suffer at a far more rapid rate than any human. The only sure way to truly slay a vampire was to decapitate them and then burn their remains to ash, thereby severing the link between the brain and the heart, and destroying anything that could possibly be revived.

At the conclusion of her explanation, Izzy slotted the crossbow bolt into the waistband at the back of her jeans, covering it with the baggy T-shirt. She bent down and slipped the throwing knife into her right boot. Then she looked at Grace and held her gaze for a moment.

"Look, Grace, I know this guy, Pieter, has saved us all from a pretty horrific situation, but I don't trust him," Izzy stated.

"But—" Grace was about to protest when Izzy cut her off.

"Hear me out, Grace," Izzy said, raising her hand. "Look, that girl in there was fed on by a vampire and he was the only one to come in here after them. When he came out, he had blood on his collar and his eyes still had a red tinge to them. Like a vampire who has just fed. He opened my shackles with his bare hands; no human has that strength. Believe me, Grace, I know what I'm talking about. I've been hunting these things all my life. He's a vampire."

"Then why did he save us?"

"I don't know. It's either some kind of trick to prolong the pleasure of hunting us or it's some kind of vampire clan war. Either way, we are still in a lot of trouble. And we have to be ready to act if we want to get out of here alive. My people are on their way, but it will take them time to get here. I need to know I can rely on you when the time comes to make a move. Can I, Grace? Can I rely on you?" Izzy asked, looking directly into Grace's eyes and holding her attention.

"Well, you seem to know what you are on about so… Yes, but how much use will I be? I don't know. I'm not much of an action girl. I'm more of a studying girl."

"Not to worry, Grace. You just keep following my lead and I'll do my best to get us both out of here alive," Izzy said, placing both her hands on Grace's shoulders.

"Okay, thanks, Izzy," Grace replied.

"Here, take this. It's not a great weapon, but it's something." Izzy handed her the cheese knife they had found.

Grace took the knife and slipped it into her right boot, copying the way Izzy had stored the throwing knife. "What about the other girls, though?"

"They will just have to fall in with us or risk finding out that Pieter is not who they should be trusting. I don't have the time or energy to explain everything to them, too. Sorry, Grace, but it's the fortunes of war. We are going to be flat out trying to get away ourselves," Izzy explained. She was now watching for Grace's reaction to the cold, hard facts she had just delivered. She had already considered her options carefully and had made her choice of partner. The old girl with the big chest was going to be way too slow, and the traumatized blonde would be an even worse choice, who would do nothing but slow her down. The girl they called Ronnie would have been a good option, but she was already involved in looking after the blonde, and seemed to have clicked on some level with this vampire Pieter. Grace, she figured, was just a little bit slower than she was in a chase, and she did as she was told. If Izzy was going to make it out of this situation, she knew that certain sacrifices might be necessary. Those sacrifices may mean Grace, too. They would be tough choices to make, but she knew she could make them without hesitation if she had to.

"Okay, whatever you say, Izzy," Grace replied.

"Good girl, Grace. Now, let's go see what's going on in the other room," Izzy said, leading the way back to the main room.

Chapter Ten

Revelation

A s he re-entered the room, Pieter saw Ronnie and Roxanne look up in shock from helping the blonde girl into a green dress. He waved and smiled at them, and they relaxed and returned to their task once more. Both exchanged looks of relief that it was Pieter who had returned. His grey sweatshirt had momentarily confused and panicked them. The poor blonde girl they were attempting to help showed no emotion and was almost like a limp rag doll between the two of them. Pieter knew that she was not in a happy place right now and wouldn't be for some time. As he approached, he looked around the room for the other two girls. With no sign of them, he decided to ask where they were.

"Where are the other two?" he said, a little worriedly. He was suddenly thinking about what Jurgen had said about the hunter and not trusting her.

"Oh, Grace helped the chained-up girl into that other room to sort out some clothes," replied Ronnie.

"She's up and walking around okay now?" Pieter probed.

"Yeah, she's got her whole attitude back pretty quickly," added Roxanne with barely disguised distaste for the attitude Izzy had cast her way.

Pieter smiled. Obviously, Roxanne and the hunter had already had one of those subtle little cat fights women seemed prone to. *Okay*, he thought, *at least I know where she is now*. Changing the subject, he looked at the girls and nodded toward the blonde-haired girl as he asked in lowered tones, "How's she doing?"

"She's doing okay. Ole Roxy is looking after her, and with a bit of TLC (tender loving care), she's gonna be just fine," Roxanne answered, giving the blonde girl a gentle hug.

Pieter caught sight of Ronnie shaking her head, confirming what he sensed that the blonde girl was not in any way okay. "Okay, I've got some rather grisly work to do. I'll try to do it out of line of sight. Will you guys be ready to move out when I'm finished?" he asked, knowing the answer to follow.

"Can't be soon enough for me," replied Ronnie.

"Amen to that," added Roxanne.

"Be as quick as I can." Saying that, Pieter headed for the first alcove he'd visited and the two youngling vampires. He pulled the vampires into position on the floor and took a quick look to make sure that the girls were unable to view what he was up to. No point in traumatizing them any more than they had been already. He wasted no time in placing the saw to each of their necks, and after a dozen or so backward and forward movements to each one, the heads were disconnected from the bodies, and he moved on to the next alcove.

He was careful not to slip on the floor with its large puddle of semi-congealed blood. Moving swiftly, but carefully, around the chair, past the companion he'd slain, he took in the sight of her and immediately bristled at the view. His knife was missing. There was only one person he could think of who would have done such a thing—the hunter.

Just then, the door to the toilet/lounge room opened and he saw first the hunter and then the Asian girl enter the main room once more. The hunter looked a little better, though still pale and tired. Jurgen's warning was nagging at the back of his mind now, and as he looked, the hunter seemed to stagger a little, quickly aided by her Asian accomplice.

Suddenly, Pieter remembered that his jacket, crossbow, and the gun he'd acquired were on that side of the room. Rather than leave them there to be found by the hunter, he figured he should reclaim them himself. The thought of Jurgen's wrath if he let the hunter use his own weapons on him brought a smile to his face as he walked across the room and retrieved the items. He put the gun into the outside pocket and wrapped the crossbow and its holster inside the folded jacket. He then carried the whole bundle back across the room to the second alcove once more.

As Izzy and Grace emerged from the other room, Izzy caught her foot on the carpet edging and almost fell. Grace quickly lent her a helping hand, thinking that she'd fainted. The two girls then slowly started walking across to the middle of the room and the other group of girls. They saw Pieter walk across the room in front of them and stop at a chair by the wall close to the main entrance. Izzy saw what he was doing and clenched her teeth in anger at her own stupidity. All the weapons she would have needed to put this vampire in his place had been sitting there, ready for the taking, and she'd been too weak to notice them. Still, she thought to herself, the vampire had been stupid enough to leave them there in the first place. Either he wasn't too bright or he thought her still completely weak and incapable of defending herself. Best she play up to that second part and keep him thinking she was weaker and feebler than she actually was. Thinking that, she feigned weakness and almost fell again, only to be quickly supported by Grace once more.

Once at the second alcove again, Pieter took a backward glance at the two girls crossing the floor. He noticed the hunter dragging her right foot slightly, and then she appeared to stumble a little. Pieter noticed that it was her left side she'd fallen to and quickly surmised that she was putting on a show for him. He was sure that she was planning to make a move on him and was trying to lull him into thinking that she was still too weak to do so. He opened up his jacket and took the crossbow apart once more, and then he put the shoulder holster back on and inserted the parts of the crossbow into it. Next, he pulled out the pistol and made a show of unloading it, checking it and reloading it. He then replaced the pistol in the right outer pocket of his jacket, which he then draped over a nearby chair.

That done, Pieter returned to the grisly task of removing the dead companion from off her vampire lover's body. Since she was close to the edge of the couch, he raised his foot and, placing the sole of his shoe against her rump, he simply pushed. The body slumped to the floor with a heavy, wet slap landing as it did in the pool of sticky blood. Pieter moved around the couch so he could grip the vampire's hair with his left hand while sawing with his right hand. As he looked up to check on the girls' line of vision, he felt that they'd seen too much of what he was about to do, so he tipped the couch over, spilling the vampire's body onto his companion. The couch, now turned onto its side, prevented the girls from viewing the scene. The vampire's body was over his dead companion with his neck extended and head tilted back to the floor, the perfect angle to assist Pieter's sawing.

He positioned the saw just below the vampire's Adam's apple and quickly sawed through it. That done, he proceeded to the last alcove he'd entered and the two female vampires. Once again, he made a show of draping his jacket over the chair at the entrance to the alcove. He was smiling to himself as he played out this teasing game with the hunter.

The first of the vampires laid face down on the floor, so he simply put the saw across her neck and made quick work of the decapitation. As he moved around to the second vampire, he noticed that her eyes were no longer scarlet in bloodlust, but were brown once more. They were also moving. Pieter looked once more at the position of the protruding crossbow bolt, and saw what had happened. The bolt had obviously glanced off one of the ribs as it entered the chest and had only just caught part of the heart. Luckily, it had been enough to almost completely paralyze the vampire, but as Pieter looked on, he could see that the vampire was breathing now. The initial pressure on the heart caused by local tissue swelling had obviously been to his advantage, but over time, the swelling was reducing and the vampire would eventually recover more movement and, in so doing, be able to remove the bolt. Pieter saw that the vampire's right hand had moved slightly by way of the smeared blood spilled from the human the two female vampires had fed on. He leaned over the vampire to look her in the eye, as he grabbed the protruding end of the bolt.

"Sorry about that, not one of my better shots. Allow me to assist you," he said, sharply twisting the bolt in toward her midline and pushing it deeper into her heart. He was just about to go through the task of decapitating the last remaining vampire when he became aware of someone approaching from behind.

"You should have let her suffer, as you sliced her head off," Izzy stated with barely concealed contempt for the now immobilized vampire. She wearily sat down on the chair close to the end of the bed, but on the other side from Pieter.

"Not my style. I prefer a quick, clean kill," Pieter replied nonchalantly as he positioned himself, ready to apply the saw to the vampire's exposed neck. He'd heard Izzy's approach from about twenty feet away; the rubber sole of the baseball boots she was wearing made small, squeaky sounds on the polished wooden floor even as she tried to sneak up on him.

"So what's the score here, vampire clan wars or are you really just a hunter in makeup to fool these idiots?" Izzy asked inquisitively while holding his gaze over the bed.

"I think we both know I'm not a hunter in disguise, and there hasn't been a clan war in over two hundred years, but as I keep telling you, young lady, I'm not a vampire," Pieter replied matter-of-factly.

"I'm not a young lady. I'm a hunter. And my name is Izzy, you pale-faced fuck," Izzy stated sharply. She stood up suddenly as she spoke and leveled her arm with the pistol she'd removed from his jacket pocket, which she aimed at his chest. She stood there, legs spread to shoulder width, knees slightly bent. Both her arms were extended, but bent slightly at the elbows.

However, rather than cupping her left hand under her right, Pieter noticed that her left hand was clenched into a fist with the right hand resting on top of it. He'd seen this type of grip used only once before in the past six hundred and forty-six years. That knowledge caused him to smile a little as he put together some pieces to a puzzle. Ever since the first moment he'd seen her, he felt she reminded him of someone, but he couldn't think who. Now he knew who and why and he was secretly laughing to himself about it.

"You're not a very good hunter if you got caught, though, are you? Not exactly born to it were you?" Pieter pointed out as he continued to saw at the final vampire's neck.

"What the...? Get the fuck up when I'm talking to you. I know this gun won't kill you, but it'll sure hurt a lot as I fill you full of holes and incapacitate you enough to stick you through your fucking cold heart and cut your head off," Izzy added angrily.

"Hang on a minute, Isabelle. Look, I'm kinda busy right now doing a dirty job that's gotta be done. If you want to chat while I do it, that's fine, but don't go getting angry and raising your voice while you're pointing an empty gun at me. Because that's just stupid and it's also very, very rude, even for an arrogant French-born hunter like you," Pieter stated, his voice remaining calm and even.

"Nice try, fang face. I saw you do the reload when you thought I was out of it with that ragtag group of girls over there. By the weight of this pistol, I've got fourteen pieces of lead ready to put a whole lotta hurt into your hide," Izzy said confidently.

"Well, once you've clicked away a couple of times and realized I'm not lying about the gun, can you reach down into your right boot and give me back my throwing knife before you cut your ankle? And I'd take that crossbow bolt out of your waistband at the back because when you feign weakness and lean over, it juts out behind and it's really easy to see," Pieter said, smiling like a Cheshire cat.

Izzy squeezed the trigger. Click! She cocked the weapon and sent a cartridge flying out, then looked inside the breech. He'd reversed the top few rounds; he'd fooled her. He'd seen she was faking her lack of recovery and had set a trap for her, one she'd walked right into. Damn him, he was a clever one. Had she been so easily fooled or was it just the fatigue of her ordeal? No time to worry about that now, plan B with the knife and crossbow bolt, but first she had to distract him and get him on the defensive. "Shit!" she exclaimed as she threw the pistol at him. She reached down with her hand to her right boot for the throwing knife, while her left hand sought the crossbow bolt at her back

Pieter batted the gun away from his face and, losing patience, raised his voice at her. "Isabelle Brigette Lancar, will you kindly stop trying to kill me before I lose my temper?"

Izzy was shocked, and left dumbfounded. No one had called her that since her father in her youngest days. None of her friends knew her by her full name. How did he know her name? It was impossible for him to know it. "H-how do you know my name?" Izzy asked, her voice trembling and her eyes wide in shock as she stood suddenly immobilized.

Pieter, having completed the final decapitation, stood up and tossed the saw away. Grabbing the bedsheet, he wiped his hands then looked Izzy in the eye. "Because you hold that gun exactly like your mother, and you still have the faintest trace of your French accent, young lady," he said flatly.

"You know my mother?" Izzy's voice was trembling and tears began to flood her eyes.

"I knew both your parents, Isabelle. I was the man who helped you bury your father and got you and your mother out of Europe," Pieter said quietly, breaking eye contact and looking down.

"Oh my God! Y-y-you're 'the Sunny Man,' Izzy exclaimed in shock.

"Yes, I'm the Sunshine Man," said Pieter.

Izzy fell back into the chair, the emotion of the moment and her physical and mental exhaustion finally taking its toll on her. As she fell, she dropped the knife and the crossbow bolt to the floor. Pieter signaled to no one in particular in the group of girls to come over and assist him.

Grace rushed over, a worried look on her face. "What is it? What's wrong?" she asked, concerned at the state she saw Izzy in.

"Isabelle just had a really big shock and could do with someone to comfort her. She won't let me give her a hug because, as she'll no doubt tell you, I'm too cold to hug," Pieter said as he stooped to pick up his knife and walked away to the middle of the room and the other girls.

Ronnie looked at Pieter as he approached the group of girls and noticed a far-away look in his eyes. She'd only caught the tail end of the confrontation he and Izzy had gotten into and was slightly confused by it all. "Wow! You sure know how to handle a woman trying to kill you, don't you?" she said in an attempt to break the mood he was in.

"Yeah, I sure do," Pieter replied, smiling weakly as he stopped thinking about the past and started focusing on the present again.

"Want to talk about it?" Ronnie offered.

"Some other time, Ronnie. Some other time and some other place," Pieter sighed, giving her a weak smile.

Chapter Eleven

Escape

Pieter suddenly snapped out of his melancholy mood and started looking around and thinking as he planned his next move. As he fidgeted, he remembered that he still had the bunch of keys he'd taken off Roberto. Perhaps there was more to be gained from this mission yet.

"Okay, I'm just going to pop upstairs to quickly check out the office for any useful information. Give those two a moment together, and then all of you start making your way down the stairs to the basement. I'll catch up with you all there. Wait for me before going outside, though," Pieter instructed before heading over to Grace and Izzy. He retrieved his pistol from where it had landed on the floor and reloaded the top few rounds correctly in front of them. "I'm going upstairs to see if I can gather any intelligence on their organization. I'll meet up with you all in the basement," he told them matter-of-factly.

Turning once more, Pieter headed toward the doors, which he jammed open using the master key he'd located on the bunch he had lifted from Roberto. Heading out to the main entrance once more, he bounded up the stairs two or three at a time, and upon reaching the top floor, he noticed that there was only one doorway blocking what used to be the corridor.

He tried the door but it was locked, as he'd expected, then he tried the keys from Roberto's collection, but none fitted either of the two locks on the door. He stepped back a little then raised his right foot and kicked the door just beside the handle. He heard the wood splinter and a slight gap appeared between the frame and the door. He raised his foot again and kicked in the same position. This time, the inner frame split and the heavy door swung open.

Immediately, he knew he'd done the wrong thing. He heard the high-pitched trigger clearly, even though it was at a frequency most humans could not detect. If there had been any dogs nearby, they would have been alerted too. Pieter took a quick step backward then dived to his left, down the stairway he'd bounded up. He was just in time as the blast rocked the whole of the top floor. A large mass of flames shot out of the open doorway and set all the walls alight as well as the upper balustrade railings.

Pieter rolled up to his feet from his position on the lower level, took one look back upstairs at where he'd stood only moments before, then turned and headed back to the girls. He suddenly feared that if they had booby trapped the office above, then maybe they had linked the rest of the building to the same system. He decided that it was time to leave, and leave quickly.

As he entered the room, the girls were all looking worriedly at him, having heard the explosion and felt the whole building shake. He raced over to the blonde girl and scooped her up into his arms in one swift movement.

"Time to go ladies, *now!*" he bellowed as he spun around and led the way out.

The girls all followed him out the door and down the corridor to the stairwell. Bright orange embers were already floating down from the fire above. Pieter gently laid the blonde girl down on the floor by the stairwell entrance, where she remained motionless and curled up into a fetal position. He quickly grabbed the heavy table the two guards had been playing cards at, and heaved it up and turned it over. Then he slid it over the balustrade and lodged the legs back under the railing with the table resting against the wall on the far side of the stairwell. It was a makeshift canopy that he hoped would protect the stairwell below from falling debris as he and the girls descended.

Pieter once more gently picked up the blonde girl and began a rapid descent down the stairs, followed by the ragtag group of girls. About two-thirds of the way down, he heard an object thump down onto the table above and quickly stole a glance upward. The table was holding, but whatever had fallen down was on fire, and so the table covering the stairwell would be soon. He hoped that nothing too big fell onto the table, as should that give way and fall down, they may all get trapped inside. *At least there has been no secondary explosive device*, he thought to himself.

On reaching the basement, he quickly made his way past the furnace to the back door, which he opened in one swift movement, and as he emerged from the building, he used his remote control to open the locks on the four-wheel drive. He leaped up the few steps to ground level, opened the back door, and gently swung the blonde girl inside. He put her down across the backseat for a moment while he took stock of the situation. Ronnie emerged from the basement next and he sent her around to the other side of the car at the back. Then Roxanne came out, huffing and puffing as she clambered up the few steps from the basement, complaining about the exertion the rapid descent had put her through. Her coat was open and her oversized bare breasts were heaving as she tried to catch her breath and stagger toward the car.

"Jump in the front, Roxy. It's going to be a bit of a squash in the back," Pieter said, turning and expecting the other two girls to be following.

After a few moments, when no one emerged, he turned to Roxanne and asked, "Where are the others?"

Roxanne took a moment to compose herself and restore her modesty, wrapping the coat across her front once more then stated in between gasps for breath, "They got off at the landing above and must be heading for the front door."

"Shit!" Pieter exclaimed. The thought of Grace and Isabelle running to the front door and detonating his booby trap suddenly hit him. He was about to race inside to try to stop them when the building was rocked by the blast. He knew in the confines of that narrow corridor and the fact that they would both have been trying to move the dead weight of the bodies, there was no chance that either of them would have survived the blast or the chemical cocktail he'd prepared.

He stood there frozen for a moment, regret washing over him for the two lives lost and the one of them who would never know her part in his past. Then just as quickly, he was startled into action. He heard the sounds of cars and heavy, booted footfalls as well as the crackling of the fiery building echo around the streets and alleys. Someone else was here at the front of the building and there were more than one or two of them. It was time to go.

He jumped into the car and started the engine, gunning it as he sped off down his preplanned escape route. Roxanne and Ronnie were about to question him on what was going on, but he cut them off as he spun the wheel to avoid the pickup truck full of armed men that came around the corner they were approaching.

"Buckle up and keep your heads down, girls. This is going to get rough," Pieter stated through gritted teeth as he straightened the vehicle up. He glanced in the mirrors and saw the vehicle had mounted the curb and hit a lamppost to avoid them. The armed men in the back were too shaken to get off a shot at him yet. As he steered the vehicle around the next right turn, though, he saw the pickup's reversing lights flick on. The driver had recovered and would soon be chasing them, and his cab passenger would be on the radio to alert any other hunters in the area, too.

Once around the corner, he gunned the engine again, and as he was about to turn left, he noticed the chasing vehicle's one headlight just coming into view. He pressed his foot hard into the accelerator and the vehicle surged forward, pushing all the occupants back against their seats and head restraints. Roxanne was silently gripping the side of her seat in stark fear, ignoring the fact that her coat was once again open and her chest was on full display. Pieter expertly handled the car through the twists and turns of their route, braking and accelerating like a professional racing driver. Ronnie sat half hunched protectively over the blonde girl, who remained silent in the back of the vehicle and oblivious to all that went on around her. Pieter's skill at the wheel was leaving the other vehicle struggling to keep pace.

Suddenly, Pieter leaned across Roxanne and opened the glove box. He pulled out a small, black remote control and flicked on a switch, which illuminated the small, green screen and a red LED (light-emitting diode) light on the top. As he turned into the next alleyway, he waited until he was well over halfway along the narrow passageway, and then stopped the vehicle. He turned to look back out the rear window, and just as he saw the headlight of the trailing vehicle, he pressed the switch on the remote. A series of small explosions on either side of the alleyway fired off one after another and the walls on each side collapsed in on the alley, blocking it completely. There was no route through for their pursuers and by the time they found a way around to the other side of the block of buildings, Pieter knew he would be on the freeway and could be going in any number of directions at the major intersection close by.

Without explanation, Pieter exited the vehicle and quickly removed the magnetic panels on either side and on the bonnet of the car, revealing silver and white stripes. The vehicle he had been seen driving from the vampire club had been completely black; now, he was driving a custom-painted special edition. Both were easily recognizable, but were unlikely to be confused with each other.

As he climbed back in the car, he casually remarked, "Okay, ladies, we'll drive a bit more sedately now. And, Roxy, you can relax your grip on my leather seats with those nails of yours."

"Well hallelujah to that!" Roxy said, leaning over and planting a big, sloppy kiss on the side of his cheek.

Even Ronnie, in the back, smiled at the release of tension and the shocked look on Pieter's face at Roxy's move on him. Pieter cast a glance at her as he shook his head in disbelief.

"There's a fleecy thermal blanket you can put across Blondie in the back there, Ronnie. Otherwise, sit back and relax, and I'll have you all somewhere warm and safe just before sunup," Pieter said in a more relaxed manner.

"What about Grace and that other girl?" Ronnie asked worriedly.

"Sorry, Ronnie, they didn't make it. I'd rigged the front door with a booby trap in case I didn't make it out myself. All I can say is that they wouldn't have suffered," he answered apologetically.

"Hey, don't beat yourself up about it. You got us out, and they made their choice. Me, I'm just grateful to be alive after all this," Ronnie responded positively.

"Me, too, and I think today is going to be a beautiful day," stated Roxy, smiling broadly with her hand on Pieter's knee.

"Amen to that, sister," added Ronnie as Pieter engaged the gears and drove the car away to the large traffic junction ahead.

Chapter Twelve

Blast

As they approached the ground floor level, Izzy held Grace back and let Roxanne continue on down the stairs past them. The older lady was struggling to keep up and looked a sight, flapping her arms and coattails as she did her best to descend as fast as she possibly could.

"Now's our chance, Grace. We can go out the front as they go down the back," Izzy instructed.

Izzy waited as Grace headed down the long corridor toward the front door. She leaned over the balustrade to look down just in time to see Roxanne reach the basement level and head off in the direction of the others. Izzy looked around for something she could use to block the way back up the stairs, so Pieter couldn't possibly come after her or follow her to the front door, but there was nothing. Looking up at the table propped against the wall and covering the stairwell, she could see it was burning at the edges now and would probably soon drop and seal off the basement. Perhaps that would work to her advantage. Just as she was about to move, she heard Grace grunting and calling for her help to move something, so she swung around to follow the Asian girl to the front door when—boom!

Izzy was knocked back from the edge of the corridor with the force of the blast. A moment or two later and she would have been struck by it in the corridor. She picked herself up, her ears ringing a little and smoke filled the air around her, making it difficult to breathe. She coughed a couple of times then peered around the corner at the corridor, or what was left of it. Flames were spreading rapidly and the whole of the front end of the corridor was engulfed already. On the ground by the wall, in front of where she stood looking, she saw half an arm with a small hand on the end of it. The arm was blackened and charred, but the fingernails were still painted brightly in light-blue, silver, and gold.

After a moment of looking farther down the corridor, Izzy knew that Grace was dead, and with the fire now getting a hold on the ceiling and walls, she knew she would have to exit through the basement after all. Realizing her sudden predicament, she spun around and quickly headed down the stairs. All of a sudden, the creaking above became louder, causing her to speed up her descent even more. Not daring to look up, she leapt down two or three stairs at a time until she reached the bottom, and headed for the open doorway. Halfway across the basement to the door, she heard an engine burst into life and roar off. Confusion set in for a moment, and she slowed her approach to the exit. She heard the squeal of tires and a thump of a car colliding with something, followed by the tinkle of shattered glass hitting the floor. She slowly peered around the corner from her sunken position at the basement door and saw a white pickup truck reversing off the pavement and turning to give chase to the pair of red taillights turning the corner farther down the road.

She waited silently in the doorway for a few moments, looking up and down the road for any sign of activity. Suddenly, she heard the table on the ninth floor give way and start to tumble down between the stairs, bouncing from floor to floor. As it hit the basement, it sent a shower of sparks toward the boiler room and Izzy figured it was time she moved out. She headed across the street, where she hugged the shadows and kept low, trying to stay concealed from anyone who might be lying in wait. She was still not sure what was going on and felt that the vampires might just be playing a game with her in an effort to break her spirit. After taking no more than ten or twelve careful steps, she caught sight of a red light on her right shoulder. As she watched, the red dot, no more than the size of a shirt button, traveled across to the middle of her chest, where it stayed wavering ever so slightly. Izzy immediately slowed all her movements and then lowered herself down on to her knees, linking her fingers and placing her hands behind her head.

Four men came wheeling around the edge of the building ahead of her, as another two remained crouched on either side of the road. The four men approached in a diamond formation. The man in front trained his weapon on Izzy; the two men at the side hugged the sides of the buildings and looked up as well as forward. The guy at the rear spun around and checked behind and up on either side. The man at the corner, on the opposite side of the road, kept his weapon trained on Izzy while the one on her side was looking up and around at the rest of the street. All of the men carried weapons fitted with laser sights and all moved silently and swiftly.

The point man came within ten feet of Izzy and barked his orders at her. "Lie face down on the ground and spread yer arms now, would ya, darlin'?"

"Get fucked, Patrick. It's freezing bloody cold and the floor is soaking wet, you dumb Irish bastard," Izzy snarled back at him.

"Jeez, Izzy! What da fook are yew doin' here in Boston, when it's not even St. Patrick's Day?" came the surprised response from the lead man as he lowered his weapon. He raised his arm to signal all the other men to hold their fire as he approached her.

"Long story, Pat, but I'll gladly tell it to you over a drink or three," Izzy stated wearily as she sat back on her haunches and slowly dropped her hands to her sides.

Patrick turned to the rest of his team and signaled two of them to him as he yelled, "It's okay. Stand down. She's one o' ours." He let his submachine gun swing down to his side as he reached into his pocket and produced a silver colored hip flask, which he offered to Izzy. "Here, looks loike yew could be using a drop or two o' this."

"I could indeed. Thanks for the rescue, Pat," Izzy replied, taking the flask from him and downing a large slug of the burning fluid. She coughed and spluttered at the strength of the fluid. She also winced at the feel of the burning it caused upon coming into contact with her split lip.

"Well, now we know yew ain't a vampoire, if yew can drink that stuff and not shrivel up and die," Patrick added, laughing.

"Yeah, as if all these cuts and bruises don't give it away already, eh?" Izzy said displaying her wounded arms.

"Well, yews are still a foine-lookin' gal under all that, ya know?"

"Patrick fat bastard Feeney, are you hitting on me?" Izzy said, looking at him brazenly.

"Well, as yew said…oi did just rescue yew, didn't oi?" Patrick argued unconvincingly.

"Give me a hand up and get me out of here before I lose my temper, ya big lug," Izzy said, extending her hands.

"We're going to hug here, fellas. She's an old friend and not a vampoire that's feedin' on me, so don't be doin' anythin' stoopid loike shootin' at her," Patrick yelled out to the men around him. He stepped forward, took both of Izzy's hands, and helped her to stand up. The two of them then hugged each other as old friends.

Izzy held him tightly and buried her face against the taller man's shoulder in order to hide the tears that were suddenly welling up in her eyes. Patrick was about to try to say something clever and flirty again, when he thought better of it. He felt her sob a little and heard the sniffle, and understood the relief she was probably feeling right now. Also knowing Izzy the way he did, he figured it was better to quit while his testicles were still hanging between his legs rather than get her angry at him and lose them.

After a few minutes of just holding her and letting her settle, then allowing her to compose herself a little, Patrick introduced Izzy to the hunter team around him. Izzy put on a brave face to greet them and thank them for coming to her aid, before Patrick barked some orders at them to get back to their positions and continue to secure the area. Izzy told him a little about the layout inside and where she knew the fires to be raging. Patrick then took her to the team leader, who was at the front of the building. She quickly briefed him on what had occurred that evening, or at least all that she was aware of.

While she was with the commander, news filtered back that the vampire who had rescued her and the other three girls had gotten away, courtesy of a pre-prepared demolition road block. Izzy was to be taken to the Boston Group Headquarters, or the BGHQ, as it was known, for medical treatment and a proper debriefing. The hunter organization was very interested in what had transpired here tonight, especially if a vampire clan war was about to break out.

So far, she had failed to mention anything about the vampire rescuing her possibly being an old family friend she'd vaguely recognized as the sunshine man. She was still processing her thoughts on what had occurred and didn't want to say anything until she was sure about what had happened.

During the journey back to the BGHQ, as Izzy was curled up in a blanket on the backseat and almost drifting off to sleep with fatigue, she heard one of the men ask how Patrick had known she hadn't been turned into a vampire when he approached her. The driver explained that apart from not being able to stomach strong alcohol, vampires repaired their injuries really quickly and didn't show up with bruises. Also, their cuts heal without scabbing and show no trace of a scar no matter how deeply they are cut. As could be seen, the poor girl here had been through a bit of a rough time over the last four days, since she went missing.

Izzy shivered, not because she was cold, but because the conversation reminded her of some of the things that had been done to her. When her team had followed the girl they suspected of being a companion home to her vampire lover, they had unexpectedly walked into a whole nest of vampires. Her team of five was totally outnumbered and she had been overpowered while the rest of the hunters had been slain. Unfortunately, the leader of this little gang of fangs realized that as a hunter, she was worth something more than just a quick meal. He had allowed his followers to feed off her, beat her, and repeatedly rape her, but he had not allowed them to get any of their saliva into her wounds. The anticoagulant contained in vampire saliva would have caused her to bleed to death, and it would also have anaesthetized the pain she felt at each wound site. Her ordeal had become that much worse once chained up at the club, with the rape and beatings being continued, but always under the supervision of the old vampire, Roberto. He took great joy in telling her how her pain and suffering was only just beginning and that his master, the great Lord Dimitri, would be back to deal with her personally.

She knew it wouldn't take that long to heal all her wounds, but she also knew that the internal scars to her mind, after the cruel, twisted ways she had been dealt with, would take far longer to heal, if in fact they ever would. Had that hell she'd been through really only lasted four days? She thought it had been longer than that, much longer.

Chapter Thirteen

Awakening

Annie-May Redfern had always been a sound sleeper. Hardly anything would ever wake or disturb her once her head hit the pillow. Not the sound of her daddy cutting the lawn in their paddock with his ride-on mower. Nor the sound of the overloaded washing machine thumping around the laundry situated in the room below hers. On school days, she had a clock radio that was set on almost full volume and her mother had positioned it on the other side of her room to stop her hitting the snooze button and sleeping in. Her favorite way to wake up, though, was to the smell of her momma's cooking of fried bacon and eggs on a Sunday morning. As she laid there now, though, she thought about how the bed was particularly hard and the burnt bacon smell that was assaulting her nose was a bit too burnt and crispy for her liking.

Then Annie-May woke up, startled as she was at the sudden pain in her legs. She looked down at her shins and screamed. A big lump of burning wood was lying across her lower legs, and she could see the skin dry and crackle as well as feel the agony at the edges of the charring flesh. One of the timber support beams in the roof had burnt through and collapsed down onto her legs, pinning her to the floor. All around her, the room was filling up with smoke and the crackling of burning wood was louder than the biggest bonfire she had ever been to. She continued to scream as she hit out and kicked at the beam lying across her legs, her motions controlled by nothing more than blind panic.

Surprisingly, she managed to wriggle free from the heavy beam quite easily. She had simply kicked and hit at it in her frenzied movements and moved her legs from under it as it rocked away from her. She stood up in the corner of what was left of the toilet cubicle. Her legs and the soles of her feet were charred and burnt, as were her hands, after the struggle with the burning beam. The one side of the cubicle had collapsed with the weight of the beam falling onto it, but the tilt of the side panel had given her some protection from anything else falling on her upper body. Another beam suddenly creaked and collapsed into the room, sending sparks flying everywhere. Suddenly, she became aware that her hair had caught fire, and she quickly batted at it with her burnt hands to douse the flames. She screamed again, more in frustration of not knowing where she was and what was happening. Was she in Hell? Was this what you got for wanting to become a vampire?

All these questions raced through her head, just as the ceiling shifted slightly, causing a pipe to twist and rupture. Suddenly water began spraying around shattering the glass at the window with the sudden change in temperature. The room began filling with smoke and steam, along with more falling beams and orange-colored burning embers floating around. Annie-May then came to her senses and realized where she was and the situation she was in. She quickly put her hand to her mouth and felt her teeth. Instantly, as she peeled her lips back, her canines slid down longer and sharper than before. She thrilled at the touch of her new fangs and became excited at the idea of what she had become. Then she refocused on her current situation. She had to get out of there, because one thing she had learned about vampires was that they could be burnt to death.

She thought for a moment about where she was and the layout of the room. Then with her mind made up about the direction she must go, she swiftly burst into action. She ignored the pain of the fires, the steam, and the embers floating around her and leapt over fallen beams and batted falling debris out of her way. She ran, jumped, and skipped through the carnage that was her old playground as she reached the door to the club room. Once into the club, she was relieved to see that the way to the exit was clear of both fire and falling debris. She swiftly ran to the entrance and was even more grateful to see that the doors were both stuck open. Running through them, she turned left into the corridor and headed down toward the stairwell.

The heavy table still protected the stairwell below, but not for much longer with the flaming debris that had fallen onto it setting it alight. Annie-May leapt down the stairs one landing at a time, until she had traveled down to the third floor. Here, she paused to look up for a brief moment as the table covering her escape creaked loudly. She moved along the corridor on this level rather than trying to continue down the stairs. Her hearing had warned her that the sounds above were the signals that the table was about to fall. From her relatively safe position farther back along the corridor, she watched as the table and even more debris fell from above, clattering down and bouncing from side to side on each landing. As it passed, a cloud of smoke and bright-orange embers floated down behind it almost gracefully, swirling in the heat-induced air flow.

Walking along the corridor, she selected a door on the left side, knowing that the room beyond would back onto the alleyway behind the building she was in. She tried the door. It was locked. In her anger, she turned the rounded handle as far as she could and it broke off in her hand. Shocked at the strength she had just displayed, she stood for a moment, dumbfounded in wonder. Then she struck the door with her open hand in a solid pushing movement; her hand smashed through the wooden panel. The splinters of wood scratched her forearm and lodged in the flesh. She winced slightly at the pain and withdrew her arm from the hole she'd made. She looked at her arm and then removed the one large splinter that remained lodged in her skin before tossing it away over her shoulder. She paused to think for a moment then hit the door again near to the door frame, just above the handle and lock. This time, the door surround itself splintered and the door swung open. It smashed against the sidewall inside, and the top hinges buckled and snapped as it fell to the floor, also ripping the screws to the lower hinges out of the woodwork.

Annie-May smiled to herself, looking at her burnt and bloodied, but powerful, hand as she casually walked into the room. She headed straight for the back of the apartment and looked through the window. She was pleased to see she had judged things correctly, this was the one used to gain access to the fire escape outside. She was just about to open the window, when she noticed some movement down in the street below. Looking down in the dark, she noticed a single man at each corner of the building opposite, and a team of four men, all dressed in military fatigues, and carrying automatic weapons, advancing towards someone hugging the wall, on the other side of the street. Annie-May pulled back a little from the window, so she could still observe what was going on down below, but was less likely to be seen herself. She watched the interplay between the lead soldier and the girl she now recognized as the hunter that had been held captive in the club. A few minutes passed before she saw the girl introduced to and then led away, by yet another man. This man appeared to be the one in charge, judging by his manner and the way the men around him reacted. Annie-May was relieved to then see the team of men follow them. That was all except the one who had embraced the hunter girl, he moved off alone, and took up his post on the corner of the building opposite sending the man stationed there away on an errand. Annie-May continued to watch both him, and the one remaining at the other corner, hoping for an opportunity to escape the burning building. The man closest to her spent a few seconds fumbling about in his pockets, before his face became brightly illuminated by the lighting of a cigarette. Acting quickly, Annie-May flicked the lock open and carefully slid the bottom panel up, opening the window. Luckily, neither of the men noticed the slight creaking of her opening the window, covered as it was by all the noise from the fire above and below at the other end of the building. She looked around more carefully now checking the second man, at the other corner; luckily he was busy watching the team walking away with the girl.

Realizing that she was still naked, she thought for a moment about how, although blackened and charred, she was still likely to draw attention to herself pretty quickly once outside. She focused on the problem for a moment, weighing up the situation. She figured that the club must have been attacked by the hunters. She'd heard stories about them, and how they viewed companions and vampires as one and the same thing: targets. The men at the corners were there to kill any survivors who made it out of the building, of this she was sure. As she looked again, the man at the furthest corner to the left was now occupied with watching the newly arrived firefighters going about their task, while the other was now opening a flask and was about to have another drink.

Annie-May, sensing her opportunity, quickly climbed out of the window and onto the fire escape, then leapt out onto the street below. She hit the ground running, speeding along in graceful, long leaps. Her eyes never left her prey ahead. As she had landed on the floor, she'd seen him take his first gulp; upon covering half the distance between them, she'd seen him swallow. His eyes had closed as he savored the warmth the spirit brought him. Finally, as he lowered the flask and began closing its lid, she was on him.

Her left hand struck him under the chin, forcing his head back against the wall and knocking him unconscious. The force of the impact of her body slamming into him carried them both back around the corner and a few paces along the side of the building. Quickly, she dragged his limp form with her down the nearby stairs to the building's basement entrance. Reaching out, she turned the door handle, marveling at her newfound strength as the metal pin sheared off in her hand. She braced herself against the door and pushed it open almost silently, the two bolts across the top and bottom inside easily bending to her force of will. Once inside, she paused for a few moments to close the door behind her and to prop a nearby mop and bucket against it to hold it in position. This simple act would cover her forced entrance to anything but a close inspection. She'd dragged the limp form of the hunter inside with her, then she made her way across the boiler room and out the door on the other side. Still dragging the unconscious body with her, she headed toward the stairwell. Once she was sure she had enough distance between herself and her point of entry, she stopped. She had placed the metal bucket across the door not just to stop it swinging open, but also to warn her of any pursuit from the other hunters. It would make plenty of noise should anyone be following her route through the basement, as opening the door would push the bucket noisily across the rough concrete floor. Such a warning, she figured, would give her ample time to effect an escape up the stairs and over the rooftops. Happy that she had considered all she needed to consider, she turned her attention to her captive, who was beginning to stir.

"Well, hi there and welcome to the 'pardy.' You're gonna be my first, so you better pucker up some, honey," Annie-May said in her bright and happy Southern accent. She kept her right hand cupping his jaw and supporting his head while twisting him slightly to his left. Grabbing at the collar of his shirt with her other hand, Annie-May ripped it away to expose his neck.

Patrick suddenly became aware of his predicament, still dazed and groggy after being hit for six. It had taken him a while to gather his wits about him once more. As he felt the cold hand holding his jaw, twist his head over to the side, and his shirt being torn away from the right side, he quickly began to fumble at his belt to try and withdraw the knife he had sheathed there.

Annie-May, upon seeing his hand going toward the knife, wrapped her own hand around his as he grabbed the hilt. She helped him withdraw the knife and brought it up between them before slowly crushing his hand and fingers with her vise-like grip.

Patrick groaned loudly with the pain as each of the bones in his hand gave way to the pressure being exerted upon them and splintered.

"Oh, come on now, suga, at least give me a scream. Goddamn, that's gotta hurt havin' all the bones in yer hand crushed like that," Annie-May taunted.

She loosened her grip on his hand and the blade dropped to the floor, with Patrick's hand now limp and unable to grip it. Immediately, Patrick tried to swing a left hook at her face and brought his knee up to strike her in the thigh. Annie-May laughed at him as she slammed her free hand into his crotch and grabbed him there. Patrick inhaled sharply and tried to double over in pain, but Annie-May still kept him held in position with her right hand on his chin.

"There, that's a whole bunch better. No more of that darn punchin' and kickin,' and tryin' to stab me. 'Cause, that's just downright rude of ya doin that," Annie-May said, cruelly chastising him.

Patrick had no fight left in him. The pain in his groin was excruciating and prevented him from resisting her anymore. Held as he was, pinned against the wall, he realized that he was done for and tears began to well at his eyes, and a sob escaped his mouth as he began to pray, taking what comfort he could in his faith.

"Oh, sweetie, I'm sorry. I didn't mean to make it hurt so bad, what with y'all bein' my first and everythin'. Here, let me kiss it better and take all that pain away for ya."

Her excitement grew as she opened her mouth and peeled her lips back in a sickly grin. Her fangs slid down into place and her eyes turned crimson red. She fell on him and took a ferocious bite out of his neck. She tore at the skin in her unfamiliar feeding frenzy, removing a large mass of flesh that she turned her head and spat away. Patrick tried to struggle once again as this new area of pain exploded at his neck. He tried to turn his sobs into a scream, but her right hand was holding his jaw, which also muffled his attempt to make himself heard. Then she covered the gaping wound with her mouth, feeling the ruptured vessels below pump the rich, red fluid almost into the back of her throat. She sucked, slavered, and swallowed as their bodies slowly sank to the floor to-gether, the little escaping blood she missed smearing a trail down the wall be-hind them, marking their slow descent.

As she continued to drain the blood in noisy, rapid swallows, she took pleasure in the feeling of power it gave her. She felt the energy bursting into her body and the warmth spreading to all of her limbs, but most of all, she was suddenly aware of the alertness it brought to her senses. Each moment she fed, she could hear, smell, and sense more of the world around her, and the ache she had felt in her stomach, almost like a feeling of dread, was rapidly disappearing. She liked the sensations that feeding gave her; the sense of empowerment it suddenly sent wash-ing over her was second to none. As poor Patrick's heart gave out with insufficient blood left to circulate around his body, Annie-May knew she enjoyed feeding on human blood and that she definitely wanted more.

She released her hold and let the lifeless head drop the remaining few inches to the floor, and commented, "Guess ya momma never told ya that smokin' and drinkin' would be the death of y'all, Mr. Hunter."

Rising from the body, Annie-May stretched out her limbs as if coming out of a deep sleep, and as she did so, several pieces of charred flesh fell away from her hands to slowly float to the wooden floor at her feet. She lowered her arms and turned her palms outward as she opened her hands. Looking down, she saw that the burns were completely healed. The dry, charred, and damaged flesh was now simply falling away to reveal the perfectly supple pale skin below. She looked down at her shins and saw that they were almost completely repaired, too. She could see the flesh growing back, and the discolored and damaged tissue was sim-ply dropping away.

Her fascination with her new powers of recovery was interrupted by the static and crackling from the hunter's walkie-talkie radio.

"Eagle Two, this is Eagle One. Do you copy? Over," the voice inquired.

Time to go, she thought. *Best get to high ground and hide out undercover on the rooftops somewhere.* She bounded up the stairs with the energy of a young child, and almost flew through the door onto the rooftop. Dawn must be approach-ing, as she saw it was starting to get brighter in the sky. She knew the old vampire films had gotten it wrong about sunlight killing her, but she also knew that it would hurt her eyes and almost leave her blind. It had something to do with the different types of light receptors in human and vampire eyes. The balance of what they called rods and cones was now different in her eyes. Where vampires were mainly nocturnal hunters with a keen sense of vision in the darkest of nights, bright sun-light was too much for them to deal with. Hence, the real reason vampires didn't go out in daylight. They also had no tanning factor in their skin to protect them from being sunburned, something she felt she would miss, but not enough to want to change back from the all-powerful being she had now become. All the knowledge she'd picked up from hanging around with vampires was suddenly going to become very useful to her.

As she no longer felt the cold, she would simply hide out for the day in one of the numerous derelict buildings around in this area. Then at nightfall, she would go hunting for some new clothes and something more to eat, or maybe she'd kill the two birds with one stone. Whatever she did, she was sure that she was going to get a big thrill out of it.

Chapter Fourteen

Arrival

At a little after 7:30 in the morning, Pieter used the touch screen on his in-car entertainment and satellite navigation system to initiate a phone call. The phone only rang twice before he heard Jurgen's voice clear and alert at the other end.

"Hello, Pieter. I take it you're close by."

"Be with you in about five minutes. We've just passed the bakery on the corner," Pieter replied.

"Okay, I'll disengage the security and initiate the sprayer now. Mechtild and I will meet you at the door. Are any of our guests in need of medical attention?" came Jurgen's next calm response.

"Nothing serious really, just scratches and scrapes. I think some breakfast followed by a warm bath each and a decent bed will help them all go a long way to feeling better." As he said his last comment, he looked around the four-wheel drive at his passengers.

Roxy and Ronnie had been sleeping fitfully, and were waking at the sound of his voice. The blonde girl, he noticed, had not slept at all. She was just staring off into space, as if mesmerized.

"One more thing, Jurgen. There will only be three guests. The hunter and one other didn't make it," Pieter added in more somber tones.

"Oh dear. Okay, Pieter, we're ready for you here."

Pieter pressed the button to end the call, his eyes now fixed on the road ahead as he gripped the leather-bound steering wheel a little tighter. The sight of Izzy's face as he confronted her with her own name popped back into his mind. He thought with regret how she had died not knowing all that he had done for her in the past, and of how their destiny had been previously intertwined.

Jurgen had picked up on Pieter's change of tone when he had mentioned that the hunter and one other had not made it out of the building alive. While he had told him to expect trouble and not to trust the hunter, he knew by Pieter's regretful tone that something had gone wrong and he felt responsible in some way.

In all their years together since Pieter had rescued him and Mechtild, their relationship had grown from that of a father to a pair of orphans, to now being his closest friends and confidants. Jurgen knew Pieter was deeply saddened by something that had occurred earlier that evening and would need some time to sit, talk, and analyze it, as he always did. Killing vampires and their companions was something he had never had a problem with. On the few occasions he'd had a run in with the hunters, he'd managed to get away without having to resort to deadly force. Obviously, something had gone wrong, and now, Pieter was about to start beating himself up in guilt again. Both Jurgen and Mechtild knew how Pieter strived to make everything right, and to be the perfect knight in shining armor. They also knew from their own experiences that the world is a very imperfect place, and no amount of preparation and planning could possibly account for every conceivable event.

"Pieter has had a bit of a setback in the final stage of his rescue attempt. There are only three lost sheep with the shepherd after all," Jurgen said softly to Mechtild.

"Oh my. Once we get them settled, then perhaps you and Pieter should spend some time in the library," Mechtild suggested knowingly.

"I think so. Now to the door; they will be here in a moment."

Jurgen, upon approaching the door, entered a code into the push button panel by the side of it. At the end of the long driveway, the two large iron gates began to swing open automatically. Jurgen remained by the door, watching the car approach from the small crossroads at the edge of the estate. He could see them clearly via the hidden security cameras concealed along the outside wall surrounding the grounds. Once the car was on the homeward stretch along the narrow road leading to this and the several other large properties, Jurgen checked for any other vehicles or people on the monitors. Seeing no one and no other vehicles, he initiated another series of codes and, instantly, a fine, mist-like spray began to rain down from the level of the junction all along the road and up the driveway.

Pieter was turning on his windscreen wipers when Roxy commented, "Will you look at that a clear blue morning sky? And it's raining."

"That's not rain, Roxy. That's a special chemical bath for the car so no vampire can scent where you've been or gone," Pieter corrected, glad to be able to speak about something other than the regret he felt over Izzy.

"Oh!" mumbled Roxy, the memories of the previous few days suddenly rushing back into her mind.

"So, are you saying those vampires can smell us all the way out here?" asked Ronnie.

"Those small cuts each of you have on the wrist, they are scent marks," Pieter explained. "The vampires take a small sample of your blood and can use it to trace you should they decide to release you, and then enjoy hunting you down. In the old days, vampires would very rarely kill their victims. They would happily feed on them for several weeks or months, and also, more than one victim at a time. Mainly, they would prey on children, as they can be easily coerced with a few sweets or gifts. Younger, more adventurous teenagers would also be romanced for their younger blood and boundless energy.

"Back in the 1200s and 1300s, when parents discovered the bite marks on their children, they would send them away or to a neighbor's house or close relative for protection. Meanwhile, the windows and doors to all the village houses would have crushed garlic smeared onto them to try to put the vampires off the scent of their victims. The men of the village would then go out, seeking any poor soul not known to them in the village and hack off their heads. Gypsies were the most common targets, as they moved around so much and a fair few of them were indeed vampires, but it was usually the travelling companions that the villagers would slay and the vampires themselves would escape.

"More often than not, the vampire was someone known and living around the village outskirts. Usually, it was a reclusive loner or a distant couple, but in most cases, it was someone still well known to the rest of the villagers. If they were a couple, it was likely that one was a human companion, who would assist in the entrapment of the victims and be the more often seen of the two of them."

"So it's true, like in the films and books, vampires don't like garlic," Ronnie stated, thinking she had put things together.

"Not really, Ronnie. Vampires have no fear of, or particular dislike for garlic. It's just something that smells strong and interferes with their very well-developed sense of smell. It simply makes it difficult for a vampire to scent where their victims are," Pieter answered as he turned in the gateway and headed up the long driveway.

"Oh well, I can't say I was looking forward to using garlic as my preferred perfume anyway," chipped in Roxy.

"Don't worry. I have one or two things to help you out in that direction. That's for when you are all recovered and ready to go back to a new life, though. It can all wait for the moment. Meanwhile, welcome to my home, ladies," Pieter said as he swung the vehicle around to halt in a position close to the front door.

Ronnie and Roxy both looked out in awe at the size and grandeur of the building Pieter had bought them to. It was at least three stories high and looked like something out of a hotel brochure.

"So, I take it this is Wayne mansion," Ronnie quipped sarcastically.

"More like Rockefeller's," added Roxy.

"I just call it home actually," Pieter replied. "Come on, let's get you all inside."

Pieter opened his door and stepped out into the still-falling mist. He came around to the other side and opened the door to gently lift out Blondie. Ronnie and Roxy both exited the vehicle and followed him into the house through the big stone archway.

Once inside, they were met by and introduced to Jurgen and Mechtild, who were prepared with large, fluffy blankets to wrap each of them in. Then they were led to a large, warm room with a fake open fire. Although it was a fake, the electric fan behind it had warmed the room and the smell of warm toast, coffee, and scrambled eggs had an instant effect on the mood of at least two of the guests.

Over the next twenty minutes or so, Ronnie and Roxy told their stories to the ever-attentive Jurgen and Mechtild as they ate and drank their fill. Pieter was also most interested in the way the girls had been abducted.

Roxy had unfortunately proven to be an easy target as a stripper touring some of the seedier clubs and bars; she was used to unwanted attention. Her problems started when she refused the advances of a particularly unpleasant club owner with a body odor and sweat problem. She remembered seeing him hanging around her vehicle just as she was leaving, but thought nothing more of it. People often wanted an autograph in private, away from their judgmental friends' prying eyes. Having rebuffed his crude advances in the club, Roxy had figured that he was about to try again, but to her great relief, he'd simply walked away. Unfortunately for her, though, she'd gotten no more than ten miles down the road when her car broke down. The club owner and three accomplices were in the next vehicle that just happened to come along the road, and their offer to help was just a setup for a particularly violent gang rape. Then she was beaten, bound, and gagged before spending an awful long time in the trunk of a car. After a couple of changes of vehicles, she wound up at the club.

Luckily for her, she'd been ignored the previous night and was the sole survivor of that evening. While none of the vampires had taken a shine to her on the previous night, it hadn't stopped the companions from teasing her and leaving her in no doubt about her upcoming grisly fate. They happily hung around her as they pointed out what was happening to the other girls who had been chained up with her. The vampire called Roberto had also made a point of mentioning that were she to be left alive by the end of the second night, then he would be taking her to his own more private quarters to deal with her personally. The cold way he'd told her this and the giggling of the companions also left her in no doubt that this would not be a particularly good thing to happen.

Ronnie's tale was not so different. She'd just finished running a relaxation class and was heading home when an old client showed up, looking to rebook her. She had dropped the client some time previously, due to his pestering her for more than relaxation therapy and his shortfall on payments. She'd heard from others at the company he used to work for that he'd been sacked and was rumored to have some big gambling debts. When he showed up out of the blue, paid all his previous debts in cash, and prepaid for the next session, which they had organized for the following Thursday evening, she'd thought he must have had a change in his luck. On arrival at his apartment, Ronnie had accepted a drink of mineral water while she was setting up the massage couch. The next thing she knew, she was naked, covered in dye, and chained to the column with the other girls.

Roxy filled her in on how she had arrived. She had been seen to simply walk into the room, and at one of the vampire's suggestion, she began shedding her clothes then laughing as they daubed her in the dye and chained her up. The guy she had arrived with was in the same happy frame of mind and had immediately gone off with the two female vampires. Ronnie confirmed that the guy's body she'd seen next to the two female vampires wasn't that of her old client, but was someone else.

Then Ronnie told Grace's story, about how her abduction had been organized by the man she trusted and was expecting to marry. He had been a friend of hers since childhood and, moreover, was a trusted friend of her family, too. Jurgen and Mechtild both looked to Pieter as this new tale unfolded and saw his reaction. To anyone else, it would seem as though he'd simply heard it all before, but Jurgen and Mechtild knew him better than anyone else, and knew what that kind of betrayal meant to him. They saw him shift in his seat a little and how his grip on the chair had turned his knuckles even whiter.

For the most part, Pieter had sat silently, taking in all the information as the two girls spoke. He'd let Jurgen and Mechtild do the egging on and encouragement. Little did the girls know that they were already starting on their road to recovery. Just by talking about their traumatic experiences, they would be starting to deal with it all. It seemed to him that there was now an underground network of people smuggling that had been developed here in America. He knew a little about the Russian gangsters who were involved in taking over the Hollywood prostitution trade, and he had some police contacts who might be able to gather more information on the matter for him.

The step up from forced prostitution to vampire food showed the same disregard for human life and greed for money. This, he felt, was his next area of investigation, shut down their food supply, and flush the vampires out into the open. Once openly pursuing their prey, they would generate police reports and could be localized, and then his special senses could locate them. If there were other humans making a profit from this arrangement, then they were no better than the companions or vampires themselves, and he would show them the same kind of mercy they were giving their victims, which was simply none at all.

Blondie had remained curled up in Pieter's arms, hugging him tightly, but after a while, with the relaxed tones and talking around her, she seemed to relax.

She had even accepted some warm, malted milk drink Mechtild had specially prepared for her. She also accepted a half piece of toast covered in strawberry jam. Like Jurgen and Mechtild, though, she had sensed a change in Pieter as the story of Grace's abduction was told. Pieter realized that his reaction had made her uncomfortable, and he had stroked her hair to calm her as much as himself.

Once the conversation had died down and the breakfast had been consumed, along with the milk drinks and coffee, Mechtild suggested she take the girls up to the guest rooms and get them sorted out and into bed for a few hours. They had all been through a lot and were overdue for some much-needed rest. With a little gentle coaxing and some reassurance from all present, Blondie was able to walk with them up the stairs. Mechtild would stay with her until relieved, so she was not left alone while in such a state.

Once they had gone, Jurgen turned to Pieter. "How bad is your thigh injury? Do you need to replenish your strength?"

"No, I'm fine. I had to do some running repairs, but there were several sufficiently twisted companions available," he replied wearily, thinking back on Annie-May Redfern.

"You made the morning news anyway," Jurgen mentioned matter-of-factly.

"Yeah. They had a security system on the door to the upstairs apartment used by Dimitri. Luckily, I heard it trigger as I entered, or I'd be a little more singed than I am. They are starting to get a little more hi tech—no cameras or anything too fancy, but they are definitely stepping up their guard."

"It had to happen. Just as the hunters are getting more organized and having greater success, so the hunted will respond in kind. Hasn't it always been the way? The vampires have become lazy and let their guard slip, but they are old and wise, as well as cunning and ruthless. There will be a backlash to all the hunters' recent victories, and you are going to be right in the middle of it all, if you're not careful," Jurgen lectured sternly.

"I know, old friend, I know. Come, we have work to do." Pieter led Jurgen out into the hall once more.

Pieter flicked a couple of switches by the door and went back outside to the car. Jurgen followed him out and both men opened the doors and got into the car. Pieter started the engine and shifted into gear, then proceeded to park the car inside the garage. Once inside and with the door closed, Jurgen began the cleanup operation on the inside of the car with a spray bottle and cloth while Pieter removed the large canvas bag from the back of the vehicle.

"Is that what I think it is?" asked Jurgen.

"It is. Lord Dimitri's personal assistant, for want of a better title," Pieter confirmed.

"You were able to prepare it for captivity?" Jurgen probed, displaying his obvious dislike for the vampires in his tone and by calling Roberto an "it."

"I was. Just to save you the problem of hiding his scent in the furnace. I'm going to get him set up in the dungeon. Can you do me a favor and contact Fran for me? I think we need to get Blondie some professional help as soon as possible," Pieter asked, changing the subject.

"Good thinking. We don't want Mechtild getting too attached and go missing out on her cooking duties, do we?"

"You mean you don't want to end up cooking, don't you?" Pieter teased.

"Go on with you, you've got work to do." Jurgen smiled in response before returning to his cleaning operation.

Pieter walked to the back of the spacious garage and opened a door there that led back into the main building and the central corridor. He swiftly walked along to the main stairwell in the middle of the house and opposite the front door. Here, he opened another door around the side and underneath the stairs that led down into the cellars. He closed the door behind him as he began to descend the stone stairway, still carrying the large canvas bag with him.

Chapter Fifteen

Reunion

"Miss Lancar, I'm Dr. Scott Lawler, the head analyst here at the BGHQ," the short man entering the room stated in a businesslike manner.

Izzy looked up from staring into her coffee, but said nothing.

"Sorry to keep you waiting," the man added, smiling. He pulled the chair back from the opposite side of the table and sat himself down, and then proceeded to remove his glasses from a small pouch inside his jacket pocket. He put them on as he opened the cardboard folder he'd brought in with him and began to flick through the notes inside. After a few more minutes reading, he laid the folder down on the table, but still continued to flick from one piece of paper to the next, carefully putting each piece of paper he'd read face down on the left side of the folder as he picked up the next from the pile on the right. He had just finished reading the last sheet of A4-sized paper and was placing it carefully on the pile when Izzy, who was staring at the clock on the wall above him, tipped forward and spilt her three-quarter-full cup of coffee all over the table and his folder.

"What the—?!" he exclaimed, suddenly pushing his chair back and standing up as the hot coffee spilt onto his lap.

"Think yourself lucky, pencil neck. If I hadn't been kept waiting so long, that coffee would have burnt what little you have between your legs. You would really be up shit creek without a paddle if that had happened, wouldn't you, short, no manners, balding, wasting my time, and completely dick-less?" Izzy stated venomously while staring coldly into the man's shocked face.

Dr. Lawler was just about to say something else when the door to the interview room suddenly opened and a much taller and heavyset man entered. He looked first at Dr. Lawler, seeing the wet coffee stains across his light-tan trousers, and then turned to look at Izzy.

"I see you've met the charming Miss Lancar, Dr. Lawler," the man stated impassively.

"Indeed I have, Commander McHugh," came the indignant reply as the shorter man picked up his notes, still dripping with the coffee, and headed toward the door. "I'll do the debriefing later, when she's had a chance to settle back into human society a little more," he added as he swept past the commander and exited the room.

The commander turned to watch him go through the door and continued to watch as the door swung to and closed behind him. "I see you haven't lost your touch for impressing the 'geeks' on the team," he stated, turning to face her once more.

"Well, the jerk off kept me waiting here for over an hour then proceeded to read his notes in front of me, and I'm too tired to deal with all that bullshit at the moment," Izzy replied exasperatedly as she sank her head into her hands.

"Too tired to give an old family friend a hug?" he inquired, stretching his arms out toward her.

Izzy looked up from her hands, and as the tears began to form in her eyes, she quickly pushed her own chair back and stepped into his embrace. She held him tightly as she felt his big, strong arms surround her and hold her close. Burying her head into his chest to try and stop him from noticing her tears, she found that she couldn't control herself and the sobbing started. Salty water flowed freely down both her cheeks and into the commander's shirt.

For his part, the commander might not have known the details of what she'd been through, but looking into her eyes as she had stepped toward him, he knew that it had been a version of hell. What she needed more than anything else at the moment was to be held and to be allowed to get all that pent-up emotion out of her system. He'd known Izzy for over fifteen years now, ever since she and her mother had come over after the incident that took her father from her. He remembered taking her and her mother to Orlando, Florida, to the theme parks for a holiday to cheer them both up after the loss of her father. Then he remembered the photo they had taken with the space shuttle taking off into the clear, blue sky behind them. He recalled how they had all been affected that day, too, and he'd ended up hugging both Izzy and her mother as all three of them wept at the news that the space shuttle had exploded, killing all the crew on board.

It wasn't until they had the photo's developed a few days later when they saw that the pictures they took had caught the explosion and the three trails of smoke in the background as they stood smiling for the camera. He still had the photo at home on his desk; it was one of the few he treasured. He'd taken ages to carefully cut around the edges of the three of them in the picture and set the photo against a different background, so there was no reminder of the terrible incident with those smoke trails in the sky behind them.

He stood there just holding her for what seemed an age, gently stroking her back as she heaved in great sobs. Her emotion had completely taken over and she was soaking the front of his shirt as the tears poured down her cheeks. Then all of a sudden, the door opened behind him. He turned his head sharply around to scowl disapprovingly at whoever had entered and disturbed them. Upon seeing the lady who had entered in her smart business suit, he softened his scowl as he gave a casual greeting to her. "Hello, Maggie. It's good to see you."

"Hello, Ian. I wish I could say the same. I see my daughter is soaking your shirt again," came the terse reply.

Upon hearing her mother enter the room, Izzy began to pull herself together, stepping back away from Ian and turning her back to the pair of them as she wiped her eyes on her sleeve. Ian walked across the room and retrieved a box of tissues off the top of a filing cabinet and brought them back over to Izzy.

"Here you go, kiddo," he said, passing her a couple of tissues he'd pulled out with one hand as he passed her the whole box with the other.

"Thanks, Ian," Izzy said, giving him a weak smile as he leaned forward and brushed her hair off her face and kissed her on the forehead.

"I'll give you two ladies some privacy," he stated as he turned and headed toward the door. He opened the door, and just before he stepped outside, he turned back to look at Izzy and said, "I'll be right outside if you need me." Then he looked at the other woman and curtly nodded to acknowledge her. "Maggie." After closing the door behind him, he gave an audible sigh of relief. He stepped toward his own office and the spare dry shirt he was sure he had hanging up in his locker.

Back inside the room, the tension was palpable between mother and daughter. Margeurite, or Maggie, as she was called by her close friends, as well as, it seemed, those no longer quite so close, stepped across to the table. She pulled back the chair a little and was just about to sit down when she saw the coffee pool on the seat and chose not to sit down after all. Instead, she walked across to the window and opened the venetian blinds to view the world outside. As she looked across the car park, she saw a small bird hopping around the front of her car and pecking at the insects that she'd obviously hit as she drove along in the early morning light. "So, how are you Isabelle?" she asked without emotion.

"Just a few scratches and bruises, Mother. I'll be fine," Izzy responded.

"You look pale. Did they feed on you?"

"Yes, Mother, they fed on me. And, no, none of their saliva entered the wounds. They used knives and had their companion bitches collect my blood in wineglasses," Izzy stated as she started to lose patience with her mother's cold attitude.

"Well, don't say I didn't warn you this would happen," her mother retorted, starting to get angry herself.

"I never said that, Mother, and that's not why I contacted you and asked you to come here," Izzy said, her own anger also rising.

"Why exactly did you ask me here then? I haven't heard from you in over three years. I get a call at the beginning of the week to tell me you've been taken. So I have to grieve quietly, so that Stuart and your brothers don't catch on. I start making all the preparations to move, in case they turn you and you come after us. All the while thinking, I'd never get to see you and give you a decent burial. I was imagining everything they would have done to you as a hunter, and of how they would have disposed of your body. Then you turn up out of the blue and expect me to drop everything and come running," Margeurite said, almost ranting in her own rising mix of anger and frustration.

"I called you here today, Mother, because I need to talk to you about the Sunny Man," Izzy stated forcefully, locking eyes with her mother.

"The Sunny Ma…you mean you've seen Pieter?" her mother replied, suddenly looking shocked at this new revelation.

"Yes, I've met him, and I need to know more about him before I go through the debriefing process here."

Margeurite quickly walked the short distance to her daughter and clasped her hands between her own. She held her daughter's eyes with equal determination as she pleaded with her. "Forget all about the differences we've had in the past, and if you still honor the memory of your father, you must never tell them anything about the Sunshine Man, not ever, do you understand? Never!"

Izzy was shocked at her mother's reaction to the name. She had thought that she would be able to coerce her mother to tell her all about him, but upon seeing this response, Izzy knew that would never happen. It was no secret where Izzy got her stubbornness from, and her mother was easily a match for her in that category. She knew that her mother only brought up her father in the most serious of circumstances, and she knew better than to try to argue around this situation. "So what am I supposed to say when they ask me how I got away from a vampire stronghold? Especially after being locked up, beaten half to death, and tortured for days," she replied, trying a different approach to get the information she wanted.

"Make something up, lie, say you had a blackout, whatever, but don't ever mention Pieter or anything about him," Margeurite demanded.

"There were other girls he took away with him. What if they turn up and get questioned? My position within the hunter ranks would be jeopardized. They would never trust me again and they'd probably think I'd turned sides to save my own life," Izzy pointed out.

"You will never see any of those girls again. Pieter will set them up with new identities and move them interstate for their own protection. Listen to me, Isabelle. This is the most important task I have ever given you, and one your father would turn in his grave over if you failed to complete it. The hunters are to know nothing about Pieter—not now, not ever," Margeurite stated even more forcefully.

"But, Mother, I need to know about him. I need to know about what he does." It was Izzy's turn to plead now.

Her mother sensed the change in her attitude toward her, but couldn't fathom why. So she asked, "Why do you need to know, Isabelle?"

Isabelle turned away from her mother as a tear started to form in her eye, and she began to explain. "There was another girl who was rescued along with me, but I talked her into getting away from the man you call Pieter. She didn't make it and I think it may be my fault she's dead."

"Oh, Isabelle," her mother sighed, grabbing her and spinning her around before wrapping her arms around her daughter, and holding her for the first time in a very long time.

Izzy turned into the grasp of her mother and let the floodgates open, sobbing uncontrollably once again. Her mother held her tightly as her own tears began to flow.

Chapter Sixteen

Interview

Five minutes passed and they were still holding each other, with neither wanting to be the one to let go. Suddenly, they were disturbed by a knock on the door.

After a short pause, the door swung inward and Ian popped his head inside the room. "Sorry, ladies, can we move you down the corridor to another office, so they can get this one cleaned up?"

"Certainly, Ian. I was just about to leave, as I'm sure you'll want to debrief Isabelle and get the whole story from her." Margeurite spoke casually, and as she did so, she pressed her thumb into Isabelle's wrist. This was an old signal between the two of them to say she should play along with whatever her mother was about to suggest. "Isabelle and I will catch up later, when I take her home with me after she's answered all the little men's questions. For now, though, I'm going to leave her in your care and go and sort out some suitable accommodation for us."

"We have plenty of accommodation here, should you need a place to stay, and I can guarantee your security, too," Ian offered.

"Thank you, Ian, but that won't be necessary. I have my own security and your accommodation is a little too far below what I'm used to," Margeurite argued, almost snobbishly.

"Okay, as you wish, Maggie," Ian said, capitulating to her argument.

"Can you give us a moment? I'd like a little privacy to say good-bye to my daughter before I leave."

Ian nodded and stepped back outside, closing the door behind him.

Immediately he had done so, Margeurite pulled Isabelle close and spoke softly, but urgently, in her ear. "They wanted us to move rooms because they were trying to listen in on our conversation, and I'm using a jamming device to stop them. The girl who got killed is your alibi. She rescued you and led you out, and she's the only one you saw or had contact with. You were weak and kept blacking out, and remember nothing but bits and pieces. Don't mention Pieter by name, if at all—or anything about anyone else. You never saw them. The guy who rescued you may or may not have been a vampire is all you have to say, as you were weak and confused. Call me when you are free, and I will come and collect you. They will plant a bug or two on you so don't say anything until you are with me and I can shield you again. Do you understand?"

Isabelle nodded her head in agreement, and the two women embraced as a mother and daughter for only the second time in a very long time.

"Be strong, Isabelle. A lot more than you could ever know depends on you now. I'll explain it all to you later." Then Margeurite broke the hug and strode toward the door. Opening it, she turned back to her daughter and spoke once more in her haughty manner. "Call me when you've finished with the little men and I'll send a driver to collect you." She then brushed past Ian with a curt nod, and swept along the corridor and out of sight.

"You okay kiddo?" Ian asked as he came back into the room.

"Yeah, I'm okay. Let's get this over with, Ian. Looks like I've got a long night ahead of me, as I'll be interrogated by my mother too. God, she gets up my nose with her snotty French arrogance, and the way she tries to control me. She thinks she knows everything and that she's in command. Well, I've got news for her, I'm my own woman and I don't need her telling me what to do," Izzy ranted angrily.

"That's the Izzy I remember. Welcome back, young lady. Now, let's go see the little guys," Ian said, stretching out his arm to indicate the way to the room where Dr. Lawler was waiting.

Meanwhile, outside the building, in her chauffeur-driven limousine, Margeurite was dialing a number she had been given many years ago. It was a number she never expected to use again. The phone rang three times and then it was answered.

"Hello? May I help you?" the male voice answered at the other end.

"Hello, Jurgen. It's Margeurite," she answered casually.

"Margeurite! Oh my, how are you, dear?"

"I'm well. Thank you, Jurgen. Is Pieter available?" she asked, cutting through the small talk.

"Yes, certainly. I will just get him for you. I won't be a moment," Jurgen replied politely.

After a couple of minutes left twitching on the line, Margeurite heard the phone being passed over to someone before a familiar voice answered the phone.

"Hello, Margeurite," Pieter said simply.

"Hello, Pieter. I just wanted to thank you for saving Izzy. I've just left her being debriefed at the Boston headquarters of the hunter organization. I thought you should know that I have instructed her to keep everything she knows about you secret and I will debrief her myself later," Margeurite said gratefully.

Pieter paused for a moment on the other end of the phone while he took in what had just been said. "She survived! She wasn't killed at the front door by the booby trap that someone triggered. Is she okay? Is she burnt at all?"

"No burns, just cuts and bruises from the beating and the feeding they took out on her. I'll get the full story later, but I'm going to have to bring her up to date on the family history in order to protect you," Margeurite answered.

"I think that's probably wise, since she tried to kill me as I was rescuing her," Pieter told her.

"Really?"

"Really."

"Well then, it seems I didn't teach her as well as I should have," Margeurite quipped.

"You taught her just fine, Margeurite. In fact, I don't think she would have survived the ordeal of her capture if not for your training. It was the way you taught her to hold a pistol that helped me recognize her, too."

"You always were one for silly little details, weren't you, Pieter?"

"I still am, Margeurite. To be honest with you, I thought she'd been killed when she went off on her own, and I was avoiding making the phone call to you. I was dreading having to tell you what had happened, especially after what happened to Jean-Paul. So I'm very relieved to hear that she is still alive."

"I take it you didn't want to tell me someone I loved very much was dead again," Margeurite said in a more somber tone.

"Something like that, Margeurite."

"Perhaps it's time we should all meet and deal with all the issues that came between us once and for all," Margeurite suggested.

"Yes, perhaps it is. I have a few things to tie up at the moment and I'm sure you'll need some time with Isabelle first. How about you come to New York to help her with her recovery and I'll hear from you when you think the time is right to sit down and talk everything through?" Pieter suggested.

"That sounds like a good idea, Pieter. I'll make the arrangements and I'll be in touch when I'm sure everything is set at my end," Margeurite confirmed.

"Okay, Maggie. I look forward to hearing from you soon. Take care."

"You, too, and thank you once again for saving my little girl." Margeurite pressed the button on the phone to end the call as she sat staring out of the window at the passing view. She didn't really notice anything outside, as she was too busy thinking of the past and what had happened all those years ago. As she sat there silently, looking out the window, a single tear escaped her left eye and rolled down her cheek. She made no effort to stop it or wipe it away; she just continued to stare out of the window and off into the distance.

For the last two hours, Izzy had stuck to the story her mother had suggested. She explained to both Ian and Dr. Lawler that she had been raped, beaten, and cut, and was in and out of consciousness the whole time she had been held in captivity. That was until she had been rescued by a Chinese girl named Grace, who had helped her escape. Izzy explained how she had gone to the restroom for clothes and had seen the body of a companion when she had communicated her position on the device she'd found there. She further explained that all the vampires she saw had been slain and decapitated, as if by a hunter. She and Grace had gone down the stairs behind the other group of girls escaping and Izzy had fallen behind a little, since Grace had run on to the front door. There had been some kind of booby trap that had exploded, which killed the Chinese girl and forced Izzy to escape out of the rear basement. That's where she had met up with Patrick and been introduced to the rest of his hunter team.

"Speaking of which, where is that fat Irish slob? He hasn't come to see me again yet. Don't tell me you are still debriefing him, too," Izzy questioned them lightheartedly.

The two men then looked at each other uncomfortably, but said nothing to her. She had worked in the hunter organization long enough to recognize the glances that passed between the two men sitting on the opposite side of the table from her.

"What's the matter? Why did you two just look at each other like that? What happened?" Izzy demanded.

"I think we're about finished here, Scott. Can you step outside and give us the room? I'll catch up with you later after I've talked to Izzy some more and bought her up to date with the situation." Ian spoke in a quiet, even voice after what seemed like a long pause.

"Certainly, Sir. I'll go and get started on my report, Commander. Miss Lancar," Dr. Lawler said in an equally subdued tone as he nodded in each of their directions and left the room as quickly as he could.

"Just tell me, Ian. What is it?" Izzy asked with tears welling up in her eyes again.

"It's Patrick. He was in charge of the team left behind to secure the area. He was watching for any suspicious activity around the back of the building you emerged from…" Ian started to explain, then paused as he gathered his thoughts about how to break the news to her.

"And…? Go on," Izzy demanded impatiently.

"It would seem that there was a vampire still alive around the location, probably a young and inexperienced one, judging by the way he was fed on."

"Oh God, no, please, not Pat," Izzy gasped before clamping her hands over her mouth to smother the cry of pain, and she shook her head from side to side in denial.

Ian scraped the legs of his chair on the cold tile floor as he stood and moved around the table to comfort her again. "I'm sorry, Izzy. Patrick's dead." He said as he resigned himself to another large, wet patch on his shirt front.

Izzy bolted upright and collapsed into his embrace once more, sobbing away for a few minutes more. Ian just stood there, quietly holding her, stroking her hair in an effort to comfort her. After a while, she calmed down a little as she considered what could possibly have happened. She retraced the events of what she knew had gone on in her mind. She knew that all the vampires in the building had been slain. She had been a witness to all the decapitations herself. There had also been several companions slain during the rescue, but only one had been fed on, that cruel little bitch with the Southern accent. Either she had somehow been turned in the process or the only other explanation was that another vampire had come to the club, had seen the hunters, and attacked poor Patrick from within the shadows of the surrounding buildings. Whatever the case, she had lost yet another friend to one of those monsters and she was determined that one day, she would make someone pay for it.

Izzy wiped her eyes and stepped back from Ian as she steeled herself with her new resolve. "I want in on the follow-up hunt for this new vampire," she demanded.

"You are in no condition to get involved in hunting anything at the moment, young lady," Ian countered.

"Maybe not right now, but I will be soon, and I'm the best lead you have because if it's the companion I think it is who's been turned, I can recognize her," Izzy pointed out.

Ian paused to stop and think for a moment, looking at her seriously. "Okay, fair point. So here's the deal then. You go away and sort yourself out with your mom for a week's convalescence. Then you report back here to me and we'll see how you are, and if you are fit enough to resume duty. Meanwhile, we will keep looking, and if we find anything, then I'll keep you posted on the details. Fair enough?"

"Fair enough," Izzy agreed.

"Good. Okay, let's get you sorted out with the medical team and into some new clothes, too, or your mother will disown you looking like that," Ian added.

The two of them then headed out of the interview room and off toward the infirmary together. As they did so, the technician operating the recording device in the adjacent room turned to his superior and asked him if he wanted the recording stored on disc. Dr. Lawler told him to wipe it, as nothing of importance had been uncovered. He was then given instructions to have one of the female staff report to Dr. Lawler's office. They needed someone to go out and buy some clothes for Miss

Lancar and quickly so that the micro-transmitters could be sewn onto them. Then the technician was to thoroughly check the recording system in interview room one and find out why it wasn't working properly. Dr. Lawler was sure something was going on and he was not going to rest until he got to the bottom of the story.

Chapter Seventeen

Prisoner

Pieter quickly descended the stairs and walked along the long, dark corridor in the cellar, passing by several rooms until he reached the heavier, reinforced door blocking the end of the passageway. He reached up and unhooked a large key, which he then used to unlock the door. Pushing the heavy door open, it creaked with age and the weight bearing down on the three sets of heavy brass hinges. The room inside had a heavy timber workbench, pushed up against the left wall. Hanging from a large hook in the roof was a heavy gauge chain, about ten feet in length. About a yard of the chain lay on the ground, and at the end of it was an iron collar with spikes lining and pointing inside the hoop.

Pieter entered the room and heaved the bag up onto the workbench. He immediately unzipped it and pulled the partially folded body bag out, laying it down on the bench. Then he unzipped it and pulled the torso and head that was Roberto out, dropping it roughly onto the top of the workbench. Next, he walked to the center of the room and picked up the collar, dragging the chain across the room with it. He checked whether the lever on the clasp was still working by closing and then opening it a couple of times. Then he positioned the collar around Roberto's neck and closed the clasp once more. Satisfied that the collar was fitted correctly, Pieter took hold of the sharpened steel stake he'd earlier plunged into Roberto's chest, and with a mighty heave, he yanked it free. Pieter then checked both the stake and the still-open wound for any sign of a metal splinter remaining in the chest. Already, the old vampire's blood was beginning to slowly ooze into the opening left in the chest, and as it did so, the rapid repair began. Pieter turned and walked out of the room, taking both the canvas and body bags as well as the stake with him.

Halfway down the corridor, Pieter entered another room on the right and laid the canvas bag down on the floor before tossing the metal stake into the sink, ready to be cleaned later. He then walked over to his own large furnace on the other side of the room and opened the door. The heat of the furnace made him squint and shield his face as he lobbed the body bag into the opening. He closed the door once more and walked back into the corridor, closing the door to the boiler room behind him.

He took a short stroll back up the corridor to his right and then entered another room on his left. This was his office. On the wall was a large map of North America, and dotted here and there, using different-colored pins, were his markings of vampire movements and hunter organizations. Also included were the locations of his informants and confirmed vampire kills. It was almost a visual history of his movements around the United States. Pieter walked across the room and around a large, ornately carved wooden desk to take his seat behind it. He opened the lower-most drawer and rummaged around through all the packets of trinkets he'd collected, until he found what he was looking for. He held the packet up and took out the gold signet ring. He inspected it, and once he was satisfied that it was the correct one, he slid it onto the little finger of his left hand. He sat contemplating his next ruse for a few moments and then stood up and returned to the corridor.

Pieter walked back up the corridor, a little way to the first room he had passed on the left, and opened the door. Without pausing, he walked over to a large, white fridge on the far wall and opened the door. Inside, stacked neatly across all the shelves, were bags of blood, human blood. Each was marked with the blood type and the date it was taken. The whole store was like a wine cellar, laid out in perfect precision and the stock easily rotated. He grabbed a bag of O-positive and returned to the room he had left Roberto in.

As he entered the room, he noticed that the old vampire was regaining consciousness and starting to breathe heavily. Pieter approached him, and using a small lock knife he'd produced from his belt, he cut off the corner of the bag of blood and stood ready. As Roberto's eyes opened in shock, he screamed in a mixture of pain and rage. After a few moments, he started to gather his wits a little and looked around the room, feeling the spikes on the collar digging into his flesh for the first time as he did so. He saw the plain brick walls of the room and noticed the chain hanging from the ceiling hook, and then he saw Pieter standing close by.

"You! You dare attack me?!" he yelled in outrage as he attempted to lift himself up to confront his assailant. Suddenly, the old vampire realized what else had been done to him. "What have you done to me?!" he bellowed, his eyes widening in shock when he realized that he had no arms or legs with which to move.

"I've cut off both your arms and legs and seared the wounds closed, then taken you prisoner," Pieter answered matter-of-factly.

"You what?" the old vampire asked, spitting the question at him.

"I said, I've cut off your arms and legs, and taken you prisoner."

"Who dares such an outrage?" Roberto demanded.

"I do, and my Lord Vladimir will be much pleased with what I have managed to do. For as well as capture you and lay waste to one of Dimitri's houses, it will seem to everyone that you are dead and that the hunters were responsible," Pieter said calmly.

Roberto went silent as he thought on what had just been relayed to him. Pieter saw that his ruse in playing the part of one of Vladimir's staff was causing the old vampire to rethink his position.

"Here, drink this. Your body will need to be repaired if in your future you are to continue to serve Lord Vladimir." Pieter extended his arm and began to pour the blood out of the pack and into the old vampire's mouth.

Roberto opened his mouth and began drinking. As he silently drank the blood, Roberto was looking around at the cellar prison, and then he began to study Pieter more closely. He'd picked up Pieter's slight accent on their initial meeting, and now he was looking for clues on just how old he really was. As Pieter raised his left hand to adjust the angle he was pouring the soft plastic bag of blood into Roberto's mouth, the old vampire caught sight of the ring. As well as being an antique gold ring, it was also a symbol of one of the old Lithuanian vampire clans. The Wolfshead Clan, as it was known, had once been part of the Western European group of vampire nations. That was until they joined with the Russian organization headed by Vladimir and turned on the other vampire clans in the first vampire clan wars. Their treachery had later led to Dimitri's change in fortune and the loss of his own clan and position. They were therefore deemed responsible for his eventual flight out of Europe and across to the Americas. For them to be here in America meant that the so-called truce being observed for the ongoing council meeting was a sham. Vladimir was making his move against Dimitri once more and using the council meeting to strike while all the senior vampires were gathered together.

By keeping him alive yet incapacitated as they had, Roberto thought they had already made their move and had probably wiped out Dimitri and all the other senior vampires in America who didn't fit their plans. He figured that he was being kept alive to provide information on all of Dimitri's organization. That meant they knew his worth and would likely allow him to make a full recovery, and then reinstate him below whoever Lord Vladimir had put in charge of America. He would simply have to swear his allegiance to Lord Vladimir to recoup his old position and go about his business as usual.

Maybe this isn't such a bad situation to be in after all, Roberto thought to himself. There was no point in following a dead leader and getting himself killed in the process, and it mattered little to him who was in charge and gave the orders as long as he was still in a senior position that allowed him his little luxuries. Yes, he would willingly serve Lord Vladimir just as he had Lord Dimitri.

"That's enough for now," Pieter said as he took the drained pack of blood away from the old vampire.

"I would be far more use to Lord Vladimir if allowed to recover as fast as possible, my lord. There are many things and places of Lord Dimitri's that need to be shown rather than told, due to the traps in place to guard them from the hunters." Roberto spoke humbly with what he felt was due reverence to his captor.

"That remains to be seen, Roberto. That remains to be seen," Pieter replied flatly.

"May I ask, my lord, how long I remained staked?" Roberto probed.

"You were revived after only a week, Roberto. Lord Vladimir didn't want your brain to rot and lose any of its sharpness...if you are to be of any use to him," Pieter lied.

"Then the high council meeting will have been and gone," Roberto thought out loud.

Pieter hid his surprise at this revelation from Roberto, and turned as if to leave, but Roberto questioned him again.

"My lord, was Lady Guinilla slain alongside Lord Dimitri and the other seniors, or does she work alongside Lord Vladimir?"

"That is not for you to know right now, Roberto. It is enough that you have been spared so that you may be useful to Lord Vladimir. Pray that he continues to think you are of use to him if you are to have any kind of future," Pieter replied as icily as he could.

That said, Pieter calmly walked out of the room without another word and locked the door behind him. He then turned out the light to the cell, and walked back down the corridor and into his office once more. He needed time to think about what he had just learned and plan his future line of questioning of Roberto.

If there was to be a meeting with all the senior vampires as well as the three vampire lords, then they presented a target that was second to none. An opportunity to wipe out the vampire hierarchy was something that didn't come along very often. The meeting with Maggie and Izzy couldn't come quickly enough now, since maybe he could tip off the hunters and allow them to do the work for him through Izzy. They could work the information into something Izzy might have overheard while she was in captivity.

Pieter knew that he would have to question Roberto more carefully now and he would have to avoid asking him about the meeting directly. The last thing he wanted to happen was to raise the wily old fox's suspicious nature with his line of questioning. He had planned on engaging Roberto in conversations aimed at discovering the various strengths and weaknesses of the senior vampires and how they were perceived to have performed under Lord Dimitri's rule. Luckily, he had some reliable intelligence on one or two of them so he could engage Roberto on them first and, hopefully, the old vampire would then swing into revelation mode regarding all the others.

As Pieter began to go through his files and refresh his memory over the three vampire lords he was about to bring up in conversation with Roberto, it seemed that he was going to have a very long night ahead of him once again.

Chapter Eighteen

History

Once upstairs, Mechtild got the girls organized and they were all showered or had a bath, then it was decided that Roxy would stay with Blondie in the one guest room, sharing the large double bed. Ronnie would occupy the adjoining room, also with a large double bed she would have to herself.

Blondie was being cuddled by Roxy, as Ronnie and Mechtild left them alone and entered the other room. Mechtild was pulling back the duvet and sheets when Ronnie asked her, "How long have you known Pieter?"

"Since I was a little girl, about three or four years old," Mechtild answered with a smile, knowing that this bright, inquisitive young lady was about to discover a thing or two about Pieter she would never have suspected.

"But that's impossible. He doesn't look a day over thirty-five," Ronnie thought aloud, then suddenly realized that she was being rude. "Oh, I'm sorry. I didn't mean to suggest you are really old but..." She stammered, not knowing what else to say.

"It's all right, Ronnie. What you are saying is true. I do look older than Pieter. In fact, I'm about sixty-seven, I think. You see, my parents and all my family were murdered by the Nazis during the war, and when Pieter rescued me, he seemed about thirty or so to me then. It's hard to tell exactly as Pieter doesn't usually talk too much about his past, and I was so young and Jurgen wasn't that much older than me, either."

"So what is he then, if he's not one of them? A vampire, I mean," Ronnie quizzed.

"None of us are sure," Mechtild answered. "Even Pieter isn't completely aware of what he is. We just know that he is something completely different to them, thank God."

"Amen to that…So what happened to you? How did he rescue you?" Ronnie asked almost excitedly.

"Well, since all that coffee you drank has taken the sleep out of your eyes, I'll tell you the story," Mechtild said as she sat down on the high-backed chair, leaving Ronnie to occupy the bed.

For the next twenty minutes or so, Mechtild told her the story of how she and Jurgen came to be rescued by Pieter and ended up staying with him. It had all started one late summer's morning, which she had worked out to be around September 1943. She had been dragged out of her house along with all her family, still groggy and half asleep. The first thing she saw was her father being shot in front of her, for daring to struggle with the soldiers. Then she remembered her mother being beaten for trying to protect her as they were herded along with the other Jewish families in the village.

After her father had been shot, no one else dared to struggle or argue against the soldiers, but they still hit and beat them if they didn't move along fast enough, especially the men tasked with carrying her father's body. They were marched through the town and down to the woods where a large ditch had been dug out. As they approached the woods, Jurgen's brother, Uwe, tried to run off into the forest. The soldiers had opened fire on him, and as he fell to the ground, injured, he began screaming in pain. One of the soldiers rushed over to him then leveled his rifle at his head and pulled the trigger. Mechtild remembered how Jurgen's mother screamed and was hit on the head by a nearby guard using his rifle butt. She remembered Jurgen's tears, but also that he didn't argue or fight back; he simply helped his mother as they were herded along the road. Two of the men were sent over by the guards to pick up poor Uwe's body and carry it back to the ditch, where they were told to leave the boy's body next to the large hole in the ground.

As the full column of people reached the clearing at the side of the ditch, the soldiers instructed them all to sit down on the ground. The soldier in charge then made a point of walking over to Uwe's now lifeless body and used his foot to kick him into the ditch. He then ordered ten of the men to be pulled out of the group and made to kneel at the edge of the ditch, facing toward it. Ten of the soldiers lined up behind them, and as the soldier in charge shouted a command, they all fired at once into the necks of the kneeling men.

Mechtild told how she remembered hearing the sharp gunfire blasts, then seeing the crimson streaks spraying from the men's necks as they slumped forward into the ditch. The soldier who issued the order then walked along the edge of the ditch, looking down at the fallen men. Then after pulling his pistol out of its holster, he jumped into the ditch. A single shot was heard, followed by the soldier emerging with a smile on his face as he signaled for another ten men to be pulled out of the group.

At that moment, a big military car pulled up and a soldier with a flat hat instead of a metal one called the soldier in charge over to him. An argument ensued and the soldier with the flat hat ended up striking the one who seemed to be in charge. Later, Jurgen had told her that the man in the flat cap was actually an officer and he had told the soldier that no such killings were to take place under his command and that all the Jewish villagers were to be transported away to work in camps.

After what seemed like a lifetime of waiting, some trucks started to arrive and everyone was loaded aboard, all except Jurgen's mother, that is. They couldn't wake her after she'd been hit on the head. Jurgen had said she was asleep and some straw-colored liquid was running out of one of her ears. When she wouldn't rise after being kicked a couple of times, two of the soldiers had dragged her limp body across the clearing and tipped her over into the ditch. Jurgen had watched it all, held tightly by his uncle. This time, his uncle's hand had been covering Jurgen's mouth to stop him from screaming and drawing the attention of the guards.

The next few days had been a blur of sleep and huddled up travelling by truck or by train, until they arrived at a place called Belsen. It was a horrible place, with an awful stench in the air that you could smell for miles. Many of the people in the camp were sick, and all were hungry. Mechtild said how she always remembered what she termed as the lifeless eyes that many of the people there had.

Luckily for her and Jurgen, they didn't get to stay there long. They had arrived in the morning and were in the middle of being processed when another officer had come along and selected them both to go with him. That afternoon, they were looked after by two women who worked in the kitchens. They were washed, fed, and given new clothes to wear. The clothes were not the same as all the other Jewish people were being given. They were normal children's clothes, and Mechtild remembered being disappointed that she didn't get one of the yellow stars to wear like all the others. She also remembered the women who had fed and washed them were crying as the officer returned to take them away. It had been early in the evening, but they didn't argue with him and kept looking toward the floor in his presence. She also remembered how happy she was to go away with this officer, as she didn't like the camp at all. She had remembered how the other officer had saved them all from being shot in the woods by her village. She'd thought they were safe now.

As they drove off in the car, she remembered looking out of the window and enjoying the view of the forest. And as it grew darker, she fell asleep curled up on the leather seat. She awoke to a gentle nudge from the officer, who, she remembered, was always smiling and was always friendly toward her. Jurgen, she recalled, was somewhat unsure, but seemed happy enough to go along with them as they walked off into the woods.

After a short walk, they came to a clearing with four big lanterns lighting the whole area and a small campfire close to an old-fashioned horse-drawn wagon. The officer jumped and skipped along with them toward a woman in a chair next to the brightly-colored gypsy wagon. As they approached, the officer began calling out to the girl on the chair, almost singing in glee.

"Ute, Ute, look what I have brought you," he called.

Suddenly, he stopped cold, and his mood changed. His grip on Mechtild's and Jurgen's hands suddenly became very tight and painful. Mechtild remembered screaming as she and Jurgen were yanked up into the air and then suddenly dropped. As he looked around the campsite, she recalled seeing the officer's face through her tears as he screamed in rage. His teeth had grown large, like dog fangs, and his eyes had turned a shocking, horrible red color.

The next thing Mechtild recalled was a "thudding" sound and the officer clutching at his chest. Then another "thud," which seemed to cause him to spin around. As he spun around, she remembered seeing an arrow jutting out from the pale flesh of the officer's hand, pinning it to the middle of his chest, and another arrow slightly below it. His eyes, she recalled, were no longer angry, as he fell limply to the grass in the middle of the clearing. They were just open and red, but his whole face maintained a relaxed, plain expression, as if he were asleep.

A moment later, she heard Pieter's voice for the first time when he asked them if they were all right. Both had been shocked into silence by what they had seen, and Pieter had to speak a few times before either of them responded to him. Pieter sat the two of them down by the fire with a large blanket he'd taken from the wagon covering their shoulders. He'd told them both that they were safe now, and he would take them away to somewhere warm in a few moments. That was after he'd finished what he had to do to keep them all safe. He had told them both to keep their eyes open for anyone else approaching, and to let him know if they saw anyone, but not to look back at what he was doing.

Jurgen had sneaked a look back and had seen a little of what Pieter was doing, and had eventually told Mechtild many years later. He had seen Pieter chop the heads off the German officer and the woman in the chair before he threw their lifeless bodies effortlessly into the wagon and set it on fire. Jurgen had marveled at how strong the man had been, lifting the bodies and tossing them about like a child would a rag doll.

Having seen the officer's terrible red eyes and fangs, and how he had hurt them by squeezing their hands and tossing them aside in his rage, both the children had picked up on how different things were with Pieter. He was strong and kind, and had killed the officer to protect them, and he had a calmness that both children had responded to. Both of them were completely relaxed around him, and for the first time since being dragged out of their beds that early morning, they had both felt safe and protected once again.

"That must have been a terrible ordeal for you both," Ronnie said sympathetically.

"It was," Mechtild agreed.

"You hear stories and see films about what the Nazis did during the war, but when you hear it from people who were actually there and experienced it firsthand, it brings it home how bad it really was and how horrible humans can be to each other. Then when you think it can't get any worse, you find out that there really are vampires in the world," Ronnie commented as she looked up at the ceiling.

Chapter Nineteen

Otto

Ronnie shook herself back out of her philosophical moment and sat back up on the bed again. She asked Mechtild to continue telling the story of how Pieter had rescued them from the Nazi vampire and his gypsy girlfriend. Apparently, after dealing with the grisly task of beheading the two vampires and setting the caravan on fire, Pieter had returned to the two children. He had pulled out a bar of chocolate and broke off two small pieces. He presented one to each of them and smiled as they gladly accepted the confectionary. Mechtild remembered the smile being warm and friendly, and something about the way he spoke also made her feel safe. He told them that he was going to take them away with him into the Harz Mountains to see out the winter, and then they would see what happened in the spring. At that time, he was thinking about moving away to somewhere far from the war and all the death and destruction it was causing.

They had to walk a fair way through the forest to Pieter's car; he then hid them in the back, under some large, warm blankets. They were told to keep quiet if they were stopped on the road, which luckily didn't happen. They eventually arrived at a place where Pieter left his car in a big old barn. Next, they spent the rest of the day walking up to what became known to them as Pieter's mountain hideaway.

Mechtild told how she remembered her first sight of the log cabin set back at the edge of the woods. It had only become visible to them once they had entered a large clearing, and she still remembered how much like a postcard the setting had been. As they approached the front door, Pieter had warned them not to be frightened by the lady they would meet inside the house. He told them that she had been attacked by an animal and her neck and face had been badly scarred, but that she was a very kind lady and would look after them like a mother, along with the other boy in the house.

The older lady was indeed badly scarred around the neck and through the right side of her face. Even though the injuries had healed, the scars told how vicious the attack had been and the poor woman had also lost her right eye in the attack. Mechtild remembered being frightened of Anna's appearance at first. As she grew older, though, she came to love and trust her as if she were her mother. She was always kind to both her and Jurgen, and she was an excellent cook and teacher.

It turned out that Anna had been a school teacher in her early years in Hamburg and had been rescued by Pieter when she was attacked by a vampire. The vampire in question had been a very inexperienced killer and had simply attacked her as she walked home late one night—no finesse or subtlety that the older vampires exhibited, just bloodlust and ravenous hunger. Pieter had slain the vampire and then taken Anna away to help her recover from her wounds. She ended up staying with him and helping him for many years, tending to the wounds of Pieter and all the others he had brought back from his hunting trips. She took great joy in helping to look after other children until they could be returned to their families, but of course, with them being Jewish, Jurgen and Mechtild had no living relatives to find after the holocaust.

Mechtild and Jurgen were not the only children to come and live with Pieter and Anna permanently. The other boy who was already there upon their arrival was named Otto. He was in his mid-teens and Mechtild found him to be a very moody young man. He was a wild-eyed boy who could change from being happy and whimsical to very angry at the drop of a hat. Moreover, he was prone to throwing tools around in an instant should he make a mistake. He didn't speak much, and when Pieter talked about his temper, he described him as having a very short fuse. Anna was always very stern with him and, on occasion, had screamed in anger at his behavior, only to hug and kiss him with tears in her eyes a few minutes later.

Mechtild recalled how he was always full of anger and would lash out at the smallest thing that upset him. She also remembered how when Pieter came back from his frequent hunting trips, he would always change into a much nicer boy. He followed Pieter around everywhere and was always asking questions of him and what he'd been up to on his latest journey. Of course, now she knew that those hunting trips were trips to seek out and kill vampires, but at the time, she thought he was just going hunting for food and selling some of the things he made in the big shed next to the cabin.

One of the things she loved about that old cabin was the way all the animals in the forest would come out at dusk and feed in the troughs Pieter had built in the middle of the clearing. They used to watch from inside, pressed up against the cabin windows. When Pieter was at home, he would put on this smelly old coat and slowly walk out and hand-feed the deer. The animals had no fear of him, and she remembered the red squirrels running up his legs and searching his pockets for the nuts he would hide there.

She recalled how happy she and Jurgen had been there in those days, and how Pieter also seemed happy when among and caring for the animals as they cheekily pestered him for more of the food he had hidden about him. That was until Otto messed everything up for them, and they had to move away.

Otto's family had all been slowly tortured and drained of blood in front of his eyes by a small group of vampires. They had worked their way through his family, feeding on them one at a time as a pack. First had been his father, then his elder brother, followed by his mother and older sister. He was to be the last meal, scared out of his wits by what he had been forced to witness and with adrenalin pumping through his bloodstream. Vampires, apparently, got a kick out of drinking blood rich in adrenaline since they do not make that hormone themselves.

Pieter had interrupted their feeding frenzy and had slain two of them with his crossbow before the other three had known what hit them. The one who leapt at him, he easily dealt with, while the other two had fled out of a window and back door. Unfortunately for the two who fled, Pieter had placed bear traps for them, and they fell to his crossbow as they desperately tried to free themselves.

It was some years after this, when the war had finished, that Pieter had left for one of his usual trips, and the following morning, they all awoke to find Otto had also gone. He had packed up and left silently in the night, taking his hunting gear with him. She remembered how Anna had not slept at all while both men were away. She had taken to keeping weapons handy all around the house, and Mechtild recalled how worried Anna seemed about the situation. Neither Jurgen nor Mechtild could understand why this was so. However, a couple of weeks later, they came to understand all too well why Anna had been on her guard.

Exactly two weeks and one day after he'd left, Otto returned to the log cabin. As Mechtild and Jurgen arrived home from collecting firewood, they saw him bloodied, bruised, and battered, slumped down on one of the kitchen chairs. His left hand lay twisted and useless at his side, and Anna had begun tending to his wounds. The children sat and watched from their chairs on the other side of the large kitchen table while Anna began gently cutting off his jacket and shirt. Otto told the story of how he'd gone out and found a group of vampires, just like Pieter had told him how he did it. He'd looked for the signs and followed one likely candidate, which had led him to a small group of four vampires. They were all young, inexperienced, and sloppy about covering their tracks.

He had killed one in its bed, then another as it leapt at him. One had gotten away, leaving him to fight the other left behind. The fight had been vicious, and Otto had feared for his life at one point, as his crossbow bolt had missed the vampire's heart, but had succeeded in pinning its arm to the wooden post in the center of the room. His second bolt he managed to release, despite how his hands were shaking, and he thought he'd hit his target. Unfortunately, he hadn't, and the vampire had been far more devious than he had given it credit. Once he was close enough, the vampire, who had simply been playing possum, grabbed his arm with its free hand and pulled him in toward its wide-open mouth and sharp fangs. Luckily for Otto, he had the large hunting knife in his other hand, and as he was pulled into the vampire's embrace, the knife ended up piercing its chest. The vampire screamed in pain and rage, and twisted Otto's arm viciously, trying to turn him away, even as its fangs raked at the side of his head and almost tore his ear off. Otto had to add his body weight behind the knife, pushing it further into the monster's chest to pierce its heart. Once the vampire was immobilized, Otto desperately wriggled out of its grasp. He took a moment to compose himself then reloaded the crossbow once more. He made no mistake as he put the next shaft into the vampire's chest at point-blank range. Then pulling out the knife, he used it along with the small axe from his pack, to decapitate all the vampires he'd imobilized.

Once this grisly task had been completed, he took out a small bottle of brown fluid from his backpack and sprinkled its contents around the room and onto all the combustible material he'd managed to drag to the side of the room, where the vampire bodies were laid out. He made a trail of the liquid to the door and then produced the lighter Pieter had recently given him. It was an American soldier's lighter. He tipped the lid open and flicked it alight, then applied the flame to the trail of chemicals. Whoosh! A stream of flame leapt across the room, and within a short space of time, the whole dwelling was ablaze with flames leaping up to lick at the roof. Otto slung his pack on his back and winced at the pain it caused in his damaged arm. Then he patted the makeshift bandage he'd put around his ear. The bandage was blood soaked and still oozing more blood down his neck, soaking into the shoulder of his shirt. He would need to attend to the wound more thoroughly later, but for the moment, he needed to get away from this place and the possibility of the fourth vampire returning.

Otto thought he had made good time on his return journey. His ear was still bleeding a lot, but he'd reapplied a fresh bandage each day and had burnt all his discarded dressings in his small campfire he made each night. He knew that once he got home, Anna would be able to patch up his wounds, just like she had done with Pieter each time he came home from a hunting trip. As he approached the log cabin, he was filled with an immense feeling of pride. It had been his first hunting trip and he'd returned triumphant. Three vampires were slain and the other was, he surmised, still running around, scared out of its wits.

Upon seeing the state of him as he arrived home, just after mid-afternoon, Anna had at first burst into tears, then she had steeled herself to the task of sorting him out. The arm, she knew, was badly broken by the way the hand was twisted outward. It would need to be manipulated and set into position then splinted. The ear and the tear in his scalp would need to be cauterized. Vampire bites did not heal on their own because of the anticoagulants secreted in their saliva as well as the anesthetic properties, which had prevented Otto feeling how bad the wound really was. If she didn't seal the wounds, then he'd continue to lose more blood and probably get an infection to go with it, as vampires were not known for their oral hygiene.

Pieter had always let the children see his wounds and how Anna cleaned and treated them; he felt it was important for them to learn at an early age how to deal with the evils of the world, and not be hidden away and kept ignorant of them. Anna wasn't so sure it was a good idea, especially for someone as young and sensitive as Mechtild. However, as both Jurgen and Mechtild had instantly jumped into action to assist her while she tended to Otto's wounds over those few hours, even she had to admit that it had made sense in the end. The two of them had been only too keen to help whenever she needed passing something or Otto's broken arm held in a particular way as she applied the splints. Even mopping the sweat from her own and Otto's brows had come in handy, and both children had more than proven their worth as medical assistants.

Chapter Twenty

Burn

It was early in the evening, by the time the entire patch-up work on Otto had been completed and supper had been finished. Otto was asleep on the couch in front of the large fire in the lounge area of the cabin. Mechtild was also asleep, seated on the rug in front of him, her back propped against the couch. Jurgen was washing the dishes and Anna was sat at the table. Her eyes were wide and she reacted to every crackle and snap from the open fire with a start. She had a large glass in front of her and a bottle beside it, but she hadn't drunk anything from the full glass yet. Also on the table and scattered around the room were several oil lamps, the type that had a wind-up wick. The lamps were all alight and the wicks pushed up too high without the glass covers over them.

Jurgen had noticed how skittish Anna was, and that she had two crossbows ready and set at the table. Pieter had always taught them never to leave such weapons armed and lying around, but he knew when not to get into an argument with Anna. Many a time, he'd tried to get away without washing before a meal or going to bed, and many a time, Anna had berated him and used that stern, no-nonsense look of hers on him. While this wasn't that particular look, it was one that Jurgen read as having no room for compromise or argument, either.

Jurgen was hoping for the squirrels to come up to the window and start making a noise so he could go out and feed them, along with all the other animals that came out of the forest at this time. For some reason, though, they had not come out to play tonight, so Jurgen was stuck doing his chores again.

A loud knock at the door startled them all. Mechtild and Otto simply stirred at the sound, while Anna's hand shot out to grab the crossbow.

Jurgen turned from his position of doing the dishes. "Pieter's home," he exclaimed excitedly.

It was a natural thing to think as Pieter was the only other visitor to the log cabin. Jurgen began to head for the door, but Anna grabbed him as he tried to rush past her. She held him tightly for a moment and then released him as she put one index finger to her mouth to signal for him to remain quiet. Then she pulled him close and whispered in his ear to go and sit with Mechtild and keep her safe. Suddenly, Jurgen understood what was going on. There was danger and he needed to do as he was told without question, just as Pieter had taught him.

Otto sat up and grabbed his crossbow off the small table between the couch and Pieter's armchair. A look passed between Anna and Otto; both knew exactly what had happened and both knew that there was no time to place the blame or argue. Time enough for that later…if they survived.

There was another knock at the door, then a woman's voice broke the awful silence. "Help! Please help me. I was attacked in the woods and I'm hurt."

Mechtild shot a pained look over to Anna, who remained motionless and her jaw clamped shut with a steely determination. "Anna, she's hurt," she exclaimed, not understanding why kind Anna wasn't rushing to help.

Once more, Anna held a finger to her lips as she furrowed her brow at Mechtild. Jurgen's hand was about to come up and cover her mouth when another voice came from outside.

"Sounds like a sweet little girl for you, Renate," came the rough male voice.

"I want the hunter. I can smell his blood. I want to drain him slowly and watch the light go out in his eyes as we feed on his family," a second male voice added.

"Mmmmmh! I can smell Anna's fear," the female voice added once more.

Anna reached for the glass on the table with her free hand then took a large mouthful from it. Then without any further talk or comment, and before anyone inside could react to the situation, the front door handle was yanked on. It held for the first pull, but on the second pull, the handle creaked and split as the door was swung outward. Most doors swing inward, but Pieter had built this one to open outward for two reasons. Firstly, in case of a fire, it enabled a faster escape to simply push the door outward rather than have to pull it inward and move around it. Secondly, though, and the main reason, it was far easier to set up a booby trap mounted on the roof to swing down as the door opened outward.

The second the female vampire had yanked open the door, she had expected crossbow bolts to be fired at her. She'd held a small wooden log across her heart to fend off such an attack. Unfortunately, what she hadn't expected was a paddle of seven, evenly-spaced, two-foot long, sharp wooden stakes to drop from the ceiling on a cantilever system. The paddle had been set up to pierce anyone setting off the trap at chest height. As she had forced the door open and suddenly became aware of the trap sprung above her, she had instinctively raised her arms to fend off the cantilever. In so doing, she had raised the small wooden log she held in front of her chest. The stakes pierced her arm and pinned the small log against her chest, and two of the stakes pierced her heart, immobilizing her. She'd had time to let out a short shriek just as the stakes hit, and was now left hanging limply on the swinging arm of the cantilever.

The remaining vampires let out an animalistic roar of anger and launched their attack, no longer interested in teasing and inciting fear into their intended victims. They were now in a rage of bloodlust and sought revenge for the impudence of such a trick. One ran at the window and leapt inside, smashing it and tangling himself in the drapery as he landed on the floor close to Otto. Pieter's booby traps were sometimes subtly hidden from view, and in this case, the wires threaded through Anna's fancy net curtains at the window were enough to entangle the vampire and slow it down for a few moments. Without hesitation, Otto leveled the crossbow and shot the vampire in its chest. It slumped to the floor and remained there motionless. Another two vampires entered the house, one by the window, now shattered and clear of any obstruction, and the other through the front door, sliding past its immobilized female accomplice.

Anna marveled at the considerable grace and smoothness the vampire's movements exhibited as it entered the cabin. Then she fired her crossbow and sent it sprawling backward, awkwardly flailing its arms as the force of the bolt piercing its chest sharply changed its direction of movement. The vampire at the window leapt across the short distance between itself and Otto, who was struggling to reload his crossbow, hampered as he was with his injured arm. The vampire grabbed at Otto's throat with one hand and Otto's arm with the crossbow with the other.

Just as Anna was reaching across the table for the other crossbow, the kitchen window exploded inward and another vampire was upon her. Jurgen had left the drapes open so he could see the animals as they came down to feed, so nothing remained at the window to entangle this vampire. Anna was flung to the floor with the vampire on top, pinning her down. Both vampires now stopped and exchanged glances, and upon seeing no more danger to themselves, they both laughed.

The one holding Otto then spoke. "Feeding time. We drain these two then pull the stakes from the others, and they can fight over the two children."

"Agreed," came the response from the one holding position above Anna.

The vampire holding Otto looked at the crossbow still held in his hand and smiled—an insidious and cruel smile. He watched Otto intently as he tightened his grip on the young man's arm. Both Jurgen and Mechtild heard the bones snap as Otto screamed in pain and the crossbow dropped to the floor. The vampire slowly twisted Otto's head over to the left, exposing his neck, then slowly leaned forward and licked the skin. It was a long, slow lick, which sent shivers through Otto and sent his heart racing with fear. The adrenalin pumped into his blood at its highest rate. Then the vampire bit and tore at his throat, all teeth and savagery. Blood rained down and splattered onto Jurgen and Mechtild, who screamed as she closed her eyes and covered her ears, trying to block out the sight and sound of it all.

The vampire above Anna was also holding her by the throat and one arm. It now leered at her, looking straight into her eyes as it opened its mouth to show the sharp canines that it intended to use to rip out her throat.

"So, Anna, I see you've been kissed by one of us before. Tell me, do you still have nightmares about it?" The vampire spoke slowly and cruelly, watching for the fear in her eyes. "Don't worry, Anna, I'm going to stop those nightmares for you now," it added, but there was no kind intent behind what it had just said.

As it spoke, it lowered its face toward Anna, expecting her to turn either left or right to avoid its intended kiss, and in so doing, she would present her neck for it to feed on. Instead, Anna kept facing the vampire, and as she judged it to be in range, she spat the contents of her mouth onto its face. She had swallowed some of the fluid in the struggle, but there was enough in her mouth for what she intended. The vampire yelped in pain and recoiled, releasing its grip on her arm and throat as the fluid stung at its eyes. Anna desperately wriggled over to the right a little and stretched out to grab one of the oil lamps now tipped over onto the floor. Ignoring the pain, she grabbed at the still-burning wick and threw it into the vampire's face. The fluid on the vampire's skin ignited, turning the whole front of its head into a ball of flame.

"Burn in hell, fang face," she retorted with no small amount of venom in her expression.

The vampire began to madly flail around the room, bouncing from wall to wall and tripping over objects in its frenzied path. It bounced off the back door, the impact dislodging the latch and opening it, causing the cantilever system to activate and deliver the same imobilizing blow as the one at the front door had done. The wooden spikes pierced the flaming vampire through the side of its body, but one of them had still found its mark in the vampire's heart. Anna had been caught watching and was mesmerized by its wild thrashings for a moment. Then as the trap was sprung and it became paralyzed, she gathered her wits. At the same time, the vampire who was feeding on Otto realized that there was a problem. As Anna quickly tried to get to the other crossbow, which was now lying on the floor beside the table, the remaining vampire dropped Otto into a lifeless heap. It then leapt across the room like a graceful, giant cat, to land on top of Anna and send her sprawling to the floor, away from the crossbow. Anna steeled herself when she felt it was about to lunge at her exposed throat, but it suddenly stopped and turned back to look toward the children.

There, standing protectively in front of Mechtild, was Jurgen, with Otto's crossbow in his hand, still leveled at the vampire. As Anna caught sight of him, she suddenly understood what had happened. Jurgen had recovered Otto's crossbow, reloaded it, and then fired the bolt into the vampire from behind. As the vampire continued to turn, Anna saw the bolt protruding from the right height, but in the dead center of its back. The bolt had failed to pierce the spine and enter the heart. Now, the vampire was angered once more, and as it looked around it saw the other loaded crossbow lying on the floor. A wicked smile crossed its face as it decided how to spread the most fear into all its victims before feeding on them.

"So the little boy likes to play with toys does he?," it stated, as it first assessed the situation and any further threat Anna might pose, then it moved toward the crossbow.

Anna, understanding the vampire's intent, desperately looked around for another weapon as the vampire slowly, almost casually, moved across to the crossbow. "You leave them alone, demon," Anna raged as she leapt toward the vampire.

The vampire caught sight of her movement and extended its arm to catch her by the throat while she tried to intervene and prevent either of the children from being shot. In one hand it held the crossbow, now aimed at Jurgen, and with the other, it held Anna at arm's length. Her arms and legs were flailing away, trying to spoil its aim. The vampire realized what Anna was trying to do, so it swung her back against the table, to knock the wind out of her and calm her down. The vampire made a point of then raising the crossbow up and slowly lowering it as it steadied its aim. Anna, though winded and in pain, grabbed the bottle, now tipped over, and chugging its contents out onto the tabletop. She held it by the neck and swung her arm around, smashing the bottle on the back of the vampire's head, spilling the remaining liquid onto its hair and down its neck.

The vampire turned in anger and fired the crossbow. The bolt hit Anna in the stomach and pinned her to the heavy, wooden tabletop. Everything seemed to stop for a moment as Anna laid almost motionless on the table, a pained expression on her face. She was gasping for air and her eyes were rolling in their sockets, unable to focus on anything but the pain. The vampire looked back at the children once more to see that they were both transfixed by what they saw. They posed no further immediate threat, the vampire thought. Then it lowered itself next to Anna and whispered in her ear.

"Anything you'd like to say to your beloved children before I feed on them?" Its voice was now sweet and mocking, with no trace of anger. It reached out and twisted Anna's head to the side, forcing her to look at the children's frightened faces, as it pulled back its bloody lips to reveal its fangs, ready to feed once more.

"Jurgen!" Anna yelled. "Let it burn!" she added, as with all her remaining strength, she wrapped her arms and legs around the vampire, pulling it in closer as if embracing a lover.

Jurgen understood what she meant, and with tears already forming in his eyes, knowing the terrible thing she wanted him to do, he grabbed the uncovered oil lamp closest to him and threw it toward the table. The lamp bounced off the vampire's back, sending sparks flying across the table and floor. Immediately, the liquid from the bottle ignited, sending flames billowing up from the floor. A sheet of flame spread across the table and the vampire's head, neck, and shoulders were like a large, rounded torch. Both the vampire and Anna were screaming in pain. The vampire pushed with both its hands on Anna's head to break her hold on it. Anna's neck snapped and her hold relaxed, freeing the vampire to run around, trying to douse the flames. It was a futile effort, Jurgen knew all too well. When Pieter had made up that fluid, he told Jurgen all about it, especially that it wouldn't go out until all the fuel was gone. No amount of water or smothering would help; it would just keep burning. He remembered the last words Anna had screamed to him, and though he had the crossbow loaded once again, he held off firing it. He'd let the vampire continue to run around and struggle with the flames until it was dead. He understood all too well what Anna had meant by "let it burn."

After the vampire had finally stopped moving and thrashing around, Jurgen took charge of the situation. He told Mechtild to grab what she could out of the house while he dealt with the paralyzed vampires. What they had gathered was now laid at their feet as they stood together, hand in hand, watching the cabin burn. Both faces were streaked with soot and blood, except for a trail of tears down each cheek that neither had tried to brush away or hide.

Two days later, Pieter returned home to find them camped out in the barn. The next morning, they all left to go to France. Pieter initially left them with friends there who were part of a group of vampire hunters. He had some kind of connection with them and trusted them to look after Jurgen and Mechtild while he was away. They didn't see him for several years, until he eventually sent for them to join him in America. Once there, they saw a bit more of him, he still moved around, but he based his center of operations out of the house they were now staying in.

Both Jurgen and Mechtild had attended school in America, and then later, college, and had lived an almost normal life for a time. They had eventually married in the early 70s, and although they never had any children, they had looked after plenty, thanks to Pieter and his work.

As Mechtild finished telling the story to Ronnie, she suddenly realized that she had tears rolling down both of her cheeks. "*Ach, mein gott*. Look at me, a blubbering wreck, when it's you who's just been through it all," she said, wiping her eyes and then blowing her nose.

Ronnie reached out her hand to pat Mechtild's, and said softly to her, "Thank you for being there for us, too."

"You're welcome, sweetie. Now, I'd better go and get more food prepared for dinner and let you get some rest," Mechtild replied as she stood up from the chair and headed toward the door.

Ronnie just nodded at her as she walked across the room and opened the door, then closed it behind her. All of a sudden, Ronnie was tired and she felt a few hours' sleep would be good for her, so she stripped off the towel and got into the bed. She then noticed that the curtains to the large bay window were open a little and light was flooding into the room. She decided that they could stay open; she didn't want to sleep in the dark, not at the moment anyway.

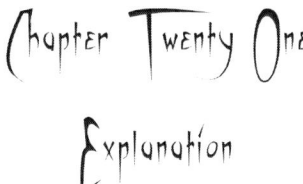

Chapter Twenty One
Explanation

The large limousine pulled slowly up against the curb, and the hotel doorman quickly stepped out to open the door at the back. Izzy stepped out and walked directly into the hotel without acknowledging the doorman's polite welcome.

Once inside the hotel lobby, she strode purposefully across to the reception desk, where a brightly smiling young lady met her. The receptionist greeted her with another polite and well-practiced welcome. Izzy treated her with the equal amount of disdain she'd shown the doorman.

"Mrs. Lancar-Jones's room?" she demanded rather than asked.

Once she had the room number, she instructed the young lady to call ahead to inform her mother of her imminent arrival.

The short time she spent in the lift with the busboy was long enough for him to form the opinion that she was not a friendly or talkative person. Also, that she considered herself far superior to someone like him.

Arriving at her mother's suite, the door opened before she could knock and the security guard, Johnson, ushered her in without any change in his expression. Once inside, her mother strode forward to greet her and grabbed both of her wrists as she spoke.

"Isabelle, you still look so gaunt and tired, dear. Come with me. I've arranged a spa treatment, and some food and wine, to help put some color back in your cheeks."

"Oh, Mother, you shouldn't have, really. I'm too tired and all I want to do is get some sleep," Izzy replied.

As she held her daughter's wrists, she pressed her right thumb firmly into her as she spoke. While her voice was jovial and even a little patronizing, the look

Izzy received from her mother's eyes was deadly serious. So Izzy decided it would be best to play along no matter how she felt.

"Nonsense, dear. You'll feel so much better after some wine and nibbles. Besides, we need to get you out of these awful clothes they've given you and get you into the ones I've been out and bought for you."

"You didn't have to do that, Mother," said Izzy.

"Well, I had to do something while I was waiting for your call."

"Well, I take it you have one of those big spa baths in this overpriced suite. So I suppose I can relax in a bath while you do your usual interrogation." Izzy pretended to give in wearily.

"There's a good girl. Now go and get changed in that room over there. I've already laid out a bathrobe on the bed for you, so go and get out of those cheap clothes and I'll have Johnson send them out to a charity shop somewhere."

As she spoke, Margeurite gave her daughter's hands a gentle squeeze and nodded her head at her. Izzy proceeded to go to the room that her mother had indicated and stripped off, discarding the clothes she'd been given at the BGHQ, leaving them lying on the floor. She put on the toweling robe and then came back out into the suite's main sitting room. After a quick nod at her mother, she went through into the large bathroom. Her mother paused to say something to her bodyguard before following her into the large, bright room. Once she had entered, her mother began to engage her in idle chitchat as the housemaid finished running the bath and adding the bath salts to the water. Once her duties were completed, the maid excused herself and exited the bathroom. She walked back into the main sitting room and was then escorted out of the suite by Johnson.

After the maid had departed, Margeurite continued to hold her daughter's hands and prattle on about nothing for a few minutes. Johnson then came into the bathroom, holding what looked like a small television remote control. There was a wire coming out of its base, which trailed up to an earpiece in his left ear. He proceeded to walk around the room slowly, waving the remote around. At first, he just waived the contraption around the room, then he pointed it at and around Izzy. After a short while, he looked over at Margeurite and gave a terse nod.

"Thank you, John. Once you've finished with the clothes, you can go and catch up with your sports channel in the downstairs bar if you'd like. Isabelle and I are likely to be some time," Margeurite said to her bodyguard.

"Yes, Ma'am. Nice to have you back in one piece, Miss Isabelle. You had your mother really sick with worry. No matter what she tells you in here." Johnson spoke with genuine warmth as he left the two women to chat.

"Thanks, Johnny, it's nice to be back," Izzy replied with a smile.

As the door closed behind them, Margeurite helped Isabelle out of the robe and into the bath. Her mother had to stifle her own gasps at the state of her daughter's body, with the many cuts and bruises she was covered in. She saw the pain on her daughter's face as she lowered herself into position in the bath and saw her start to relax once submerged up to her neck in the warm water. Immediately after Isabelle was settled, her mother opened the bag she had brought with her and started to arrange the medical supplies along the marble sink top. Her daughter's cuts would require new "steri-strips" and dressings, and possibly a couple more sutures once the medicinal soak was over.

"So how did it go with the little men?" Margeurite asked as she began to make proper conversation.

"I did exactly as you said, Mother. It wasn't too hard to convince the pencil necks that I'd been too weak and was fading in and out of consciousness all the time. I told them I couldn't recall too much of what was going on around me, other than pain, cutting, and more beatings. It was actually true for the most part. I just left out one or two of the details to the story," Izzy explained.

"Do you think they bought your story?"

"I'm pretty sure they did."

Just then, there was a knock at the door, and Margeurite walked over to it and opened it just enough to chat to Johnson.

"Just like you said, Ma'am, the top button on the coat and one of the decorations on the belt are microphones," Johnson told her.

"Thank you, John. You can dispose of them down in the lobby as you go to watch the game." Margeurite closed the door and returned to sit down on the chair by the bath to carry on her conversation with her daughter. "So they may or may not still trust you, but your hunter organization is definitely trying to eavesdrop on our little chitchat."

"Why would they do that?" Izzy asked, frowning.

"Because I think someone in the upper echelons of your organization may suspect something of what I'm about to tell you. That's why they were so set on recruiting you when you left home for college. Especially after I'd left them and took all my money with me," her mother stated flatly.

Izzy looked puzzled. "You never did tell me why you left the organization, even after what they did for dad."

"I know I didn't, Isabelle, and I had good reason not to. You were going through a particularly difficult, rebellious teenager period of your life. You were floundering around, looking to latch onto any father figure you could find. In a way, I was happy for you to find that in Ian. The problem was that I soon discovered that Ian was not entirely genuine in his friendship toward us both. I caught him snooping around our house a couple of times and then realized what was going on. I couldn't tell you at that time, as you were far too wild, and likely to spill any secrets we told you at the slightest hissy fit you threw, for whatever reason. I chose to keep what I'm about to tell you secret because I didn't feel I could trust you at that time."

"And now?"

"Now, it would seem I have no choice. Having met Pieter again, I'm sure if I didn't tell you about him, and the big secret our family has kept for over six hundred years, then I have little doubt that the stubborn streak you inherited from me would cause you to push and pry, and involve every resource that the hunter organization has to find him. So I think it is better that I bring you into the family trust and explain everything to you."

"Okay, fire away. What's the big secret? I'm all ears," Izzy said, suddenly intrigued and eager to be let in on the big family secret.

"Well, you first met Pieter when you were very young, about four or five, I think it was. He had just returned to stay with us after a trip to Italy, where he had been involved in a very dangerous mission. He was recovering from his injuries and taking some time to catch up with your father and I. It was while we were all sitting around the pool when you came up with the name the 'Sunny Man.' Pieter, like a vampire, is pale skinned and does not tolerate a lot of sun. You commented on his pale complexion and told him that he worked too hard, and should get out and play in the sun more often. Then whenever you saw him after that, you called him the Sunny or Sunshine Man."

"So he is a vampire then," Izzy stated.

"No, not really. We're not really a hundred percent sure what he is. I need to start this story way back in the beginning to explain it as it was explained to me." Margeurite paused for a moment to gather her thoughts, and then she began to tell the story that had been passed down to her by her ancestors.

Throughout time, with the many wars and the subsequent redrawing of the European maps, the borderlines have changed a great deal. Over the centuries, Margeurite explained, her family had ended up travelling farther west, like many others who were considered wealthy. Eventually, they had ended up in France, where both she and Izzy were born. Back in the mid-1300s, though, their ancestors were not one of the more affluent families around. They were based in the mid to East European lands, somewhere close to what is now Romania, but, at that time, was part of a much larger Lithuania.

One of their forefathers, named Pavel Kushenko, was a bright student who had excelled at school and was especially gifted in matters related to science. He, along with the professor he was studying under, were recruited into a team of equally intelligent men, all of whom together formed what was considered the earliest recorded hunter organization.

At the time, there had been a change in both vampire numbers and their feeding habits, which brought them more attention than usual. This was mainly affecting the Central and Eastern European countries. Warring vampire clans sought to boost their numbers and had turned more victims into vampires. This, in turn, led to there being more young, inexperienced vampires about. These new vampires exhibited no subtlety or finesse in their feeding habits. Rather than feed from a human and leave them alive to feed upon another day, they viciously killed their prey, like a wild animal would. Initially, these vicious attacks were thought to be the work of wolves or other wild animals, such was the ferocity of the attacks and the damage done to the victims. With the increased number of attacks and the lack of animals tracked in hunting parties and the empty baited traps, the vampire's existence was brought to the attention of the authorities. With public awareness now gathering pace, steps had to be taken to fight back against them. Certain local authorities had no choice but to act, despite how many bribes had previously been paid to turn a blind eye.

The story went that two of the larger vampire clans joined forces to wipe out all of the other clans. Once these two clans took command a return to the old secretive ways was initiated with the culling of their own youngling vampire army. With the numbers reduced to a more sustainable level, the two clans involved then turned on each other. It was then that the senior vampire in charge of the vast area of Lithuania had been targeted by the hunters. He had apparently not fared too well against his Russian counterpart and was caught on the run. There were even rumors of collusion between the Russian clan leader and some members of the hunter organization that provided much of the information used in flushing out the Lithuanian clan leader.

They had almost killed him during a fierce battle in his own home, but unfortunately, the hunters had suffered heavy losses during the fight. Five of the eleven hunters died, with a further three receiving serious wounds, and in the process, they had only managed to cut off the vampire's left hand at the wrist. This, however, flushed him out into the open and left him exposed and on the run.

He was being chased through the forest by a group of hunters on a particularly stormy night, when somehow, he managed to double back on his pursuers. He had returned to a small village, where he had fed on a child and a villager a day earlier. Their ancestor Pavel, had stayed behind in that very village with his ageing professor to study the bodies of the slain and to study the vampire hand that had been cut off. The ageing professor wasn't quite up to the more physical task of chasing down a vampire through the woods.

Apparently, one of the women of this village was with child, but unfortunately for her, she had gone into premature labor at the news of her husband's death. He had died a most horrible death at the hands of the injured vampire, after unwittingly disturbing him as he fed on a child from the same village the day before.

The baby had been delivered something like eight weeks early, but was far too small to thrive, and the mother was left too weak and sickly after her ordeal to be expected to survive the experience either. The attending midwives from the village had done what they thought best and wrapped both mother and baby up warmly. They had then left them alone in a bedroom, to share what precious little time they had left together.

Unfortunately, this was where fate decided to lend a hand to proceedings. Injured and almost exhausted, the escaping vampire, perhaps attracted by the smell of blood, came upon the house and broke in. He fed on the mother, draining her, before being disturbed and, once again, had to flee the village. Pavel had then been called to the scene with his professor due to what the midwife had discovered. The baby, although dropped to the cold floor, was still alive. It was both cold to the touch and pale of complexion, but against all the odds, it had survived the ordeal. Around the baby's mouth, there was both caked, dried blood and also darker, still-liquid blood. The two men of science surmised that there was both blood from the mother and the injured vampire as the blood they had extracted from the vampire hand was of similar consistency. These facts remain the only clues as to what may have happened to Pieter.

From the position of the mother's body, it appeared that the vampire had forced his entry via the window and fell upon his victim from behind. He had bitten into the left side of her neck and fed on her from the left common carotid artery and the left jugular vein. Perhaps because of the injury to his left hand, he had used his right hand to force the head across to the right and had exposed the left side. The baby, being held against the left breast of the mother, was directly beneath the wound to the mother's neck and had probably been spattered by some of the mother's escaping arterial blood flow.

The vampire was known to have received several deep wounds, as well as the removal of his left hand, during the initial battle with the hunters. We now know that vampires have a rapid healing factor about them, but also that the new flesh could be very fragile and easily damaged initially. It seemed likely that if the vampire had so many injuries and was forced to flee, he would not have been fully recovered from those injuries. Hence, his need to feed and the risk he took in returning to the village. Perhaps in her struggles, the mother had opened some of the vampire's wounds and caused some of his blood to escape and be ingested by the baby.

It would be impossible to guess as to how the ingestion of vampire blood by an underdeveloped human baby would affect it. The only thing Pavel and the professor knew was that the baby, surviving as it had, meant that it was abnormal in some way, and therefore merited some kind of further study.

They kept the survival of the baby a secret from everyone, and the two midwives were paid off and sworn to secrecy. The rest of the hunters continued the chase after the vampire, but Pavel and the professor chose to depart from the group and return to the city with the baby. They made the excuse that it was to make further study of the vampire hand before it rotted and could provide no further clues as to the nature of the vampire. These were the early days and science was quite primitive at the time. The knowledge of the vampire was also mainly still based on rumor or superstition.

"So now you know our family secret and as much as any of us do about Pieter's origin," said Margeurite.

Izzy was deep in thought for a moment and then looked at her mother with tears welling up in her eyes. "If only I'd known, poor Grace would still be alive. I was so afraid that he was a vampire trying to con me into going with him," she said before her emotions welled up in her again and she began sobbing.

Her mother moved forward off the chair and knelt down beside the bath, and completely ignored the water as she took her daughter in her arms so she could hug and comfort her.

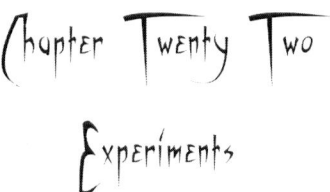

Chapter Twenty Two

Experiments

Margeurite held her daughter in silence for a few minutes; the only noise heard between them was the large sobs and gasps for breath in between them from Izzy. Gradually, the sobbing subsided and Izzy recovered enough to break her mother's hold and wash the tears from her face with the bath water.

"It's been a few years since you've soaked me like this, young lady. I remember trying to keep dry with you splashing away anytime you were in any kind of water," Margeurite said as she rose and reached over for the towel to dry herself. Both women laughed at the break in the tension. Then Margeurite sat back down and continued to tell Izzy the story that had been passed down to her regarding Pieter.

Once Pavel and the professor arrived back in the city, they were quick to make a startling discovery. The vampire hand they found had decomposed at a far slower rate than normal human flesh. However, this particular hand also had another secret to give up. There was a signet ring on the fifth finger that appeared plain and of little or no value. Once it was removed and studied, though, the family name inscribed on the inside of it would lead Pavel to a startling new discovery.

The ring's inscription read "Vasolo," which led the ever-inquisitive Pavel to follow up on the family name and history. To his surprise, he discovered that the local records had been tampered with. Moreover, it seemed that the same changes had been made regularly as far back as the records went. This intrigued Pavel, and he decided to investigate the matter further. Upon arriving at the vampire's family home, he found that it had been completely destroyed. The villagers, upon learning from the hunters that it was a vampire's lair, had reportedly ransacked and then burnt the place to the ground. Upon his further investigation, Pavel discovered what no one else had managed to find—the secrets to the vampire lord's wealth and prosperity.

The tampering with the records had been done to show a fictional history of the various deaths, births, and marriages within the family. Yet the firstborn male had always been called Dimitri. This had been done to prevent the locals from becoming suspicious over the continued existence of one man. When Pavel broke into the family crypt, his suspicions were confirmed, as no rotting corpse had ever been contained inside any of the coffins. What they did contain, though, were riches beyond his belief. Rather than telling anyone about what he'd found, it became another secret that was kept and passed on down through his family. The vampire clan leader had kept his treasures well hidden, so that he could one day return to them. Those treasures were what the Kushenko ancestors had used to set up and keep the family wealthy and prosperous over the years. It had also been used to help fund the continued hunting of more vampires.

As for the baby, it was a boy, and he was also found to be something unique. Initially, he wouldn't feed properly from the wet nurse Pavel and the professor had employed. So a second wet nurse was sought. It was the second nurse that led to a startling discovery about the baby. She was suffering from mastitis with cracked and bleeding nipples, something she initially kept secret from her employers for fear of losing the extra income her lactation afforded her. The baby, however, was far more settled with her and thrived under such conditions, which included his growing at an extraordinary rate.

Within the month, the baby had almost doubled in weight and had already developed a full set of teeth. It was when the baby next fed that the situation with the teeth took on a somewhat strange twist. As it fed, Pavel and the professor came running to investigate the screams of the wet nurse, only to discover that the baby's canine teeth had enlarged and developed into fangs as it fed. It had pierced the wet nurses flesh and was now suckling directly on her escaping blood. Upon further questioning of the wet nurse, the facts about the mastitis and the earlier feeding on blood were uncovered.

The wet nurse was once again paid off to ensure her silence. The baby was then fed on blood paid for and collected from the local peasants. The peasants were told that the blood was to be used in experiments by the professor, which, in a way, was true. The baby rapidly grew to child size within a few months. Then Pavel and the professor started to move around and set up their science laboratories in different locations in an attempt to avoid comments over the child's rapid growth.

Because they were involved with the secretive hunter organization and because of the wealth Pavel had secreted away from the clan leader's family tomb, all such movements were easily facilitated. The need for blood for their anti-vampire work was then further helped by the capture of a vampire by the hunters. This became the single most important factor in the child's development. Until then, they had presumed that the child was a vampire and they would be able to study it for weaknesses and develop a way of destroying the creatures. With a real vampire now being held, they could experiment on it, and then attempt the same experiments on the child for comparison. This led to the startling discovery that where they had similarities, the vampire and the child were not the same.

The vampire had no discernable heartbeat, whereas Pieter, as they chose to call him, did have a very loud and rapid heart rate. The vampire, when cut, lost very little blood, which failed to coagulate outside of his body, yet the wound repaired rapidly, especially when human blood was ingested in sufficient quantities. Pieter bled profusely from any cuts, although he also healed very rapidly under basic first aid treatment. His blood was also very slow to clot and, strangely enough, he also healed at an even greater accelerated rate, when fed more blood. The vampire could regrow a severed limb, and again, more rapidly so when fed on human blood. Pieter, however, could not regrow his limbs, and to this day, the tip of his little finger on the left hand is a shorter stub. Both had excellent night vision and both had trouble seeing in full sunlight, although Pieter, it seemed, was a little more tolerant and still able to function with good color perception. The vampire, it seemed, had none or very little color perception in full sunlight, but fared better in dim or even dark situations. Pieter was equally adept with his own night vision.

The strength of the vampire was judged to be almost four times that of an average man, where Pieter was shown to be slightly superior to this, at around five times stronger than the children they tested of similar size to him. The vampire showed much more stamina, and where Pieter would tire at a much slower rate than any human, this was still faster than the vampire would tire. Both had an incredibly sharp sense of smell and could discern the tiniest change in scents. Upon further investigation, it was found that they could both match the human blood they were fed on with the person it came from.

The captured vampire could not tolerate any human food at all; even the bloodiest of steaks made him vomit the food back up within seconds of its ingestion. Luckily, Pieter had no such problem and could easily tolerate human food without any problem. He was, however, seen to thrive on the blood he was given, both in terms of the energy he displayed and the repair it afforded him after any test or injury. In fact, one test they put him through proved that he needed the blood, as when deprived for a whole week, he became listless and tired—and his concentration lapsed considerably.

Their hearing was also extremely acute, and they could quite literally hear a pin drop or conversations held at great distances away, even behind closed doors. Along with all the other senses being heightened, their sense of taste was especially well developed, and they could go as far as to tell blood groupings and rhesus factors, although that fact wasn't discovered until more recent times, when human science had advanced. They could, however, both detect the sex of the supplier and certain blood-borne diseases such as anemia and malaria by taste. The one superstition that they did manage to dispel was that of the virgin and non-virgin source of blood. However, they could quite accurately guess the age of the supplier.

During their studies on the captive vampire, many of the myths and superstitions surrounding them were found to be untrue or even misleading. No religious effigy, ornaments, trinkets, or symbols ever had any effect on the vampire, as was the case with holy water and garlic. The burning of vampire flesh with caustic acid had a similar effect to human flesh, but the vampire would recover from such wounds without scarring. The naked flame, however, was not something the vampire tolerated as easily. In fact, even the smallest flame was judged to be far more painful to a vampire. Where humans tend to blister, the vampire's flesh tended to blacken and char. If not fed, the vampire's burns remained as they were, and only when they fed would the rapid repair occur.

Sunlight was seen to have a slightly different effect upon each of them, too, as the vampire's skin showed very obvious signs of burning at the slightest exposure and developed no discoloration or pigmentation to protect itself. Pieter showed markedly less effect from the burning after a normal day in the sun, but still didn't go brown. The effect of burning the vampire with a magnifying glass was almost the same as using a naked flame, where Pieter developed just a small blister.

The only superstition held about vampires that was found to have a modicum of truth about it was silver. While it did not burn or injure them in anyway, the vampire did cause the surface of any silver worn against his flesh to turn black. Pavel and the professor assumed that it had something to do with the difference between vampire and human skin secretions and acidity. Again, this was seen as a difference between Pieter and the vampire, as he could wear silver without causing it to discolor in any way.

Once it was concluded that Pieter was not a vampire, but some kind of hybrid, which provided him with certain vampire traits, he became more of a son to Pavel and was looked upon kindly by both him and the professor. They hoped to be able to raise and train him, so that he would be able to lend a hand in the fight against the vampires. In the short time he had been with them, he had already grown to the size of an eight- or nine-year-old boy, and he had been a willing student who learned everything they had tried to teach him very quickly.

On an evening of relaxation together, they had taken Pieter to a travelling circus, and the following day, both Pavel and the professor had marveled at his ability to juggle and his acrobatic prowess. They were both stunned later that day at his knife-throwing ability and accuracy. It seemed all Pieter had to do was watch something, and he was pretty much able to pick it up and do it. This became a new area to venture into for him, as he was given lessons in fencing and archery, which he took to just like he had with the circus performers.

After six months of studying the vampire they held in captivity, the type of tests they conducted were no longer being reproduced on Pieter. This was when the studies progressed to how the vampire could recover and repair himself from injury. They used various sharp implements to cut the vampire and finally started to pierce his chest and interfere with the heart to immobilize it. Any object that pierced the heart caused the vampire to become paralyzed, not just wood, as superstition suggested. Study was also made of the time it took a vampire to recover once the stake or spike was removed. Here, it was discovered that the longer the vampire was staked, the longer it took for it to recover. But again, this healing factor could be reduced if the vampire was fed human blood.

Initially, the captive vampire had been willing to cooperate with the tests and received blood as his reward for doing so. As the tests became more serious and aimed at finding a way to hurt or immobilize the vampire, he had become more withdrawn and unwilling to assist. He had not long been a vampire when captured, and the elder vampire who had sired him was destroyed during his capture. Originally born a peasant living in a small farmstead close to the Carpathian Mountains, he was neither very bright nor experienced in the ways of being a vampire.

Over the short period of time he had remained in captivity, though, he was seen to become more animalistic and vicious. He had also developed a very cunning mind and great care was needed for him to be taken around, or he would strike out to injure his captors. This last trait could have been a reaction to the constant experimentation and torture, of course, but both Pavel and the professor surmised that it was more likely to be the vampire in him becoming fully developed. Unfortunately, the professor had fallen foul of this situation when he got too close to the vampire. While thinking that the vampire was still recovering from being staked, the professor had been careless in his approach. The vampire had taken the opportunity quickly and, without mercy, had muffled the professor's cries for help almost immediately, and in the process, he had snapped the frail old man's neck and then continued to feed off him.

Upon the discovery of what had occurred, Pavel decided that they had learned all they could from this particular captive vampire. The vampire was first staked by crossbow, then he was decapitated, and the body parts were burned. Where the loss of the professor had been a terrible blow, the information they had gathered from the captive vampire had been invaluable. Pavel's final gift to his old professor was to publish a secret manual in the professor's name. It was to be distributed among the hunters, and detailed all their findings about the vampire; in particular, its weaknesses and how it could be fought, immobilized, and destroyed. The book was titled *The Hunter's Guide to the Vampire*, by Professor Abraham Van Helsing.

"So there really was a Van Helsing," Izzy exclaimed.

"Yes, Isabelle, there really was a Van Helsing, and it's a fitting tribute to the work he did that he is still remembered, even if the Hollywood version is well wide off the mark of what he was actually like. The work he and Pavel started has been continued by others, but it was the start, and the discoveries they made helped take the vampire out of being a creature of superstition and into one of scientific fact," Margeurite confirmed.

"Wow! What a legacy. So our family fortune is built upon the stolen wealth of an ancient vampire lord, and our ancestor was Professor Van Helsing's right-hand man," Izzy said, barely concealing her own joy at the news.

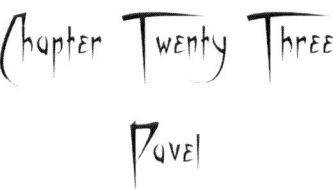

Chapter Twenty Three

Pavel

"So what happened after Professor Van Helsing was killed?" Izzy asked impatiently.

"All in good time, young lady. Let's get you out of the bath and dried off so I can take care of those wounds that need redressing. Any longer in the bath and you'll shrivel up," her mother instructed. Then she continued the tale about Pieter's upbringing as Izzy emerged from the bath and she helped gently towel her daughter down.

A short while after the publication of the manual, Pavel decided that it was time to move on again. Despite keeping themselves separate from the general public, one or two people they came into contact with on a semi-regular basis had noticed Pieter's rapid growth. This, along with his pale skin and extraordinary abilities, had led to a situation where questions were starting to be asked. For his part, Pieter appeared to be a young boy of around twelve to thirteen years, when in reality, he was only just approaching his first year. He was very bright and energetic, and so far, he had shown none of the vampire's sadistic or cunning traits.

They moved to Hamburg in Germany, where Pavel took up a teaching position, claiming Pieter as his orphaned nephew. Once settled into life there, Pavel started to take Pieter's education and skill development more seriously and was pleased to see him excel in virtually every subject he took.

It was a month after their arrival in Hamburg when Pavel noticed that Pieter had stopped growing. This came as a great relief in one way, as it meant they could mix in with the local populace and go unnoticed. It also took away the fear in Pavel that Pieter was destined to appear to grow older than him within two years and possibly die of old age two or three years later. Pavel concluded that Pieter had grown at an accelerated rate of one month equaling a year's normal human growth. Now, at around thirteen to fourteen months, when his body should be going through the puberty changes, he had suddenly stopped growing.

After two years of no further growth, Pavel decided that it was time to move away, as some of their close friends had started to comment on Pieter's pale complexion and dislike of sunlight. They had surmised that he had some kind of ailment and Pavel's more learned colleagues were all badgering him to allow them to examine the boy. One thing that Pavel had noticed was that Pieter's heart rate had slowed considerably and was barely audible now. Also, when he drank blood, his eyes developed a crimson tinge about them, which remained for a minute or two after he'd fed. Further to this, when Pieter hadn't fed on blood for a while, the anticipation of it as he smelled the blood led his eyes to turn red and his canine fangs to extend. Much to Pavel's relief, Pieter still exhibited none of the animalistic or cunning behavior of the vampire they had held captive.

With both Pavel and Pieter being multilingual, they chose to move down to Venice in Italy, where Pavel took up a teaching position once again. Making contact with the local hunter organization helped to smooth the transition, and there were never any questions asked about the need for blood for his secret experiments. Pavel claimed that he was attempting to find a way to poison the human blood against vampires. This was something he received great support for—and the hunter organization also provided him with any captured vampires to experiment with. While the capture of a vampire was rare, over the next year or so, he did receive a total of three to work on, and although he didn't learn anything new about the vampires biologically, Pavel did get to know a lot more about how their minds worked. He found that they were always very clever and cunning in both their actions and their conversations.

The hunters had discovered a brothel that had been catering to a particular type of client some time ago, but rather than storm in and kill everyone involved, they had been far more subtle for once. They had sent in two of their most experienced and capable hunters, who then identified and befriended all the girls with bite marks on them. Through these contacts, they had been introduced to a pale-skinned, middle-aged gentleman named Tibor, who frequented the brothel at least two or three times per month. He was very interested in purchasing some orphan children the two men claimed to have access to. For the right price, there would be no questions asked and as many as ten children were available for immediate delivery.

The two hunters had insisted on going to somewhere more private to discuss matters further, claiming that whores had a habit of overhearing things and selling that information to anyone who would pay for it. Tibor understood their concerns and mistook their raised heart rates to be a result of talking about the shady deal. Upon leaving the establishment together, they had walked no more than two streets away when both of the hunters attempted to thrust a dagger into Tibor's heart. The first hunter's arm had been caught by the vampire mid-thrust and his throat ripped out before he knew what was happening. The second, however, had succeeded. His blade had luckily found its way between the ribs and pressed on into the vampire's heart. The vampire had then toppled forward, immobilized as it was, and had pushed the stiletto even further in upon impacting with the ground.

When the vampire had been delivered to Pavel, he soon discovered that he was the oldest vampire he had ever encountered and that he was completely devious. Pavel always started any interaction with newly captured vampires as if he were ignorant and could easily be fooled. Tibor had feigned fear and pain at the presentation of a crucifix, obviously hoping that Pavel would use one to guard against his escape, rather than the metal collar and heavy chain linking his neck to an anchor point on the dungeon wall.

Once the elder vampire caught on to the fact that Pavel had a very detailed understanding of what could and could not hurt a vampire, he changed his attitude toward him greatly. Rather than engaging him in conversations aimed at confusing him with false or misleading information, Tibor chose to threaten him with what he would be doing to him once he gained his freedom. Pavel then chose to demonstrate to the vampire that he was not afraid, and in a show of power between them, he shot the vampire in the chest with a crossbow bolt to immobilize him. Pavel then cut out Tibor's tongue to teach him a lesson before removing the bolt from his chest and allowing him to recover. Tibor was not pleased about this turn of events and began to plan his revenge carefully.

Foolishly, after the incident with the tongue removal, Pavel chose to goad Tibor and often threatened to shoot him in the heart again whenever he became a nuisance. Pavel felt that he had shown the vampire who was in charge of his present situation, and that he was powerless against him. Tibor knew only too well that sometimes, in anger, people did silly things, like maybe lower their guard.

The cellar where they kept the vampire was spacious enough to have a large desk and various cupboards and instrument racks at one end, with the bare captive area at the other end. Over the years of its use as a dungeon, it had housed many different occupants. Mostly those who had been held there were humans, and it was only recently that it had been used to hold a vampire prisoner. The chain had been replaced with a somewhat stronger one, and the anchor point on the wall had been equally upgraded. One of the things that hadn't changed was the marks on the floor. Where the same anchor point had been used for so long, an area on the floor had subsequently been worn away, showing the extent to which the chain would allow the captive to walk to. Once upon a time, a white line had been painted on the floor to indicate this area. The idea of the line was to show the jailer the limits to where the prisoner could extend their hands or feet to, and therefore a safety zone beyond which they could not be grabbed, kicked, or head butted.

Since the incident that led to the death of Professor Van Helsing, Pavel had taken the precaution of securing any captive vampire's hands behind their back with iron manacles. With Pavel's insistence, that fresh pine sawdust be used to cover the floor and give the jail a more pleasant aroma, the cunning plan the vampire formed to get his revenge could not have been simpler. As Pavel entered the room, ready to feed the vampire the small amount of blood required to keep him functioning, he barked out his usual instructions. Tibor did as instructed and knelt down at the limit of the chain pulling taunt on the wall. He then opened his mouth like any trained animal, ready to receive a reward from its master. Pavel moved forward with the jug in his right hand and a small crossbow in his left, leveled at the vampire's chest.

The vampire's fangs had extended and its eyes were crimson red in anticipation of the feeding he was about to receive. As the semi-congealed blood began to flow out of the jug and into Tibor's mouth, he prepared to make his move. Pavel, being somewhat half asleep after the celebrations of the previous evening, hadn't noticed that the white line on the floor had been completely obscured by the fresh sawdust. He didn't notice the angle that the chain held tight against the wall was slightly lower than usual, as the vampire was merely holding it as high as he could behind his back with a loose loop of chain hanging between the collar and his hands. Pavel didn't notice the smile forming at the sides of Tibor's mouth as he stared at him, knowing that his plan was about to come to fruition.

"I need more blood," the vampire demanded as the last few drops of blood landed on his tongue and Pavel righted the jug in his hand.

"That's all you are getting, Tibor. You should be grateful that I allow you any at all," Pavel responded.

"With more blood, my mind would be able to work better and I'd be more than a match for you intellectually. Are you afraid that I'm intellectually superior to you after all, child?" Tibor goaded.

Pavel took a half step closer toward the vampire, pushed the crossbow firmly against his chest, and stared into his red eyes as he replied through gritted teeth, "I'm no child, and you are not as bright as you think you are. I'm growing tired of this endless baiting and bickering between us. It serves no purpose. Perhaps, I should just paralyze you and dissect you instead of trying to learn something knew from you."

"Ha, I'll teach you something now, human."

As he spoke, Tibor released the chain he held taunt behind his back and twisted his body a little to the left as he lunged forward the extra distance allowed him by the loop of chain he'd held behind his back. The sudden movement caught the hungover Pavel completely by surprise, and he instinctively fired the crossbow.

The bolt merely grazed Tibor's right shoulder and then clattered harmlessly into the wall behind. As he dropped his head forward, Tibor drew his lips back, opened his mouth as wide as he could, and bit into Pavel's forearm. The vampire's sharp teeth easily penetrated the flimsy material of Pavel's expensive shirt and held his arm in a vise-like grip. The sudden force of the bite on his forearm caused Pavel to drop the crossbow, which clattered noisily on the stone floor. The pressure exerted by the vampire's jaws broke one of the bones in Pavel's forearm and left the hand hanging limp and useless below. Next, Tibor began to viciously tug at Pavel's arm, pulling him back into his domain, and at the same time, the vampire struggled to his feet. With nothing to grab hold of and no weapons to use, Pavel was quick to realize that all of his resistance would be to no avail against the stronger vampire. His own overconfidence and the vampire's cunning had turned this situation to his prisoner's advantage; he had indeed been outwitted by someone he'd judged inferior to himself.

Pavel, realizing the severity of his situation, continued to struggle as much as he could and began to scream for Pieter. He had very little problem with screaming as loud as he could due to the pain he was feeling with each pull on his arm.

Tibor, knowing that there was only the young boy likely to be able to assist Pavel, grew in confidence. *This is all too easy*, he thought to himself.

Once the vampire was properly on his feet again, he pulled and swung Pavel around against the wall. Pavel was almost knocked senseless with the force of the impact and was certainly winded. Then, Tibor kicked his legs from under him, breaking the tibia and fibula in Pavel's left leg as he did so. The pain stopped Pavel blacking out from the impact with the wall, and he could do nothing but continue to scream as he crumpled to the floor and the sharp ends of the broken bones in his legs burst through the skin's surface.

The vampire took a few more large mouthfuls of blood from the wound he had torn into Pavel's arm, then released him. Pavel's arm dropped at his side, limp and useless. He was barely coherent as to what was going on around him, overwhelmed as he was by the pain in both his arm and leg. The vampire laughed as he collapsed the full weight of his body down on top of Pavel. Again, Pavel screamed as the weight of the vampire landing on him sent another jolt of pain through his shattered leg.

"Not so boastful now, are you, child?" Tibor taunted.

The vampire began to squirm around on top of Pavel as he sought to bring his arms around to the front of his body. Each struggle by the vampire caused more pain to shoot through Pavel as he was shaken and moved by the vampire's body still lying on top of him. The vampire began to strain as he tried to get the manacles past his feet. Suddenly, even Pavel heard a mighty "pop!" as the vampire dislocated his own shoulder, allowing him to bring his arms up in front at last. That done, he crawled up into a kneeling position, and with a grimace, he shook his arm vigorously to relocate the shoulder joint back into position; the vampire growled in pain and anger through his own gritted teeth as he did so.

Then looking back down at Pavel again, Tibor saw that he was barely conscious and had gone pale with shock. Seeing the pool of blood soaking into his trouser leg for the first time, the vampire tore away the cloth and fell upon the wound, twisting the leg mercilessly to get a better position upon which to feed on the blood escaping from the wound. Tibor was quite happily gorging himself on Pavel's blood when, all of a sudden, he heard the rushed footsteps coming down the stairs and along the stone corridor. The vampire stopped feeding as he adjusted his position and prepared for the next phase of his plan.

As Pieter entered the room, it only took him a moment to understand the situation. Somehow, the vampire had gotten hold of Pavel and had either killed him already or incapacitated him. It had been no more than a minute or two since he'd heard the scream and cry for help, but still, it was long enough to possibly be too late. The vampire stood with his back against the wall and was holding Pavel up as a shield in front of him, protecting his chest. His left arm was looped around Pavel's neck, supporting him and holding him as if he were a small child. He was holding Pavel's left arm against his mouth and was continuing to feed as he watched Pieter's every movement while he decided what to do.

Through his superior hearing, Pieter could just pick up Pavel's heartbeat, then he noticed the awkward position his left leg was twisted into. Looking down at the torn trouser leggings and the blood from the open fractures, Pieter knew that Pavel was in a serious way. He immediately realized that he needed to get Pavel away from the vampire, who was continuing to feed on him, if he were to stand any chance of survival. Looking over at the desk at the end of the room, Pieter saw the tools they had used to fix the manacles and collar around the vampire's hands and neck. He knew that the vampire would need them to effect his escape. Even if he killed both Pavel and Pieter, he had to be able to remove the chains to get away, so just killing them both was not really an option. Pieter first picked up the tools then grabbed one of the spare crossbow bolts from the quiver set upon the chair and turned to face the vampire.

"You let him go and I give you the tools you'll need to break your chains and free yourself," he stated calmly, holding the crossbow bolt, ready to stab the vampire, and looking him straight in the eye.

The vampire thought for a moment, then paused from his feeding to answer him. "Put the tools down where I can reach them, boy. Then back away and I'll release your father."

Pieter did as he was instructed, but made a point of holding the crossbow bolt protectively between himself and the vampire. He added a little shake to his arm and made sure that he went a little bit closer to the vampire than he should have, but not so close as to seem unafraid.

After Pieter had set the tools down on the floor and when Tibor judged him to be close enough to grab, the vampire discarded Pavel, who slumped to the floor like the proverbial "sack of potato's". He suddenly lunged toward Pieter, intent on grabbing him and feeding on him, too. Pieter timed his anticlockwise turn to perfection, and as he pivoted around on his right heel, he dropped into a crouch and struck upward with the crossbow bolt. The direction and speed of the thrust and the force of the blow caught the vampire completely off guard, and with his arms reaching forward to grab the boy, the vampire's chest was left completely unprotected.

The arrowhead pierced the vampire's skin just below the bottom of the sternum, in between the inverted "V" of the lower rib cartilages. Its upward angle sent the tip of the arrow into the left ventricle of the vampire's heart, completely immobilizing him. Tibor slumped forward, and as he did so, the chain at his neck pulled tautly, causing him to swing around in an arc to the right before falling to the floor. Pieter ignored the vampire and quickly went over to Pavel. He took a few seconds to view the wounds and then sprang into action. Having fed on both the arm and the wound around the protruding bones in Pavel's lower leg, Pieter knew that the vampire's saliva and the anticoagulant it contained would prevent the blood from clotting. He knew that he had to cauterize the wounds to stop the bleeding and give Pavel a chance at surviving this ordeal.

Luckily, with Pavel's scientific, biological, and medical background, Pieter had been well tutored in such situations. Pavel himself was going in and out of consciousness, and was of no use when he was awake due to the delirium the pain and the blood loss was causing him. Pieter set about his task swiftly and efficiently by firstly applying tourniquets to slow the blood flow to the affected limbs. He then sealed the wound to the arm using a red-hot poker, being careful to cauterize only the flesh he needed to. He knew he needed to stop the bleeding, but also prevent too much scarring and restriction of movement later on. He would splint the fracture later, but the blood loss was the most important consideration at the moment.

Then came the more involved operation with the leg. Firstly, Pieter had to tie Pavel to the table to restrain him, lest he struggled too much and ended up falling onto the floor. Then Pieter had to cut the flesh around the fracture site and peel it back a little to expose the broken bones. He used the poker to cauterize the major blood vessels as he exposed them to prevent more blood loss and blood pooling that would remain inside the flap. He then took the surgical-type saw to the main bone of the lower leg, the tibia. He cut across it at a right angle to the main shaft, and then did the same to the smaller fibula bone, but slightly higher up the leg. As the fibula is an accessory bone and not essential to weight bearing, if left at the same length, it would cause irritation once a "peg leg" was applied.

As soon as the task with the bone was complete, Pieter carefully sliced through the flesh with a surgical-type blade. The lower part of the leg, the ankle, and the foot had been without proper blood supply for too long and could not be saved.

They therefore needed to be amputated; otherwise, infection would set in. Once removed, Pieter rolled the outer flesh back down into position and carefully cut around the edges to match them together, which he then both stitched and sealed by carefully using the poker once more. By the time he started to do this final part of the operation, Pavel became more restless and started to regain consciousness. Luckily, Pieter had prepared him well and all his struggles against his restraints were to no avail. The soft wooden bit, placed between his teeth and strapped around the back of his head, hadn't been required half as much as Pieter had expected. This was due mainly to the speed and precision of Pieter's work.

The only two fears he had now were that Pavel may have lost too much blood to survive the next few days or that later, an infection might set in. It was some six hours later before Pavel fully regained consciousness and could speak coherently. Pieter had to tell him what he had done and why. Pavel smiled weakly and tried to squeeze Pieter's hand as he thanked him, and told him that he had done well.

Over the next few days, Pieter continued to nurse Pavel, leaving his side only to go out for fresh food supplies. Pieter had to crush the food up and spoon it into Pavel's mouth, as well as keep offering him sips of water and freshly squeezed fruit juices. Earlier on, Pieter had tried half chewing the food for Pavel, but unfortunately, upon swallowing the food, Pavel's throat was left anaesthetized and he'd almost choked on the drink Pieter had given him to wash the food down. It was another lesson learned about the similarities between himself and the vampire. On the sixth day, Pavel showed an improvement in his pallor and wasn't so sleepy. The wound showed no sign of swelling or infection and Pavel claimed that his toes were tingling constantly. He was out of immediate danger of infection and was starting to heal.

"Ow! I know just how he felt," Izzy moaned as her mother tugged on the loose ends and snipped off the final stitch she had applied to the wounds on her daughter's body.

"There you go. That's much better. Now, hold still while I put some dressings over these," Margeurite instructed her daughter.

"I don't know why you bothered, Mother. The steri-strips were holding fine," Izzy stated in a slightly disgruntled manner.

"Bah! An active girl like you would tear them off in half a day and end up with much larger ugly scars. One thing you can thank Pieter for when you see him again is that he taught your mother how to stitch a wound perfectly."

"How much time did you get to spend with him then?"

"Enough that your father became jealous of us," Margeurite replied with more than a hint of remorse.

"How come?" Izzy asked.

"You have to remember, dear, your father was much older than me when I met him. At first, the age difference wasn't a problem and we were very much in love. Unfortunately, your father became very insecure about his appearance as he got older and was always frightened that a younger man would steal me away. When Pieter came to stay with us that last summer, your father had a lot of pressure on him and was drinking a little too much too often. Pieter was a good friend and I confided in him a lot during that time, and we became very close. Your father took that closeness to be something completely different and reacted very badly to it," Margeurite explained.

"Dare I ask what he did?" Izzy asked nervously.

"This is not the time or the place for that particular story, young lady. All you need to know at the moment is that a vampire killed your father, and at that time, Pieter saved you and me," Margeurite said sadly.

"Oh, no wonder you never told me what really happened if he was involved," Izzy exclaimed, sitting back down on the edge of the bath, shaking her head.

"It was better you just thought it was a simple vampire attack that killed him rather than knowing the complicated truth of the matter. Like many other people who should have known better, he let his guard down and lost everything he had," Margeurite said, stroking her daughter's hair.

Chapter Twenty Four

Sireling

After a few minutes of silence between them, each lost in their own thoughts about the past, Margeurite suggested that they make a move to get dressed. She and her daughter emerged from the bathroom and crossed the living space in the plush suite to enter the master bedroom. There was a trolley covered in small canapés and three large jugs of freshly squeezed fruit juice drinks that Margeurite had ordered earlier. The two women then lounged on the large, king-sized bed, drinking and eating as Margeurite continued the story of the secret kept by their family for so long.

It wasn't until the ninth day after Tibor's attack on Pavel when Pieter returned to the dungeon to deal with him. While he was angry at what the vampire had done to Pavel, he also accepted that the vampire was only doing what he could to escape. Tibor was wise enough to know that he would eventually be killed once all the information had been extracted from him. It was simply a kill or be killed situation, and there could be no middle ground between a hunter and a vampire.

Pieter pulled the stake out of Tibor's chest and sat back, awaiting his revival. He took the time to reflect upon what he was about to do, mulling over the decision and the possible outcome of it all. Without Pavel to guide him, he had to try to think of everything and make the right decision on what to do by himself. Two or three minutes after the stake had been removed, Tibor began to stir. The vampire's eyes opened with a squint even in the subdued daylight of the cellar, and he looked around the room to see where he was. Upon seeing Pieter sitting at his chair, looking back impassively, Tibor locked his gaze upon him and they became entangled in a staring competition. Eventually, Tibor blinked and, in so doing, realized that Pieter had outlasted him. Tibor continued to watch Pieter's every move intently, but said nothing. After an hour or so of mind games, Tibor slowly pulled himself up into a sitting position and shuffled to lean back against the cellar wall.

After a few more minutes of silently staring at each other, Pieter leaned across the desk and, without breaking eye contact, picked up a jug. He then walked across the room, almost casually, toward the vampire. Pieter made no attempt to skirt around the vampire or stay out of his reach. He simply strode forward and laid the jug down beside him. Only then did he break eye contact as he turned and walked away at an even pace. The vampire reached out warily and picked up the jug. Then sensing and smelling no danger to himself, he attempted to drink thirstily from it. After the time taken for Tibor to recover and the delay since the blood had been taken, it had started to congeal. Though not the best of meals to drink, the vampire wasn't about to turn his nose up at what it smelled and tasted to be human blood. Tibor was careful not to spill any of the blood, and fought against his own hunger to keep control and drink steadily. He was all too aware that his every move was being watched and studied by this strange and powerful young boy sitting silently across the room from him.

A few minutes after he had finished drinking and draining all the blood that he could from the jug, Tibor spoke, breaking the silence between them. "What are you, boy?"

Pieter smiled as he replied, "You tell me."

"I cannot, for I have never met anything like you before."

"What do you mean by that?" Pieter asked inquisitively.

"What I mean is that you do not have the smell of a young human about you. Young humans of your appearance and age are notoriously smelly, as they change to become men and grow beards. You do not smell at all, and you have a much slower than normal human heartbeat that I can barely hear. You are only a slip of a lad yet you possess strength and speed greater than mine, and I dare say even greater than any vampire I have yet encountered," Tibor explained.

"And that bothers you?" Pieter replied flatly.

"It does, for I wish to escape my captivity and continue to hunt, kill, and live a normal life for a vampire. However, you pose a somewhat insurmountable obstacle to my plans, one that I have never had the problem of dealing with before."

Pieter allowed himself another smile, and then he sat forward on his chair to engage the vampire in further conversation. He knew that Tibor was trying to flatter him, so that he would lower his guard and provide the vampire an opportunity to escape. "So you have never come across anyone like me before?"

"Never," Tibor confirmed sharply.

"So, how were you turned into a vampire?"

"The same way any other vampire is sired, of course," Tibor responded, looking somewhat puzzled.

"Sired, you say? Explain this term to me." Pieter's attention was now hanging off each word from the vampire, but he struggled not to show it.

Tibor quickly realized that the only way out of this current predicament involved either fighting or befriending this somewhat strange boy. Since his first rather foolishly overconfident attack on the boy had ended with a stake thrust into his heart, he decided to try the friendship route first. Maybe he could coerce this especially astute young man into aiding him with the promises of things yet to come should they join forces. Plus, he was in no condition to try the option of force at the moment, as he was still trying to recover from being staked. He began to tell the story behind being sired. "Once you are selected to become a vampire, you are taken away to somewhere safe, somewhere where you will not be interrupted, usually deep in the forest. Your vampire elder then bites and feeds upon you until you are close to death. The elder will then make a cut about their own body, usually into their wrist, and allow the selected human to drink of his or her blood. Both the vampire and the human then continue to feed on each other's blood until the human can feed no more and dies. The elder vampire then guards the sire-ling and waits until he or she awakens as a newly sired vampire. The process is entirely dependent upon the size of the human being turned, and the amount of the elder vampire's blood they can ingest before dying. Hence, the reason for going to somewhere out of the way, where you will not be disturbed, as the vampire elder can be considerably weakened by the ordeal too, and will need time to recover.

"Because of the elder vampire's recovery time, and the requirement of the newly sired vampire to feed, it is not uncommon for a captured human to be taken along with them. Then the elder vampire can recover faster and the newly sired vampire can complete their first kill upon this captive human. For this reason, the chosen captive is most often someone the sire-ling vampire considers an enemy or holds a particular grudge against. It's very common in such situations for the elder vampire to feed a little upon the captive to aid their recovery and then allow the sire-ling only a mouthful of their victim's blood so they can scent them. The captive human is then released and runs away, usually terrified, while the newly sired vampire is held back for a moment or two with their bloodlust at its highest point and its newly heightened senses screaming the directions of where their intended victim has fled. The sire-ling is then released to hunt and chase their first victim. With their improved sense of smell, acute sense of hearing, and increased speed and muscle power, the newly sired vampire soon captures and savagely kills the human, completing the transformation from human to vampire.

"The older, more experienced vampire then teaches and guides the new vampire they have sired, showing them how to live, hunt, and feed as a vampire. The elder and the sire-ling are forever linked, as the vampire bloodline contains a particular scent, which is passed down and links the individual members of any one vampire clan together. In such a way, the seniority of the various vampires is based on how strongly associated with the clan leader their individual scent is. For example, I am but two positions below the head of the Venetian Clan leader and my scent marks me as such. Also, it is very uncommon for the more senior vampires or the vampire lords to sire any new vampires, as they would be granted a higher position within a clan because of it. Such duties are delegated down through the ranks of a particular vampire clan."

Pieter nodded his head in understanding as he carefully thought about what Tibor had just told him. "So, do I carry a scent?"

"I'm not sure, I understand what you are asking. If you are not a vampire, why would you think you would carry a scent?" Tibor asked, almost mocking the idea, but thinking better of it upon noticing the change in Pieter's position in the chair.

Pieter was now leaning forward more expectantly, and was far more enthusiastic in his questioning of the topic, rather than being laid back and almost nonchalant in his approach as he had been earlier in their conversation. There were no longer any drawn-out pauses in between his questions, while he pondered what had just been said. "Because it has been explained to me, that my mother gave birth to me prematurely, and we were both left to die. Then a vampire, desperate for blood, broke in and fed upon my mother. In doing so, and during her struggles against the vampire, it seems some of his blood and my mother's blood spilled into my mouth. Now, I'm still alive against all expectations and I have certain 'abilities,' but I have no explanation as to how or why. So, if what you say is correct, then the vampire who fed upon my mother, and whose blood I drank by accident, may have left its scent upon me?"

"It is possible that there is a trace of the scent in your blood, for as I have already explained, I cannot detect even the normal human scent upon you," the vampire replied.

Pieter used one of the tools on the desk at the end of the room to cut into his finger; he then impatiently strode back over to the vampire and halted close by, holding his hand up above the vampire. Tibor tilted his head back and opened his mouth, allowing the blood to drip onto his extended tongue. After allowing a few drops to fall, Pieter pulled his hand away and wrapped a small piece of cloth around the wound to stem the bleeding.

"I did not need to taste your blood to know its origin, youngling. I detected the scent in your blood well before tasting it. You are closely bound to the deposed Lithuanian leader, Dimitri Vasolo. Maybe it was he who fed on your mother; the scent is so strong," the vampire explained.

"Tell me about him," Pieter demanded, maybe a little too eagerly.

"I could, but my mind is still somewhat foggy from my recent spell of inactivity. I need more blood to help me recover and to sharpen my senses to all the times I have been involved with Dimitri, Vladimir, the Wolfshead Clan, and, of course, the vampire wars," Tibor said craftily. He was beginning to warm to this new task and had already developed a plan of befriending this youngling and gaining his confidence, then seizing any opportunity to escape when it presented itself.

Pieter pondered upon what the vampire had said for a moment, then turned and walked out of the room. Tibor heard Pieter open another heavily bolted door somewhere down the corridor toward the right-hand side. He then heard a slight scuffling sound and a female voice protesting about the rough treatment she was receiving, before the door was closed once more. Then came the sound of a woman being dragged unwillingly along the floor, kicking and struggling as she was being manhandled and forced along, against her will. After a few more seconds, they came into Tibor's view. Pieter had a companion with him, held tightly by one arm. She was one that the vampire recognized and had often fed upon at a local brothel. Pieter simply dragged her along as she helplessly continued to try to free herself from his grasp. Once within Tibor's reach, Pieter gave her a last shove into his open embrace. The vampire smiled and held the girl protectively, and she responded by accepting his protection, glad of a seemingly kind and familiar face.

"Here, feed on this, and I'll be back in a few minutes. I have to go and change Pavel's dressings, and when I return, we will talk further about this Dimitri," Pieter stated coldly.

"What would you like to know about him?" Tibor asked as he gently caressed the companion's exposed neck.

"Everything," Pieter said as he turned to leave.

Swiveling on his heels, Pieter marched purposefully out of the room once more. Swinging the door closed behind him, he threw the bolt across just as the girl saw the vampire smile at her with his crimson eyes ablaze. Tibor opened his mouth wide to reveal a pair of sharp, yellowed canine fangs extending from the roof of his mouth, and the girl suddenly realized what was about to happen to her. Suddenly, in desperation, she began to struggle and scream, but it was of no use. She was held tightly in the smiling vampire's powerful grasp and there was no one who could save her now.

"Out of the frying pan and into the fire, my dear," Tibor said before lunging at her throat.

"He killed all the companions where I was held captive, too," Izzy interrupted.

"Yes, he would have. Pieter has no compassion for either vampire or those who would serve them in any way. It's the one thing that he matches them for in cold-bloodedness. In many ways, he can be very funny and sweet, but not when it comes to vampires, guards, and companions. On that issue, he is completely black and white, and there are absolutely no shades of grey," Margeurite confirmed.

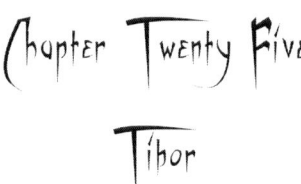

Chapter Twenty Five

Tibor

Margeurite replenished the fruit juice in both her own, and her daughter's glass before she continued the story.

Upon his return to the room in the cellars, Pieter found the companion dead and slumped against the wall. The girl's skin was almost pure white; she had been completely drained of blood, and her eyes looked lifelessly off into the distance. Pieter walked across the room without comment and grabbed her by the foot. Then he simply turned and dragged her lifeless carcass behind him to the end of the room. Picking up an axe from among the tools on the bench, he changed his grip on the body to hold her up by the hair. Then Pieter lopped off her head with one clean swipe of the axe. Still holding the head by the hair, he then grabbed the foot once more as he used his knee to push open the door. As he left the room and turned into the corridor, the girl's trailing leg thumped against the door frame; Pieter gave a sharp tug to flick the body around and continued on his way to dispose of the girl's remains.

When he walked back into the room a short while later, Tibor posed a question to him. "Did you cut off her head because you feared I'd turned her while you were away, boy?"

"Not really. You're too clever to be that obvious, and it would be a sign of desperation on your part if you had turned her. You think too much of yourself and your own superiority to ever be reduced to such a desperate ploy," Pieter answered

"Maybe that's what I thought you'd think, so I did it anyway to see if you'd get careless, like your father did," the vampire countered.

"That's why I chopped her head off, so that you'd know I don't leave anything to chance and I'm not likely to make such a stupid mistake."

His answer and the unbridled arrogance Pieter showed toward him stunned Tibor into silence. The boy showed wisdom beyond his years and he did not seem the least bit bothered by anything the vampire said or had already done. *This one will not be so easy to overcome*, Tibor thought to himself.

Once more, Pieter settled back down in the chair and looked over at the vampire still chained to the wall, and then said, "Now, as you were saying about Dimitri Vasolo."

For the next few hours, Tibor outlined what he knew of Lord Dimitri Vasolo and of how he knew so much about the history involved due to the vampire wars. He wasn't sure of when Dimitri had been sired or by whom, but he was sure that Dimitri had risen through the ranks of his own vampire clan rapidly. Apparently, he was an ex-military leader and of noble birth. He had been an exceptional strategist as well as a skilled swordsman, if the tales told of him were to be believed. He had helped his own clan rise to absolute power over the whole of Lithuania with both his cunning and military strategies. Previously, the Wolfshead Clan had ruled over that area, but under Dimitri's eventual rule, his clan had pushed the Wolfshead Clan out and forced them further east, into Russian lands.

Because there were so many different vampire clans around in Europe, each sought to control its own area, and therefore the human population contained within it. This had led to many arguments and even all-out conflicts between the various clans on more than the odd occasion. In order to improve their chances of winning in such conflicts, the individual clans had set about boosting their numbers. Many strong young human men and women were sired into the clans, but because of their inexperience and lack of training in the secretive ways of the vampire, they had been less than discrete in some of their feasting.

One of the greatest weapons we vampire have in our favor is secrecy, and the fact that the truth of our existence lies hidden in myths and legends. The vampire elders were more than happy to keep things that way and disliked anything that drew attention to them. The younglings' indiscretions were leading to a raised awareness among the human prey. In fact, it was around this time that the hunter organizations had started to form. There were groups of humans who had witnessed vampire slayings or had seen the dead bodies with their throats ripped out and bodies drained of blood. These groups then banded together to track down the vampires; most were either unsuccessful or were slain themselves, but this, in turn, led to more awareness of what was occurring, as grieving relatives spread the word on what they were doing. The outcome of all of this increased activity was for the humans to start becoming organized as they became more aware of the vampire's existence.

Dimitri had risen in power too fast and his expansion to control the whole of Lithuania had destabilized the status quo, with various smaller clans being wiped out, overtaken or pushed out of their own location and into another. This was what caused the wars among the clans, and because of it, Dimitri was both hated and feared among his own kind.

Worse was to come as Dimitri approached the Russian clan leader, Vladimir Shestakov, offering him a partnership in order to wipe out the other clans or take control of them all. Vladimir was a true elder and had taken his time to ascend to his clan leader position, but he saw the merits of Dimitri's plan. So with the added manpower of Vladimir's Russian vampires, Dimitri swept through middle Europe and killed all the other clan leaders, putting only those loyal to him in their place. A great many of the youngling vampires sired to boost clan numbers were then selectively culled. Basically, any young vampire not associated with either Dimitri or Vladimir was destroyed. The younglings from Vladimir's and Dimitri's clans were then spread around, replacing the older vampires slain in the war. They were put under the guidance of those elder vampires who had both survived the wars and had switched loyalties to Dimitri and Vladimir. The younglings then became those elder vampires' responsibility to be instructed in the stealth-like ways of the true vampire, almost as if they had sired them. The younglings remained loyal to Dimitri and Vladimir, and they were strategically placed in a position to be able to spy on those who had switched their allegiance. Acting on behalf of the two leaders, they helped to ensure the other elders' continued loyalty. So the numbers of vampire were normalized once more and their feeding habits were returned to the old and secretive ways.

Some time after the vampire wars were over and a semblance of peace among the clans had been restored for a few years, Vladimir chose his moment to strike out and destroy Dimitri. Vladimir had long been associated with the Wolfshead Clan, due in part to his early days as a minor clan leader in a neighboring area. He had given them safe haven in his lands when Dimitri had cast them out of Lithuania, and they had, in turn, amalgamated their clan with Vladimir's own. They had further promised their loyalty and servitude to him in return for revenge upon Dimitri. To everyone else, it appeared that the Wolfshead was no more and that its surviving members had joined another clan, as was the way when such things occurred. However, the Wolfshead was a particularly proud clan of warrior breeding, and they were simply playing along and biding their time while remaining ready to strike. Once Vladimir granted them permission to act, the Wolfshead Clan secretly positioned their agents and then retook their lands, slaughtering most of those loyal to Dimitri in one night. Because Dimitri's rapid rise to power had upset many of the elder vampires, they were all too keen for revenge upon him and his clan for their arrogance. They were especially keen to act in Vladimir's favor and, in so doing, possibly position themselves to their own advantage. Many minor vampire lords had suddenly shot up the rankings during the vampire wars, and they all saw the possibility of doing so again with this latest power struggle.

However, Dimitri himself had been left for the hunters to deal with. Each vampire lord had given his word in the pact between them, that they would never raise a hand against each other directly. The pact was well known to all, and as the ruler of the largest of the vampire clans, Vladimir could not be seen to go against his own word. So no vampire was ever sent against Dimitri, but a fair few of them, it was said, passed on information about Dimitri's location to the hunters.

It was said that the hunters attacked Dimitri in his own home, and that he fought against them ferociously and with great skill. He killed almost all of them, and left those who survived with many a scar or loss of limb to remind them of his strength and swordsmanship. During the fight, Dimitri himself had suffered many sword cuts to his body, and in particularly to his face and neck, as the hunters had tried to behead him. The biggest problem he'd had, and the point where the hunters almost took him, was the loss of his left hand and the second sword he had been wielding. This event had caused Dimitri to withdraw from the fight and flee his estate through secret passages he'd had built in anticipation of such an event ever occurring. Presuming the security of his other estates would also have been compromised and without a base of operations to return to, Dimitri had been forced to flee into the open countryside.

While a vampire can regrow a limb, it takes time to do so, or a lot of fresh young blood, and while the bone and the deep tissues are being repaired, the outer skin repair is compromised. So Dimitri couldn't hide very easily with his battle scars on show until he'd fed enough to repair his hand, which made it easy for the hunters to trail him. He probably did manage to escape the hunters, though, or Tibor would have heard about it. All that Tibor knew for certain was that Lord Dimitri was being chased by the hunters when he disappeared.

Tibor believed that Dimitri had eventually fled across to the west of Europe, where he was thought to be still in hiding. Vladimir restored the Wolfshead Clan to rule over Lithuania, while all of the East European clans were now united under his rule. Some of the other younglings had also escaped and fled across to the west, but they were of little or no significance. They had either established themselves there independently, had joined other clans, or ended up dead at the hands of the hunters, Tibor surmised. The only negative thing to survive the wars, as far as the vampires were concerned, was the new hunter organizations. However, the elder vampire council members considered that the humans, in having such short life spans, would quickly die off and the old stories would soon be forgotten, or become nothing more than late-night horror stories told around campfires. The threat they posed would shortly pass away and would only be continued if the vampires actively took a stance against them. There would be no long-term threat once the old ways were restored and the vampires once again became both selective and secretive in their feeding habits.

Once Tibor had completed the story, Pieter left to take a walk and ponder on the matters told to him. As he strolled among the shade of the estate's olive trees, he mulled over what he had just learned, along with what he knew about his origin from Pavel and the professor. He had half expected Tibor to simply lie to him and twist and turn the truth to confuse him, or make him angry and careless, as he had done with Pavel. Pieter had fully intended to shoot an arrow into Tibor's heart, and then decapitate and burn his body the moment he felt he was being lied to and given no useful information. The realization that he had gathered far more about his own existence in half an hour of talking to this captive vampire than in all the time spent with Pavel and the professor was unsettling.

Over the next few days, Pieter talked at length with Tibor, learning what he could about the vampire's method of operations and how they were organized. After each session, he would wander off into the gardens and think for a while on what he'd been told. Then he would go to Pavel and discuss everything with him.

Pavel was making slow but steady progress with his recovery, and most importantly, he had no signs of any infection from his injuries. He was back to being his sharp and intelligent self once more and had been thoroughly impressed with Pieter's performance in both his rescue and his surgery, as well as his continued useful observations over the interrogation of the vampire. Pieter had another theory regarding Tibor, which he told Pavel about. He thought that Tibor was trying to befriend him and mentor him, in an effort to turn him over to assist in a possible escape. Pavel agreed that this was indeed likely, and that while the information was flowing, Pieter should appear to go along with things in an effort to obtain even more information. However, the utmost care should be taken, as Tibor, despite his middle-aged appearance, was still far older and far wiser than the both of them, and his cunning and guile were second to none.

Pieter agreed, but was also quick to point out to Pavel that as with any vampire or companion he would ever come across, Tibor's days were numbered. Moreover, when it came time to end this particular vampire's existence, he would happily carry Pavel back down to the cellars so he could pull the trigger on the crossbow himself. It was then that Pavel noticed a subtle change in Pieter's attitude toward the vampires and their companions. Whereas before, he seemed to accept that they were evil and needed to be killed, now he seemed to hate them with a vengeance. Maybe it had something to do with the revelation that the monster that had killed his mother and father and helped shape his own very different existence could still be at large. Or it could be that the vampires considered themselves superior to their human prey, and since he wasn't one of them, he wanted to prove his worth against them, and then to better them in every way. Or maybe it was seeing firsthand what a vampire was capable of doing to someone like Pavel. Whatever the cause, it was something Pavel would need to keep an eye on, in case it blinded Pieter to other opportunities to gain an advantage over the vampires.

Something else Pieter had noticed about this particular vampire was how Tibor was quicker to respond and less worried about the consequences of the information he gave away when starved of blood for a longer period between questioning. Could it be that the older vampires required more blood more often to keep themselves as sharp and youthful as they appeared on the outside? He discussed this matter with Pavel, and between them, they came up with a way of experimenting on Tibor with not only longer periods of time between feeding but also by using different age groups of blood donors.

"So it was because he discovered how his family had been slain and how he'd been somehow changed from human to a kind of half human, half vampire that he became a hunter," Isabelle surmised.

"One thing you should never call Pieter is a 'hunter.' He has no love for the hunters. He has assisted them without their knowing in the past and accepts that they do a job, but he knows they would just as soon treat him like a vampire and put a stake in him. Even you picked up on his vampire traits and were ready to slay him at the drop of a hat, young lady," Margeurite said, chiding her daughter.

"But that was before I knew about him and what he's been through," Isabelle replied, defending herself.

"You reacted like the hunter you've been trained to be, nothing more and nothing less. And as a result, someone is dead. Like I told you when you joined the hunters, they do not know everything and their methods are sometimes found wanting. Perhaps now you'll listen to me and pay attention to what I say. Revenge is a terrible thing to run your life around."

Suddenly, the guilt of what she had done and how it had led to the death of Grace washed over Izzy and she turned away from her mother to hide a tear welling up in her eyes.

Her mother, sensing the mood change her words had precipitated, checked her watch and then made a suggestion. "Get yourself dressed, Isabelle, and let's go out for some air. A walk in the park will do us both good. Hurry up now, before it gets too cold. I'll let Johnny know what we're doing." She left Izzy alone in the room to get dressed.

Chapter Twenty Six

Brothel

Once outside in the afternoon sun, Izzy felt the whole weight of the world lifting off her shoulders. She was still sore and certain movements pulled on the stitches and steri-strips her mother had redressed her wounds with, but being in the sun still made her happy to be alive. When they had crossed the road from the hotel to the park, she and her mother had linked arms and continued to walk side by side. Johnson, the bodyguard, walked a few meters behind them, with his earpiece in his right ear, and inside his jacket pocket, his right hand held yet another electronic device. This one was used to detect any listening devices being activated around them. Along with the detector, Johnson also had a keen eye to spot anyone taking more than a casual interest in his boss's conversations or actions. Margeurite knew that if she and Isabelle kept walking, it would be doubly difficult for anyone to intercept their conversation. So she kept walking at a slow, steady pace while she continued the story passed down to her regarding Pieter's earliest days.

The hunters had continued to monitor the brothel Tibor used to frequent; they had also coerced away some of the women working there with promises of better pay and conditions at another establishment. Of course, once the girls were taken from the brothel, they were never heard of again. They were all incarcerated and sadistically tortured by the hunters for information. If they survived, they were sent to Pavel for his use in feeding and experimenting upon the captured vampire.

Finally, on one particular night at the brothel, the hunters became aware that three vampires were visiting the establishment. So while one of the hunters remained to monitor the situation, the other left on the pretense of feeling ill. Once on his horse, he raced back to the city, where he raised the alarm to his superiors in their group. This led to fifty or so trained hunters being mobilized and heading out to the brothel within the hour. Upon their arrival, they put into practice all the training they had done over the past few weeks in preparation for such an event. Every door and window in the establishment was covered by at least four men with crossbows at the ready. The leader of the hunters, an ex-military captain, and three other men entered the brothel and stood in the center of the main downstairs room. The captain then spoke in a clear, controlled voice to all who could hear, which, of course, included the three vampires, who had far more acute hearing than everyone else.

"All vampires and those who bear the marks of consorting with vampires are hereby under arrest. All exits to both windows and doors, have my men posted at them, armed with crossbows. Anyone attempting to leave will be shot on sight. You have one minute to get dressed and show yourselves."

One of the vampires immediately attempted to flee, and had been immobilized by the hunters, shooting him with crossbows as he tried to climb out of the window. Another had proved himself far more capable than those hunting him. First, he had forcibly gained access to the room next door, and then he ordered the senior school teacher there, to try to exit the window and climb up to the roof. The poor teacher had little choice, but to do as he was told, with the vampire baring his teeth and snarling his instructions at him. The frail older man hadn't heard the details of the captain's declaration from his location in an upstairs room, so he wasn't aware of what was waiting for him outside. He just knew that a very frightening-looking man was physically manhandling him out of the window. The vampire still had blood dripping from his chin and his eyes were of the darkest red. The teacher didn't need too much coercing; he wanted to be anywhere but in the same room as the vampire. He had just managed to get one leg out of the frame and was sitting on the windowsill before being struck by the first of several crossbow bolts. The vampire held him by his trailing leg until he figured that all the men with a line of sight to that particular window, had unloaded their weapons. The vampire then released the teacher, allowing him to topple forward to his death on the ground below, if the crossbow bolts had not already taken his life.

Not giving the hunters the time required to reload their weapons, the vampire had quickly exited the same window and then climbed up onto the roof in an amazing display of gymnastics and upper body strength. Once on the roof, he was free to run the length of the building and jump across to the lower roof of the adjoining stables. He then ran along the stables until finally, he leapt off at the end and ran in the direction of the nearby woods. One of the hunters guarding the back door had caught sight of him and launched a crossbow bolt that had barely missed its target. The vampire, with his far superior running speed, had left all the hunters behind him, and soon disappeared off into the safety of the forest at night.

The third vampire had also tried to be clever, as having only a small window in the room he was in, he had been forced to come out into the main corridor where the hunters were waiting. The vampire had the young lady he had been feeding on positioned in front of his body as a human shield, and was trying to use her to protect himself while looking for another possible exit. The captain, on seeing what was happening, strode forward, raised his crossbow, and shot the girl in the chest. Momentarily shocked at the cold-blooded action of the captain, the vampire released his hold on the young girl and let her slump to the floor. The moment the vampire's chest was unprotected, two of the other hunters sent their crossbow bolts into the exposed target. One of the other girls, on seeing her friend and the vampire shot at close range, screamed in shock and horror.

The captain walked purposefully toward her and drew back his hand before slapping her across the face. "Quiet, bitch, and pray you have no vampire bite marks upon your pretty flesh, or you'll be next."

The madam of the house came forward, and wrapped her arms around the girl to console and calm her. At the same time, she kept her gaze low to the floor and offered no argument to any of the hunters. She knew only too well who they were and what they were capable of doing to them all.

The captain then barked more orders to his men and, before long, all the ladies of the house were bundled together into one upstairs room. Two of the hunters remained in the room to guard over them and prevent them from talking to each other. Meanwhile, all the other patrons of the brothel were to be individually questioned. One by one, each of the men were brought before the captain, who questioned them on what they knew of the vampires frequenting the establishment. Once convinced that none of them knew anything of the brothel's special patrons, they were released and sent scurrying on their way home to their wives and families.

After about half an hour of being cooped up in the room together, the madam and her girls were taken out individually to a room farther down the corridor. Here, two women they had not seen before were waiting. Neither smiled or offered any kind of greeting to the whores and staff of the house as they entered. Upon their arrival in the room, one of the two women simply barked a single instruction to them: "Strip."

When one girl tried to argue the point, the older and shorter of the two women, the one who had barked the order, approached her and grabbed a handful of the girl's long, dark hair. Twisting the hair roughly in her grip, she pulled the girl down to her direct eye level. Then she looked straight into the young girl's eyes and stated coldly, "Take all of your clothes off, now, or I'll have two of the men do it for you."

The manner and attitude of the older woman left the frightened young girl in no doubt about how serious she was with her threat. She quickly began to take her clothes off, as instructed. Once she was naked, the two women walked forward and started to inspect her, using small, handheld lamps to illuminate the skin surface.

Those girls found to have bite marks or scars from previous bites were separated from the others, along with the madam of the house. Kept under close and constant guard, they were led outside and loaded onto the wagon containing the two bound and immobilized vampires.

The captain informed those left behind that they had a few minutes to gather up their belongings and vacate the premises. He also told them why they were being released, and why the others were not. Any of the girls who showed signs of consorting with and allowing a vampire to feed upon them were taken away to be dealt with. Further to that, since most of them would likely end up in the same line of work elsewhere, the girls were informed that if they ever came across a brothel that catered to such clients, they were to report the matter to the captain, any of his men, or the other local authorities immediately. They were told that they would be both well rewarded and protected for any such information they provided. Failure to pass on what they knew about any vampires, though, would have dire consequences.

Having said his piece and given out his final instructions to the remaining men, the captain had left to escort the wagon containing the two immobilized vampires, the madam, and the vampire consorts away. Immediately after he left, the remaining hunters set about looting what they could from the brothel. The girls who had been released found themselves pushed out of the way or manhandled as the hunters searched for items of value as well as the alcohol. One of the more senior men in the group did not seem particularly impressed by the behavior of his men, but he knew that there was little he could do to curtail it. So he concentrated on assisting with getting the girls out of the house as quickly as he could. Once he'd accomplished that task, he gave the order for the men to evacuate the building, then had them set fire to it. Within minutes, the fire had taken hold and the building was beyond saving. Satisfied that his job was done, the sub-commander gave the order to leave, and the ragtag group of men and women, carrying all that they could muster, headed down the road toward the city.

After about twenty minutes or so of walking, one of the hunters was struggling to keep up with the main group. He was attempting to carry a large drape he'd pulled from a window and had filled with bits and pieces from the brothel. He was also trying to shake off the effects of the bottle of alcohol he'd been tipping back into his throat as he went about his looting. No sooner was the man out of sight of the others, as they turned a bend in the road ahead, than a dark shadow raced out of the woods to stop beside him. Whatever it was quickly ran up to him and knocked him off his feet by hitting him in the chest. He found himself on the floor, gasping for breath for a few moments, looking up at the full moon, high in the night sky above, unsure of what had just happened and blissfully unaware that he had a crossbow bolt sticking out of his chest.

Meanwhile, one of the other hunters, who had been busy trying to strike up a conversation with one of the girls, noticed that his friend had fallen behind. On being made aware of the situation, the sub-commander dispatched two of the hunters on horseback to go back for him. As they approached their comrade, they were joking about how drunk he must have been to fall over and smash his bottle in the middle of the road, but as they got closer, they noticed the crossbow bolt protruding from his chest. Then as one rider dismounted, he gasped in shock when he saw that the man's throat had been ripped open. Before he could say anything, though, his still-mounted colleague toppled from his horse and landed upon him, pinning him to the ground. Both horses then ran off down the road toward the main group and the city beyond.

The second hunter, who was knocked down from his horse, had a crossbow bolt protruding from his right ear, and the man underneath was struggling to get his arms into a position of leverage to move the dead weight off him. Before he could organize himself, though, his comrade's body was lifted off as if by magic. Then before he knew what was happening, he was grabbed by the collar and pulled up off the road. Suddenly, standing with his feet on solid ground again, he was confronted by a tall, lean, and muscular man, stripped down to the waist, with blood spattered on his chest as it dripped from his chin. The crimson eyes stared at the hunter mercilessly and the lips curled back in a snarl, exposing the protruding fangs from the upper jaw. The hunter tried to reach for a dagger in his belt with his right hand. The vampire intercepted the movement with its left hand, holding the man by the wrist. The hunter then tried to punch the vampire with his left hand, and again, it was intercepted as the vampire released his grasp on his collar and grabbed his other wrist with uncanny speed. The vampire paused a moment, looking deep into the hunter's now terrified eyes. Then the vampire smiled before rapidly rotating both his own wrists and forearms outward. In so doing, the vampire twisted the man's arms forcefully outward, dislocating both of his shoulders from their sockets in the process. As the vampire released his hold, the hunter screamed in pain and slumped down to his knees with his arms falling limply to either side of his body.

The vampire then stepped behind the hunter and grabbed him by the hair with his left hand, pulling his head across to the left. His right hand yanked and ripped the shirt collar away to fully expose the hapless hunter's neck.

"Aren't you sorry you didn't have a last drink at that brothel like your two friends here? With so many people to kill, and so many hunters to avoid, I couldn't drink too much of their alcohol-filled blood. Lucky for me, you had your eyes on the whores. I wonder how long it will take to send the next ones back to check upon you, and whether you'll die from me snapping your neck or drinking my fill of you. Let's see, shall we?"

The vampire fell upon the hunter's exposed neck and tore into him viciously. With his fangs piercing and ripping great gouges out of the soft flesh, the underlying veins and arteries were also sliced open, allowing the blood to rush out in great spurts of crimson into the vampire's waiting mouth. The hunter screamed again and kept screaming for a minute or two as the vampire continued to feed upon him, until he neither screamed nor moved anymore. Once the man's body had gone limp in his grasp, the vampire was able to listen to what was going on farther down the road.

The whole of the group fleeing the brothel heard the first scream, and all the men looked to the sub-commander for instructions on what to do. The commander paused to think for a moment about what had probably occurred, and surmised that the vampire who escaped earlier had probably returned and attacked the man who'd fallen behind. Then he had waited and ambushed the two men sent back to check upon him. In this light and with the vampire's superior night vision, speed, and strength, plus the element of surprise, the men hadn't stood a chance. A couple of the hunters dropped their loot into the back of the single wagon that remained with them and prepared their crossbows once more.

Just as they were about to ride back, the sub-commander barked out his orders. "You men, hold your ground. We are not splitting our forces. If we do, we'll be picked off one by one."

"But there is only one of them and so many of us, we can take him," one of the men argued.

"We don't know how many of them there are, and they are faster and stronger than us, plus they can see better in the dark. We stick together and make haste back to the city. You women, throw away anything that slows you down. We will be going as fast as we can. Men, empty that loot out of the wagon and put the slowest of the women in it. The rest of you women, follow behind the wagon on foot. You men on foot, get your crossbows ready and walk at either side of the wagon and flank the women at the rear. You on the horses, four to the front and the rest bring up the rear."

The men did as they were told, suddenly shaking off the effects of the alcohol they had consumed, as their situation was made startlingly clear to them by the sub-commander. The joviality they had all expressed along the way home was now replaced by a sudden sense of fear and dread. Once they had finished quickly dumping their possessions by the side of the road and organizing themselves in and around the wagon, the driver flicked the reins and they set off at a brisk pace. The sub-commander rode back to the group of horsemen at the rear and gave one of them separate instructions. The man passed his pack and crossbow to another beside him and raced off at a gallop toward the city.

"Keep your eyes peeled, men, and shoot at anything that moves in the forest," the sub-commander said as he nervously scanned the tree line himself.

After another quarter of an hour of nervous riding down the road, the sub-commander was suddenly called to the front by the wagon driver. There, in the middle of the road in front of them, was the head of the rider sent to the city for reinforcements. The road was covered in blood, and a heavy trail continued towards the city. It appeared the rider had been decapitated, and his body was probably still in the saddle of the fleeing horse.

Immediately, the sub-commander barked out the order, "Stand ready!"

The men all suddenly sharpened their postures and their eyes started scanning the woods at either side of the road. Those on horseback sat up in their seats, crossbows in one hand at the ready, reins in the other. Those walking put both hands on their crossbows, now held pointing at the surrounding tree line of the forest. Suddenly, a man at the back and left of the column toppled forward off his horse. His hands were clutching at his throat as he writhed around on the road, desperately trying to breathe. As he fell, his horse reared up and a wave of fear spread through all the other horses, as if they could sense something was about to happen. The men tried to settle and steady their mounts. By the time the sub-commander had ridden up to his position, the man on the ground had stopped gasping and writhing, and was dead in a pool of his own blood. The crossbow bolt had entered from the left side of his neck, cutting across the major blood vessels, then the windpipe, and finally, into the major vessels on the right side as it came to a halt.

"Keep moving. Don't stop for anything. If you fall, you're dead," barked the sub-commander as he turned his horse around toward the city once more.

Fear gripped everyone, but in particular, the sub-commander, who realized how serious their situation was. If he stopped the column and went off into the woods, chasing the vampire, he knew it would pick his men off easily. If he kept them all moving, he would lose several more men or women to the vampire's sniper attacks, but more of them would survive. Keeping the column moving made the targets more difficult to hit, and once they were in the city, the vampire would be less likely to follow without the woods to hide his location. That was, if there was just one vampire; if there were more than one, then their situation was even more dire, but the choices were the same.

"One of you men or women on foot, up on that horse; in fact, double up where you can. We need to move quicker," came the sub-commander's last order before a crossbow bolt pierced his thigh and entered his horse's right flank. The horse reared up in shock and pain then waddled off to the side, slamming against another horse and rider. Then another crossbow bolt struck it between the ear and the eye. The horse dropped to the floor, dead, trapping the sub-commander's leg beneath its body as it did so.

The sub-commander yelled to the others, "Keep moving; don't stop. It's your only hope. Get to the city, where there are no woods for him to hide in and pick you off. Don't worry about me or anyone else who gets hit. Save yourselves. Go! Go!"

Just as he finished speaking, another man was hit in the shoulder by a crossbow bolt, then another in the stomach. Either there was more than one assailant or the vampire was using more than one crossbow. He probably had all three from the men he had killed already, and that meant he had plenty of ammunition. All the men on the right side of the road shot their crossbows at the forest where the crossbow bolts had appeared to come from. Then the sub-commander heard the snap of the reigns as the wagon driver encouraged his horses to pick up the pace. Several of the men on horseback spurred their mounts on and those on foot started to run. The whole group fell into panic and disarray as fear took over. With all of them travelling at different speeds, the distance between them was stretched out. As the sub-commander watched on helplessly, trapped as he was beneath his fallen horse, he feared for them all. This vampire had military skills and knew where to press his own advantage.

Over the next half hour or so, the ragtag group of exhausted and frightened people suffered more injuries as they ran along the road. Almost all of the men were hit by crossbow bolts, but amazingly, none of them were mortal blows, except for the one hit in the stomach. That poor fellow had keeled over and died within minutes of being hit. None of the women who reached the outskirts of the city were hurt, apart from having grazed hands or knees where they had stumbled and fell as they ran. No further attacks had been made upon the group once they were clear of the forest and within sight of the city itself.

Nearly an hour after his horse had been killed and fallen to the ground, trapping his leg beneath its body, the sub-commander still laid there, trapped on the side of the road. He could no longer feel the pain of the crossbow bolt in his right leg, just the cold throughout his whole body. In his almost semiconscious state, he failed to hear the vampire approach. Before he knew it, or could react, his hand holding his own crossbow was pulled away from the handle as effortlessly as an adult pulls a toy away from a baby. He looked up groggily to see the face of the vampire looking down at him. The vampire had an impassive look upon his face as he knelt down in front of him.

"You did well. Most of those people you commanded made it back to the city. Of course, I injured most of the hunters, just so I could scent their blood. Now, I'll just take my time finding each one of them, and their families, and feed on them. It could have been much worse, though. If you'd have been foolish enough to chase me into the woods, as I'd hoped, then you'd all be dead already," the vampire said calmly.

The sub-commander relaxed at the news and his eyes closed as his head fell back. Suddenly, he was snapped back awake as he felt the vampire's hand close around his hand and squeeze. The pain of his hand being crushed and the individual metacarpal bones breaking under the pressure pulled him painfully back into the land of the living.

"Don't die on me yet. I want some information on your group of hunters. Like where they meet and drink, so I can catch up with those I've scented. Plus, it would be pointless to kill you at the moment, as I'm quite full after feeding on some of your men earlier," the vampire stated casually.

"Go to hell," the sub-commander retorted.

"Oh, come now, there's no need to be like that. Let's have a nice little chat and you tell me all I want to know, and maybe you'll get to die of your injuries rather than having me rip your throat out and feed on your last few drops of blood. The alternative is far less pleasant for you. Here, let me show you." The vampire grabbed the sub-commander's other hand by the wrist. He then grabbed just the little finger with his other hand. "Now, here's how it works. I ask you a question... like for instance, at which bar in the city do most of the hunters drink together? And then you tell me the answer. Or...I do this." As the vampire finished his sentence, he snapped the sub-commander's little finger backwards, dislocating it from the joint.

The sub-commander screamed in pain.

"You see how painful that would be? And to die is one thing, but to die in screaming agony like that is far worse, believe me." The vampire paused for a few moments to allow the sub-commander time to recover a little from the pain in his hand. Then just as savagely, he pulled the finger back into its original position. "So are you ready to tell me what I want to know, or should I continue to play with the rest of your fingers?"

"Wh-what do you want to know?" the sub-commander stammered.

"That's the spirit. Now, Oh, how rude of me. I should really introduce myself shouldn't I. My name is Marco Brescati, but you can just call me Marco. So let us begin, shall we? You just tell me everything you know about your little hunter organization, and as long as you keep talking, and you answer any of the questions that happen to pop into my head along the way, we'll get along just fine," the vampire answered jovially as he took a seat on the fallen dead horse.

For the next two hours, before he died, the sub-commander told the vampire everything about the hunter organization he'd been recruited into. He went into detail about the training manual he'd received and where they'd completed most of their training, as well as those who were the main organizers of the group. Most interestingly, he mentioned a doctor who had taken up residence nearby after moving here from Germany. Specifically, he mentioned how this doctor had taught the class of hunters he attended all about vampires, and what could and couldn't hurt them. It was to his estate that the captive vampires would have been taken, as the doctor was conducting experiments upon vampires. The vampire had been most interested in hearing all about this Dr. Pavel Kushenko.

Once the vampire had extracted all the information he required from the sub-commander, he simply leaned across and twisted his neck sharply. He had become terribly weak as the blood loss from his leg wound took its toll on him, and Marco was tired of snapping his fingers to keep him conscious. Marco stood up, stretched his long limbs, and squinted as the sun began to rise in the eastern sky. *Time to return home, for the moment, and then in a few weeks, after the human hunters think they are all safe again, a trip into the big city seems to be called for. That could then be followed by a visit to this Dr. Kushenko's estate, to see how my two sire-lings are faring in the good doctor's care,* he thought.

"So the hunters' letting that one vampire escape had proven to have terrible consequences. There's nothing new in that, Mother," Izzy interrupted.

"I know, dear, but it's what happened a few weeks later that caused the prob-lem. Come, let's sit a while on that bench over there as I continue the story," Margeurite suggested, pointing to a vacant park bench out in the open.

Chapter Twenty Seven

Marco

Johnson nodded at Margeurite as he continued to walk and check the surrounding area once more. On receiving the bodyguard's assurances that they were not being overheard or monitored in any way, she continued with the story.

Among the men who had raided the brothel with the hunter organization was one of the local blacksmiths named Angelo. He was a big man, standing over six feet tall with particularly broad shoulders and powerfully built arms. During late-night drinking sessions at the local tavern, he would often take on two opponents at a time in an arm wrestling competition and win. As he stood in front of the furnace, pumping the bellows system and turning the metal he was working on, until it glowed almost white hot, he failed to hear the man enter his workshop behind him. As he turned to start hammering the metal rod into shape, however, he suddenly became aware of the other man's presence.

"My apologies, Sir, I did not hear or see you enter," Angelo said before quickly turning back to insert the metal rod into the hot coals once more while he discussed business.

"No matter, my good man. I could see you were busy," the stranger replied.

Angelo wiped his right hand on a nearby cloth before extending it toward the man in greeting. The man extended his own hand and they shook. Both men had the kind of firm handshakes that set them apart from most people.

"I'm Angelo. How may I assist you, Sir?"

"Well met, Angelo. My name is Marco Brescati. I was actually walking past and thought I recognized you, so I figured I should at least pop in and say hello."

"You have me at a disadvantage, Sir, as I don't recall meeting you before. Have I done some work for you in the past that I've forgotten?" Angelo asked, slightly puzzled. While he was a busy man with a great many customers, he prided himself on remembering all of his clients by name and by what job he had completed on their behalf. To have someone recognize him but he not them was most unusual and perplexing. Perhaps it was in a social setting they had met, he thought, as he was quite famous in the local area as a man of strength in the bar games and challenges. Again, though, with his size and not being a heavy drinker, he was not one to get drunk and fail to remember the people around him. Especially when so much of his work came from people he met and chatted with in the local tavern.

"Aha, I can see by your furrowed brow that you do not recall meeting me, Angelo."

"My apologies once more, Sir, for indeed I do not recall our previous meeting at all," Angelo said, more than a little flummoxed at the situation.

"Oh, that is most disappointing, Angelo. Usually, people have no problem remembering me at all. In fact, most people I've met can think of nothing but me for a long, long time. Indeed, most men I meet have me fixed in their minds for the remainder of their worthless lives," Marco explained with a little more jovial bravado.

Still, Angelo could not recall the man standing in front of him, talking so relaxed and pleasantly. Then the fact that the man had mentioned that most people didn't forget him and could think of nothing but him triggered a response, and the hairs on the back of Angelo's neck suddenly stood up.

Marco heard the sudden increase in the heart rate of the big man across the room from him and decided to take his little cat and mouse game to the next level. "So tell me, Angelo the blacksmith, do you often fire a crossbow bolt at someone and not recall what he looks like, or was it simply too dark at the brothel for you to see me?" he said, maintaining his calm and almost friendly composure.

Angelo suddenly had his worst fears confirmed. The man in his workshop was the vampire who had escaped the brothel and terrorized him and the other hunters all the way back to the outskirts of the city. With his heart now racing, Angelo grabbed the iron rod he had been working on out of the fire and held it up with the glowing, hot end pointing at the vampire to ward him off. Angelo began circling toward more of his tools that could be used as a weapon against the vampire, but as he moved, so did Marco, heading him off. The two men were now silent as they locked eyes, moved, and counter-moved around each other. Marco's eyes had gone crimson red and his teeth had extended to give him a toothy smile with his fangs protruding.

Every time Angelo tried to move one way or the other to reach his other tools, Marco would casually stride one or two paces to the side to counter his move. Marco had stood at the back of the workshop, watching the blacksmith for at least ten minutes, and in that time, he'd looked around at all the equipment and tools hanging on the walls and propped up against the sides. He had worked out his plan of attack carefully.

Angelo knew that he was a strong and capable man, but he also knew that his strength would be no match for that of a vampire, and coupled with the increased speed and reflexes of a vampire, the advantage was clearly his opponent's. He knew he needed something to even up the odds or even tip them in his favor. Then he realized what Dr. Kushenko had taught him and the other hunters about vampires; they had a fear of fire, as they could be burnt to death. Angelo quickly used the small shovel he kept in the coal bucket to scoop up some of the hot coals and cast them at Marco. The vampire tried to parry them off with his hand as well as duck under the spray of red-hot coals, but one caught him on his right cheek as well as two or three hitting his hand. The pain of a burn to a vampire was roughly ten times the intensity that a human feels, and Marco snarled in anger at such an affront.

Marco was no longer content to play the game of cat and mouse and leapt forward across the room at the blacksmith as he turned to scoop up another load of coals. Marco grabbed Angelo by the throat and held him firmly with the fingers of one hand digging in around the bigger-built man's windpipe. His other hand grabbed at the bar in Angelo's hand and twisted it out of his grip as easily as taking a toy off a small child. Marco spun the blacksmith around so that he was leaning back toward his own forge. Angelo, desperate to breathe and escape, had both of his hands trying to remove the fingers from around his throat.

Marco loosened his grip very slightly to allow the man to breathe, but not to escape. Then he slid the metal rod back beneath the coals and raised his arm to pump the bellows as he had seen the blacksmith do earlier. Recovering his breath a little, Angelo was suddenly aware that his hair was beginning to singe at the back of his head. Realizing the position he was in, he began to panic and struggle, but the vampire was too strong and easily held him. Marco extended his arm to push Angelo further over the fire and soon noticed the man's hair starting to shrivel and smoke. Withdrawing the metal rod once more, Marco brought it up to inspect its orange, glowing tip. He intended to tease Angelo with it before slowly plunging it into his chest. Angelo suddenly and unexpectedly grabbed at the rod with both hands, ignoring the burning pain of holding it in the middle, and pushed it toward the vampire's face with all his strength.

Marco gave an animalistic growl of pain as the red-hot poker caught him across the bridge of his nose and seared a line across his face and through the middle of his ear. The pain caused him to lean backward and release his grip on the blacksmith's throat. Angelo took the opportunity to quickly run to the left side of his workshop and grab the axe propped against the wall. Although a heavy, cumbersome weapon to most men, in his strong arms, the axe was Angelo's best available choice. He cut an arc through the air with the axe at the height of the vampire's neck as he recovered and quickly advanced toward him. Unfortunately, Marco had anticipated the move and ducked under the swing, and then struck upward with the rod he still held. The point of the rod entered beneath Angelo's chin, in the middle of the "V" of his jaw. It pierced first his outer skin, then continued upward through his tongue, then hard palate, and on up through the nasal air passages and ethmoidal sinuses, before piercing into the frontal cranial cavity and Angelo's brain.

The axe clattered to the floor as it dropped from the blacksmith's lifeless hands, and Marco stood for a moment, supporting the full weight of the man's dead body with his one hand. As he twisted the metal rod in his hand to the left or right, the vampire found that he could move and tilt Angelo's head around like a glove puppet. Marco smiled as he walked back over to the forge and lifted the blacksmith up onto it. He then spent a few minutes packing more coal around the body of the blacksmith and operating the bellows to bring it up to maximum heat. Noticing the legs were hanging over the edge, Marco used the axe to cleave into them at mid-thigh to break each of the femurs. He then folded them up on top of the body to ensure that they would be burnt with the rest of him. Next, the vampire took a moment or two to put out the two small fires that were struggling to stay alight from the coals that Angelo had thrown at him. Once he was convinced that all was well and that the body of the blacksmith would soon disappear, he left for his next port of call.

The street was quiet in the middle of the evening, with no people out walking or carriages passing by, and Marco made good time striding out as he did with his long legs. He arrived at the carpenter's house to see the lamps inside the house glowing brightly through the thin curtains covering the windows. Marco was well aware that the carpenter had been one of the hunters at the brothel that night, but on scenting him and following him home, he had been pleasantly surprised to see that one of the young whores had taken up residence with him. While outwardly, the pair were being very discreet about the situation, they had been unable to keep their little secret from a senior vampire like him. The fact that the whore concerned was the one he had been about to taste that very night pleased Marco greatly.

After first checking the street to make sure he was not being observed, Marco knocked loudly on the door. After a few moments, he heard two chairs moving back from their position at the table and one person going down into the cellar while the other approached the front door.

"Who is it?" the voice nervously requested.

"Open up. I have an urgent message from the captain," Marco bellowed loudly.

The door was then quickly unbolted from behind, and as soon as it was opened slightly, Marco slammed his hand against it, as he forcefully straightened his arm. The man behind the door was caught unaware and sent sprawling backward into the room with the force of the blow delivered through the door. Marco then entered through the open doorway and turned to close and then bolt the door behind him.

"Who the hell are you? And what do you think you are doing, barging in here like that?" the young carpenter demanded.

Marco walked purposefully over to him, just as he was getting to his feet. He grabbed the young man by the hair and started to drag him across the room almost nonchalantly behind him. The carpenter made an effort to pull against him and raised both of his own hands to try to twist Marco's hands off his hair. The vampire ignored the man's struggles and pulled him over toward the large, wooden table. Once at the table, Marco simply smashed the man's head down hard against the corner edge of it. He felt the man's skull crack like an eggshell as he did so, and he released his hold on the hair bunched up in his hand and let the body slump lifelessly to the floor.

Marco then strode over to the door at the top of the stairs leading into the cellar. Lifting the latch, he swung the door open and began walking down the stairs, into the darkness. As he descended the cold stone steps, he began taking his shirt off, allowing it to drop to the stairs behind him. On reaching the bottom step, he paused a moment to take off each of his boots and the remainder of his clothing. Standing there naked, he looked around in the darkness and spotted the young girl attempting to hide herself away in the farthest corner of the room. It didn't help her, as he could see her perfectly as she sat hunched in the corner, the unlit lamp still cradled in her hand.

Marco silently walked over to her and took the lamp out of her hand. The girl's heartbeat was racing now as she had obviously heard a bit of the struggle from above and he had not tried to hide his descent down the stairs from her. Without saying a word to her, he gently took hold of her hands and pulled her up onto her feet. Once she was standing up in front of him, he leaned forward and gently kissed her. She tried to pull away, but he held her and forced his attention upon her. After a few more moments of trying to resist his advances, the girl stopped fighting him and gave in, allowing his tongue to enter her mouth as she kissed him back. He began to tear her clothes off as he continued to kiss her. She started to sob and he felt the water of her tears as they flowed down her cheeks. Once she was naked, he pushed her down onto her hands and knees. Then kneeling down behind her, without any further preamble, he pushed his manhood forcefully into her. She gave a small yelp of pain and tried to pull away again. Marco grabbed her tightly by the hips, digging his powerful fingers into her flesh as he did so. She now tried to struggle away more forcefully and began to cry and scream. The vampire pumped his hips backward and forward with mounting vigor and ignored her screams as he cruelly satisfied his lust.

Luckily, the girl's torment didn't last long. The vampire reached his climax quickly. Pausing to regain his senses for a moment after his climax, he released the girl and let her fall forward onto the cold floor, still sobbing at his frenzied attack upon her. Then after a short pause, he reached forward and grabbed her by the hair, viciously pulling her back toward him again. The girl screamed in both shock and pain at the renewed attack, as Marco twisted her head slightly to one side and brought his other arm up to grip and pull her shoulder down, exposing her neck to him. He opened his mouth wide and slowly bit her neck, making sure that he sealed the wound he'd made with his mouth. He didn't want to let any of her blood escape as the burns on his face were going to need all of it so he could repair himself and look as handsome as he usually was once more. He ignored the girl's screams and her feeble attempts to struggle free of his grasp, and concentrated on savoring every last drop of blood he drained from her sweet, young body.

Marco used every trick he knew to keep her blood flowing into his mouth, and even after she died, he kept massaging the limbs and compressing the chest to squeeze more blood around her arterial system. Once he'd finished his feeding, he cleaned himself up and dressed, then spent some time looking around at the handiwork of the carpenter. He still had some time to kill before the tavern's patrons would be thrown out onto the street. He hid the body of the young whore inside a chest he found in the cellar. He'd had to break a few of her bones to make her to fit in, but once finished, he was pleased to think that the body wouldn't be found for some time. On returning to the carpenter, he placed a chair on top of the table and arranged the man's body to make it look like he'd been doing something with the lamp suspended from the ceiling. Whoever discovered the body would assume that he had simply lost his balance and fallen down, smashing his head on the corner of the table in the process.

Happy with the way he had arranged everything, Marco carefully left by the back window. He had left all the doors locked from within and managed to bump the window hard enough to make the latch fall back into position, securing it as well. So the way he figured it, no one would ever suspect foul play had occurred or even discover the body for a very long time. Looking up at the position of the moon in the night sky, Marco judged that he had plenty of time for the short walk over to his predetermined vantage point, looking onto the old tavern. Once again, he checked up and down the street for any sign that his actions had been witnessed. Seeing nothing but a scrawny alley cat that took flight upon seeing him, he began the journey to his next port of call. That whore had been extremely young and nutritious, he thought to himself as he stroked the freshly repaired skin on the side of his face with a smile.

Arriving at his lookout post opposite the tavern a short while later, Marco stayed hidden within the shadows. The fact that it had several smaller side streets branching off from it made this place exceptionally good for late-night stalking, and particularly so if you were a vampire hell bent on bloody revenge.

As the two men spilled out onto the street in their drunken state, Marco held his position hidden among the shadows and downwind of them. As he breathed in the night air deeply, he recognized the scent of both men. They had both been at the brothel that night, and both had fled. They had considered themselves lucky to make it back alive and had virtually forgotten the injuries they'd received during the escape. Both, however, had tended to drink a little more than usual since that night. This was mainly in an effort to drown out the nightmares that persistently interrupted their sleep. As the two men staggered off home together, Marco slowly emerged from his position and began to follow them. He was almost like a cat, silently sneaking up on an unsuspecting mouse. He was enjoying this part of his revenge, feeling as he did that this was where he truly shone as a vampire, a creature of stealth and silent hunting. Hugging the sides of the buildings, he carefully trailed in their wake until they separated at a street junction ahead of him.

Then swiftly making up the distance between them, he ran and leapt upon the one who had turned to the left. Before the man could scream or yell, or even knew what was happening in his "well-oiled" state, Marco had a hand on either side of his head, covering his ears, and he savagely twisted the man's head around to the right. The man fell completely limp before Marco tossed his body into a pile of wooden staves leaning against the front of the nearest of the houses lining the street. To the people who discovered his body the next morning, it appeared he'd tripped and fallen in his drunken stupor and had broken his neck in the process.

Marco then quickly turned and sped off after the other man, again using the available shadows to hide his movements from any who may see him. The second man was standing atop a small bridge and relieving himself of a full bladder into the fast-running river below when Marco caught up with him. One moment, he was standing feet apart, a hand on his hip with the other holding himself as he sprayed a pattern across the water's surface, the next he was flailing his arms as he attempted to keep his balance and himself out of the cold water. He had been so drunk that it had only taken the slightest of pushes to topple him into the water. Marco smiled to himself as he wondered if the man might have actually fallen anyway; he was that drunk and unsteady.

As he broke the surface and gasped for air, the man tried unsuccessfully to put his feet down on the solid bottom of the river. Immediately he sank back under the water. Coughing and spluttering, he came back up once more as he kicked his legs and tried to use his arms to stay afloat. The cool water had something of a sobering effect on him, and after looking around and seeing that he was being swept farther along the river, he started to swim across to the nearest side with the flow. Luckily, he was sober enough to realize that the current was too strong to swim against it. Marco, from his position on the bridge, watched and waited to see which side the man would head for. Once he saw the man heading to the left side of the river, he slowly paced off along the river bank, ready to intercept if he emerged.

Almost totally exhausted with his wet clothes pulling him down and catching in the river's flow, the man felt a loose pebble or two as he swept his arm in a tired arc, making contact with the bottom at last. Immediately, he brought his legs down and flopped around, and fell over a couple more times as he dragged himself through the shallows. Almost crawling out on his hands and knees in his exhausted state, he just managed to pull himself up onto the riverbank. As he reached dry land, he collapsed into a heap and rolled over onto his back, gasping heavily. He looked up at the night sky. With the moon and the stars twinkling in the distance, he felt his heart rate still racing madly. He took a few long, deep breaths as he tried to recover from his ordeal. *No more drinking*, he thought to himself, realizing how close he'd just come to drowning. Suddenly, a shadow loomed above him and he felt a pair of hands grab him by his jacket lapels. A moment later, he was lifted up onto his feet in one smooth movement.

"You should have stayed in the water. You would have been safer there, as I really don't want to get my feet wet," came the dispassionate voice.

The next moment, the man was lifted high up into the air, suspended above the vampire's head, before being tossed back into the middle of the river. In his near-exhausted state, this time, the man only surfaced twice as he tried weakly to swim to the shore again. The area he landed in was moving much faster than before, and he was soon dragged under. The vampire shook himself and swept his hands back through his hair to remove the water that had dripped down onto him. He looked up and down the riverbank once more to check for any witnesses, and upon seeing no one else, he turned and walked back the way he came. It was now time to go and visit this Dr. Kushenko, he decided.

Chapter Twenty Eight

Captain

Over the past couple of weeks, with the two new vampires to experiment on, along with Tibor and the girls of varying ages that the hunters had delivered as blood donors, Pavel was able to discover that the younger the human blood donor, the better for the vampire. This was particularly true for older vampires like Tibor, who was far brighter and attentive to his questioning when fed blood from the youngest of the girl prisoners. It seemed that the blood from older humans, such as the madam and the much older whores, was less nutritious to a vampire. This also tied in with their sleep patterns. The younger vampires tended to sleep far less when given young human blood, but slept longer when fed on older human blood. The gender of the human donating the blood was not found to have any effect upon the vampires at all.

Pavel was pleased to be able to throw himself back into his studies at long last, and working made him feel useful once more. While he harbored more than a little resentment toward Tibor after what the old vampire had done to him, Pavel accepted that it was his own overconfidence and foolishness that had cost him his leg and partial use of his left arm. Luckily, Pieter was proving himself to be an invaluable assistant and picked everything up incredibly quickly. He also had the additional effect of controlling Tibor's temperament just by being in the room with him. The old vampire was keen to be seen as compliant whenever Pieter was around.

It was now late in the evening and Pavel had been working by candlelight for a few hours so his eyes were becoming heavy. Pieter was on the other side of the room. He sat reading in one of the large, comfy chairs almost hidden in the shadows, as he required no additional light by which to read the text in front of him.

Suddenly, Pavel was startled by a knock at the door. Pieter immediately put down the book he was reading and went to answer it.

"That sounds like our friend, the captain of the guard, and two of his thugs," Pieter stated as he passed Pavel on his way to answer the second, more insistent, series of impatient knocks on the door.

It was indeed the captain of the guard and two of his men. The captain demanded to see Pavel immediately in his usual impatient manner. Pieter ushered them into the living room at the front of the house as he went to assist Pavel, who was not yet fully ambulant on his new leg and single crutch. Once they were all seated in the room, Pieter took his leave and went back out into the corridor, closing the door behind him. He could still hear everything that went on inside the room, but Pavel felt it was better to keep his extraordinary abilities and involvement a secret from the others in the hunter organization, just in case he drew attention to himself.

The captain was by no means a stupid man and had worked out that something not quite right was going on of late. In the last week alone, he'd lost eight of his men. All of the men had died in apparent accidents, but the fact that all of the men concerned had been at the brothel that night concerned him. All of these men had been injured during the course of their eventual escape, and all had spilled some of their blood in the process. The captain was sure that these accidents were the work of the lone vampire who got away. Pavel agreed with the captain about the likelihood of such a set of accidents befalling only his men who had been at the brothel. It was obvious to Pavel that those who had been injured had actually been scented by the vampire concerned.

Secretly, Pavel felt he should kick himself for trusting these hunters not to bring trouble to his own door. By holding out on the information about the vampire who had escaped and not confiding in him, the captain had made a stupid mistake. Pavel further surmised that the vampire would doubtless have studied his quarry long enough to pick up their habits and also spotted those associates that he hadn't scented that night. So now all of the captain's men were in danger, as well as Pavel, Pieter, and the captain himself. Doubtless, the vampire would be keen to free his friends if given the chance to do so. Worse still, the vampire may be part of a larger coven and could have involved them in the situation, too. So there could be any number of vampires out hunting the hunters.

Pavel explained to the captain his understanding of how the vampire's scenting worked and how, if he'd been told about the escaped vampire, he could have helped mask the men's scent and thereby possibly offered some kind of protection to them all. He further explained how the vampire was likely to operate and pick off his quarry one by one as the opportunity arose.

The captain, upon thinking on the matter for a few moments, then scribbled a letter of instruction and sent one of his men off to gather all the remaining hunters and to bring them here to Pavel's house. He explained that he intended to lure the vampire in and to take care of it once and for all. Meanwhile, it was time to kill the other captive vampires, as the risk of them running free again was too great to allow. Pavel reluctantly agreed to his proposed course of action, and called out to Pieter to come and guide the captain and his remaining aide to the cellars.

As Pieter, the captain, and his aide entered the room, all three of the vampires laid asleep, slumped against the back wall. They were on minimal rations of blood so were not particularly alert. The captain of the guard strode purposefully forward, leveled his crossbow, and shot the first one in the chest before it could react. The two remaining vampires were on their feet in a moment and moving as much as their chains would allow them to spoil the shots they knew were to follow. The captain fired his reloaded crossbow at the second vampire. The vampire growled in pain and anger through clenched teeth as the bolt struck its hand as it tried to swat it away. Seconds later, the captain's aide sent his own crossbow bolt into the vampire's chest and it slumped to the ground, immobilized.

Both the captain and his aide were now busy reloading their crossbows when suddenly, the last remaining vampire, Tibor, swung his arm, releasing the small rock he had managed to work free from the cellar wall over the last few weeks. The rock hit the captain's aide on the temple and embedded itself there. The man dropped to the floor instantly, his eyes remaining open and staring off into the distance. The captain halted his own reloading to check on the man's condition. When he rolled him over and saw his eyes, he instantly knew that the man was dead. Anger now welled up inside the captain as he returned to finish reloading his crossbow. During the pause, however, Tibor had grabbed the immobilized body of one of his fellow vampires and was now holding it up in front of his chest as a shield.

The captain, once he reloaded, looked up at Tibor. Upon seeing how he was holding the other vampire, he smiled wickedly. "So you think your friend will protect you, do you?" he stated as he walked back and placed the crossbow on the bench at the back of the room. The next moment, he swept his long coat to the side and withdrew his sword from its scabbard. The captain swished the sword about, slicing the air a couple of times, then he began to advance toward Tibor.

"I wouldn't be so worried about me, Captain, but more about the vampire boy at your back," Tibor stated calmly.

"What do you mean?" the captain asked, momentarily stunned and surprised.

"The boy beside you, does he not look a little pale? Do his eyes not squint like mine in the bright lights of the lamps you've used to light your way down here?" Tibor continued quickly, sowing the seeds of doubt in the captain's mind.

"You lie, vampire. You just seek to confuse me," the captain spat back as he advanced once more.

"No, I'm not lying at all. You see, now, my little friend has to make a choice. Does he let me die at your hand, and then have you keep a closer eye on him, knowing as he does that you will eventually realize what he is, and either chain him up or kill him, or does he kill you to protect his secret and come away with me, so that I can show him the joys of being a vampire and feeding and living forever?" Tibor said, holding eye contact with Pieter.

Pieter was suddenly confused about what to do. Everything Tibor had said was true. The captain was an intelligent man, and now that the first seeds of doubt had been sown, he would indeed be keeping a closer eye on him. Pieter was suddenly confronted with the possibility of being shackled and experimented upon, just like a vampire. On the other hand, he was being given the opportunity to go out and live as a vampire, feeding and living as free as he could ever want and to learn more about himself. Hadn't he already learned more about himself from Tibor than anyone else? Could it be that this was how he was meant to live? As Pieter was caught in his own moment of indecision, the captain had once again turned to look at him, and in that moment, he'd seen the look of confusion on Pieter's face and known that what Tibor had said was true. Pieter hadn't expected anything like this situation to occur and had been caught completely unprepared. In that moment of confusion, he'd played perfectly into the old vampire's trap and given himself away.

The captain instantly tried to swing around and slice Pieter's head from his neck. Pieter saw the move coming and ducked below the arc of the sword, and continued rolling forward. The momentum carried his full body weight into the captain, his right shoulder hitting the man's legs at the knee joints and buckling them backward. The impact sent him screaming in pain to the floor. Although in agony, the captain kept hold of his sword and brought it up protectively to keep Pieter at bay. Unfortunately for the captain, when Pieter had rolled into him and knocked him backward, he'd been pushed over the white line etched into the floor. No sooner had he landed than Tibor seized upon his opportunity; he dropped the other vampire he was using to protect himself and pulled the crossbow bolt from its chest. Then Tibor stabbed the crossbow bolt into the captain's right shoulder and used it to drag him back across the floor into his own clutches. The captain's arm went limp, and he dropped the sword as he felt himself pulled back into Tibor's grasp. Tibor then grabbed him by the hair and pulled his head to the left, fully exposing his neck. Tibor paused for a moment to smile up at Pieter before opening his mouth and sinking his fangs viciously into the captain's neck.

Pieter was struck dumb once more as the captain's eyes locked on his. He saw no plea for mercy in those eyes, just cold-blooded hatred staring straight back at him. Pieter sat back against the wall in desperation and confusion, not knowing what to do. Then the door swung open and a tall, pale man entered, carrying Pavel roughly. As the man entered the room, he dropped Pavel on the floor to the left by the bench.

"Marco!" the vampire beside Tibor from whom he'd withdrawn the crossbow bolt exclaimed as he was becoming aware of his surroundings once more.

"Alfredo and Tibor, and if I'm not mistaken, that's Carmine with his hand and chest impaled," Marco stated as he scanned the room..

"Well met, my friend," Tibor said, blood dripping from his smiling mouth.

"And who might this be?" Marco asked, looking at Pieter.

"He's food for the taking. But be careful. He is not without the strength and speed we possess, but nothing the great Captain Marco Brescati cannot deal with, I'll wager," Tibor added as he returned to feed on the captain.

"So, little one, you have some of our abilities, yet you are not one of us, because I can hear your little heartbeat in terror," Marco said menacingly.

Pieter, realizing the danger he was in, tried to roll forward to gather up the captain's fallen sword. Marco was quick enough to intercept him and used his superior bodyweight to wrestle him to the floor.

"My, my, you are a strong little fellow, aren't you?" Marco stated as he continued to try to subdue Pieter.

Marco's eyes turned red and his fangs extended as he tried to get Pieter into a biting position. Just as his larger bodyweight and higher position was about to give him the final advantage, he suddenly yelled in rage and twisted to look back toward the entrance. Pavel had grabbed the captain's crossbow from the table, and although his hastily aimed shot had missed the vampire's heart, it had pinned his shoulder blade to his chest and caused him considerable pain. The distraction and loss of the use of his right arm meant the advantage had returned to Pieter, who wriggled, punched, and kicked the vampire until he could no longer hold him pinned to the ground.

From his position propped up in the corner of the room, with the wall on his left and the bench behind him, Pavel could just reach one or two of the tools. He grabbed a hammer and tossed it across the floor toward Pieter. This time, Pieter was the quicker of the two to react. He grabbed the hammer in his left hand and swung it against the vampire's forehead. Marco was momentarily dazed by the blow, which was immediately followed by another stronger blow that hit him just behind the ear and ripped part of his ear off. The vampire rolled back, trying to get away from the possibility of a third blow as his own blood slowly flowed down into his eyes, making it difficult to see.

As he shuffled backward across the floor, Marco suddenly felt the sword by his left hand. He grabbed the sword hilt and lifted it, thrusting clumsily toward where he thought Pieter was. The sword cleaved nothing but air. Pieter had seen the vampire grab the sword and anticipated the desperate attack. He'd regained his footing after landing the second blow to the vampire's head. He'd then swapped the hammer over to his right hand just as the vampire's sword thrust began. Pieter spun around on his left heel and extended his arm from the shoulder, and as he completed the full clockwise circle of the spin, he snapped his elbow straight just as the hammer contacted the side of the vampire's head. Pieter held nothing back;

he put all his strength and all the power of the momentum of his spinning movement into the blow. The vampire's head was caved in like an eggshell and he fell unconscious to the floor.

The sword clattered noisily to the ground, released from the vampire's grip. Pieter calmly picked it up and then lifted the vampire's head by his blood-matted hair. With one clean sweep of his arm, he severed the head from the body. Then Pieter strode over to Alfredo, who was just lying propped up against the wall, taking the time he needed to recover from his crossbow bolt impalement. He raised an arm weakly against Pieter, who cleaved it off mid-forearm. The young vampire barely had time to scream before Pieter thrust the sword into his heart to immobilize him again. Withdrawing the sword after a few moments, Pieter grabbed Alfredo by the hair and pulled him forward. Now held in the perfect position with the back of his neck exposed, Pieter cleaved his head from his body. He then made short work of decapitating the third vampire, Carmine, leaving only Tibor alive. Tibor still held the dead body of the captain protectively in front of him and watched silently as Pieter turned and walked back toward the entrance to the room. He dropped the sword and stood in front of Pavel, who was still propping himself up against the wall and table.

"Tibor told the captain that I wasn't really human, and then I hesitated as the captain considered the facts laid before him. He decided in that moment that I was a vampire and he struck out against me," Pieter explained.

"It was always a risk that one day, someone would see you as something you are not, Pieter," Pavel surmised.

"I wasn't prepared for the situation and my reaction caused the captain to act the way he did," Pieter added.

Pavel reached out and put his arm on Pieter's shoulder. "There was nothing you could be prepared for; we both knew keeping Tibor alive was a risk. He is without doubt the cleverest and most cunning individual I've ever had to deal with. So it's no shame, nor is it a surprise that he managed to twist and turn things on you, too. What we both have to do is learn from our mistakes so that we don't end up repeating them."

"What do we do now?" Pieter asked wearily after a short pause.

"Well, the vampire who killed all of the captain's men may or may not have acted alone. So we have to consider the fact that the safety of this house might be compromised. My work on the captive vampires is complete, and I think the hunters have proven too dangerous to be associated with any longer. If they are not leading vampires to our doorstep with their incompetence, then they are starting to look at you questioningly. I think it's time for us to move on and start somewhere new," Pavel answered.

"Any idea where?" Pieter inquired, intrigued by the idea.

Pavel smiled. "I think you need to brush up on your German. I have some distant relatives who I think we should go and visit."

Pieter gave Pavel a hand and supported him back upstairs, where he hastily put together some travelling bags and packed a few essentials they would need. This included the old wooden chest they took everywhere, with all the gold and jewelry Pavel had liberated from Lord Dimitri's family tomb. About an hour before dawn, Pieter had the small wagon and two horses set ready to go. He also had his own favorite horse tied to the back of the cart. The remaining two horses and the other livestock, he had released.

Supporting Pavel once more, they returned to the cellars and entered the main room where Tibor was still incarcerated. Helping Pavel to sit up on the table near the door, Pieter then picked up the captain's sword and strode down the corridor to the room that housed the captive whores and the madam. After a few moments, Pavel heard some screams and a little shouting, then complete silence. When Pieter returned, Pavel noticed that there was blood smeared down the length of the blade and dripping from the hilt of the sword. Seeing Tibor still chained up and holding the captain's dead body in front of his chest as a shield, Pieter was about to step forward to deal with the old vampire when Pavel stopped him with an outstretched arm.

"No point risking injury against someone as cunning as Tibor," Pavel said. "I think it's time to try something new." He reached out across the table and removed a large jar from the wall-mounted shelf. He passed it to Pieter, and instructed Pieter to spread it around Tibor and up the walls. Pavel also made sure that Pieter remembered the instructions on how to use this particular oil.

Pieter remembered that he shouldn't get any on himself, not even the smallest splash or drop. Once his task was complete, Pieter went back up the corridor, returning a few moments later with an unlit torch and a small glass candle lamp, which was lit.

Pavel took both from him and placed the lamp on the table, where he carefully took off the glass cover then used the naked flame of the candle to light the torch. Then Pavel hobbled toward the door and told Pieter to throw the two remaining jars high against the wall Tibor was chained to. Pieter did as he was instructed, and each jar smashed against the wall, showering Tibor and the area his chain would allow him to walk to in the oil.

"Forgive me for not taking the time to kill you more humanely, but sometimes revenge is an emotion that gets the better of us humans," Pavel said, almost apologetically.

Tibor knew he had no chance of escape and his search over the captain's person had not been of any use in providing any other weapon he could use on Pavel or Pieter. The two crossbow bolts he'd recovered from Carmine's corpse would only be of use in close-proximity fighting, something that he'd been prepared for when Pieter started to walk toward him with the sword. Now confronted with the oil spilled all around him and Pavel holding the torch, he knew he was about to meet his end. "Ha! You'll be joining me soon enough, human. That boy of yours will show his true nature, and then you'll be sorry when he puts an end to you," he spat out his final words before he slammed one of the crossbow bolts into his own chest.

The old vampire dropped to the floor, paralyzed. Pavel took a moment to reflect upon what the vampire had just done. Rather than die a horrible death, writhing in agony as he burnt to a crisp, he'd chosen to paralyze himself and not wake up from the stake. In one way, Pavel felt robbed of the revenge he'd sought. He wanted to see the old vampire suffer, just like he would with the injuries Tibor had given him, injuries that would stay with him for the rest of his life, especially on cold, damp mornings. In another way, he saw a certain sense of nobility in the act of choosing the way he would exit the world.

Pavel tossed the torch as far as he could to the end of the room. Immediately, the far end of the makeshift dungeon exploded into a fiery furnace of incredible intensity. Pavel quickly turned away and was assisted along the corridor and out of the house by Pieter.

Once he'd helped Pavel take his seat on the cart, Pieter skipped around to the other side and, a short while later, the two of them were riding off to the northwest, with the house ablaze behind them. They stayed on the more minor roads and kept to themselves as they journeyed up across Europe, until they reached Pavel's cousin's home in the Harz Mountains in Northern Germany.

No one from the hunter organization knew anything of their current location; they had surmised that all had died in the house fire, along with the captain and the prisoners. The other hunters had found the messenger the captain had sent with the handwritten letter detailing what he feared was occurring with the vampire. The instructions never reached his men due to Marco intercepting and killing the man. Though the remnants of the hunter organization stayed on alert and searched for the vampire responsible, he was never found. In fact, no vampire sightings or incidents occurred in the area for some ten years or so after that night.

The hunters came to the conclusion that the vampire had attacked the captain at Pavel's house and that rather than allow the vampire to free the others, the captain had engineered a trap and sacrificed himself in the resultant fire. His actions had therefore saved the people of the city from the threat of the vampires. He was considered a hero and used as an example to all future trainee hunters on what was expected of them.

Chapter Twenty Nine

Marguerite

Because of what almost happened with Marco and Tibor, Pavel chose never to work with the hunter organization again. Nor did he take up another teaching position. Instead, he chose to stay in Northern Germany, hidden away in secret and known only by his close relatives. He and Pieter moved out to a small and private homestead close to a river and on the edge of a dense forest, from which he could call down and feed the local wildlife. The Harz Mountains provided a scenic backdrop and a secluded-enough spot to keep their privacy. Here, he could spend more time with Pieter and they could go off fishing together, as he and his father had done during his own childhood.

Pavel had come to the conclusion that he was sick and tired of dealing with vampires and the misery they had brought upon him. He decided to retire, relax, and most of all, enjoy his life as best he could. He and Pieter had no problems with regard to money, as they still had more than enough to live on as well as plenty to invest from the funds they had liberated from Lord Dimitri. Pavel was also mindful that Pieter's pale complexion would have eventually raised further comments should they remain in contact with the hunter organization.

"So that's why he's kept himself secret from the hunters, for fear of being mistaken for a vampire himself," Izzy deduced.

"That's not the only reason, but it's certainly the main reason. Pieter is well aware of the inherent problems of such a large organization as the hunters. By remaining a secret, he can do the most damage to the vampires. Can you imagine either of them ever resting in pursuit of him, if knowledge of his existence ever got out?" Margeurite quizzed her daughter.

"No, you're right. Both sides would never stop searching for him. I can see he needs to be kept a secret," Izzy agreed.

"Not just for his own safety, Isabelle, but also those he has rescued and protected, too, which includes both you and I. Pieter still has contact with most of the people he has saved from the vampires. The vampires would torture that information out of him, no matter how long it took."

"Why would they want to go after those people? Surely, they would all be prepared in some way and the vampires would likely suffer losses in such a situation," Isabelle pointed out.

Margeurite smiled at her daughter as she explained. "That's your military strategist coming out in your thinking. The elder vampires care little for any loss of the younger, inexperienced vampires who would be sent out to do any such dirty work. What they do care about is keeping their existence a secret. Every person Pieter has rescued is someone who knows that vampires really do exist. The elders want to keep their existence a secret rather than risk an all-out war against them."

"I've always wondered why don't the hunters expose them and parade a captured vampire around on television?"

"There are three reasons that prevent the hunters from exposing them really. Firstly, the hunters kill companions, assistants, and anyone else involved with or helping the vampires. Remember, anyone involved with the hunter organization has likely been exposed to vampires in one way or another. That means they will have probably suffered some kind of tragedy based on that experience, and the driving force behind their involvement with the hunter organization is therefore likely to be revenge. People whose sole purpose in life is revenge are both reckless and uncompromising in their methods, as you should be well aware of, since it's the reason you went against my wishes and joined them, too.

"That's not politically correct in the climate of modern society. If the hunter organization were to go public, they would likely lose a lot of people on murder charges, as hunters operate without courts and lawyers, and sometimes even without proof. If there is one thing that the vampires love, it's the stupidity of the human race and its willingness to judge others by their own humane standards. All those bleeding heart pacifists who would want to forgive and make excuses for the companions, consorts, guards, and even the traitors within our own governments and big corporations who are doing the vampires' bidding, they would want to forgive and understand the traitors to the human race, who have sold millions of human souls to the vampires. That alone is something the hunters will never allow to happen.

"Secondly, any attempt to expose the vampires on television or some other media would be ridiculed and never taken seriously, especially with modern-day special effects to explain away their appearance. The general public would just never accept the possibility and would label it as nothing more than a publicity stunt. Worst of all, the vampires would be forced to mobilize themselves against such an act. They would start a massive recruitment campaign under such circumstances and kill thousands of people before the general public did eventually believe the truth of the matter.

"Thirdly, even the hunters don't know how deeply involved the vampires are in our own political and financial institutions, as well as possibly our military organizations. They have been around forever and have exerted their influence on us for far longer than we will ever know. So any outright confrontation would be a disaster for either side. As humans, we would lose billions of people in the fight, and if we lost the eventual war, we'd possibly end up as some kind of cattle, kept and bred only to be fed on. The vampires would have to face up to the possibility of extinction, or even if they won such a war, then a complete change to their way of life. So neither side wants to change the way they operate and fight against each other, as to change the way they go to war could mean they end up losing such a war," said Margeurite, sharing her philosophy on the situation.

Izzy thought on what her mother had said for a moment or two, and then asked, "So both sides are happy to fight the silent war against each other in order to protect the way they both operate?"

"Exactly. The status quo that exists suits both sides for their own particular reasons."

"But what about Pieter, where does he fit into all of that?"

"He doesn't, and that's why we have to protect him. He is a surgical instrument that takes out vampires, where the hunters are a hand grenade that quite literally blows everything up around them. He rescues people and helps put their lives back together, but if either side became aware of him, they would destroy him," her mother answered, a little more passionately than she should have.

"Do you have feelings for him, Mother?" Izzy asked her mother flatly, acting on a hunch.

Margeurite turned to look at her daughter angrily, shocked at the question she had dared to ask. Then she turned her head away to look off in the distance and paused for thought for a moment.

Izzy had met the look from her mother with one of equal determination and she wanted answers.

"I loved your father Isabelle, and in a way, I grew to love Pieter. As your father grew old and insecure, and the alcohol took more of him away, Pieter was my rock for a while. Pieter has lived over six hundred years and has had one of the loneliest lives imaginable due to the accident and circumstances of his birth. We comforted each other and we crossed a line. That line we crossed set your father on a path of self-destruction that he never turned back from. Both Pieter and I regret those actions and the tragedy that they led to, but, yes, after all that has occurred, I still have feelings for him," Margeurite confessed.

"So you had an affair with him and Daddy found out and freaked. Is that what you're telling me?" Isabelle pressed.

"No, Isabelle, it wasn't like that at all," Margeurite insisted.

"Then tell me, Mother, how was it exactly?" Isabelle demanded.

Margeurite looked into her daughter's eyes once more and saw that there was to be no walking away from this confrontation. As much as she hated the idea, she was eventually going to have to explain everything about what went on to her daughter. "You are going to have to wait for that explanation, Isabelle, as I need to tell you more about Pieter and Pavel before I start telling you how we became involved with him," she said, attempting to skirt around the issue.

Isabelle was about to argue and press her mother for more information, but Margeurite raised her hand to cut her daughter off.

"Not another word on the matter, Isabelle. I promise you, all will be revealed, but not until you know and understand the full back story to everything," Margeurite stated.

Isabelle said nothing in reply; she just stared off into the distance like her mother. She thought about what had happened to her childhood after her father died and how her life had changed so dramatically. The two women remained silent for what seemed an age, both lost in their own thoughts and both with slightly watery eyes. Despite the sadness of the thoughts each were dwelling on, they both fought to control their tears and blinked them away.

Margeurite resolved to do better for her daughter now that the truth was finally to be revealed, and then she reaffirmed to herself that she would continue to help protect Pieter no matter what. For her part, Isabelle planned to ask this Pieter a few questions of her own, preferably while holding a large-caliber weapon to his head. She was both angry and frustrated now, and she wanted to get to the truth of the matter. She knew her mother well enough not to press the issue at the moment, so she would change her methodology and carefully cajole the information out of her rather than clash heads and tempers with her. Isabelle had come to recognize that both she and her mother had a very stubborn streak in them, and no amount of arguing and shouting would help her break down her mother's resolve.

After a few more minutes of silence between them, Margeurite gave a big sigh and stood up. She then turned and extended her hand toward her daughter to assist her to stand. "Now come along, let's go and get some dinner before it gets too much colder," she suggested.

Both women then walked off to the hotel once more. They trotted along arm in arm, with their ever-present but discreet bodyguard trailing a short distance behind them.

Chapter Thirty

Dragica

After they returned from their walk in the park, Margeurite ordered dinner via room service. Then excusing herself for a few minutes, she had attended to some other business by phone in the privacy of the main bedroom. Isabelle had taken the opportunity to catch up with Johnson and see the family pictures he still carried around in his wallet, to show off to anyone who cared to see them. Johnson was fiercely loyal to her mother, but had always been kind to Izzy. Even when she'd stormed out after a heated argument, he never took sides. Izzy knew she could go off in a huff and be striding down the road, yet within five minutes, Johnson would pull up at the curb side next to her. He had a calming influence about him and she found it impossible to be angry with him. The way he talked to her had an almost magical way of settling her down and stopping her mid-tantrum. The fact that he was the driver as well as the bodyguard meant he could then take her wherever she wanted to go after to drown her sorrows.

The two of them were laughing and joking together when Margeurite came back out of the bedroom. Then all three of them continued the conversation, reminiscing about Isabelle's famous temper tantrums. Twenty minutes or so into the conversation, the dinner had arrived with a knock on the door. Once it was set out and Isabelle and Margeurite had taken their positions at the table, Johnson took his leave.

"I'll let you two ladies enjoy your dinner while I go pick a spot in front of that plasma TV in the bar," he said as he led the maid who had delivered and set out the meal away with him.

"Thank you, Johnny. Enjoy the game," Margeurite replied as she poured her daughter a glass of red wine.

As soon as they were alone, Izzy used the small black box Johnson had given her to check for any hidden electronic surveillance devices on or around the trolley. Once she was sure it was all clear, she started to chat openly once more. "So come on then, Mother. I'm not getting any younger. What happened next?" She had decided to change her approach on the subject from being confrontational and demanding to that of simply being eager to hear the story.

"Well, before we get up to date on what you really want to know, we have to tie up the loose ends regarding Pavel. You see, the move to the Harz Mountains was the starting point for a big change in both Pieter and Pavel's circumstances. Initially, all was going well. Pavel's family readily accepted them both, and eventually, Pavel and Pieter came to trust the family enough to reveal their secrets to them. Pavel even married and settled down with a wife named Ute. She had started out as the maid who cooked and cleaned for them, but a relationship had developed. His wife often joked that she had swapped a decent wage for being married and having more work with less pay, but she was only joking and they were all very happy together. Pieter would go off on jaunts around the place to do some hunting of his own, then report back to Pavel on how things had gone. Pavel could relax, read, and study all he wanted now. He could also spend some of his time inventing traps and devices that would assist Pieter and protect their base of operations should a vampire ever manage to follow his trail home. Pavel and Ute were also lucky enough to be blessed with the birth of a baby boy. They named the baby Dieter and it was he who went on to continue the family line all the way down to us.

"Pavel's cousin, Heinrich, and his wife, Bettina, had a daughter, Dragica, named after Pavel's great aunt. The aunt was renowned for her free spirit and had left the family home in Lithuania to travel across the whole of Europe. She had eventually settled in Northern Germany upon taking a husband and retiring from a very active social life. The young Dragica grew up a very bright and happy girl, despite having the misfortune of losing both her mother and father at an early age to disease. Pavel and Ute took her in and brought her up as if she was their own child, and Pieter was a reliable and friendly big brother, with Dieter being the baby of the group.

"It's here where things started to go awry, as over time, Dragica grew up to be a very attractive girl, with a free spirit equal to that of her ancestor. At sixteen, she and Pieter could almost pass for non-identical twins; they were that close and in tune with each other. Unfortunately for all concerned, that closeness developed further, and they fell in love. It was not something they had planned on; it was just a natural progression of things. Neither Pavel nor Ute were aware of how far the situation had gone; they only saw a brother and sister at play as they had always done.

"The story goes that Dragica, fearing she would age and lose her good looks, and therefore, Pieter, in the process, talked him into trying to turn her into what he was. She was a bright girl and reasoned that as he wasn't a proper vampire, then she wouldn't develop into one, either. Initially, Pieter resisted the temptation to try, but eventually, after persistent pressure from the girl he loved, he gave into her and they tried an experiment. Dragica drank of Pieter's blood without him drinking of hers. They reasoned that it was the best way to repeat what had happened to him, and as she wasn't drained of blood herself, she wouldn't die and they could see what effect it would have upon her.

"The night they performed the deed, all seemed well enough. Dragica and Pieter had waited until after the evening meal and had ventured out to feed the forest animals at sunset, as they usually did. They had walked some distance away from the cabin to a clearing in the forest they had often visited and sat talking in the long grass. Pieter had opened a cut on his wrist, which Dragica had then fed on. Tentatively at first, and then once she was used to the taste, Pieter had let her drink her fill from him. They stayed awake until late in the forest to see what effect the blood would have upon her, only to be disappointed when nothing seemed to occur. They had returned to the cabin and gone to bed as normal, but due to the loss of blood from his system, Pieter had fallen deeply asleep. He was in such a deep sleep that he didn't hear Dragica get up in the night and start rummaging around the kitchen. Ute had heard her, and worried that she may have been ill, she'd gone to see if she could be of assistance to her stepdaughter. As Ute came upon Dragica, she saw what she was doing. She'd caught a chicken from the pen outside and had sliced its head off. Holding the chicken up in the air, she was drinking the blood as it drained from the severed neck. Ute screamed at the sight, and upon being disturbed, Dragica suddenly threw the chicken aside and, instead, set upon her stepmother with the same knife.

"Dragica wrestled Ute to the ground, pinning her down so she could get at the blood seeping from the cut she'd sliced across her stepmother's forearm. She had just begun to drink thirstily from the wound when she'd heard Pieter and Pavel start to respond to Ute's screams for help. Dragica immediately stopped what she was doing and thought frantically for a moment. Then she had leapt up, turned, and ran out of the house, off into the woods. Pieter was the first to reach Ute and hear what she said as Pavel came hobbling into the room, supporting himself on the walls. Ute exclaimed almost hysterically that Dragica had attacked her, and that she looked like a vampire. Ute recalled seeing the blood red of Dragica's eyes as she pinned her to the floor with incredible strength.

"Pieter quickly grabbed a crossbow and a small quiver of crossbow bolts, and ran out of the cabin after Dragica. As she run off, she had left a scent trail of Ute's blood dripping from her chin. Then she'd trodden on something sharp as she ran speedily through the woods and opened a cut on the bottom of one of her own bare feet. Following her proved simple for Pieter with his acute sense of smell, but she was travelling almost as fast as he could. After about an hour and a half of steady pursuit, Pieter caught sight of her running uphill in the clearing ahead. He called out to her, and she stopped momentarily to turn to look toward him. Then she ran off at an even faster pace than before. After an even longer chase, Pieter caught up to her atop of one of the mountain ledges. She'd been running blindly and had cornered herself, with nowhere else to go. As Pieter tried to slowly approach her, she backed up against the cliff top, looking desperately for another escape route. Her head darted from one side to the other, trying to spot a way past him, but she realized that he had positioned himself too well for that.

"With no escape route available to her, Dragica quickly started to scramble over the edge of the cliff and try to find a way down. The granite rocks were jagged and brittle on her bare hands and feet, but still, she desperately tried to find a way down. She reached a small landing area a few meters below and was trying to work out which way to go next when Pieter caught up to her. As he approached her, Pieter started to try and talk to her and to calm her down, but as he got closer to her, she turned and looked at him, her eyes blazing into his eyes. With the sun just starting to send it's warmth out and in the dawning light of the new day, Pieter saw and recognized that terrible crimson hue, which sent a shiver down his spine.

"Then without warning, Dragica screamed and launched herself toward him, and in that one terrible moment, all his training and instinct took over and he fired the crossbow, sending a bolt thumping into her chest. The force of the arrow slamming into her stopped Dragica's forward momentum and twisted her off to the right. Pieter watched in horror as she tipped over the edge and fell bouncing and smashing off the rocks on the way down the almost sheer slope, before she landed in the water below. The river was swollen by the warm spring weather melting the winter's snow and ice, and Pieter looked on as Dragica's body was swept away face down and lifeless among its turbulent flow. There was no way for him to get down to her, and the flow was carrying her away far faster than he could catch up with the terrain he'd have to cover. Within a minute, she was gone from sight and lost to him forever.

"He fell back against the rocky wall and slid roughly to the ground, tears welling up in his eyes uncontrollably. He sat there just looking out at the river for what seemed like an age. Eventually, he picked himself up and began to climb back up the rock face. It took Pieter half the day to walk back home, and when he got there, he had to explain to Pavel and Ute what they had done. Pavel had been most disappointed with him, and Ute wouldn't talk to him for over a month. Pieter, it seemed, was just numb to everything. Even Dieter couldn't raise a smile out of him, as he tried on occasion to get Pieter to play a game with him.

"The final outcome, however, would be to push Pavel back into his experiments. Six months after the incident, Pieter had moved out of the house, leaving Pavel and Ute alone with Dieter. He'd built his own cabin higher up in the woods and was busy clearing an area all around it when one day, Pavel rode up to see him. The fact that drinking Pieter's blood had affected Dragica in such a way, although upsetting at first, was now burning in Pavel's mind. It had reawakened the scientist in him once more. The two men chatted about the consequences as men of science and agreed that it was something they needed to study and understand better. They kept Ute completely in the dark about what was going on and worked out a series of experiments to see what effect Pieter's blood would have on another human. Once they had their experiments all planned out, all they needed was a companion to experiment on.

"Pieter made a longer than usual trip away and had ended up somewhere in Hamburg. The brothel he chose to frequent was the perfect lair for a vampire to do some hunting. Being a busy city and trade center, it had a great many people coming and going, and new faces were nothing out of the ordinary. Sure enough, Pieter discovered that a couple of vampires frequented the place, looking for people who wouldn't be missed. Pieter took his time so as not to arouse suspicion, but started flashing a bit of coin around, and his youthful looks made himself seem like an easy target.

"The two vampires didn't take long to try to make his acquaintance and share in his generous company. After several hours of drinking and singing together, each of the three men went off to more private chambers with one of the ladies of the house, at Pieter's expense. Pieter had noticed that one of the girls was only too happy to go along with one of the vampires. He noticed that she had one or two scars from previous feedings, and had been more than keen to accept his money. The trap was now set. All Pieter had to do was continue to play his part until the vampires tried to feed on him. Firstly, he made sure that he took his time pleasuring and being pleasured by the girl he'd chosen to go with. Then as he walked back down the stairs and into the main bar once more, Pieter attempted to bid his new friends good night. He used the excuse that he had to go and find lodgings for the night. The two vampires had then offered him the hospitality of their own abode, and then all three left together.

"The route they took him was down some of the darker, more out-of-the-way backstreets and alleys leading to the docks. Pieter walked with his hands in his jacket pockets as he prepared himself for the attack he knew was about to come. Turning one corner and starting to walk under a bridge, Pieter's nose was assaulted by the unmistakable smell of old and dried blood, and lots of it. At this point, one of the vampires fell slightly behind them and crouched down, feigning having a loose shoelace that needed tying. Pieter stopped and turned to watch what was going on. The other vampire immediately leapt at him from behind and tried to push his head across to the right to expose his neck for the first bite.

"Instead of resisting against the push to the side, Pieter rolled his whole body off to the right as he dropped to one knee. He shrugged the vampire over his left shoulder, using his own bodyweight and momentum against him. The result was that the vampire fell forward, landing face first onto the floor. Before the vampire he'd downed could react, Pieter completed his clockwise rotation and dropped his full weight onto the vampire's back knees first. He then plunged the sharpened iron spike he'd manufactured with a wooden handle into the vampire's back, just off to the right of his spine and angled toward the middle to pierce his heart.

"The second vampire proved less valiant than his cohort and immediately tried to make a run for it. By the time he stood up, turned, and had run twenty paces, Pieter had caught up with him. As the vampire turned around to look over his right shoulder and see if he was being chased, Pieter was level and then passing on the vampire's left side. Pieter swept his right arm across the front of the vampire's body and the point of the second iron spike found its mark. The sudden impact caused the vampire to stop in his tracks and collapse backward to the ground in a heap of loose limbs.

"Pieter looked around quickly to ensure that his actions had not been witnessed. Then sure that all was still quiet and peaceful, he dragged the second vampire back to the body of the first. Looking around, he saw an old wooden cart with one of its wheels missing. It was collapsed against the outside of one of the nearby sheds, and gave Pieter exactly what he needed next. He pulled the heavy cart away from the shed as quietly as he could and then tossed any other pieces of wood he could find lying around into the back of it. Opening a small bottle he'd pulled from the inside breast pocket in his jacket, and being especially careful not to spill any of the fluid on himself or his clothes, he splashed the brown fluid all over the back of the cart and the piled-up wood. Satisfied that he'd prepared everything correctly, Pieter retrieved each of the vampire's bodies and heaved them one by one into position on top of the makeshift pyre. Next, he used his tinder box and flint to spark a small, flaming torch he'd rapidly put together with a splinter of wood and the last drop of the fluid from the bottle. Once alight, he flicked the splinter into the back of the wagon and stepped out of the way. A whoosh of flames erupted almost immediately, sending a wave of heat exploding outward. He watched the fire take hold of the whole cart within a few seconds. Happy that his work was done, Pieter turned around and headed back to his overnight lodgings.

"The next night, Pieter made a point of visiting the same brothel, where he sat back and keenly observed the other patrons. Once the clientele had reached its peak and he could detect no other vampires were present, he made his move. Where he'd paid for the two vampires to enjoy the company of the whores the previous night, he'd made a note of which girls had gone with them. He was quick to spot one of them and made a play for her. The girl seemed quite shy, far more so than she had been the previous evening. In fact, she was most reluctant to accept his advances. The madam of the house had spotted her reluctance and had virtually twisted her arm off as she dragged the girl back over to Pieter. She had sensed that there was money to be earned and wasn't about to see the opportunity pass. Pieter had gone upstairs with her, and once there, he discovered the problem. The girl was in servitude to the madam to pay off debts her family had amassed when her father had been injured and couldn't work for an extended period of time. She was new to the game of prostitution, and also quite innocent and naïve. The vampire feeding on her the night before was the first such experience she had encountered, and she was now both shocked and scared at what went on in the outside world. Pieter had calmed her down and informed her that he could help her situation improve in return for information on everything he needed to know about the brothel.

"During the next half an hour or so, Pieter gathered all the information he needed to make his choice of companion. It seemed the other girl from the previous night, who had willingly gone with one of the vampires, was in fact his regular whore. Not only this, but she had been pointing out the clients she'd serviced who had a few more coins to spend than the regular visitors. The two vampires had been befriending those pointed out to them for at least all of the few weeks this new girl had been in residence at the brothel. No doubt the vampires had been feeding off these poor, unwitting souls and killing them for their money, too.

"Pieter had arranged to meet with the innocent girl the following morning, when she was tasked with going to the market. He had escorted her back home to her family and provided enough coin for her father to pay off his debts, which he had duly done while accompanied by Pieter. As he left them, Pieter provided the family with enough money to move elsewhere and to start anew, since once labeled a whore, Pieter knew that the girl stood little chance of living a normal, respectable life should they stay in the same place.

"Once the two vampires had been dealt with and were out of the way, it had been an easy ruse to sweep back into the brothel and suggest a similar arrangement with the whore involved. The only difference was that they were to take the con on the road, with Pieter playing the part of her son. The whore was only too keen to get away after the madam of the house had turned up dead, with her throat ripped out and the body drained of blood. It was something Pieter had a hand in and was designed to draw the brothel to the attention of the local hunter organization.

"No sooner had Pieter and his pretend mother, Dagmar, worked their way back toward the Harz Mountains when Pieter had bound her wrists and gagged the girl, then forcibly dragged her along behind him as he marched back to his own cabin deep in the forest. Once there, he and Pavel set about their experiments.

"The first thing they noticed about the experiment was that even the smallest amount of Pieter's blood had an effect upon Dagmar. Usually, within an hour of being fed with his blood, she developed her own hunger and her eyes became crimson. The funny thing was that the less blood she ingested, the quicker she showed the effects, and this was only slowed if she had already eaten a normal meal. While they could not fathom a logical reason behind this, they did complete several more experiments to confirm it. One thing that they did understand was that the amount of blood ingested was proportional to the amount of time it took to return to being a normal human being again.

"As well as the crimson-colored eyes and the sudden craving for blood, the ingestion of Pieter's blood also gave Dagmar a big boost in her strength and senses. However, once she had returned to normal, she'd be overly weak and tired until she'd had a chance to sleep and recover. Each time she recovered, she would also be extremely hungry for normal human food and thirsty for water.

"The final test they had designed was to see if she would be completely turned into a vampire and stay that way if she was drained of blood and died with Pieter's blood in her system. She did indeed change into a vampire and was kept alive to test her relative strength against that of the other vampires they had captured and experimented on. Here, again, they had some interesting news, as this new vampire was far stronger and faster than a normal vampire and was almost as strong and as fast as Pieter himself. In fact, in all the tests they ran, when they compared the results to those of their earlier captives, the girl showed her abilities were a step above all the other vampires, but still a small step behind Pieter himself.

"Unfortunately, before they got a chance to do any more experiments, Ute discovered what they were up to and insisted that they destroy the monster they had created, and further, that Pavel should move the family away, back to the city. This they did, but Pieter remained in the cabin he'd built and stayed in touch with Pavel only by letter, and the very occasional visit on his way out to hunt.

"Pavel passed on all his notes and family secrets regarding the wealth and everything else to Dieter, who became Pieter's only link to normal society. In time, Pieter withdrew more and more into himself as he became more and more the hunter. He developed a kind of bitterness toward all the vampires and their companions due to what he felt was his enforced loneliness, caused by his mixed heritage. The fact that he had fallen in love and seen that person destroyed because of it made him hate himself almost as much as the vampires.

"Many years later, our family name changed to Lancar, and my Great-great-grandfather Luke spent quite a lot of time befriending Pieter and helping him deal with a great many of his personal demons. At this time, Pieter spent an extended summer in Paris and was introduced back into society as much as possible. Apparently, Pieter became something of a ladies' man around Paris and was invited to a great many parties and theatre outings. It was while attending one such evening theatre when Pieter discovered a vampire operating within the throng of Gypsies and exposed his presence to Luke, who had never seen a real vampire despite all he knew of the family history. The result was that Luke then joined up with the hunters and pulled our whole family back in with him, too. Ever since then, the Lancar family has been closely linked to, first, the Paris hunters, and then the Boston and New York hunters as we stepped across to America after we lost your father.

"During your childhood, Pieter used to come and visit us for the summer as he had with all our ancestors since Luke. While he was with us, he would fill in the present head of the family on the intelligence he had gathered on the vampires and where he had slain them. Because you were always playing in the pool and running in the sunshine, you were always of a darker complexion and your skin tanned easily in the sun. Once, when you were on Pieter's lap, you noticed how pale his arm was in comparison to yours, and you made a comment about it. You said he should get out more and enjoy the sunshine, so he wouldn't be so pale. From then on, we always made a joke of it, and you nicknamed him the Sunshine Man or the Sunny Man."

"Oh, wow," Izzy exclaimed as the tears began to well up in her eyes.

"That's not all. When we lost your father, it was Pieter who saved us and got us out of France, and helped with the move over here to America, but you were so young then and I'm sure you probably don't remember it all."

"I remember some of it, Mother, just not the right bits. I remember the Sunny Man and how pale he was, but I also remember the vampire who attacked us and killed dad, and how pale she was, and I think I got the two muddled up over time. When Pieter told me who he was, I was shocked and weak, and all I saw was the pale skin. I didn't trust him when I should have. I got someone killed because of that, Mom. I got someone killed!" Izzy began to sob uncontrollably as her mother reached out and wrapped her hand around her daughter's to comfort her.

"Oh, Isabelle, one thing you learn when dealing with vampires, dear…someone always gets killed."

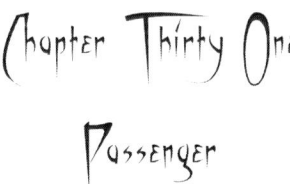

Chapter Thirty One

Passenger

The shiny, black stretch limousine slowed as it approached the traffic intersection and halted at the white line, as the lights turned from amber to red. The blackened glass hid the occupants from the loiterers around the twenty-four-hour grocery store on the corner.

"Really, Joshua, you should have put your foot down and gone through on yellow," chided the lady in the back in a haughty manner.

How Joshua would have liked to have given her a different answer to the one he chose. "Yes, Ma'am. Sorry about that. Didn't want to have you bumped around in the back, though." What he really wanted to say was, "Shut the fuck up, you stupid, snotty, drunken bitch, and let me do my job properly without all your snapping and moaning in my ear all the time."

Joshua had been working as Mrs. Van Dyne's personal chauffer for eight months, two weeks, and three days, and he'd disliked her and her haughty, better than thou, pompous manner for around eight months, two weeks, and two days of that time. The fact, however, was that the money was too good to turn down. The Van Dynes had to be seen to be the richest, so they paid the best rates, and he got meals thrown in at the house with the other servants and a room of his own.

He figured he'd continue working for her for a year or so more. Then once he'd saved up enough money for a deposit, he'd get a loan for the rest and buy his own limousine. He planned to set himself up in business with the rich contacts he'd made and been sure to impress while working for Mrs. Van Dyne. He could look forward to society weddings on weekends and socialite evenings during the week, as well as city tours organized through the big hotels during the days. Of course, there would be business expenses to take care of to get the right people to use his service, but his hotel and club contacts would receive ample reward for their recommendations. Joshua had it all planned out and nothing was going to stop his dream of becoming his own boss. Nothing he'd expected or considered anyway.

As he applied pressure to the gas pedal, the car smoothly pulled away through the intersection, gathering speed as it continued up the road toward the on ramp to the highway. Joshua knew this part of town well; his dad used to work at one of the local factories. That was until he got laid off and died of a heart attack some five years later. Joshua had taken Mrs. Van Dyne to one of her homeless charity events and watched her give her charitable speech and donation, then retire to the back room to start getting drunk. She always made her excuses and left before her alcoholic state became too apparent, but Joshua knew. His father had gone the same way, and he knew that all the money in the world wouldn't save her from the road she was heading down.

Just as he was going past the last set of buildings on the right, he saw a young woman run out and stagger onto the road in front of him. He slammed on the brakes and the car came to a rapid, but smooth, halt about a foot from the woman. Joshua noticed that she was only covered in what looked like a bedsheet as she appeared to collapse onto the hood of the car.

"What is it, Joshua? Why did you stop?" came the irritated response from the back.

"It's a young girl, Mrs. Van Dyne. She ran out in front of the car. I think she may need some help," Joshua stated as he unclipped his seatbelt and began to get out of the car.

"Well, don't be too long…and be careful, Joshua. This is not a good area," she called after him.

"Yes, Ma'am," Joshua replied, looking back in the direction the girl had appeared from in case trouble was following her. He knew only too well how bad an area this had become, and thoughts of how the girl had gotten into such a state raced through his mind. He kept an eye out for the likely cause of her trouble, half expecting someone to come running out to attack him, too, if he wasn't careful. "You okay, Miss?" he asked in a gentle voice.

"Oh God, it was horrible," she blabbered. "They must have slipped something into my drink at the club. When I woke up, there was a gang of them… Oh God, what they did to me…" she added, breaking down into tears and sobs.

Joshua took off his jacket and draped it over her shoulders; he then wrapped an arm around her to comfort her, saying, "It's okay, Miss, you're safe now. Come on. Let's get you into the car and out of here."

As he approached the passenger-side door, the rear window smoothly slid down and Mrs. Van Dyne poked her head out of the window. "What is it, Joshua? What's going on?" she asked in her usual impatient manner.

"It's a young girl, Ma'am. I think she's had a bit of a rough time and needs some assistance," Joshua answered in his usual respectful manner.

"Well, don't just stand there with her. Help her into the car then," she replied briskly.

"Yes, Ma'am. I was about to do just that," Joshua replied, hiding his anger at her superior attitude. He opened the front passenger door and suddenly got another earful of Mrs. Van Dyne when she's had a little bit too much to drink.

"Not in the front, you buffoon. Put her in the back with me, so I can take care of her," she chided sharply.

Joshua rolled his eyes and did as he was told, while ever so gently biting his lip to avoid saying anything more that would invite a further rebuke from Mrs. Van Dyne. Once the girl was safely in the car, Mrs. Van Dyne began her interrogation into how she got into such a state. Joshua took another look around to see if anybody was about, or if any likely threat existed. On seeing no one, he walked around to his door, got back into the driver's seat, and started the car.

As he drove the car off toward the highway on ramp, Joshua looked into the rearview mirror and the back of the car. Mrs. Van Dyne was still chatting away with the young lady, hardly giving her a chance to get a word or an answer in before she fired the next question at her. He caught a glimpse of the girl in the rearview mirror before Mrs. Van Dyne flicked a switch in the back and the screen slowly rose between them with an almost silent hum. This effectively cut him off from the conversation and the details about what had happened.

She sure is an attractive little thing, though, he thought to himself.

Joshua drove on along the highway, for about another three quarters of an hour, without any incident. Then suddenly, he was startled to hear a sudden thumping sound from the back. He was about to lower the screen when it came down under the control of someone in the back.

"Can we pull over into the next rest stop please, Joshy?" the girl asked, speaking softly.

"Certainly, Miss. Is everything all right back there?" Joshua inquired.

"Yeah, the old lady polished off the rest of the brandy and dropped the decanter as she passed out," came the calm response.

"Oh, she does that, I'm afraid. There's a rest stop about a quarter of a mile up the road. We'll be there in a minute."

"Thanks, Joshy. You're a life saver, honey." The girl's voice was now calm and much more controlled.

With that said, the screen slowly hummed back up into the closed position. No sooner had it closed than Joshua saw the lights up ahead of the rest stop, so he began to slow down, ready to pull over.

Once parked, Joshua got out of the car, intending to walk around and open the passenger door for the young lady. Before he could do so, the door was open and the young lady was out and on her way across toward the ladies' room. Just as she was about to disappear inside, she swung her head back around to call to Joshua.

"Hey, Joshy, the old lady's still fast asleep, so best not disturb her. And do you think you could get me something sweet to drink from the shop?" she inquired cheekily.

"Yeah, sure," Joshua replied as he briskly set off to do her bidding.

The guy behind the counter at the service station shop was one of those people who loved to chat about anything and everything, so Joshua's shopping ended up taking much longer than he cared for it to. So much time that as he was leaving with the soda pop bottle and the gum he'd purchased, the girl was just getting into the back of the car again. Upon seeing him approaching, she looked inside the back of the car as if to check on Mrs. Van Dyne, and then abruptly closed the back door and moved to the front passenger door.

As Joshua approached the car, he stretched his hand out to pass her the drink he'd purchased for her. She reached out to receive the bottle, but fumbled and dropped it. It bounced a couple of times before Joshua managed to stoop down and gather it up, just before it rolled under the car.

"Oh sorry, Joshy, guess I'm still a little bit shaken," the girl said apologetically.

"No harm done, Miss. These plastic containers are near indestructible. Although, you may want to hold off on opening that one for a while, as it's going to be pretty shook up," he said, passing her the drink once more.

"Yeah, good advice, Joshy. I just got some water while I was in the little girl's room, so that won't be a problem," she replied. "Mind if I sit in the front and keep you company?"

"Sure thing. Always nice to have some company, especially when it's an attractive young lady like yourself," Joshua replied, watching for her response to his subtle flirty approach.

If she reacted in any way, Joshua didn't detect it as he opened the door for her and she stooped down and slid into the plush leather seat. He closed the door, went around to the driver's side, and got back in. He started the engine and reversed the car out of its parking position, then smoothly guided it back onto the highway to resume the journey back to Mrs. Van Dyne's house.

After several minutes of driving, the silence between them was broken when the girl sniffled as if she was about to start crying.

"You okay, young lady?" Joshua asked.

She silently nodded at him, but sniffled again.

Joshua thought she was trying to hold back the emotion of what had recently befallen her. He'd heard stories about guys using date rape drugs on girls and doing all kinds of things to them. Some had even used videos to record what they had done to the girls and taken some sick pleasure in posting them on the Internet.

Most of the victims had been unaware of what had happened under the influence of the drugs until they had been shown the footage. This poor girl had been abused by a group of them and had actually been aware of what was going on at the time.

He thought to involve her in conversation. What was it his army counselor had told him on his return from the first Gulf War? Guys needed to be made to talk about things to get them out in the open and dealt with, while girls just needed an opportunity to talk and it would all flow freely. It was the big difference between the two sexes, as guys, acting all macho, bottle things up until they explode, but girls share and deal with it in the process.

"Anyone you need to call, to let them know you're safe?" he asked.

The girl shook her head, and then turned away as if to hide her tears.

"Hey, it's okay. Don't cry. You're safe now. No one's going to hurt you. What about your parents? They must be worried sick about you."

"No, they don't care," she said as she brushed the loose hair from her face and rubbed her eyes.

"There must be someone, though…boyfriend or flatmate?"

"No, just me, all on my own," she said, turning to face him and forcing a smile.

"Okay then, what do you want me to do? There's a police station not far from here I can turn off to, or if we go a little further into the city, we can get you to an emergency medical center I know of," he offered.

"Can't I just stay with you, Joshua? It's nice and warm in here, and I felt so safe when you put your arms around me. I really don't want to go through all those police questions and medical examinations right now," she said as she moved closer to him.

Joshua couldn't believe his luck. Was she coming on to him? He stole a glance at her and noticed for the first time that she was no longer wearing the bedsheet— and that his jacket had opened slightly and revealed most of her left breast.

She smiled at him seductively.

"Well, okay…if that's what you want," he stammered.

"Yes, Joshua, that's what I want, someone big and strong like you to take care of me," she said with almost a hint of a tease.

He was trying to keep his eyes on the road, but she was all he could think about. His heart was racing as he thought about what might happen when he got her back to his room in Mrs. Van Dyne's house. He had to wriggle in his seat to prevent his rising erection from catching in his boxers. Each time he turned back to glance at her, she would smile that innocent smile. He had never wanted someone so much in his life; the effect this poor girl was having on him was almost hypnotic.

He smiled to himself as he pressed harder on the gas pedal, speeding the car up. As he glanced at her once more, he saw that she had his jacket wrapped tightly around her and was looking at the road ahead. He was sure he detected a hint of a mischievous grin on her face for a moment.

She was certainly something special, he thought as he weaved and sped on through the other traffic. He couldn't return home to Mrs. Van Dyne's house quickly enough now, and he would certainly heed his boss's words and put his foot down, through any further yellow lights.

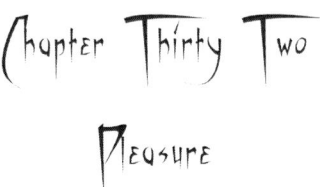

Chapter Thirty Two

Pleasure

A s Joshua pulled up to the large, wrought-iron gate at the Van Dyne estate, it smoothly and silently slid open, allowing him to drive through and head up toward the house. He parked in front of the large doors and was about to get out of the car to assist Mrs. Van Dyne when his young lady passenger suggested that she would wake the "old biddy" and get her into the house for him. He could then park the car in the garage and deal with the cleanup in the back. That way, they would have more time together for chatting during the rest of the evening.

Let her deal with the miserable old bitch, then we get more playtime together, sounds good to me, Joshua thought to himself. "Okay, sounds good to me. You sure you can handle her?" Joshua inquired.

"Yeah, piece of cake honey," she replied, winking at him. The girl was out of the car and had Mrs. Van Dyne leaning on her for support as she led the older woman toward the door within moments.

Joshua marveled at his luck as he looked in his wing mirror to see Mrs. Van Dyne slumped in the girl's arms and almost being carried away. *Let her deal with that snobby idiot of a butler, Rene, and his disapproving looks at the state the old bitch had gotten herself into once more*, he thought to himself.

As he approached the garage, Joshua flicked the switch on the remote and the door lifted automatically. He drove the car in and parked it in the usual spot. Then he began his ritual cleanup and restocking of the bar, ready for the next trip out. On opening the door, the stench hit him. *That senile old bitch*, he thought as he walked over to the cupboard at the back of the garage and pulled on a pair of rubber gloves. He poured some disinfectant into a bucket and then half filled it with warm water. Grabbing a large sponge, he returned to the car and began to clean up the urine from the leather seat. She'd also spilt a fair amount of the brandy into the carpet and it was difficult to tell which smell was the most pungent. He blotted the carpet with some newspaper to suck up the brandy and then wiped over the leather seats once more, this time with the special protectant he had purchased just for such occasions.

Then he noticed that the old biddy had cut herself and spilt some blood on the back of the leather seat. Joshua chuckled at the thought of the silly old cow falling asleep and leaning her head against the seat, and those awfully big, spiky earrings of hers slicing her neck open. Shame she hadn't cut her throat open and bled to death. Then he thought about who would have to clean all that blood up, too, and figured it was better she hadn't. Finally, with the cleanup done, he sprayed the back of the car with the deodorizer. Once his daily ritual was complete, he flicked the switch to close the large garage panel door, and he headed into the house through the internal entrance that was connected to the servant's area of the house. It was then he started to think about the night ahead and what pleasures might lay in store for him.

As Joshua entered what was the combined staff dining room and main kitchen, he was surprised to see the young girl sitting at the table, mulling over a cup of what smelled like Rene's famous Italian coffee.

"You'd better not let Rene see you drinking from his favorite cup, or there will be hell to pay," he said as he walked across to pull a beer out of the fridge. He twisted the top off and took a long slug of the beer, before sighing in appreciation of the cool liquor hitting the back of his throat.

"Oh, he won't say anything to me," the girl added with a confident smile.

"Don't you bet on it, honey. He's a genuine French stick up the ass; arrogant asshole, that one," Joshua replied, barely concealing his distaste for the European butler.

"Well, don't you worry about him. The old biddy put him in his place when he tried to look down his nose at me. She sent him packing off to bed after he fetched me a towel so I could take a shower and freshen up a little. Then the old lady told me to get you to help me out with whatever I needed," the girl explained mischievously.

"Being put in his place will just get him angry, and the rest of the staff are the ones who'll cop it off him tomorrow."

"Yeah, maybe, but I'll bet a big, strong guy like you could put him in his place if you needed to," she added as she stood up and began to walk around the table in his direction.

The way she moved lithely toward him got him aroused immediately. She almost glided over the floor, and though she was still wearing his jacket, she had obviously been given one of Mrs. Van Dyne's expensive silk blouses to wear, too.

She spread her arms out and dropped her shoulders and arms behind her as she approached him. This simple movement allowed his jacket to slide from her shoulders and end up crumpled on the floor behind her. The cream-colored blouse was almost sheer, and clung to her body as she moved. It was unbuttoned almost to the bottom, and showed off her cleavage as she walked. Her nipples were stiff and jutted out into the fabric, drawing his attention to them. She came to a halt just in front of him, placing her cool hands on either side of his chest, just below his collarbones.

Looking up into his big, brown eyes, she asked him teasingly, "See anything you like?"

Before he could answer, she spun around and backed her hips into him, slowly sliding her backside to the left and then the right repeatedly across his crotch. She was teasing him and he knew it as he felt her pressing against his stiffening erection. Her right hand came up and slid behind his neck, pulling his head lower into the nape of her own neck. He smelt the expensive perfume that until now he'd never much cared for, since he had always associated it with Mrs. Van Dyne. Now he could appreciate the musky scent and revel in the feeling it gave him as he breathed it in. Her left hand snaked around his back to squeeze his left buttock, and pull him tightly to meet the movement of her hips as she ground back against him. Joshua was swept up in the moment and began to kiss and nuzzle at her neck. He brought his hands up to cup her breasts, and felt the hard nipples as he massaged and squeezed the ample mounds of flesh through the thin material covering them.

"So, Joshy, is there anyone else we have to worry about disturbing us, honey?" she inquired, almost breaking the mood.

"No, baby. Rene sleeps in the room next door to the old bitch upstairs, on the third floor, in case he's needed during the night, and Conchita, the housemaid, is on the other side of the bathroom down the hall from my room. She's either out at the movies or stays in her room. She always sleeps listening to her Latin American music; says it's so she won't hear me shouting and whooping when I watch the game. The cook, Cassie, won't be in until about 6:30 in the morning. So we can make as much noise as we want without any worries at all."

"Mmmmh! Sounds good. Let's get started then. Wouldn't want to waste any time, would we?" she said as she spun back around to face him again. Just as he began to lean forward with the intention of hugging and kissing her, she lifted her hands to deflect his arms out to the side. A confused look crossed his face as then, placing her hands against his chest, she pushed him back toward and onto the table forcefully.

Joshua was caught unaware by her sudden movement and fell down lying on his back, staring up at the ceiling, momentarily dazed. As he recovered from the shock of her sudden movement, leaving him spread across the table, a look of genuine surprise crossed his face at her strength. For such a little thing, she sure had some muscles. Maybe, he thought, he'd just been caught off balance at her unexpected movement. "Oof! Easy, baby. You trying to kill me or something? You almost broke my back there," he said, laughing nervously, trying to make light of the situation.

"Oh, I'm sorry, Joshy, but there are two things you should know that I really like. One is to be on top and the other is…I like it rough. So I hope big, tough little Joshy here is ready to come out to play."

As she spoke, she slid her hand up and over the mound at his crotch. Then she pulled the zipper down and slowly slid her hand into the opening to grab and hold his manhood firmly while she undid the top button to his trousers and freed him from the restrictive clothing. She was impressed by his size, and after a few strokes with her hand, she leaned forward to take him into her mouth. She bobbed her head up and down a couple of times, getting him to maximum hardness, and enjoyed licking at the sides, feeling the veins bulging along his shaft. Then she clambered up onto the big, heavy wooden table to straddle him. He took the opportunity to lift his hands up to open the blouse and expose her breasts. His rising passion made him forget the damage to his male pride, at being thrown onto the table so easily. Leaning forward, he kissed first one nipple then the other, his hands holding each breast and squeezing them roughly. He'd never been with a woman who liked the rough stuff before, although he'd read about them in men's magazines. Because of that, however, he wasn't quite sure how to proceed and how physical he should get with her.

Still holding his fleshy weapon firmly in her hand, she locked eyes with him and then guided him into her as she lowered herself down. She slowly rode him up and down for a few strokes, enjoying the feeling of him thrusting up to meet her downward movements. Then she began to increase the momentum of her up and down movements until she was riding him as fast as she could. She was enjoying being in control of the situation, and even when he began to moan and attempted to slow her down so he could last longer, she continued to set the pace. Joshua knew that he wouldn't be able to contain himself much longer at this pace, and felt his orgasm start to rise. He furiously started to flex and extend his ankle joints, and circled his feet around—first, clockwise, then anticlockwise—in time with the pelvic thrusts down onto him. One of his high school friends had told him about this technique years ago. Supposedly, it had something to do with the acupuncture points or meridians and the nerves entering the spine close to each other. This meant you could reduce the sensation of the friction at the head of the penis and help delay the male orgasm by wiggling your feet in this way. While he wasn't sure of the details of how it worked, Joshua simply knew that it did work, and had used it to great effect previously. Right now, he was thankful that it was helping him keep pace with this gorgeous young thing above him and help to prolong the intercourse between them.

Suddenly, the girl began to moan loudly and her movements on top of him became much shorter as she seemed to almost hold him in one position, and simply pulse her hips against him. Then she leaned forward more as she gasped loudly, planting her palms down onto his upper chest, supporting herself as she gripped him deeply. She curled her fingers around to grip the outer layer of his skin. He felt the sharp pains of her pinching his flesh as she also pulled on the chest hair trapped and curled between her fingers. Then she became much louder and more vocal, issuing a long, drawn-out grunt cum squeal as she started to shake and her body convulsed in orgasm.

After a short while of shaking and trembling above him, Joshua felt her start to relax her hold on his chest, and he began to think about the next position he wanted to roll her into so he could reach that same plateau of sexual bliss. He figured that doggy position would be the best way to go, so he wouldn't have to worry about losing anymore chest hair in the process, and he'd really be able to thrust into her the way she seemed to like it. He was just about to suggest a change of position when she recovered from her "thrilling moment" and pushed his head back hard against the table again. Before he could say anything in protest or suggest a change of position, she fell completely forward onto him. Clamping her hand onto his chin, she twisted his neck over to the right and began to lick and kiss his neck. She began teasing him with little nips and bites before sucking at his flesh and threatening to give him the mother of all "hickeys." Joshua brought his arms up to massage at the sides of her breast in preparation for rolling her to one side, but the girl slid her arms down to grab his hands and pulled them off her breasts, then stretched and held them out to the side of his body. He laid there across the heavy oak table, head to one side, arms extended out like he was about to be crucified. The girl on top of him paused for a moment as she wiggled her hips a little, still feeling his manhood aroused and ready for more inside her; she was going to enjoy this, she thought to herself wickedly.

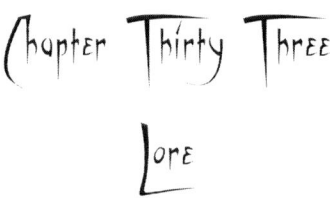

Chapter Thirty Three

Lore

Ronnie couldn't sleep for long. The events of the last few days kept playing on her mind, and although she hadn't woken up screaming, suffering from a nightmare, she was still unnerved by the situation she found herself in. She felt safe in Pieter's house, away from what she now knew was walking around in the big, bad world outside, but still couldn't close her eyes for any decent length of time, as she had so many unanswered questions popping up into her mind. She'd tossed and turned around on the big four-poster bed until eventually, she'd given up and decided to go down into the library to see if she could find a book to read, anything to stop her mulling over everything. As she turned the handle and pushed the door open in front of her, she was relieved that it didn't creak like one of the big, old doors that the horror movies always used. She entered the room and flicked on the light switch with her right hand. The recessed lights in the ceiling all began to glow dimly, only just illuminating the room.

"What the heck? Jeez, some crappy lights for a library," she said out loud to no one but herself.

"Sorry, Ronnie. I've set the dimmer on to the lowest setting, and these new, energy-efficient globes take a while longer to illuminate the room as they warm up," Pieter stated, reaching for the remote control on the small table beside him. He pressed a button on the little black box to alter the brightness setting in the room to its highest value and then quickly put on the nearby mirrored sunglasses to protect his eyes from both the increasing glare of the lights and to hide the red tinge in them, since he had just finished feeding.

"Oh! I'm sorry, Pieter. I didn't think anyone was in here," Ronnie replied, startled. Luckily, she recognized Pieter's calm voice as he spoke to her, and although shocked at someone else being in the room, she hadn't gone into full panic mode. She considered that a blessing after what she'd been through, and was relieved to be feeling her heartbeat return to normal.

Pieter was also listening to her heartbeat, and was also pleasantly surprised to hear only a small speed increase in the beats per minute. He also noticed that it was almost back to normal again already. He stood up and walked forward and to his left a little, trying to shield Ronnie's gaze from what he'd been doing. Too late. With the room now fully illuminated, she'd caught sight of the drip stand and associated bits and pieces by the side of his chair.

"I didn't mean to disturb you, Pieter. I just couldn't sleep and wanted to see if there was something I could find to read and occupy my mind," Ronnie said.

"Well, all of Mechtild's romance novels are at the end there and all of Jurgen's sword and sorcery novels are at this end here, and then in between are a lot of older books and reference manuals, and various first editions," Pieter explained as he pointed out each section.

"Anything you'd recommend? Since Jurgen told me you've read them all," Ronnie asked as she walked closer to the shelves of books.

"Well, actually, I haven't read any of Mechtild's old romance novels, but *Magician* by Raymond E. Feist is an excellent start for a fantasy series, and the follow up novels, co-written with Janny Wurts, are also very good. For an interesting biography, *Parky*, the story of the famous English television interviewer, Michael Parkinson, is good, as he seems to have met and interviewed everyone who was anyone in the last forty-odd years," Pieter replied, warming to the conversation.

"What's that you're reading at the moment?" Ronnie asked, seeing the large-format book positioned on the small table.

'That, oh, it's a...er...it's a graphic novel of one of my favorite recent books. It's called *Legend* by David Gemmell," Pieter stated almost shyly.

"You mean to tell me you read comic books?" Ronnie said, almost laughing.

"They are not comic books, they are graphic novels, and some of the artworks in them are quite amazing actually," Pieter said defensively.

"So the super vampire slayer, in reality, gets all his moves from reading Superman and Batman," Ronnie stated, grinning wickedly at him.

"No, actually, I've read very little of the Dark Knight and the Son of Krypton. I'm more of a Marvel comics fan, so it's the Avengers, Hulk and Spider-Man that I relate to," Pieter replied, not so seriously.

Ronnie ribbed him again. "So let me guess, they have more vampires in them, like that cool vampire slayer, Blade, who Wesley Snipes played in the films, as I recall, and my kid brother used to read all his *comic books*!"

"They do indeed have more vampires in Marvel comics, but unfortunately, they are all wrong about what can and cannot affect a vampire. They are not mythological creatures; they are real as you've now seen and they do pose a real threat to the human race," Pieter answered more seriously.

"Yeah, you don't have to remind me about that," Ronnie stated with a sudden shiver.

"Sorry, Ronnie, but it's now part of my job to help prepare you for going back to some semblance of a normal life, and that involves educating and reminding you all about vampires and how to steer clear of them in the future," Pieter said apologetically.

"So, were you actually reading in the dark?"

"No, I was actually just, er…just about to clear up after feeding on some blood. I topped up on the red stuff to help me get over the bullet wound while thinking about my next move against the vampires," he said nervously, unsure how Ronnie would react to his requirement for blood to top up his normal food intake.

"So, you like your blood at body temperature then," she said, looking at the tubing wrapped around the blood-warming machine and the display in the center showing a temperature of thirty-six point nine degrees Celsius. She recognized the machine from the time her brother had been in a bad automobile accident and had required several units of blood transfused into him after his operation.

"Yeah, it's the most natural form that I've acquired a taste for over the years as, unfortunately, there was no refrigeration when I started feeding on it."

"So tell me, what's the difference between you and the other vampires? Oh, I'm sorry, that came out wrong. I didn't mean to call you a vampire," said Ronnie apologetically.

"That's' all right, Ronnie. I won't bite you for calling me a vampire. Well, not on the first occasion anyway," Pieter said jokingly.

Ronnie gave him a puzzled look, not sure if he was really joking or not, and Pieter picked up on her sudden unease.

"Kidding! Honest, I only bite companions and guards who associate with vampires. Here, take a seat, there's no time like the present to fill you in on vampire lore one oh one, and I can answer any other questions you may have, too."

Ronnie took a seat in the big, leather easy chair a short distance away from Pieter's own chair, as he began to fill her in on all things vampire.

"Firstly, all vampires used to be human beings, or should I say, they are humans who have died with vampire blood in their system and have then metamorphosed into a vampire. I was, as far as we can tell, born prematurely, and when a vampire fed on my mother, some of both his and my mother's blood ended up being spilled into my mouth. Then rather than dying, as most premature babies did back in those days, I somehow thrived and survived."

"So how old are you then?" Ronnie asked, intrigued to know the answer.

"How old do you think I am?" Pieter replied, smiling.

"Well, I know from what Mechtild informed me that you looked about the same age when you met them back in the 1940s, so I'll say about a hundred as a rough guess," Ronnie said, very pleased with herself that she hadn't said the obvious early 30s as Pieter appeared to be.

"Oh, to be so young again… I was actually born in 1362, so this year, I will be six hundred and fifty-one years old," he said, looking her in the eye to gauge her response to the information.

"Oh my gosh! I take it you moisturize and exercise regularly then," she added flippantly.

Pieter just smiled at her response. She was quite a woman, he thought. Even after all she had been through, nothing had really fazed her and stopped her rolling with the punches. She even managed to keep her sense of humor intact. "True vampires don't age at all. From the day they are 'sired,' they remain the same in both appearance and youthfulness. Consequently, if they are sired when they are in their twilight years, they will remain looking that way."

"What do you mean by 'sired'?" Ronnie asked.

"It's the term given to how you become a vampire. Unlike in the movies, just being bitten by a vampire does not turn you into one. Being bitten by a vampire simply makes you anemic or dead, depending upon how much blood the vampire takes. To become a vampire, you have to be selected by a vampire as someone he or she wishes to adopt and teach the ways of being a vampire. Firstly, they feed on the subject until they are close to death, which may take two or more feedings, depending on the vampire's feeding pattern. Then they open up a wound on themselves and allow the human subject to feed on their blood. Once the human has ingested a few mouthfuls of vampire blood, the vampire will continue to feed on them until they lapse into unconsciousness and die. Then usually, somewhere between one and five hours later, the human will awaken as a newly sired vampire. They immediately have all the traits of a vampire, which include increased strength, speed, and stamina. They have sharper night vision and the ability to repair their injuries, and a vastly improved sense of smell and hearing."

"How come, though, if they were really humans before, they suddenly have super strength, speed, and night vision?"

"It's all part of the vampire blood and how it constantly repairs and changes the tissue it comes into contact with, and then passes that change on at a cellular level. The muscles are the same but with much stronger contractive ability, and the reflexes are sped up by the nerves being chemically changed to be faster. Within the eyes, the numbers of the two types of receptors are changed. Humans have pretty much an equal number of rods and cones. The rods are responsible for black and white perception, and the cones are for color distinction. Vampires have far more rods, which gives them far greater eyesight in the dark, but means they are more sensitive to sunlight, so they avoid it. They also have no protection against sunlight, as they no longer produce melanin, the color pigment in human skin, so they will burn very easily in direct sunlight."

"So there is some truth in the old films after all," Ronnie said.

"Yes and no. They certainly burn in sunlight, but they don't burst into flames or die from it, and a sip or two of blood and they repair pretty quickly. That's also why no Negro or even Hispanic people become vampires; they would stand out as virtual albinos among their own kind with the eventual loss of their natural skin pigmentation. That's why a large movement of vampires aligned themselves with Hitler's Gestapo and SS (*Schutzstaffel*) during the Second World War, as to all intents and purposes, vampires have to be racists, as only Caucasian-born vampires can go unnoticed and blend in."

"So you're saying Wesley Snipes should have been painted white for the film to be accurate then," Ronnie joked.

"Not only that to make it authentic. But, yes, he should have been made albino. The best example of a film vampire I can name is *The Omega Man* with Charlton Heston; it was based on an interesting book by Graham Masterson called *I Am Legend*. They also filmed it with Vincent Price as *The Last Man on Earth*, and more recently, with Will Smith, using the book title. In *The Omega Man*, however, there is a stunning African-American girl who catches the vampire virus and is turned albino. I actually wondered if Masterson had been exposed to either the vampires or the hunters before he wrote that book, as it is far closer to reality than all the old Hammer horror films ever were."

"So it was more science-based than mythology-based is what you are really saying," Ronnie surmised.

"Most of the mythology surrounding vampires is actually based on fact, but as it's been passed down over the years, each new generation has embellished the story a little and the legend has grown proportionally. For instance, vampires have no fear or problem with garlic. In the old days, when a child was found to be lethargic and pale, and bite marks were found on them, then it was known to be the work of a vampire. So the children were sent away to stay with another relative or at least to another home to recover, and all the villagers would daub garlic around their windows and doors to prevent the vampire from finding the child by his or her scent. You see, once a vampire feeds upon you, it can scent you and your location from a great distance. So over the years, out of that, we get that vampires are supposed to be warded off by garlic."

"Well, as I said before it was never going to be my perfume of choice, so I can't really say I'm sorry you've dispelled that particular myth."

"They also have no fear of any religious artifacts, but one well-recorded incident, way back in the twelfth century in Lithuania, can account for the reason people started to believe they did. A few vampires were terrorizing a small village where all the men had been conscripted away for some war or another. All the villagers left behind, mostly women, children, the old, and infirmed had been herded toward and sought refuge in the church at the center of the village. The priest, being a very passionate believer in his God and all that the church stood for, decided that they were evil creatures and pawns of Satan. He took it upon himself as a servant of god to go out, confront them, and cast them out. So taking his Bible and holding his large holy cross high in front of him, he bravely started preaching at them. The story goes that the vampires then all took flight and ran away from the scene as fast as they could. He was actually a big, burly man and intended to use the cross as a weapon to bash the vampires' heads in, as I recall. It was written about at great length at the time and it was wrongly surmised that the vampires had fled from the large cross the priest carried before him. The man who raised me and his professor studied the case and discovered that only five to ten minutes after the vampires had fled, a sizeable column of soldiers had ridden into the village on horseback. The vampires would have heard the approaching men on horseback with their keener sense of hearing, and rather than risk losing one or two of them in a fight against superior numbers, they had simply chosen to flee."

"So they ran off and got everyone believing that they are scared of crosses. I'll bet they were laughing about that one for a while," she said, shaking her head in disbelief.

"It's funny you should mention that, Ronnie, because the vampires themselves are more than happy to have all these mythological ideas floating around about them. They are very secretive and wish to remain hidden from the general population."

"But why? If they are so much stronger, faster, and harder to kill, and with less weaknesses than all the movies suggest, then surely they have very little to fear from us?"

"Well, what you say is true. They are stronger, faster, and harder to kill, but there are far fewer of them than there are humans, and the one thing they fear most is the ingenuity of the human race. Imagine what would happen if the whole of the world suddenly became aware of their existence. Suddenly, every arms manufacturer would be designing weapons to use on them, and every scientist would be studying their blood and genetic makeup, trying to come up with a biological weapon to defeat them. In order to deal with that situation, they would have to create a massive army of vampires to fight a global war, and they would have to feed that army. What happens when all the humans are defeated and turned or fed on? It's a no-win situation for the vampires and they know that. So instead, they control their own numbers and keep hidden, and are quite happy to coexist, picking off a meal here and there."

"So why don't the hunters expose them and rally everyone to their cause?" Ronnie inquired.

"The hunters are all people who have had their lives affected in some way by vampires; they want vengeance, not war. They know all too well that if a war broke out with the human race against the vampires, then they would also be looking for all the vampire-friendly servants and guards who are hidden in our society, too. They wouldn't be able to just go around killing and torturing anyone they suspected of being a sympathizer anymore, either. There would suddenly be rules involved. At the moment, their silent war is having an effect on the vampires at last, and they are attracting more and more people to their cause all the time. With more people comes more funding and better organization, but they still want to keep outside of the law. They don't want a bunch of tree-hugging pacifists getting involved and sympathizing with the vampires or their companions and guards; they want their revenge. Both sides know that keeping things the way they are is the best situation they can be in. Anything else would destroy the so-called status quo and may tip the balance one way or the other, and that would change everything about the way we live and may be not for the better."

"What a crazy situation. I was better off when I didn't know anything about it all," said Ronnie wistfully as she shook her head.

"I hate to say it, but I agree. You are far better off being ignorant of what's going on around you. However, since that's no longer an option, its best we get you prepared to avoid any further confrontations. So as you already know from what went on at the vampire club, to immobilize a vampire, you need to stake them through the heart. Once staked, a vampire is both paralyzed and unaware of what is going on around them. The stake doesn't have to be wood, as any tough and sharp material will do. I tend to use hardwood stakes, as they don't set off metal detectors, and once you've staked a vampire with wood, there's a good chance it will splinter in them, which means simply pulling out the stake may not be enough to allow them to recover. I use steel spikes if I'm likely to want to revive them at any stage for questioning. After you've staked a vampire to immobilize them, then you need to either decapitate or incinerate them. Once you do either of those things, they cannot be revived or repair themselves. Obviously, if they are burnt to a crisp, then there is nothing to repair, but as far as decapitation goes, the nervous system link between the heart and brain, if cut in a vampire, is the only thing that they cannot self-repair. I usually do a combination of decapitation followed by incineration, just to make sure."

"What about them turning into bats or wolves or mist?" Ronnie asked him.

"Those are all just stories that have been passed down through the ages and added to, in turn, by each generation. Probably, a vampire was being chased by a mob and climbed a tree to escape them, and when out of sight of the mob, it disturbed a bat. The mob then saw the bat fly off and jumped to the usual superstitious conclusion. Same goes for the wolf. A vampire being chased disturbs a wolf and hides himself while the humans watch a wolf run off and assume it's a supernatural beast after all. If you were to chase a vampire into a mist or fog, then you really are at their mercy, as with its greater speed and heightened senses it can run silently past you and escape or take it's time to kill you and anyone with you. I can imagine that there have been times when a group of hunters or a mob of angry villagers chased a vampire into such a situation and were left dumbfounded when they never found him or her, despite thinking that they have them surrounded."

"Okay, what about holy water?" was Ronnie's next question.

"That one was fairly recent actually, but falls in with the old magician's trick of substituting one thing for another. Back in the seventeenth century, a Spanish monk discovered a small den of vampires operating somewhere on the outskirts of Madrid, and linked up with the local hunter organization to deal with them. They captured one of them and the monk wanted to give hope to the local populace that had been so terrorized by the vampires, as well as bring them back to the Church they had lost faith in. The vampire was taken out of the jail he'd been held in and chained to a set of gallows. The monk then went about putting on a show of blessing the vampire to purify its soul before it was destroyed. The blessing involved anointing and casting holy water upon the vampire, all of which appeared to burn the vampire's skin as it came into contact with it. So the vampire was then staked, his head lopped off, and his body burned, so everyone was convinced that the holy water had burnt the vampire's flesh. Unfortunately, the monk concerned, a Brother Alfonso, later admitted to being a bit of a fraud, in that he had splashed acid on the vampire rather than holy water to get the dramatic effect. However, the story survived him and, over the years, has been turned into yet another falsehood that actually assists rather than hinders the vampire movement."

"So what's the explanation behind mirrors and silver then?"

"Well, vampires are far quicker at moving than normal humans, so you could be looking in a mirror and by the time you turn your head to look behind you, a vampire could be there or vice versa, so that's one possible explanation, and silver has always been the poor person's metal for their crucifix and other such holy symbols. So it would stand to reason that people would consider silver as being poison to a vampire if they thought a crucifix scared them away, too. It's all just centuries of urban legends and old wives' tales mixed in together really. Although silver does turn black, if worn by a vampire, something to do with the changes in skin chemistry I believe."

"So apart from the pale skin and squinty eyes in bright sunlight, how can you tell if someone is a vampire?" Ronnie asked more seriously.

"Well, one way is to offer them a strong drink of alcohol; they can tolerate a beer and most wines, but any strong spirit served up neat without any mixer to water it down will burn their throat and stomach, and give them a pretty strong reaction, which is your indication to get away."

"Isn't it a bit too late if you're having a night cap with them?" she pointed out.

"Okay then, when you first meet someone, do the old method of detection and shake their hand, as their skin temperature is a bit of a giveaway. Vampires are neither warm blooded nor do they feel the cold, so if you go into the mountains and one guy is happy enough to lie in the snow without feeling cold or even getting breathless in the rarified air, then he'd be the best candidate to fit the bill. I've worked out that it's something to do with the vampire proteins and enzymes in their blood not being temperature dependent, and also an ability to absorb oxygen through every pore in their skin rather than needing to inhale it into their lungs like normal humans do. This is also why they can repair themselves so effectively and recover from virtually any wound, as the proteins and enzymes are far more active than their equivalent in humans.

"On dissecting a few captives over the years, I've also discovered that vampires develop far more valves in all their blood vessels, and not just in their veins, but in their arteries, too. This means any movement will help propel their blood around their body and reduce the reliance on the heart muscle as a pump. So if you get pale-skinned super athlete with incredible stamina who doesn't ever get out of breath, again, you'll know what you are dealing with."

"I'll keep that in mind if an albino starts chasing me for no reason," Ronnie joked.

"Actually, do that, as the reason you all have those small cuts on the back of your hands was what they call a scenting procedure. Once a vampire tastes or gets a good, long smell of your blood, he can trace you almost like a bloodhound. Sometimes, the vampires like to do a little hunting themselves, so they'll let a captive go and then a vampire will be given a drop of the blood sample that was taken from them, and it will then chase and hunt them down like an animal."

"So now that the building we were held captive in has been burnt down, I take it all of those blood samples would have been destroyed, too, yes?"

"I would hope so, Ronnie, but there is no way of being certain until I can worm that question into the interrogation I'm conducting on the old vampire who was running the club you were held in."

"You used a metal spike on that creepy old guy, the one who showed you around, didn't you?" Ronnie asked, suddenly far more interested in the topic.

"Yes, I did," Pieter answered.

"So where is he now?" she asked, her voice a little nervous.

"He's locked up and in shackles down in the cellar. I'm in the process of playing a trick on him to try to get him to reveal more information on what is going on with the vampires," he explained.

"How long before you get all the information you need out of him?" Ronnie pushed.

"Probably only another few days. Why do you ask?"

"Because when you are done asking him all those questions, I want to be the one to fire the crossbow bolt into that creep's heart, and I want him to know that it's me who is doing it to him. Then after that, I want to be the one who cut's off his head and throws it onto a fire, so he can never come back." As she spoke, Ronnie's eyes were welling up with tears through her anger.

This left Pieter in no doubt that while Veronica was showing positive signs of coming to terms with what had gone on during her captivity, she had nonetheless still been badly scarred by what had been done to her. Roberto would indeed be made to pay for his part in her pain. Standing up, he walked over toward her and offered his hand to her.

She accepted his hand and stood up.

"Come here you," he said as he wrapped his arms around her and gave her a hug.

She relaxed into his arms and brought her own arms around him, too. They stood there for a few minutes, with Ronnie silently crying in his arms. Then as she sniffed a little, Pieter broke away to reach across to the table and passed her a box of tissues. Laughing at herself for getting emotional, Ronnie accepted the gesture and took one of the tissues out of the box. She blew her nose and took another tissue to wipe her eyes. Pieter sat back down in her chair and gently pulled her down to sit on his lap and lean against him.

"Good job I'm not wearing any mascara or I'd be a bit of a sight at the moment," she joked.

"It's only natural to be going through these emotions at the moment, Ronnie. You've had a huge, life-changing experience. The good news is that you'll come out of this stronger and better able to cope than most," Pieter said, taking her in his arms again and stroking her hair as she leaned closer into him and placed her head against his chest.

Reaching up, Ronnie gently took his hand and brought it to her lips as she kissed it. Then looking him in the eye, she spoke softly to him. "Thank you, Pieter, for everything."

"You're welcome, young lady," he said, smiling back at her.

"I suppose I really am a young lady to you, aren't I?"

"Well, yes, I suppose you are actually, come to think of it."

"And yet, I don't find that creepy with you. In fact, I feel completely safe around you."

"Awwww! Now you're going to upset me, telling me you feel safe around me. How can I keep up the pretense of being a dashing ladies' man and reckless adventurer if you feel safe with me?" Pieter joked.

Ronnie laughed along with him at this comment. Then while still holding his hand, she asked him, "Why are your hands so warm now? They were cold the last time I touched them."

"It's because I've just fed. In many ways, I'm like a vampire, but in other ways, I'm like a human. After I've eaten, my body temperature rises as part of the chemical reaction to digesting my food. It's the same with blood and with normal human food."

"So you do eat normal human food as well then?"

"Yes, I do. And, yes, before you ask, I do take my steak rare and bloody," Pieter stated, anticipating her next question.

"But not seasoned with garlic, I take it," Ronnie teased him a little.

"Yes, seasoned with garlic and Worcester sauce actually, but not too much garlic. I like to keep my breath fresh in case there are any pretty girls to rescue, kiss, and cuddle with," Pieter joked.

"Oh you do, do you?!" Ronnie exclaimed, slapping him playfully on the chest.

The two of them continued to talk and giggle as they sat there for the next few hours. Eventually, Ronnie, feeling warm and safe, drifted off to sleep curled up in his arms, with Pieter holding her and gently stroking her hair. Pieter just stared off in the distance through the window, watching the night sky change, re-membering the last time he'd been able to hold someone close like this. It had been a very long time, he recalled, and he had missed the feeling of companionship, much more than he was prepared to admit to himself. In fact, now, he realized, with this striking young woman curled up asleep on his lap, he had missed it a lot.

Chapter Thirty Four

Attraction

onchita Alonso had come a long way since her very Catholic upbringing in Chetumal, the capital city of Quintana Roo in Southeast Mexico. Her parents had been hardworking people with their own little farm and grocery store. They mainly sold to the locals and the Belizeans crossing the border to get items not available in their own country. Her father had actually been born in America and served as a soldier in Vietnam. Once he'd been discharged from the service, he returned to his distant family in Southeast Mexico a broken man with both psychiatric and medical problems. He used to scream awake some nights, having terrible nightmares, and once he'd almost strangled his wife in his sleep during a particularly vivid reenactment of one of his wartime experiences. Conchita remembered how his skin used to bleed and how he had terrible rashes that would come and go on his hands, arms, and face.

Her parents had both been killed in a car accident when she was only eighteen, leaving her to keep the small farm and store going herself. In the end, this had proved too much for her to do alone, and she had reluctantly been forced to accept assistance from a local businessman. The local businessman was actually the local drug lord, and was using the farm and the transport of grocery items to hide other goods he was trafficking. Conchita became aware of what was happening, but felt she was powerless to do anything about it. Then, at only nineteen years of age, a little over one year since she lost her parents, she had to leave the farm and the store when she fell foul of the very same local drug lord. He hadn't appreciated her spurning his advances during the time he was helping her, and one night, after a few too many drinks, he came to visit and tried to force himself on her. To his dismay, she had not only fought back, but she had managed to trip him up and send him crashing to the floor. He was less than pleased at the humiliation of being beaten by a woman, and the scar she'd added to his face with the broken bottle he'd fallen on was even less welcome. Conchita had fled the scene immediately, taking only what she could carry and managed to get away to Cancun. There she worked for a distant uncle in his hotel and bar as a cleaner and waitress.

She thought she was safe there and had left all those problems behind her. Unfortunately, the drug lord was long on patience in his search for her and had employed the services of a local ex-cop who had a knack for finding people, particularly if the price was right. Luckily for Conchita, the ex-cop saw the benefit of a continued retainer from the drug lord, and a payoff from her as well to keep her location secret. To do so, she had to steal money from her uncle's safe, after using all of her own savings. She had not been so lucky when trying to get away this time, though, and ended up in jail, courtesy of her uncle's wife, who had never accepted her as part of the family. It was only a matter of time before news of her capture reached back to Chetumal.

She had almost given up hope until an American agent from the Drug Enforcement Administration (DEA) came to visit her. Luckily for her, the American, Mexican, Guatemalan, and Belizean governments were working in cooperation to stem the flow of South American-produced drugs being transported overland into North America. In return for her testimony, she would be given a new identity and placed in the witness protection program in the United States. Her father being an ex-American soldier meant they could treat her as an American citizen. It was too good an opportunity to pass up, and she'd been happy to go along with it to save herself. Now all these years later, she wasn't so sure she had received such a great deal.

After the trial and conviction, the Americans had kept up their end of the bargain, but with the move all the way up to Boston, her employment situation and the fact that she had no skills meant she was destined for a life of minimum wage. She was limited as to where she could go and could have no contact with any of her old family or friends. After jobs in coffee shops and hotels, she had eventually fallen into the job with Mrs. Van Dyne, and while the work wasn't the most stimulating, the pay wasn't too bad and the accommodation did at least give her the security and privacy she required.

She'd started going to evening school with the idea of bettering herself and had eventually taken up a part-time teacher's post, teaching both English and Spanish. The extra income was okay, but the main attraction for her was the chance to meet other people. In particular, she liked to meet the young females who attended the class, and especially those who were keen on some extra more private tuition. Her room on the ground floor was in the perfect location for her late-night visitors. The sliding patio doors allowed easy access without going through the house, and the fact that she constantly played her music meant that no sounds of her visitors were ever picked up by that "Neanderthal" driver, Joshua, or Rene, the butler.

As Conchita laid there on her bed, reading, she was startled to hear a woman's voice followed by the closing of Joshua's creaky door, in the short pause between the two songs playing through her iPod speaker system. The voice was definitely a young female and she was now singing a recent pop song as she walked along the corridor to the bathroom. Conchita was intrigued; she had never known Joshua to sneak a woman into the house before. She was sure that if he ever did such a thing, Rene the Rottweiler, as she called him, would have headed him off and issued one of his stern warnings.

Her curiosity got the better of her, so she jumped up and headed for the bathroom herself. Her plan was simple: sing away with her own song and try to enter the bathroom, making it out that she was unaware anyone was in there, or if the door was locked, to simply wait as if expecting Joshua to come out. She threw on the short, silk, leopard skin pattern, dressing gown and tied it loosely at her waist, making sure her cleavage was well displayed. She took the hair tie out and shook her long, dark hair loose. Finally, she checked herself in the mirror and began to sing as she exited her room, heading straight for the bathroom. To her surprise, the door was slightly ajar, so she just walked in as naturally as she could. As she entered nonchalantly, looking at the floor, she became aware almost immediately that the girl was standing in the bathtub and had just turned on the water to take a shower.

"Oh! I'm sorry. I wasn't aware anyone was in here," Conchita said loudly.

The girl in the shower continued scrubbing her hands across her face under the stream of water for a moment, then paused and turned to look at her, making no attempt to cover herself in the process. "Hi there, honey. You must be Conchita," the girl said in a chirpy voice as she continued to wash herself.

Conchita stood there for a moment, puzzled, not knowing how the girl knew her name, and drinking in the sight of her with all the water gliding down her naked body. "Y-yes, I am. How did you—?"

"Joshua, Rene, and Mrs. Van Dyne filled me in, sweetie," came the equally chirpy response once more.

"Oh!" was all that Conchita could say in reply.

"Hey, Connie, can I ask a favor of you? Can you grab me a towel, honey? I forgot to ask Joshua where they're kept before he hit the sack. Poor dear's just so drained, he's practically dead. Any chance you could spare any hair products and shower gel, too? I could have used all Joshua's sports stuff, but it didn't really appeal to me. I would have come knocking, but I didn't want to wake you to ask," the girl added, winking at her.

"Sure, I'll go grab some stuff for you. Be right back," Conchita replied, barely able to hide her grin and lustful thoughts about the way this was working out.

"Thanks, Connie. You're a real star," the girl in the shower said as she continued to rub the water across her body.

Conchita rushed to her room and quickly grabbed two of her big, fluffy towels, then a couple of the smaller towels for their hair, and finally, a short toweling robe. She thought for a moment then pulled the belt out of the robe. With nothing to tie it up, it was more likely to fall open, and give her a better view of this lovely young thing. She placed the items on her dresser then grabbed her toiletry bag and her sponge. She added the items to the pile then she quickly made use of her "Opium" perfume, spraying around her neck, her wrists, then finally, she pulled open her robe and removed her underwear before spraying across the flat of her abdomen. She glanced at herself in the mirror once more and quickly flicked at her hair. Then she adjusted her robe again to make her cleavage a little more pronounced. Satisfied with her own appearance, she then pouted and blew herself a kiss.

"You wicked lady, looking to corrupt that poor, innocent young girl," she said to herself as she grabbed all the items she had prepared and headed back toward the bathroom, with a Cheshire cat grin on her face.

On re-entering the bathroom, Conchita saw the girl with her back to the shower and her head tilted up and back, enjoying the caress of the water cascading off her head and down her body. Her eyes were closed and her hands came up to run her fingers through her hair. Conchita noticed how the movement lifted her breasts and how it silhouetted her nipples perfectly against the plain, white tiles of the bath and shower recess. Conchita continued to watch her for a while, her eyes drinking in the sight of this young nymph, the curves of her body and the smoothness of her skin. Then she thought she'd better not get caught staring for too long or the pretty young thing might get an inkling of what she was about. She didn't want that to happen before she had the opportunity to work her charms on her.

Conchita closed the door and flicked the lock over. She didn't want that pig, Joshua, stumbling in on them and spoiling the mood. She placed the towels and robe down on a stool, then took the shampoo, conditioner, and shower gel out of her toiletry bag and set them up along with the sponge on the top beside the sink. Then she selected the shampoo and crossed the short distance to the bath, and handed it over to the other girl.

"Here you go. It's for normal hair so it should do the trick for you," she said cheerfully.

"Thanks, Connie. Anything will do, I've been trying to get the smell of smoke out of my hair for days now. Have a seat and we can chat while I wash up, then maybe I can get you to scrub my back for me," the girl said teasingly as she turned with a handful of shampoo and started massaging it into her scalp.

As the girl turned her body around, leaving her exposed back to her, Conchita took in the sight of her from behind. The way her back and waist swept down then smoothly curved out to her rounded bottom and wide, feminine hips appealed to the older woman. Her youthful physique was very much to Conchita's liking, and seeing the two dimples at either side of the back of her pelvis, and absolutely no trace of any cellulite, almost made her mouth water. Seeing that the girl was now starting to wash the shampoo out of her hair, Conchita snapped out of her admiration of the younger woman's body and started a conversation as she reached over for the conditioner.

"So how do you know Joshua?" she inquired.

"Oh, isn't he a sweetie? He and Mrs. Van Dyne rescued me from the side of the road and brought me back here to help me out. They are both so friendly, and Rene, too. I always thought those European types were real stuck up and snobby, but he was as nice as pie and hit me up with a great caffeine high with that coffee he makes," came the reply.

Before Conchita could make another comment, the girl asked a question of her own. "So how long have you been working here, Connie?"

"I've been here a little over nine years now," Conchita answered, handing over the conditioner.

"Do you like it?"

"It's okay. The money is good and I have a place of my own, and my privacy, so I'm happy here for the moment," Conchita replied, taking both the shampoo bottle and conditioner tube back from the girl and returning them to her toiletry bag. Next, she pulled out the shower gel and squeezed some of the creamy, pink liquid onto the sponge, then walked across to hand it over. As she approached, the girl shook her head as she rinsed the conditioner out of her hair, sending a large splash of water over the front of Conchita.

"Oh! I'm so sorry, sweetie," the girl exclaimed, seeing what she had done.

Conchita stood for a moment in shock, feeling the water soak into the flimsy gown, making it cling to her naked form beneath. Then she laughed and both girls continued giggling.

"Here," Conchita said, handing over the sponge, then turned away and started to strip away the gown. "Well, looks like I may as well join you and scrub your back after all," she said whimsically as she struck a pose with her hands on her hips.

Now it was the other girl's turn to take in the sight of a naked Conchita. For a woman in her early forties, Conchita had a well-preserved body. She stood there with her long, dark hair cascading over her shoulders, not a sign of grey anywhere. Her large, pear-shaped breasts were topped off with wide areola and large nipples. The breasts were only just starting to show a hint of stretch marks across the top, no doubt caused by her love of dancing without a proper supporting bra to show off her cleavage to maximum effect. Her stomach had only the slightest little paunch, again due to her love of dancing and exercise, which helped to keep her trim. Below that was the tiniest triangular thatch of black hair; the rest of her pubic mound was trimmed and shaved bare. Her legs were long and slender, kept in shape by her dancing and regular bicycle riding.

Conchita saw the girl's eyes widen in delight at her appearance and both of their faces cracked into broad grins. As Conchita stepped forward to join her in the shower, the girl turned her back toward her once more and extended her arm backward to hand over the sponge. Conchita took the sponge and began to lather and caress the girl's back with firm but flowing movements.

"Mmmmh, that feels so good, Connie. I can't tell you how I've missed the feeling of another woman. I haven't had this since the girls' showers after cheerleader practice when I was in high school."

Conchita continued to lather the girl's back with ever-larger sweeping movements, going from her shoulders all the way down to the small of her back. The girl put both of her arms forward to support herself against the wall and bent one knee forward while locking the other out. The water from the shower head sprayed into her hair as she leaned forward, and then dribbled across her shoulders and down her back. Conchita placed her own left hand on the girl's hip as she turned a little to the left and steadied herself so she could apply a little more massaging pressure with her right hand. She became a little bolder with her massaging strokes and began circling around the girl's buttocks. Receiving no objections, she pushed things further still, sweeping the sponge around the right side and caressing the side of the girl's breast, then down and around the buttocks, and sweeping up and down her inner thighs.

"Why, Conchita, I do believe you've done this before," the girl purred seductively with a mischievous grin on her face as she looked back over her left shoulder.

"I think you have, too," the older woman replied, giving her a knowing smile.

With that, the young girl just giggled and leaned back into Conchita's body, pulling the older woman's left hand up and placing it over her left breast. Conchita cupped the breast, squeezed, and massaged it as she brought the other arm up and around to apply the sponge to the girl's right breast. After a few sweeping strokes with the sponge, Conchita swapped the sponge over to the left hand and applied the same technique to the other breast while she continued to play with the girls right nipple with her free hand. Conchita was pleased to feel each nipple stiffen at her touch, as well as to hear little gasps of pleasure escape from the back of the girl's throat.

After a few more minutes of having both her breasts massaged and teased, the younger girl placed both her hands on Conchita's forearms and guided them lower to her abdomen, as she leaned back fully into the older woman's body. Conchita, knowing what the girl wanted, began her own teasing game. She swept the sponge around the girl's abdomen repeatedly, each time going lower and lower, before sweeping up and around her breasts once more and then returning to her abdomen to start again. The girl began to make little moaning sounds and she swept her arms around Conchita to grab a hold of her buttocks. The younger girl pulled the older woman firmly against her as she ground her backside against her and swung her hips in time with the older woman's sweeping motion with the sponge.

Eventually, Conchita allowed her hand and the sponge to slide all the way down the front of the girl's pelvis and caress in between her thighs. As she heard the girl gasp a little, she concentrated her actions on sliding the sponge up and down over her pubic area. In response, the younger girl opened her thighs wider as she stepped her one foot forward and turned sideways a little to give the older woman better access to where she was most sensitive. Then after a few more moments of caressing, the young girl swept her arms up into a hug and the two women kissed for the first time. The kiss was both slow and passionate as both women held each other closely. Conchita now released the sponge, allowing it to drop to the bottom of the bathtub, and began massaging her fingers through the girl's pubic mound and teasing the outer lips of her labia. She bought her other hand around to lift the girl's leg up and pushed her back against the wall of the shower, pinning her there with her body as she continued to finger her and kiss her fervently.

"Oh, Connie! That's nice...don't stop...don't stop...don't...oh...oh... ooooooh!" the young girl exclaimed with a quivering voice.

Conchita was happy to continue and began to insert one of her fingers into the girl's vagina. She gently probed a little, then withdrew almost completely, then probed forward a little more. Each time she pushed her finger into the girl's moist opening, she went a little further in. Eventually, she was all the way in to the knuckle. The girl's eyes remained tightly closed as she began to squirm a little at the older woman's ministrations. Her moans and gasps of enjoyment also began to increase in both volume and tempo. Conchita added a second finger and again began the process of working them both ever deeper within the girl's warm and willing honey pot.

Conchita then began to trace small kisses around the girl's exposed neck, taking little nips or licking and sucking at the sensitive skin there. Eventually, with her fingers curling slightly inside to start to tease and massage the younger girl's "G" spot, Conchita slid her mouth down to first lick and then suck on one of the girl's nipples. After a few more minutes, the pressure being exerted on the younger girl's most sensitive area, plus the sucking on her nipple, helped to drive her over the edge and into orgasm. She trembled and moaned loudly with her eyes squeezed tightly shut. The older woman showed how much more experienced she was by maintaining a steady rhythm with her fingers and mouth, so as to prolong the event for her young plaything as long as possible.

Chapter Thirty Five

Store

"Mmmmmh! That was nice," the young girl said as she stopped shaking, turning to raise her head toward the shower and having the water cascade over her still closed eyes and face.

"I'm glad you enjoyed it. Perhaps we should get dry and go back to my room. I've got a few more moves I'd like to show you," Conchita replied huskily.

"Sounds like a plan," the young girl replied as she stepped out of the bath and moved toward the towels Conchita had brought in with her, leaving the older woman to briefly shower herself under the cascading hot water.

It didn't take long for the two women to then towel each other down, continuing to giggle and laugh as they did so. Then once they were dry, they sneaked back down the corridor and into Conchita's room, giggling. Conchita ended up wearing the short toweling bathrobe, and had her hair wrapped in one of the smaller towels. The younger girl just had the one large towel wrapped around her. On entering Conchita's room, the younger girl simply dropped her towel to the floor and dived across the big double bed in the center of the room. She rolled around giggling as the older woman released the towel from her hair and began rubbing it against her scalp in an effort to dry her hair more. She sat down on the stool at her dressing table and reached over for her hair dryer, and quickly started applying the hot air to her head as she combed her long, dark locks.

As she gazed into the mirror, she saw the young girl looking around the room, first at her pictures on the wall, then all of a sudden, she leapt up from the bed and started inspecting her ornaments. Conchita had all kinds of little knick knacks and collectibles as well as books scattered around the room. There were also several scented candles in key positions; she loved to use them to give her room a musky aroma similar to her favorite perfumes. The older woman enjoyed watching the younger girl's lithe body as she gracefully moved around the room, inquisitively checking out all her possessions.

As she turned off the dryer and put it down on the dresser, Conchita ran the comb through her hair for the last few times as the young girl came up to stand behind her. Conchita felt her cool hands on her shoulders as she began to massage her. The hands were strong for someone so slender and dainty in appearance, Conchita thought, but she was enjoying being caressed by them nonetheless.

"I see you like horror stories, Connie," the girl whispered into her ear as she continued to massage the older woman's shoulders.

"Oh yes, I love to read a good horror story, especially at night," Conchita admitted.

"Any particular favorites?"

"Something like Dracula—or anything similar that's set in the old days and has an innocent young female falling victim to a wise old predator, especially if they wear a tight bodice and are acting all prim and proper before they get corrupted," Conchita said, laughing.

"I notice you have all the Anne Rice books about vampires," the young girl observed.

"Yes, I love her writing. Her books are so much better than the films they made of them."

"Well, I have a more modern tale for you, one that I've been working on for just a little while now. Would you like to hear it?" the young girl asked, continuing to massage Conchita's shoulders and neck.

"Mmmh! Oh yes," Conchita agreed, flashing the younger girl a wide smile.

"You see, there was this car driving along the road one night, when a young girl came running out, all helpless and scared. She was almost naked, except for a single, white bedsheet she'd wrapped around herself."

"Oh! I like it already," Conchita said playfully.

"So the car stopped, and the nice driver and the old lady he was chauffeuring offered to help the poor, innocent-looking young girl. She got inside and rode in the back of the big limousine with the old lady. It was all warm and private in there with the screen up between them and the driver, so they could say and do anything they liked without the chauffer hearing a single thing. The old lady had been drinking a little bit too much and was almost out of it, while the young girl was really a hungry vampire, looking for an easy meal or two and transport out of the local area in case any hunters were looking for her. You see, she was a newly sired vampire, and although she knew she had to be all clever and secretive, she hadn't had much practice in this kind of thing before. Luckily, she had excelled at both drama and English at school and could do an accent from almost anywhere, so she chose to speak in a more refined North American voice as she conversed with the old lady, and she took the opportunity to feed on her and drain her completely. The young girl then had the driver pull over at a gas station, explaining that she needed the toilet. She had informed the chauffer that the old lady had fallen asleep in the back, so he'd best not disturb her. As he was used to the old lady being that drunk, the chauffer thought nothing of it and didn't suspect a single thing. The vampire had jumped out of the car at the gas station and quickly cleaned herself up, after asking the driver to get her a drink as an excuse to get him away from the car. She didn't want him checking the back and discovering the now dead passenger.

"When she returned to the car, she made a play of checking on the old lady in the back. Then as the chauffer came up to her with a soda pop bottle, she intentionally fumbled it. She let it drop to the floor so it would all fizz up so she wouldn't have to open it and drink any. You see, when you become a vampire, you can't drink soda pop or coffee or alcohol anymore. The vampire had then travelled in the front passenger seat for the rest of the journey, teasing the driver with promises of sexual adventures once they got back home. As they arrived at the old lady's place, the girl had fooled the driver that everything was okay in the back, and pretended to help the old lady into the house while he parked the car in the garage.

"On her arrival at the front door, carrying the dead old lady, the girl attacked and fed on the snotty French butler who had opened the door. He'd stunk of strong coffee and had a very bad attitude toward the young girl upon first meeting her. The vampire didn't appreciate his way of talking down to her and had taken an instant dislike to him, so she simply dropped the old lady, grabbed him by the throat, and sank her teeth into him in the entrance hall before he could say more than a few words to her. As she drained the old butler, she suddenly got hit with an almighty buzz, as the effects of his coffee started to affect her. The caffeine hit the vampire received, was something new and unexpected, and sent her happily skipping around the house on a mission, to see if there was anything worth stealing. She took some of the old lady's jewels and a nice silk blouse before splashing heaps of her expensive perfume on. Where the caffeine from the butler continued to kick in, it kept her all 'hyper,' and she ran around trashing the rooms in her quest for anything she wanted. As the effects of the coffee started to wear off, though, she found that she couldn't wait to feast again. It seems the effect of feeding on the two old cronies didn't provide a lasting meal to a hungry young vampire.

"Finding her way down to the kitchen, she sat down with the butler's coffee mug in her hands, pretending to drink from it as the chauffer came back into the house. She questioned the chauffer on who else was present in the house and who may disturb them for a moment or two. Then once she was sure it was safe to carry out the plan she'd formulated in the car, she continued to tease and seduce him. In no time at all, she managed to get him all worked up and excited, and she threw him roughly across the big, wooden kitchen table, ready to have her wicked way with him. Once there, she got him even more worked up and ready for sex with a little foreplay. She had taken him right there on the table, almost raping him with her wild, animal passion. Finally, she fed on him at the height of his ecstasy, holding him tightly so all of his struggling against her was a waste of effort and his fear turned his blood even tastier. Straddling him on the table, she had turned his head to the side forcefully and held his arms out wide as she ripped his throat out and fed on him, quite literally draining the life out of him.

"After that, the young vampire girl had set up a trap to lure out the only other person in the big old building, the housemaid. She was so easy to fool and had helped to while away a few minutes as the blood from the chauffer was being digested. The vampire girl had lulled her into a false sense of security by playing some hot lesbian mind games in the bathroom with this older woman. Then when it was time to feed again, the vampire girl decided to take her time and enjoy the moment, making it last for a while longer. So she teased her and told her the very story about how she was about to be slowly bitten and have all the life drained out of her. Once she had fed on the housemaid, she spent the rest of the night going through more of the house to see if there was anything worth stealing. Finally, the vampire girl fed on the cook as she arrived early in the morning to start her shift. Then she drove off into the sunrise in the big limousine with the blacked out windows and the view of the house burning down behind her in the rearview mirror.

"Now what do you think of that for a story?" the young girl asked, keeping eye contact with Conchita in the mirror. As she spoke, she lowered herself down and started to lick and kiss Conchita's neck. Her hands still continued to massage her shoulders and caress and fondle the older woman's breasts as she awaited her reply.

"Not bad," Conchita conceded, smiling back in the mirror and delighting at the touch of the younger woman. "But there are a few holes in your plot line. For instance, the vampire girl wouldn't have been able to enter the house unless she'd been invited, as vampires cannot enter a house or place where anybody lives, unless they are first made welcome by invitation. Then your idea about the caffeine is very original, but I don't believe it would have affected her at all. The next point, a real vampire wouldn't be able to stay here in my room with my large crucifix hanging on the wall over there. Then the most important thing of all that you have got wrong is if you really were a vampire, I wouldn't be able to see you in the mirror, as vampires don't cast a reflection. Oh, and the idea of riding off into the sunrise wouldn't work for you, either, as although the car windows have been tinted, there would still be enough sunlight entering to fry you to a crisp. Finally, there is no coffin with the earth of your burial ground anywhere here so you would not be able to rest and would perish in the daylight."

"Are you real sure 'bout that, Connie, darlin'? I mean, I'm pretty damn sure most of what I dun told you actually happened within the last twenty-four hours. Oh, and just between you and me, honey, I don't need no invitation to come in, a crucifix don't mean shit to me, and I reckon, for one o' the undead, I still look pretty hot in that mirror of yours," Annie-May stated, looking her straight in the eye through the mirror.

A slightly worried frown then spread across Conchita's brow as she continued to look into Annie-May's eyes.

"You should also know that when I dun get turned on like I was in the shower earlier or I start gettin' ready to feed and all, I have to keep ma' eyes closed as they go all red like this, and my teeth… Well, you'll see." As she spoke, her eyes turned crimson at the excitement of the upcoming kill, and she opened her mouth to show her canine teeth slowly extending from her upper jaw to form her fangs. Her hands and arms suddenly locked in a tight, suffocating, and unbreakable embrace around Conchita's upper body.

Conchita was momentarily stunned at what was happening, but then, as she realized the horror of her predicament, she screamed and tried to move, flailing her lower arms around and attempting to push herself back with her legs.

Annie-May continued to hold Conchita's gaze, enjoying seeing the panic suddenly written across the older woman's face. She slowly traced a long line along Conchita's neck with her tongue, watching as her frightened prey's eyes widened in fear through the mirror. Conchita kicked out with her legs, bruising them badly on the dressing table in front of her and sending all her boxes and trinkets flying off to the floor. Annie-May held her attempts to struggle free from her grasp almost effortlessly. She opened her mouth wider and slowly lowered her head to Conchita's neck. She paused a moment, hearing her victim's heartbeat suddenly racing ten to the dozen. Then she slowly and deliberately sank her teeth into the soft flesh. She felt the sudden pop as each of her fangs punctured the tough outer layer of her victim's skin. Continuing to push down harder, she felt her fangs sinking deeper into the softer, muscular flesh below, until she felt one of her fangs pierce the artery and the pressure of the blood caused it to squirt into her open maw. Then as she relaxed her bite and sealed her lips over the two holes, she took delight in the feeling of the warm, coppery liquid flowing freely into her mouth. Where in her first couple of kills she had ripped at the throats of her victims and lapped at the blood, this method, she felt, was far more refined and wasted less of the red-colored nectar she now craved so much.

Conchita, for her part, even though she was struggling to escape, couldn't tear her vision away from the image in the mirror. The sight of the vampire staring at her with those evil, crimson eyes held her gaze just like a rabbit caught in the glare of car headlights. Annie-May continued to marvel at her own strength, and how she was so easily able to hold her poor, helpless victim's most frenzied struggles, as she continued to feed on her. The image she saw kept Conchita's adrenalin pumping and her heart racing, which, in turn, kept the blood flowing faster to her major arteries. Annie-May continued to hold her gaze for the whole few minutes it took to drain enough blood to cause her to finally go limp and lose consciousness. When the blood stopped flowing, she sucked at the puncture sites until she could drain no more of the rich, dark fluid. Then she simply stood up, releasing poor Conchita's dead body to slump to the carpeted floor with a muffled thud!

Looking at herself in the mirror, Annie-May saw some of the blood had escaped her mouth, and had dribbled a little down to her chin. She brought her hand up to draw a finger across the line of blood that had escaped, then brought the finger up to her mouth to lick it clean. Then she grabbed the still-damp towel she had dropped to the floor and wiped off any remaining traces of blood.

Standing there with her hands on her hips, she admired herself in the mirror. Smiling at her own reflection, she giggled and said to herself, "You wicked, wicked little thing, Annie-May.

Chapter Thirty Six

Blood

The next morning, Ronnie was a little shocked to find herself still curled up in Pieter's lap. She couldn't recall at what time they had stopped talking; she just knew she had felt safe in his arms and had eventually drifted off to sleep. With the sunlight now starting to shine in through the window, the library was slowly becoming illuminated.

For his part, Pieter had been awake all night and had been happy just to hold Ronnie as she slept. However, he had been considering ways to gently try to wake her within the next few minutes, as the sun was creeping across the room toward him. He had no desire to get sunburn, and while he wasn't as sensitive as a vampire to the effect of the sun, it did still burn him. Luckily, Ronnie had begun to stir on her own and was now waking up. Ronnie noticed Pieter was awake and staring off at the window, in a world of his own, then as she moved to stretch a little, he turned to look at her and their eyes met.

"Good morning, young lady. I trust you slept well," he said jokingly.

"Yes, I did actually, despite the mattress being a little lumpy in places," Ronnie replied as she poked at Pieter's ribs.

Both Ronnie and Pieter then stood up and stretched themselves out, attempting to remove the stiffness of their overnight positions. Pieter caught himself admiring Ronnie's flexibility and shape as she lithely pulled herself into a couple of different positions.

"What time is it?" Ronnie asked, looking toward Pieter's left wrist.

"It's just after six," Pieter replied. He thought for a minute or two about his plans for the day, and then spoke up again. "If you'd like to go and get a quick shower, Jurgen and Mechtild usually have breakfast at around seven. If I know Mechtild, she will be up and sorting things out already. She usually goes into town at around nine o'clock on a Friday, too. So if you'd like to go with her to pick up some more clothes, I can make some funds available for you."

"What, you mean you don't approve of the baggy sweatshirt and pants look we've all adopted?" Ronnie asked him jokingly.

"Not that I don't think you can pull off the baggy sweats look, I just thought you'd like to get an outfit or two for yourself and at least your own underwear," Pieter quickly pointed out.

"Okay, that sounds like a good idea. Do you want me to tell Roxy about it, too, or should I leave her looking after Blondie?"

"Mmmmh! Good point. Yes, I think you should include Roxy in the quest for clothes, as there isn't much point to what she's trying to wear at the moment. I think she would benefit most by a new outfit or two, and it would certainly give mine and Jurgen's eyes a rest," Pieter replied, joking, remembering how Roxy had to wear the biggest top to be able to cover her surgically enhanced chest.

"And there I was, thinking you were too much of a gentleman to have noticed her hidden assets," Ronnie said, smirking.

"Oh, I noticed, but as you said, I was too much of a gentleman to comment upon them," Pieter fired back with a smirk on his face.

The two of them then went out of the library and met up with Jurgen at the bottom of the stairs.

"Good morning, Pieter, and good morning to you, too, Miss Veronica," Jurgen offered as he descended the last few steps.

"Morning, Jurgen," Pieter replied jovially.

"Good morning, Jurgen," Ronnie added with a smile.

"I was just coming to find the two of you, as there seems to be a bit of trouble upstairs with the young blonde lady," Jurgen explained.

Pieter and Ronnie both immediately started to climb the stairs rapidly, heading toward the bedrooms. Jurgen also turned and fell in behind them as he explained what was going on.

"It would seem she awoke this morning alone, since Miss Roxanne had stepped out to go to the shower. The poor thing seems to be quite upset and unsure of where she is," Jurgen added, trying to keep up with them both.

Pieter heard the screams as he got halfway down the corridor toward the room, and he seemed to take off at an even faster pace, leaving Ronnie way behind. As he entered the room, Pieter saw everything in a flash and realized how serious the situation had become. Blondie was trying to escape through the window and both Mechtild and Roxy were trying to stop her. Although only on the second floor, the fall would likely cause Blondie some serious injuries if she managed to struggle out of the other women's grasp. For their parts in the scene, both Mechtild and

Roxy were keeping a hold on one of her legs and one of her wrists between them, and in so doing, were preventing her from falling off the ledge. Blondie was halfway out of the window and was frantically kicking, clawing, and scratching at the two women, trying to break their hold on her. Mechtild was on her knees while Roxy was standing and leaning over her. The large bath towel Roxy had once worn wrapped around her was on the floor, so she was naked but for the hand towel wrapped around and still covering her hair.

Pieter leapt into action and vaulted across the bed to reach them just as Roxy was forced to let go, with Blondie's nails digging deeply into her flesh. As she winced in pain, Roxy pulled her hand out of the way and inadvertently hit Pieter in the face as he arrived to assist them. The escaping blood from the deep scratches on Roxy's wrist splashed across Pieter's face, but he had no time to think about being hit. Now that she had her arm free, Blondie was falling backward, and soon, her whole bodyweight and momentum would be transferred to Mechtild, who was trying desperately to hold onto her leg by its ankle. Pieter grabbed at Blondie's other leg, catching the foot and ankle firmly in both hands just as she was about to use it to kick out at Mechtild to force her to release her hold.

"It's okay, Mechtild. I have her," Pieter said calmly.

Mechtild let go and fell backward, away from the window, to lie propped up against the wall, gasping for breath. Roxy picked up the towel and sat back on the end of the bed, as she used the towel to stem the bleeding from the deep scratches on her wrist. Pieter simply stepped back while still holding Blondie's leg, and with his far superior strength, he steadily pulled her back inside. She tried to grasp the window frame to stop herself being pulled back into the room once more, but Pieter stepped forward to wrap his arm around Blondie's waist and steadily pulled her away from the window. Pieter ignored her flailing arms and legs, and held her close against him, slowly stroking her hair in an attempt to calm her down, just as Ronnie entered the room.

Ronnie saw that Mechtild wasn't doing so well and went across to assist her as Pieter was taking hits, kicks, and scratches from Blondie. Roxy was inspecting a long, deep scratch on her left forearm that was continuing to bleed, oblivious to the fact that she was virtually naked.

After a few more moments of fighting him, Pieter felt Blondie relax a little, when she realized her efforts were not getting her anywhere. She was totally exhausted after the exertions of trying to escape, and she collapsed into his arms. He continued to try to keep her calm as he sat down on the end of the bed, holding her with her back toward him.

Ronnie then turned to look at him and noticed Pieter's eyes and gasped. As he turned his head slightly to look back at her in response to her gasp, Blondie also caught sight of his eyes through his reflection in the dressing table mirror. Blondie screamed and started to struggle again, but this time, there was genuine fear in her voice and blind panic. As Jurgen managed to get to the door, Pieter looked over at him and instructed him to fetch the medical kit. Poor Jurgen had to turn around and head off to Pieter's office as quickly as he could. Meanwhile, Pieter struggled to control his bloodlust sparked by Roxy's blood splashed across his face. Some of the blood had entered his mouth, and while he had not lost control of his faculties due to his recent feeding, his eyes had gone red and his fangs had half extended. He was doing his best to calm himself down and at the same time prevent Blondie from running amok and injuring herself or any of the others.

Except for Blondie, with her struggling and screaming, everyone else in the room remained silent during the time it took Jurgen to arrive back at the room with the medical bag. As he came back into the room, Pieter calmly instructed him on what he was to draw up into one of the small syringes and what size needle he should attach. Pieter held Blondie firmly as Jurgen gave her the injection, and soon after, she began to settle down. Within five minutes, Blondie had fallen asleep in Pieter's arms. Pieter then instructed Jurgen to open the end room for him. Mechtild was about to try to rise to assist, but Pieter told her to stay and relax, and recover from her ordeal. Pieter nodded at Ronnie, indicating that she should stay with the older lady as he carried Blondie off down the corridor.

As they arrived in the room, Pieter laid Blondie down on the bed, then both he and Jurgen set about organizing things around her. They attached padded wrist and ankle cuffs to her then a single, wide Velcro strap across her waist, and raised the bars on either side of the bed. Pieter checked that all the padding was in place, then positioned a large, quilted blanket over her to keep her warm. Pieter paused for a moment as he stroked her hair away and off her face. He had hoped that they wouldn't require the use of the drugs and the restraints, as to do so would prolong the treatment required to help this poor young girl cope with what she had been through. Unfortunately, she was now in the situation where she was a danger to both herself and others, so he had been forced to act out of necessity.

"Can you try to get in touch with Fran again this morning, Jurgen? I think we need her help here sooner rather than later," Peter said calmly.

"I'll give her a call immediately after breakfast and see what we can sort out, Pieter," Jurgen replied.

"She'll need to be monitored, too, so can you set up the intercom again for me please?"

"I reloaded the batteries in the remote yesterday morning, after we settled them all down for a rest."

"As efficient and reliable as ever," Pieter said, smiling at his old friend and patting him on the shoulder.

Pieter said nothing more as he walked out of the room, leaving Jurgen to adjust the settings on what was basically a baby monitor with a remote listening device.

He walked back into the other room to find Ronnie helping Mechtild up off the floor, and he rushed over to assist.

"Good catch, you two ladies. If not for the pair of you grabbing her and holding onto her, our young blonde friend would probably be on her way to the hospital right now," Pieter announced.

"Will she be all right?" Ronnie asked.

"Well, the tranquilizer I gave her will keep her quiet for a couple of hours, and we've put her in restraints for her own safety. I know someone who can help, and we'll get in touch with her later this morning. Meanwhile, we just have to prevent her from hurting herself or anyone else," Pieter answered.

"I think she needs her nails trimmed," Roxy added as she gingerly inspected the torn skin on her forearm.

"I think I need a nice, strong cup of tea," said Mechtild, just as Jurgen came into the room and handed the remote speaker over to Pieter.

"Ronnie, would you like to give Jurgen a hand taking Mechtild down to the kitchen and see to it that she sits down and actually rests while I sort out a dressing for Roxy's cut?" Pieter asked.

"Sounds like a plan," Ronnie agreed.

Jurgen and Ronnie then both linked arms with Mechtild and all three of them headed off through the door. Just as she was about to exit the room, Ronnie spotted the toweling robe on the chair and quickly retrieved it before turning and tossing it toward Roxy.

"Here you go, Roxy. Your wound isn't the only thing that needs dressing," she said with more than a little hint of sarcasm.

"Why thank you, Ronnie, but all that excitement has left me rather hot and flushed," Roxy replied.

Whether Ronnie caught the second part of her comment or not, Pieter didn't know, as Ronnie had already left the room and rejoined Jurgen and Mechtild. He just smiled at the little bit of "cattiness" the two women displayed toward each other over him.

"Okay, Roxy, let's see what you've got," Pieter stated.

"Oh my, you have no idea how many times I've had a tall, dark and handsome man say that to me," Roxy purred as seductively as she could.

Pieter smiled and shook his head in disbelief at her brazen flirting. "I meant the cut on your arm, Roxy," he replied flatly.

"Of course you did, Doctor. I mean it's plain to see what I've got, being all naked like I am, isn't it?" she added playfully as she straightened her posture and thrust her chest out more.

"I think what you've got has had plenty of exposure in the last couple of days, and not only that, but since your arrival here, I think poor old Jurgen has almost had a heart attack or two," Pieter responded equally playful.

"What about you? Have you come close to a heart attack since I've been here?"

"No, Roxy. I'm made of sterner stuff."

"Ah, sterner stuff, eh? That must make you a *hard* man to please," Roxy said, continuing to tease him.

"It does indeed. Now let's have a look at that scratch and see how bad it is," Pieter said, changing the subject back to the matter at hand.

Pieter took up a position kneeling on the floor in front of where Roxy sat on the bed. Roxy held her arm forward and turned her head away as Pieter slowly peeled the fluffy towel away from the wound. Roxy wasn't wrong about Blondie needing to cut her nails. Obviously, one was quite sharp, as she had given the older lady a long and deep cut, which had bled quite badly. Pieter was using all his concentration to keep his bloodlust under control as he smelled and dealt with cleaning the bloody wound. Luckily, the cut did not require stitches, but after he'd cleansed it using an iodine-based solution, he did use some adhesive skin closures to seal up the lower end of the wound where the nail had cut the deepest. Roxy had kept her head turned away, not wishing to look at the wound site and her own blood. Pieter finished by applying a non-stick dressing and an elasticized netting bandage to hold it all in place.

"There you go, all finished, Roxy. I've cleaned it up as best I can, so hopefully, you won't get an infection. One of the problems with scratches like this, though, is that bacteria under the fingernails can infect the wound. We'd better keep an eye on things and do a daily redressing," Pieter explained in his best bedside manner.

"So, are you telling me, that you want to undress me every day," Roxy said mischievously.

Pieter just smiled and shook his head again as he started to clean up the packaging from the things he'd used to clean and dress the wound. "You are a worry, Roxy," he commented as he stood up and leaned across to throw the rubbish he'd collected into the small waste bin beside the dressing table.

As he caught a glimpse of his own reflection in the dressing table mirror, Pieter saw some dried blood across his right cheek. Turning back to the bag of medical supplies, he took out one of the packs of sterile gauze and tore it open. Then walking into the adjoining en suite, he flicked the mixer tap on and soaked one corner of the gauze before using it to wipe away the traces of the dried blood.

"So, do I taste any good or not?" Roxy asked him as he re-entered the room. She was now standing and had started to remove the towel covering her hair, ready to rub it dry.

"You are a typical B positive, and definitely all woman," Pieter responded.

"So you can tell my blood group just by the taste," Roxy inquired, seeming genuinely interested.

"There are a lot of things I can detect from the taste of blood, and your female hormones are obviously real. The blood group you have would only be a shock if you were a pure blood American Indian or an Australian Aboriginal, as they are predominantly O or A blood groups and very rarely do they have your B group in their makeup, so nothing especially remarkable there I'm afraid, Roxy."

"And there was me thinking I was something special with the effect I had on you. I was thinking I'd have to lock my door at night to stop you coming in to 'drink my blood!'" Roxy added the last bit in a fake European accent, trying to sound like the count on the Sesame Street TV show.

"Not necessary, Roxy. I have a whole fridge of blood down in the cellar," Pieter said, trying to end the topic of conversation.

"Well then you'll just have to come up and see me so I can thank you for rescuing me in my own special way," Roxy said huskily as she walked toward him.

"No need for that, Roxy. It's just something I do. Now, you'd better hurry up and get dressed or you'll miss breakfast. Later this morning, I'll have Jurgen and Mechtild take you and Ronnie downtown for some shopping so you can start to build up a new wardrobe." Pieter then grabbed the medical kit off the bed and quickly exited the room, leaving Roxy standing perplexed at the end of the bed with her hands on her hips.

Roxy was disappointed that Pieter had left so quickly, as she was very much in the mood to repay him for the rescue, and she was more than a little curious as to what it would be like to get this tall, handsome stranger into bed. Maybe the shopping trip would provide her with the opportunity to buy something nice that would increase her chances of that happening before that other girl got a chance to influence him. She noticed the way Ronnie had looked at him, and Roxy knew that she was going to have to flaunt what she had in her most seductive way to get what she wanted here. She was also aware that while some men might try to look disinterested, eventually, they always came knocking at her door once they were made aware that she herself definitely had an interest in them.

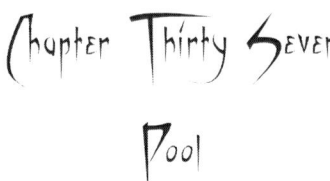

Chapter Thirty Seven

Pool

Later that morning, after breakfast had been eaten and everything had been cleaned and put away again, Pieter made the suggestion that Jurgen should accompany Mechtild and the girls into town. He was more than a little concerned about how the events of the morning had shaken Mechtild and felt having Jurgen to assist her would be a good thing, just in case.

While they were all away, Pieter had taken the time to go and sit with Blondie. He had once again injected her with the sedative after she woke up and began to panic and struggle once more. Jurgen had managed to contact the counselor Pieter had used in the past. Unfortunately, she was away for the weekend with her new boyfriend and wouldn't be back until Monday. He knew this wasn't the best situation to leave poor Blondie in, but he also knew there was nothing else he could do about it. Taking her to a normal psychiatric unit would raise too many questions about her state of mind and how she came to be in that condition. God forbid if she ever started talking about vampires in a group therapy session, as they would just lock her away forever, thinking that she was out of her mind.

When Mechtild, Jurgen, and Ronnie came back later the day, Mechtild took over looking after Blondie so Pieter could go and do his usual workout in the large gymnasium and pool set in the grounds of the rear garden. Jurgen had explained to him that Mechtild was feeling a bit weak, and that while Ronnie had bought the items she needed, Roxy was still shopping. The plan had been to return Mechtild and Ronnie to the house, and then go back to pick up Roxy with all her shopping in a couple of hours.

Pieter had then gone to his own room to change his clothes, and then he jogged to the gymnasium, where he completed an exercise program he'd designed using both the multi-gym and the free weights he had there. Once he completed about an hour of exercise, he stripped off down to his trunks and dived into the pool in the large glass house adjoining the gymnasium. Jurgen had obviously anticipated that the girls staying with them would possibly like to go for a swim at some stage of their stay at the house. The whole of the south-facing rear roof of the house had been covered with solar panels to leave them virtually independent of power bills, and the man who thought of everything had turned the thermostat up, so the water was very warm, compared to the usually unheated temperature Pieter swam in.

He had completed about forty or so laps of his usual fifty when he became aware that Ronnie was entering the pool room. He swam over to her as she entered and took in the sight of her in her new clothes. Ronnie had purchased a simple white blouse over which she wore a cream cashmere sweater, which outlined her curves nicely. She wore straight-leg blue jeans with almost knee-length, light, tan-colored suede leather boots with moderate two-inch heels.

"How'd the shopping trip go?" he asked as he reached the side closest to her position.

"You tell me," she said as she slowly twirled around, showing off her new look.

"Very nice," Pieter approved, smiling broadly at her.

"So how's the water?" Ronnie asked, making conversation.

"Actually very warm, as Jurgen has obviously turned on the heating, anticipating that some of you may wish to take a dip later," he explained.

"Well, if I'd known about it, I would have bought a costume while I was out shopping today," Ronnie replied.

"You don't need a costume. I promise not to look," Pieter quipped. As he spoke, he covered his eyes with both hands, but made a point of opening an obvious gap between his third and fourth fingers so Ronnie could see that he was looking.

"Yeah, well, it's not like you haven't seen me naked before, is it?"

"Well, truth be told, I was a little bit too busy to fully notice you that night."

"That's not what Roxy told me yesterday. She said you'd been checking me out all the way across the room as I went to find some clothes when you rescued us," Ronnie teased.

"Oh oh, guilty as charged, I'm afraid. Although, in my defense, I have to say I'm something of an art collector, Ronnie. And let's face it, you are a thing of beauty," Pieter flirted back.

Ronnie laughed again at his response, but this time, it was only a short laugh, as something changed her mood suddenly.

"What is it, Ronnie?" Pieter asked, sensing her unease.

Ronnie brought her arms up and across her chest as she rubbed each of her upper arms nervously, suddenly feeling a chill. "Just remembered something from back at the club," she said in a subdued tone.

"Care to talk about it?"

"I suppose I should, shouldn't I?" Ronnie answered reluctantly.

Pieter slapped both his hands down on the edge of the pool and pushed himself up and out of the water. He first walked over to the chair he had placed his towel on and quickly began to dry himself off as he walked toward Ronnie and gestured for her to take a seat. "Here, come and sit down," he said, patting his hand onto the upper part of the wooden sun lounger, next to where he intended to sit.

Ronnie sat down, still hugging her arms as if cold, staring at the floor.

"Okay, now would be a great time to give you a hug, as I'll actually be warm after swimming in the heat of the pool, but I'm still soaking wet so we'll just have to talk it out. So what just bothered you?"

"That old guy at the club, he'd made a point of mentioning that he saw me as a thing of beauty, too, and that only one of what he called 'the seniors' would be allowed to feed on me," Ronnie answered.

"Well, I may not disagree with what he said, but I'll wager he was referring to your blood group and not your looks. Was this at the time they gave you that scratch on the back of your hand?" Pieter asked a little more seriously.

"Yes, it was just after that. How did you know?"

"He would have tasted your blood as he took the scenting sample to see what blood group you are, and I suspect you are AB negative, which is the rarest blood group and one certain older vampires refer to as the beautiful group, as it's so rare to taste it," Pieter explained.

"I haven't got a clue what blood group I am. I've never been tested."

"May I?" Pieter asked, extending his hand to take hers.

Ronnie nodded her approval as Pieter picked at the edge of the small scab of dried blood on the back of her hand. As he stroked her wrist and hand, pushing away from her heart and toward the now open wound, a small drop of blood began to bubble up through the skin. Pieter touched the tip of his finger to the droplet and then, with his eyes closed, he transferred the blood to the tip of his extended tongue. He took a couple of seconds to compose himself and get over his bloodlust before speaking again.

"It's as I thought. You are blood group AB negative," Pieter confirmed.

"Well, at least I don't have fairy blood like Sookie Stackhouse," Ronnie replied, making fun of the situation.

"You see, that's one of the things that makes you special. Even after all you've been through, you can still make a joke about it and try to laugh it all off," Pieter said, praising her resilience.

"Yes, but it doesn't take the nightmare and the memory away, does it?"

"No, it doesn't, but it is a release mechanism. It's good to talk about it and deal with it, while just sitting around and brooding on it would be bad for you. So come on, get yourself in the pool, and get your mind off it with some healthy exercise," Pieter said, gently slapping her on the thigh. He stood up and threw his towel across a nearby chair before he ran and dived into the water again. He swam the whole length of the fifty-meter pool underwater, did a tumble turn at the far end, and managed to get halfway back to his point of entry before he had to come up for air.

Immediately, he noticed that Ronnie had stripped down to her new matching bra and G-string. She stood facing away from him, displaying her back and perfectly shaped bottom as she reached her hands up behind to undo the three rows of hook and eye clasps at the back of her bra. Then she quickly wiggled out of the G-string before running and diving off the edge of the pool and into the water. She glided gracefully along beneath the surface for several seconds before popping up close to Pieter.

"Wow, it's so warm," Ronnie gasped as she stood up and flicked her long, dark hair backward.

"Yes, I think Jurgen put it up to maximum to get it warmed up as quickly as possible. I'll turn the thermostat back down later once we've finished," Pieter replied as he walked the last couple of steps toward her.

Ronnie was head and neck above water while Pieter's shoulders were also visible. Neither said anything more as they came together close to the center of the pool. Pieter took her in his arms and lifted her up to meet him as he pulled her in close, and both their heads turned slightly to one side as they kissed. The kiss was at first slow and tentative, then they pulled apart and grinned at each other. Pieter then dropped her and leapt away backward, as he rapidly swam away, using a steady backstroke technique. Ronnie bobbed below the surface of the water for a moment when Pieter dropped her and then sprang back up to give chase in the pool. Pieter goaded her as he kept himself a certain distance away from her. This game continued for some time with Pieter cupping his hands and splashing water into Ronnie's face if she got too close. Eventually, after about fifteen minutes of the cat and mouse antics, Ronnie gave up the chase and started to swim to the side. She had enough exercise for a while and went for a rest. Immediately, Pieter changed to freestyle and started to chase her. Keeping his head above the water, he started to make the "da dum…da dum…da dum, dum, dum, dum, dum" noises from the film *Jaws* as he closed in on her. Ronnie was laughing and screaming as she realized what he was mimicking. Pieter caught hold of her left ankle just as her hand touched the side, and he pulled her back into and under the water.

He twisted her around under the water, and then surfaced, holding her in his arms. Ronnie caught her breath, then scooped her hair off her face and over her back and shoulders before playfully splashing Pieter in the face. The two laughed, with Ronnie still held in his arms tightly against his chest. They both paused silently for a moment before Ronnie wrapped her arms around his neck, and they began kissing again, this time more urgently and passionately. Halfway through the next kiss, Ronnie lifted both her legs and wrapped them around him as each continued to explore the other's mouth. After a few minutes, they parted once more, grinning and laughing at each other.

"So, do you make a habit of getting all the girls you rescue naked in your swimming pool with you?" Ronnie teased again.

"Only the stunningly attractive ones," Pieter replied in between kissing her again.

"Oh, so you use flattery to get what you want, do you?"

"Only if my boyish charm alone doesn't work," Pieter said, running a trail of kisses down her neck.

"Hey, careful you. I've seen *True Blood*, so no losing control and biting me," Ronnie said playfully.

"That TV show may be great entertainment, but as I've already told you, most of the vampire lore they have chosen to adopt for the show is based on myth and legend, and has strayed away from the real facts," Pieter explained as he continued to kiss around her neck and chin before seeking out her mouth once again.

"So, are you telling me you don't have the speed and stamina of Eric North-lander when it comes to making love?" Ronnie asked mockingly as she released her legs from around his back and slid her hands down and around to the waistband of his swimwear.

"My dear Ronnie, you only have to look at the way Eric Northlander's fangs suddenly drop into place from his second incisor teeth rather than his canines, which are the third teeth out, to know he is a fake. However, when it comes to making love like one of the *True Blood* vampires, I suggest you judge for yourself," he said in between continuing to plant small kisses all around her mouth and cheeks.

"Mmmmh, perhaps I will," she mumbled as she started to help him out of his trunks.

Pieter continued to kiss her as he stepped the last few paces toward the side of the pool he'd recently dragged her away from. At the same time, he was trying to wriggle free of his swimwear, which Ronnie had managed to push down to the middle of his thighs. Eventually, he managed to shove them down below his knees and clumsily step out of them. Since this was the shallow end of the pool, the water was only up to Pieter's waist. He lifted Ronnie out of the pool and sat her on the side before springing himself out again on his hands once more. He extended a hand to help her up and walked her over to the Jacuzzi. It was her turn to study his physique now and Ronnie liked what she saw; she liked it a lot. He removed the cover and pressed a series of buttons to start the whirlpool effect, then Pieter scooped Ronnie up in his arms again and kissed her once more as he climbed into the swirling tub.

Their kisses were more desperation than passion now as the anticipation was rising between them. Pieter lifted her up so that he could kiss and suck on one of her breasts and the now stiffened nipple. At the same time, she kissed and licked around his exposed ear and neck, and as they both knelt in the center of the large tub, each explored the other's body with their hands. Ronnie was gripping his buttocks with one hand as she started to stroke his already stiffened shaft with the other. She was relieved to feel what she thought was a normal penis of about seven and a half inches in length. She was relieved to have any thoughts she harbored about him being incompatible with her leave her mind in that instant. For his part, Pieter was gently teasing the outer folds of her labia apart to expose her clitoris, which he began to gently rub and fondle. As they continued to kiss, Ronnie became more aroused at his touch and little gasps and whimpers escaped her as Pieter progressed to slowly fingering her, pressing firmly against her anterior vaginal wall with the tip of his finger. He knew better than most that some women can experience a sensation similar to clitoral stimulation around this area known as the G spot, and sure enough, Ronnie started to respond with a lot more vocalized moans and expressions of pleasure as they continued to kiss.

Pieter, being acutely aware of what was about to happen, turned Ronnie around, helping her into a position against the side of the tub, on her forearms and knees; he stood behind her, the water up to his mid-thighs, and her firm, shapely buttocks presented in front of him. He leaned forward with one hand in the small of her back, and with the other, he guided his manhood toward her opening. Upon contacting her fleshy mound, he used his hand to gently swirl the head of his shaft around the entrance, using the escaping lubricant she was producing to coat himself in preparation for what was to follow. He then slowly began to push his hips forward and enter her. Once inside her a little, he just as slowly withdrew himself and paused a moment before once more sliding forward. His arousal was in full flow now and he experienced the reddening of his vision as his eyes turned crimson. With each slow and deliberate thrust forward, Ronnie was now counter-thrusting back toward him, and he felt his upper canines extend down as his lust and arousal caused his bloodlust to also peak. Positioning his hands on either side of her hips, Pieter struggled to retain control of himself. He knew his strength was such that he could hurt this beautiful woman, so he was ever mindful of how he held her and how he thrust himself forward into her. The slow and steady rhythm he worked to was a struggle for him to maintain, especially with her response of rocking backward and forward to meet each movement, and the contractions he started to feel her making around his member, squeezing him tightly.

Pieter was shocked when, without warning, Ronnie pushed herself up off her forearms and onto her hands. Suddenly, he could lean forward and kiss her shoulders and neck. As he did so, he could feel the pulse thumping vibrantly below the surface of her warm, smooth skin. With his bloodlust raging, he almost lost control, feeling his hips bucking backward and forward wildly. He heard her starting a low, guttural moan, which rose in volume and intensity, until she began to shake uncontrollably in his grasp. He knew he was close to raging bloodlust and the urge to bite into the neck in front of him was growing with every passing second. The thought of draining just a little of her warm, red nectar started to play on his mind, as he tried to maintain her pleasure by keeping to the same tempo and pressure of movement. Then it happened; he felt his own crescendo approaching just as she was coming down in the last throes of hers. He managed only a few more frenzied movements into her, before he, too, went into spasmic release. Immediately, he let go of her and froze as the wave of pleasure, centered at his groin, washed over him. He felt the muscles contract, and he could feel his penis throb and jerk as he came in several spasms. As he began to recover, he could relax; he had let go of her and had not gripped and crushed her as he feared he might do at the height of his passion. And now, as he breathed deeply, his eyes began to clear and his teeth retracted once more. Still positioned inside her, they were both enjoying the waves of pleasure the release had brought them, and as he once more reached his strong arms around her, they enjoyed the afterglow of their passion together. After a short while, Pieter then rolled back into one of the formed chairs of the Jacuzzi, pulling Ronnie on top of him and into his arms, and their mouths met once more and they kissed. This time, it was a gentle kiss.

"Wow!" Ronnie exclaimed, still catching her breath in a big sigh.

"Wow yourself," Pieter responded, equally exhausted.

"That was pretty amazing, and at least now I know you can outdo Eric Northlander and all those other characters on *True Blood*, and you didn't even try to bite me, either," she said, making what she thought was a joke of the situation.

If only she knew, Pieter thought to himself. One day, he knew he would have to tell her the struggle he had to go through to make love without giving in to his bloodlust, but today, he decided, was not that day. Today was a day for Ronnie to rejoice, make love, and feel alive again, and he didn't want to spoil it for her.

Chapter Thirty Eight

Gweilo

Jurgen knocked on the door as he opened it, popping his head around the door to grab Pieter's attention as he said, "I've got that information you wanted on Grace Tam."

Pieter looked up from the computer at his desk to nod at Jurgen, who then entered the room and sat down in the leather easy chair set off to one side facing the desk. Jurgen put on his glasses and began to brief Pieter on the information he gathered from the news and on the Internet.

"It seems what the girls said fits in with the news reports. Grace was indeed engaged to an up and coming young businessman by the name of Charles "Charlie" Wu. Originally from Hong Kong, he secured an American green card in 1984, in preparation for the handover from British to Chinese rule. His family currently operates two small jewelry shops in the tourist districts of Kowloon and Central Hong Kong. He originally made his own money in the clothing manufacture business, and now has several factories based in the Philippines. He's recently been gaining inroads into the hospitality industry by linking up with his fiancée's father. Mr. Alan Tam is, or should I say was, Grace's father. He owns and operates a chain of budget-priced motels and Chinese restaurants in several major cities. Since future father and son-in-law joined in partnership, they have opened a further four restaurants and now a nightclub.

"Now, this is where things get interesting, as four young ladies on the police missing persons list were last seen at that particular nightclub. The house security tapes do show each of the girls leaving the establishment on the nights they disappeared, so the police are not convinced of any involvement by the club itself, as the same statistics apply to any of the other clubs in the area.

"Young Charlie was apparently very upset at the disappearance of his fiancée and had put up a reward of one hundred thousand dollars for any information leading to an arrest for her kidnapping. This was then increased to two hundred thousand dollars, upon news of her untimely death in the fire, which, obviously, we know all about. The other interesting thing is that he would have struggled to pay such a large sum of money if someone had come forward, without the need to sell off some of his assets. Not the kind of position a wily young Asian businessman would ever put himself in unless he was completely besotted with the girl or absolutely sure he'd never have to pay such a reward.

"He's actually just taken a trip back to Hong Kong to grieve over his loss with his family. Unfortunately for him, he was photographed leaving one of Hong Kong's more famous brothels with a girl on each arm on his second night back home. So, obviously, he's recovering from his loss much faster than expected." At the completion of his report, Jurgen sat back in the chair with his hands relaxed on top of the papers he'd read his notes from, which were now lying across his lap.

Pieter sat silently in his chair, mulling over what he had been told for a few moments. Then he asked, "Do you have the details on the family jewelry shop in Kowloon?"

"It's the Wah Hing Jewelers, situated in the Miramar Hotel Shopping Arcade. I've booked you into the Peninsular Hotel and your flight leaves in four hours and thirty-three minutes," Jurgen answered.

"What made you think I'd want to fly to Hong Kong to deal with him?"

"Because I've known you almost all of my life and I know that nothing upsets you more than the act of betrayal by a family member or a loved one. I also know that you won't be able to concentrate on anything else until you deal with this matter and have laid it to rest. Plus, it may well prove to be a good opportunity to gather some information on the people smugglers, so we can stop them from feeding more poor souls to the vampires," Jurgen responded confidently.

"Sometimes I think you know me better than I know myself," Pieter commented, smiling at the older-looking man.

"Sometimes I do," Jurgen replied, very pleased with himself. He then stood up and left the room to assist Mechtild with the preparations for their guests.

Pieter remained in his study, thinking for a moment before going to prepare for his hastily arranged overseas trip.

．　．　．

Heading north along Nathan Road, Pieter told the cab driver to stop and pull over just short of the turn to Waterloo Road and the Lion Rock Tunnel. The driver duly pulled over and smiled at the hundred dollars Pieter left with him for the fare and a tip. It had only been a short taxi cab ride up from the Peninsular Hotel, but it was raining, that horrible, drizzly rain that felt like a cold mist. It was the kind of mist that soaked you if you stayed out in it for too long, so Pieter had chosen a taxi rather than walking.

Pieter much preferred Hong Kong in the winter months, as the brightness and the humidity were so much less and it was more comfortable to walk around in. He was wearing only a medium-brown suede leather jacket. It was a short, bomber style coat, with no hood, and finished just below his waist. He wore a casual, beige sweatshirt under the jacket and an old, comfortable pair of Levi's jeans. On his feet, he wore his favorite casual pair of desert boots. Despite the rain and overcast conditions, Pieter kept his mirrored Aviator sunglasses on. He kept his hands in his pockets and hunched his shoulders slightly just to keep the rain from running down his neck more than because of the cold.

He briskly walked across the road, avoiding the traffic to the Miramar Hotel Shopping Arcade. He had "Googled" its location while in his hotel room. Once inside, it didn't take him long to locate the shop he was after. He entered the Wah Hing Jewelers shop and heard the bell on the spring tinkle each time the door flicked it as he first opened, then closed the door behind him. Three men sat on the opposite side of the shop's glass counters surrounding the room; no other shoppers were present. An elderly gentleman greeted him in Cantonese.

Pieter smiled and acknowledged him with a nod of his head. "My apologies. I neglected to study your language. Do you speak English?"

"Ah, English, my English velly good," came the reply.

"Excellent, that will save us a lot of complications," Pieter commented loudly.

"You Eulopean, velly good exchange late with the Eulo at the moment," the old man added, switching into his well-practiced sales pitch

"I'm looking for Charlie Wu. I was told I may find him here. I have a business proposition for him. A very big business proposition, with lots of money to be made," Pieter explained as clearly as he could.

"You wai' here, I go see somebody." The old man nodded at him then turned and walked off toward a door in the back left-hand corner of the shop.

There was a chubby fellow with a big, hairy mole on the left side of his face, sitting behind the glass counter at the back of the shop. As the first man passed by, he spoke to him in Cantonese. "Watch the foreign devil while I go call Charlie on his mobile."

Pieter understood Cantonese very well, having spent a few months in Hong Kong when the British first took control of it and began to develop the area; he then returned for a while in the late 80s. But he didn't want them to know that he understood what they were saying.

After two or three minutes of browsing around at the various handmade items on display Pieter turned as he heard the old man re-enter the room.

"Velly solly, Charlie Wu no avaylable now. You leave numba, he call you soon," the old man said, trying to pass him off.

Pieter smiled and unzipped his jacket; he reached into the inside pocket and pulled out a thick wad of notes, which he casually tossed onto the counter in front of the old man. Most of the notes stayed on the glass counter, but a few fluttered off onto the floor. He now had all three men's undivided attention. "Call Charlie back and tell him to meet me in 'Someplace Else' bar in the bottom of the Sheraton Hotel in one hour. Tell him I'm a friend of the people he dealt with in New York and I'm looking for more girls like those he supplied. Don't forget to tell him that I have plenty of money to spend." Then he turned to walk toward the door. He opened the door and half stepped out before turning back to add, "Don't forget to describe me—brown suede jacket and jeans, and wearing sunglasses."

As he exited the building and stepped out onto the street, Pieter noticed that the rain had stopped, so he began casually walking back down Nathan Road. He thought back to the early days and the governor being ridiculed for building this road. Originally, it had been termed Nathan's Folly. No one could believe it was or ever would be of any use building a road through a mosquito-infested swamp. The road was now better known as the Golden Mile, with the major hotels and shopping districts that attracted all the tourists running off it. It had proven very important in the development of the Kowloon Peninsula on the opposite side of the water to the Central District of Hong Kong Island. The governor had made a wise decision to develop the area. He must have had a good friend advising him, Pieter chuckled to himself, remembering the conversations he'd enjoyed as he and the governor had planned the route together. He hoped that Pavel, too, would have appreciated his input into the planning of all of this. It was one of Pavel's biggest regrets that he'd never built anything for people to remember him by.

As he approached the Sheraton Hotel on the bottom left of the road, he looked over at the Convention Center, completed in the late 80s, right next to Star Ferry and in front of his own hotel. He smiled, recalling the general feeling associated with the building at the time. The roof was like a ski jump, as the cartoonists had pictured it, but the thing that annoyed Pieter the most about the building was that, here it sat, on the edge of one of the most spectacular harbor views in the world, and yet it didn't have a single window to look out and take advantage of that view.

Pieter shook his head at the folly of that building and was just about to go down the steps and enter the Sheraton's well known bar when a very well-dressed and polite oriental-looking gentleman approached him and bowed slightly in front of him.

"Excuse me, Sir. Mr. Charles Wu sends his compliments and has asked me to escort you to him," the man said in perfect, private school English.

Pieter paused to look at his watch; he was five minutes early. Pieter nodded at the man and walked in the direction he gestured to, where a metallic-red Rolls

Royce had pulled up against the curb. He entered the back of the car through the door, held open for him by another man. The man had jumped out of the front passenger seat as the car pulled over. Pieter sat back into the cream-colored leather seat as the door was closed, and his escort quickly ran around to enter and sit down in the other passenger seat behind the driver. Once the man who had opened the door for Peter had re-taken his place in the front passenger seat, the car smoothly pulled away and headed east.

"And your name is?" Pieter inquired, turning to face the well-spoken escort.

"Julian, Sir. Julian Ng. I'm Mr. Wu's personal assistant," came the reply.

"Hi, Julian. I'm Rodger, Rodger Rodgerson from Rhode Island," Pieter stated, smirking to himself at the name and location he'd chosen to use because of the local dialect finding it particularly difficult to pronounce the letter "R." Pieter extended his hand and the two men shook. Pieter made a mental note that Julian was deceptively strong and had calluses on his hand similar to those developed on swordsmen or users of other handle-based weapons.

Pieter enjoyed looking out at the many new buildings that had sprung up and even the changes to the roads that had been made. He eventually realized that they were heading toward the Cross-Harbor Tunnel. Then once they were over on Hong Kong Island, he soon recognized the route being taken to the floating restaurants at Aberdeen.

"Your first time in Hong Kong, Sir?" Julian inquired.

"No, not at all. I've been here a couple of times now. Just a few years in between so everything's changed so much," said Pieter.

"When were you last here then, Sir?" Julian asked, making polite conversation.

"In the late 80s, when the British were still in charge. The China Bank building was the tallest in Hong Kong and the Furama had the best view of the harbor from its revolving restaurant," Pieter answered, reminiscing.

The car halted in front of a small dock and the man in the front passenger seat again leapt out to open Pieter's door. No sooner was Pieter out of the door when Julian was at his side, guiding him toward the small boat waiting for them.

"I always wonder if anyone would still eat at the Jumbo if they came during the day and saw the color of the water around the boat," Pieter commented to no one in particular.

"Well, Hong Kong does mean 'fragrant harbor,' Sir. Once it's dark and the lights are turned on, this place really does come to life, and it's very popular with the tourists," Julian chipped in smugly.

"Can you still tour the lower deck where they keep the live fish tanks?"

"Oh yes, Sir. In fact, that's where we are going to meet Mr. Wu right now."

As they travelled across the small stretch of water between the dock and the famous floating restaurants, Pieter looked into the green, smelly water and saw the trash floating around in it. *How different things are between Hong Kong and*

Singapore, he thought, remembering how he'd gone from one to the other in early 1990. Singapore, he recalled, was so much cleaner and easier on his somewhat more sensitive nose than here in Hong Kong. The boat then bumped against the small platform beside the Jumbo Floating Restaurant, bringing Pieter back to the present once more.

Once off the small ferry boat, Pieter and his escort walked into the main entrance then down the steps to the lower deck. He heard the small ferry boat pull away, heading back across the water. The lower level opened up into a large space filled with small tanks of live seafood. All kinds of fish, crabs, and lobster were held in these small tanks, which kept them alive, but hardly gave them any decent amount of space to live in. The tanks were not designed for breeding, merely to keep the captive seafood alive and fresh before being selected for use in the various dishes prepared each night.

As they walked to the far end of the lower deck, Pieter saw one young Asian man, very well dressed in a shiny grey suit, flanked by two other men in plain black suits. One of the black-suited men appeared to be of Asian descent; he was short and squat, yet very powerfully built. He had a shaved head and displayed a few more scars than was normal, plus the upper half of his right ear was missing. The man reminded Pieter of Harold Sakata, the actor who played "Oddjob" in the third James Bond film, *Goldfinger*. The other man was European, possibly Irish, as he had thick, curly red hair. He was over six feet tall, heavyset and muscular, with a big handlebar moustache almost covering a scar through his upper lip and extending down to his lower jawline. Both men were obviously bodyguards who had been called upon to use their muscles on more than one occasion, and bore the evidence of such confrontations.

A fourth, oriental-looking young man in his late teens was sitting tied to a chair in front of the group. He had a rope around his chest, holding him in place against the back of the chair, and another two sets of ropes holding his ankles clamped to the front chair legs. His hands were tied behind his back, but Pieter couldn't see by what means they were secured. The younger man was wearing a yellow L.A. Lakers T-shirt and jeans, and he was bare footed. The T-shirt was covered with a number of bloodstains that had obviously dripped down from the puncture wounds to his face. The sharply dressed Asian man, who Pieter presumed was Charlie Wu, had broken off one of the bony feelers from a lobster, in one of the nearby tanks, and was taking great pleasure in stabbing the feeler into the young man's face as he questioned him about some missing drugs. The feeler, being quite brittle, kept breaking off, leaving small parts stuck in the young man's cheeks.

As Pieter and Julian approached, all three men turned to face them, and Julian made the introductions. "Mr. Rodger Rodgerson, may I present Mr. Charles Wu."

"Ah, Mistwa Wodgwason," Charlie Wu exclaimed jovially as he extended his hand in greeting.

"Please, call me Rodger. There are far less R's in it," Pieter joked as he shook hands, noticing the same calloused areas on the man's hands as his personal assistant.

Julian smiled at the joke, which was not picked up on by either Charlie Wu or his two bodyguards, who remained impassive to all that was going on around them.

"Pweeze excluze me fow wan momwent, Wodga," Charlie asked before turning to berate the young man tied to the chair again.

It seemed that the young man was a drug courier who had been caught stealing from the parcels he was employed to deliver. Charlie Wu was attempting to ascertain where the drugs were now or who he had sold them to. After another minute or two of sticking the spike into his face, along with the repeated questioning, Charlie tired of the game and handed the task over to the tall redheaded man as he stood back and watched.

Julian explained, whispering to Pieter, what was going on in his perfect English. "Unfortunately, this young man had done something similar once before and had been let off with a warning. The warning had been the chopping off of his little toe on the left foot. This time, something a little more drastic was required to send the appropriate message that Mr. Wu was not someone you should ever steal from."

As Pieter watched, the tall man Mr. Wu spoke to, called David, walked over to one of the preparation tables and came back with what looked like a large, dirty tea towel, which he proceeded to tie around the young man's mouth and neck as a gag. Then David picked up a large, heavy cleaver from the bench and brought it over so the young man could see it.

Julian told Pieter that the cleaver was used to chop the lobsters in half, but could do an equally good job on someone's toes. Charlie indicated that the other bodyguard should assist David. So the man known as Simon took up a position holding the young man's shoulders from behind the chair. With Simon holding the young man in position, he was less likely to be able to rock backward and forward on the chair, or tip it over, and so delay the inevitable punishment about to be meted out. The young man was frantically struggling against his bonds and trying to scream in protest, most of which was muffled by the gag. His eyes were wide in fear as he saw David kneel down beside him.

David placed one powerful hand on the young man's right knee, then looked him in the eye and smiled at him before raising the cleaver up slowly. He then slammed the blade down hard onto the captive's mid-foot area. The cleaver hit just behind the toes and completely severed them all from the foot. The muffled scream from their young victim had no effect on his tormentors other than to make them laugh at him. Pieter was glad he'd kept his sunglasses on as he felt his canine teeth extend momentarily out of his upper jaw. It took a moment before he got control of himself with the smell of the fresh blood escaping the wounds, causing him to flare his nostrils. Luckily, no one else seemed to notice his predicament.

Pausing just long enough to look over at Charlie Wu and see the slightest nod from him to continue, David placed his palm down onto the young man's other knee and swiftly repeated the process of severing the four remaining toes on that foot, too. The young man's eyelids were squeezed together in pain and tears were flowing down both cheeks. His pallor changed to almost white as he began declining into shock. Simon untied the gag around his mouth and the captive leaned forward in the chair as he heaved and began to vomit onto his own lap. Charlie Wu walked across and picked up one of the severed toes. He took a moment to look at it then started to recite the old children's nursery rhyme.

"Vis wittle piggy went to mawket…vis wittle piggy stay home…vis wittle piggy have woast beef…vis wittle piggy had nun…and vis wittle piggy went all the way into the fish tank."

As he spoke the last words, Charlie Wu tossed the severed toe he held into one of the fish tanks, where the fish started to nibble at it as it slowly sank to the bottom of the tank. Both David and Simon were laughing at their boss's sense of humor. Then Charlie gave them the nodding signal again as he looked over to the chute where all the fish guts and rubbish were ejected out of the preparation area and into the harbor waters behind the boat. David pulled the young man up onto his feet by his hair and Simon produced a knife to cut away the ropes that bound him. Then David frog-marched him over to the chute, lifted him onto it, and pushed him out headfirst through it.

Once they had removed the object of their attention, the two bodyguards once again took up a position to either side and slightly behind Charlie Wu.

"Now, Wodga, I bewieve you have a pwoposition for me," Charlie Wu said in his heavily accented English.

"Indeed I do… Is there somewhere we can speak in private, I'd like to make you an offer you can't refuse?" Pieter replied .

Chapter Thirty Nine

Interrogation

Charlie Wu nodded over each of his shoulders at his two bodyguards, who gave a slight return nod before departing the lower deck to take up positions in the foyer on the deck above them.

"Mista Ng hewe is my pewsonal assistant. You may speak fweely in fwont of him," Charlie Wu said.

"Very well then... I recently purchased some merchandise in Boston that originally came from you and I'm keen to purchase more," Peter stated.

"Mr. Wu handles a great deal of merchandise, Mr. Rodgerson. You will have to be a little more specific as to the product involved," Julian interjected.

"It was a special package by the name of Grace Tam," Pieter replied as he watched for a reaction from Charlie Wu.

Charlie Wu's brow furrowed and he began to snap at and argue with his personal assistant in Cantonese. Julian, for his part, was acting very sorry for himself and apologizing profusely. Charlie Wu was not happy that his ex-fiancée's disappearance had been traced back to him in any way, and was berating his assistant in a petulant fit of anger. From the conversation between the two men, Pieter concluded that it was Julian who had arranged for Grace to be taken by the people smugglers, and he had now lost considerable face in front of his employer, something the Chinese are very sensitive about.

Charlie Wu then calmed himself down for a moment and asked Julian what he knew about this "*gweilo*," or foreign devil, as the term translated. He wanted to know all about this man who had come to him wanting more slave girls. Julian had to admit that he knew nothing other than he had a lot of money and wasn't shy about passing it around. He had dumped twenty thousand American dollars onto the counter at the jewelry shop and left it as a calling card.

Charlie Wu thought for a moment and then instructed Julian to get rid of the *gweilo*, and to tell him that he had been shocked and insulted that he would think that he, Charlie Wu, would have been involved in the disappearance and death of his beloved fiancée and his own business partner's daughter. Once they had found out more about him, they would have to arrange an accident to befall him either here in Hong Kong or back in the United States, if such an act was likely to draw attention to their operation. Most of all, they needed to cut any link between Charlie Wu and his ex-fiancée's disappearance, in case her father ever discovered the truth.

Julian cleared his throat and was just about to start making the excuses when Pieter held his hand up to silence him as he spoke out of turn. "Charlie boy, there's no point in denying your involvement now. This *gweilo*, as you call me, became fluent in Cantonese way before you were even born."

Both men looked in shock as it dawned on them that everything they had just said had been understood by their guest.

"The people you sold her to didn't put her into prostitution; it was something far worse. Unfortunately, she died when I tried to free her. Otherwise, she'd be here, delivering this message to you herself," Pieter stated coldly as he held eye contact with Charlie Wu.

"What message is that, Mista Wodgason?" Charlie Wu asked sneeringly.

It was the last thing Charlie Wu thought about before the swift movement of Pieter's right arm sent the throwing blade into his forehead. Pieter used so much force in the throw that it pierced the bone just above the eyes, through the frontal sinuses, and into the man's brain. Charlie Wu's head was snapped back with the force of the blow and he slumped to the floor, dead.

Julian took a moment or two to react to what had just occurred. Then on seeing his boss suddenly struck down, he swiftly sprang into action and adopted a defensive posture. Pieter recognized the stance as a typical Tae Kwon Do ready position.

"Tae Kwon Do rather than kung fu, or even the Jiu Jitsu you obviously practice, judging by the sword hilt calluses that you and your boss both have on your hands," commented Pieter as he adopted a similar position.

"You will find I have a very mixed fighting style, Mr. Rodgerson. I've studied under many great martial artists," Julian replied confidently as he began to bob and weave around, looking for an opening point in which to launch an attack.

"Unfortunately for you, you'll not be awake long enough to show me anything but your opening attack," Pieter stated as he dropped his guard on the left and invited his opponent to strike out at him.

Julian, upon seeing the opening, launched himself swiftly forward, trying to strike at the taller man's left eye. Pieter had anticipated the move perfectly, and with his superior speed and strength, he spun around anticlockwise on his right forefoot, ending up behind Julian as the Chinese man snapped his punch into midair. Before Julian could react, Pieter had him by the neck in a choke hold and was squeezing the muscles in his upper arm to cut off the blood supply to the shorter man's brain. Pieter held on tightly as Julian struggled and tried to break free, using various techniques and moves that Pieter anticipated and reacted to before Julian could enact them properly. All of Julian's struggling was in vain as merely holding him in that position for a few seconds was enough to cut off the blood supply to his brain and render him unconscious. Once Julian stopped struggling, Pieter gently lowered him to the floor. He then proceeded to reclaim his throwing knife from Charlie Wu's forehead, which he wiped clean on the dead man's expensive suit.

Pieter quickly put Julian into the same chair as the young man he'd seen them torture to make an example of, and used the same rope to tie his arms behind his back and to the chair. Then, as Julian was starting to come back to his senses, he headed up the stairs to the foyer level. The two burly bodyguards were leaning against the desk, sharing a joke. Luckily, Charlie Wu and his assistant had been overconfident in their ability to deal with one *gweilo* stranger, and they hadn't called out or raised the alarm. However, just as Pieter approached the two men, Julian had recovered enough to start yelling for help.

Both men bristled and were quickly ready to attack him in an instant. Pieter quickly punched Simon, striking him in the temple. Then noticing the other man was unbalanced, he pushed David away and the big man stumbled to the ground. The blow he'd delivered to Simon's head had disoriented the heavyset Asian man for a moment, allowing Pieter the time to spin around and kick him behind the right knee. As Simon slumped to the ground in front of him, Pieter placed his hands on either side of the man's head and twisted it sharply to the right. The speed of Pieter's movements, and the disorientation caused by the punch to his head, gave Simon no opportunity to brace the thick muscles in his squat neck. The loud, crunching sound confirmed to Pieter that he had broken several of the man's vertebrae and severed his spinal cord successfully.

David, upon seeing the rapid assault on Simon from his position on the floor, had quickly rolled out of the way in order to buy himself the time required to remove a set of nunchaku from his rear waistband. As the red-haired man rose to his feet once more, the two of them now stood facing each other only a few feet apart. David swirled the nunchaku in front of his body in a figure eight pattern to ward Pieter off. The two men then began to slowly circle each other, seemingly both wary of each other and each looking for an opening from which to press an attack. Pieter then slowly removed his jacket and tossed it aside while continuing to keep a close eye on David, in case he tried to lunge at him. David, upon seeing Pieter remove his jacket, decided to do the same. As he continued to swirl the nunchaku in the space between them, he carefully took off his own suit jacket. Pieter noticed that the white cuffs of his shirt had actually been sown into the sleeves of his suit, and once his jacket was removed, David's arms were bare, but for the many oriental dragons and lions he had tattooed onto them.

"Wow! Who would have guessed we share the same tailor," Pieter joked.

David said nothing in response, then Pieter stood perfectly still and took his sweatshirt off to reveal the brown-colored polo shirt below. David then released the metal clip behind his tie and tossed it aside before opening the top two buttons on his sleeveless white shirt.

"Anything else you want to remove before we start, or do you need a pole and some stripper music playing to set the right tone for you?" Pieter asked mockingly.

David's face widened into a snarl as he responded to the taunt by starting to swirl the nunchaku around his body from front to back and out to the side, swapping hands and patterns as he tried his best to both impress and intimidate Pieter with his skill. After a minute or so of the twirling, Pieter suddenly stepped forward and parried the nunchaku off to the left with his left hand. He had watched David's pattern, almost nonchalantly it seemed, but in reality, he was working out when he copied specific moves. At the moment David had stretched his right arm out to its full striking length, Pieter had stepped inside the redheaded man's reach, parried the weapon away, and upset the rhythm of his routine.

Pieter struck the middle of David's lower jaw with the heel of his hand. The force of the blow split the jaw in the middle as well as fracturing both condyles just below the temporomandibular joints, where the jaw articulates with the base of the skull. The big man was knocked senseless and slumped to the ground, shaking and twitching, as if having some kind of seizure. Pieter followed this move with a downward stomp and a twist onto the man's skull. As a result, David didn't move or twitch anymore.

Pieter gathered up first his sweatshirt and then the jacket, before he headed back down to the lower deck, where he'd left Julian tied up. As he approached his captive, Pieter noticed that he had managed to tilt the chair over and was struggling to free himself. Unfortunately, when he hit the ground, it was right in the middle of the pool of blood and vomit from the chair's previous occupant.

"Since you seem comfortable on the floor among all the body fluids, I'll leave you there while we have a little chat," Pieter said calmly as he crouched down on his haunches beside the incapacitated Mr. Ng.

"You are a fucking dead man," Julian snapped angrily.

"Now, now, Julian, there's no reason to swear and spoil that toffee-nosed English accent of yours," Pieter replied condescendingly.

"Fuck you, asshole. You are a fucking dead man. No one kills a triad member like Charlie Wu and lives to tell the tale. Not in Hong Kong they don't."

Pieter, sensing that Julian wasn't quite ready for the little chat he had in mind, stood up and walked over to the same preparation bench that David had approached earlier. He retrieved the cleaver and raised it to a position Julian could clearly see. The smell of the blood on the blade made him slightly light-headed for a moment, as he felt his eyes glaze red and his fangs half extend. Pieter took a moment or two to take in a deep breath and dry swallowed in an attempt to control his sudden urge to feed. Walking back over to his captive, he made a point of showing the cleaver to Julian. Pieter left a pause between his actions to enable Julian to appreciate his predicament a little more before he stepped forward, treading on his captive's right ankle to hold it in position. He then stooped down to hold his other ankle firmly out of the way against the other raised leg of the chair. Then with one swift chopping motion, he hacked off the front end of Julian's right shoe. Pieter figured that he'd taken about two or three of the man's toes off with the cut. Julian screamed in agony through gritted teeth, then obviously a little upset, he returned to berating Pieter once more.

"You motherfucker, you are fucking dead! They are going to find you and cut you up," Julian ranted.

Pieter, having tired of the verbal abuse and obscenities being hurled at him, grabbed Julian roughly by the collar and yanked him up. Setting the chair he was tied to back on all four legs and keeping hold of his collar with one hand, he slapped Julian across the side of his face with his open palm. Pieter had made sure to slap him on the opposite side, to the one with the blood and vomit matting into his hair and staining his cheek. Julian was stunned into silence by the act, his face stinging almost as if burnt.

"Now, that's better. Let's try and keep this civilized, shall we? I want the details on the people smugglers you sold Grace to. If you give me that information, then the pain and the cleaving will stop; if not, then the next thing you feel will be your ankle being sliced off, then I'm sure you are familiar with the song, you know, the ankle bone's connected to the shin bone, the shin bone's connected to the knee bone, the knee bone's connected to the thigh bone, and so on," Pieter explained almost casually.

"So if I give you the information, what's in it for me? Will you let me go?" Julian asked nervously.

"Oh come on, Julian. I don't tell lies. You're a dead man and you know it. I'm just telling you how to make the pain stop so we can end things quickly and as painlessly as possible for you."

"Then fuck you, Mr. Rodgerson," Julian retorted defiantly.

"Well, Julian, you may wish to change your mind when you look into my eyes." As he spoke, Pieter dabbed the tip of his right index finger onto the tip of one of Julian's severed toes and brought it up to his mouth. He licked at the fingertip before he took off his sunglasses and let Julian look into his crimson eyes. Then he smiled his best toothy smile, with his fangs in full view.

Fear suddenly gripped Julian; it was a fear like no other he'd ever felt before. He started to shake uncontrollably and his stomach began churning as he lost control of his bladder and began to pee himself in fear of the vision in front of him.

Pieter could hear his heart suddenly race.

"Wh-what are you?" Julian stuttered as his heart continued to gallop.

"I'm your worst nightmare come true, little man. Now tell me how I can make contact with those people smugglers, or I'm going to cut you into pieces and feed on you slowly and painfully for as long as it takes to make you talk," Pieter said in a controlled but menacing voice.

Julian began talking as quickly as possible, all the while trying to keep his head turned and not look at Pieter, and into those terrible red eyes. He even took Pieter through the contact details stored in his Blackberry phone and gave up the password protecting certain delicate pieces of information. After a few more minutes of questioning about how he'd made contact and who the main players were in the organization that Julian and Charlie Wu had used, Pieter decided that he had obtained all the useful information he required from the frightened little man. He stood up, walked over to his jacket, and deposited the Blackberry into the inside breast pocket. He returned to stand behind and just off to one side of Julian, and picked up the cleaver once more.

"Are you going drink my blood now?" Julian asked nervously.

"No, Julian, I'm not that fond of Chinese. You know how it is. You eat Chinese, you feel full, but you're hungry again in an hour or so," Pieter replied.

Julian laughed nervously at the joke, just as Pieter's arm swept across and angled the cleaver slightly upward into the back of his skull. The blade sliced through the occipital area and came to rest embedded almost halfway into his brain, and Julian's body went limp, slumping forward in the chair.

"That's the quickest death and the fastest way I can stop the pain for you, Julian. Think yourself lucky I didn't have to spend a lot of time torturing the information out of you."

Pieter dragged the chair over to the waste disposal chute then lifted Julian's body and the chair onto it, before pushing him through the gap. He followed this by dragging Charlie Wu's body to the chute and disposing of him in the same way. Once upstairs, he was about to throw the two bodyguards over the side when he heard the small water taxi boat start up at the dock opposite. Rather than wait to be discovered moving dead bodies about, he walked out and around to the flashy, red speed boat that Charlie Wu had obviously used to transport himself, his posse, and his prisoner onto the floating restaurant earlier. Pieter had spotted that the keys were left in the ignition as he'd admired the lines of the boat when he and Julian had arrived at the dock beside it.

Pieter started up the engine and cast off the mooring lines, then turned the boat to head across toward the waiting car. As he slowed the boat on the approach to the dock, he noticed that the two men were still waiting by the red Rolls Royce. One of the men was making a phone call. Pieter then heard Julian's phone ringing in his inside pocket. As he pulled up alongside the dock, he casually handed the mooring line to the driver. He moved the short distance between the car and the dock to assist him while his colleague was trying to find out what was going on. As soon as he grabbed at the line, Pieter looped it over his wrist and pulled him over into the boat. As the man fell forward, off balance, Pieter looped his arm around to drag the lassoed wrist up out of the way as his other hand grabbed at the man's waistband and drove him headfirst into the deck. The man made no movement, and judging by the angle of his neck and shoulder, Pieter surmised that he was dead. Pieter quickly rummaged through the man's pockets for the keys to the car.

Jumping out onto the dock, Pieter casually walked over to the man with his back to him. The man was leaving a voice mail message and trying to communicate with his boss, hoping for instructions on what to do. As Pieter approached, he simply stood next to the man as if waiting for him to open the door to the car again. The man quickly looked for the driver, who was hidden in the boat below the level of the dock, out of sight. With no instructions from his boss and no one else to confer with, he chose to open the door. As he stood to the side to allow Pieter access to the back of the car, Pieter stepped forward and hit him square on the nose with the heel of his hand. As the man's head snapped back, Pieter followed up with a knee directly to the man's groin. The man crumpled forward with a loud moan as Pieter pushed and swung him around a little so he fell almost into the car. Next, Pieter slammed the door against his head a couple of times. He then picked the lifeless body up by the belt, bundling him into the car trunk before he slammed it shut.

Rather than drive back to the hotel in a car that would soon become a crime scene for the Hong Kong police, Pieter drove back to the Central District of Hong Kong, and with the privacy screen erected behind him, he pulled up into the front of one of the big new hotels built since his last visit. Stepping out, he handed the keys to the valet and tipped him a hundred dollars to put it somewhere discretely out of the way, saying that he would be at a meeting all afternoon and into the evening. From there, it was a short walk over to the Star Ferry service for the short trip across the harbor. Pieter enjoyed relaxing and taking in the views of the much-changed skyline during the trip across the harbor from Hong Kong Island back to Kowloon. Once he disembarked from the ferry, it was a two-minute walk to his hotel, where he checked out immediately after showering and changing all his clothes and footwear.

He disposed of all his clothing and shoes into one of the street trash containers and proceeded to board the Mass Transit Railway at the Tsim Sha Shui Station nearby. The train, being its usual busy hustle and bustle, with hundreds of people crushing on board, brought back more fond memories to Pieter. As he stood there almost a head and shoulders above all the other passengers, he looked along the carriage to see a virtual sea or carpet of black-haired heads with only the occasional tourist jutting up above them.

Once at the international airport, Pieter proceeded to change his flight with no problem, although he did have to upgrade to first class to get onto the earlier flight. All in all, he was happy with the way things had gone. He'd avenged poor Grace and procured some valuable information on the people smugglers. If he could follow their trail and wipe out a valuable food supply to the vampires, then maybe he could also flush one or two more of them out into the open. Once they were exposed, they'd be where he would be able to deal with them. He decided that when he got back, it was also time to get more information out of Roberto on what was happening within the vampire organization. So he settled down on the flight for some well-earned rest, as he knew he would really need his wits about him if he was to deal with the wily old vampire successfully.

Chapter Forty

Meeting

Margeurite and Izzy arrived at the small Italian restaurant five minutes before the designated meeting time. The head waiter greeted them, and then escorted them to the private room where the meeting was to be held. He offered them some refreshments, which they both accepted and ordered from the drinks list on the menu provided. Johnny had been politely asked to occupy one of the small booths out in the main restaurant area, which he did after receiving a nod of agreement from Margeurite. As he sat there, Johnny realized that the position he'd been given provided him with an excellent view of the comings and goings into the establishment via the main entrance. Also, with a large wall mirror being used to make the small restaurant appear much larger, he could see toward the back and the door to the room where Margeurite and Izzy had been escorted. He had just been served his large glass of ice and the dry ginger ale to go with it, and held the bottle poised ready to pour into the glass when he heard a familiar voice beside him.

"Glad to smell there's no whiskey in that glass, young man."

Johnny looked up to see a face he hadn't seen in a very, very long time. Despite the time, however, the man looked exactly the same as the day they had met almost twenty years previously. "Hello, Pieter. Good to see you," he said with a smile as he stood and extended his hand to greet the other man.

They shook hands firmly then Pieter sat down next to Johnny for a quick catch up before he had to go join Margeurite and Izzy in the other room.

"You're still looking fit and healthy, Johnny. How's the family doing?" Pieter asked.

"All good, thank you, Pieter. Here, I've got some pictures," Johnny said as he reached into his coat to extract his wallet.

Pieter took the time to flick through the pictures one at a time and study the faces. How he envied Johnny and his beautiful family of a wife and two girls. As he looked at the cherished photos, he saw how Johnny's two girls were now growing into very attractive young women, much like their mother. "You're a lucky man, Johnny. Marsha is still far too good looking for an ugly bugger like you, though, and how Kate and Joanne ended up looking so gorgeous, I'll never know. Are you sure Marsha didn't fool around on you with the milkman?" he asked mockingly.

"I am a lucky man, Pieter. And all joking aside, please don't think that I don't know I'd have nothing if it weren't for you," Johnny said, changing the tone of the conversation.

"Nonsense, Johnny. You'd have pulled yourself together eventually. I just pushed you in the right direction a little bit earlier, that's all," Pieter replied, slapping Johnny on the shoulder, trying to keep the conversation light and jovial.

"No, Pieter, if it weren't for you, my life would have been headed in a whole different direction. Marsha and the girls wouldn't even be alive right now if it weren't for you. You make a difference, man. In this crazy, fucked-up world in which we live in, you make a big difference, and to a lot of people, too. You turned a snot-nosed weasel of a hunter, who was drowning his sorrows in a bottle and killing anything and everything in his path, into a sober, responsible family man. You saved my wife from becoming some fang's dinner. You introduced us and whenever we've needed anything, you have always been there for us. Now, I don't know what's going on with you, the boss lady, and Izzy, and I'll keep our relationship a secret from them for as long as you require me to do so. I'll continue to protect them as if they were the first lady and the president's daughter, just as long as you know that it's for you, man. The whole reason I do this is out of respect for you, and what you've done for me and my family. When Joanne almost lost her leg after that car accident, Margeurite wasn't the one who coughed up the money for the medevac flight down to that specialist in Washington, you were. It was you who supplied the dough for that, and the operations, the rehab, the wheelchair, and everything else. If it weren't for, you my daughter wouldn't be able to walk on her own two legs, Pieter. As long as you know that you can rely on me for whatever you need and whenever you need it…" Johnny's words trailed off as emotion got the better of him and his eyes began to fill with tears, his voice quivering to a halt.

Pieter slipped his arm from patting him on the left shoulder across to his right shoulder to pull him in for a hug. "I know I can trust you, Johnny, and I know you are always there if I ever need you for anything. Seeing you turn your life around and giving Marsha something to live for again are all the rewards I need. You have the family I can never have, and you are a good man, a good husband, and a great father; don't you ever forget that. Now, I've gotta go talk to 'da boss lady' and clear a few things up with that headstrong daughter of hers. If any of Izzy's hunter friends show up unexpectedly, you just play dumb and head back to the hotel. This is one of the old 'speakeasies' from back in the Prohibition days, and there's a secret way in and out of here if required. The owner's a kindred spirit whose daughter got fed on a while back, so we are in safe hands. If anything happens, I'll get them back to you in one piece one way or another. Okay?" Pieter said as he moved to stand and leave.

"Okay, Pieter, whatever you say…and Pieter," Johnny called after him.

"Yes, Johnny?" Pieter replied, turning back to look at the bodyguard once more.

"It was good to see you again," Johnny said, smiling, as he dabbed a paper napkin at his watery eyes.

"Good to see you, too, Johnny," Pieter said with a nod before turning around and heading toward the back room where Margeurite and Izzy were waiting for him.

As he headed toward the door, Pieter thought twice about entering, and considered the fact that he'd chosen not to wear a Kevlar bulletproof vest. That might well have been a very poor choice on his part. Luckily, he didn't have to worry about making an entrance, as just before he reached the door, the young waitress walked out from behind the service area into his path. She was carrying a tray with two steaming cups of coffee on it, and she proceeded to knock twice on the door before it was opened from the inside. Pieter followed her into the room to be greeted loudly and jovially by Paolo, the owner whose daughter Pieter had rescued some years earlier. While Paolo was saying hello and making a fuss of someone he considered to be an old family friend, Margeurite and Izzy sat silently looking on and smiling politely. After a few minutes of welcoming, Paolo left them alone and closed the door behind him as he and the young waitress exited the room.

"Margeurite, Isabelle." Pieter nodded his hello as he sat down opposite the two of them at the large, round table.

"Hello, Pieter," Margeurite offered in return.

Isabelle merely glared at Pieter.

He could sense the animosity and hatred being directed at him by the younger of the two women, and wondered again if he should have worn a bulletproof vest. "So here we are. What would you two ladies like to talk about?" he asked, trying to break the ice.

"Well, first of all, I'm sure Isabelle would like to thank you for rescuing her, wouldn't you, Isabelle?" Margeurite said as she turned to look at her daughter sternly.

Izzy paused for a moment before breaking eye contact with Pieter to look at her mother, and realized that she was being chastised for being so rude. "Okay, thanks for the rescue, fang face," she said angrily, staring at him once more.

"Isabelle!" her mother scolded her.

"It's all right, Margeurite. Let Izzy get it off her chest," Pieter interjected, holding his palm up toward the older lady.

"I'll tell you what I want, you pale-faced fuck. I want to know what happened to my father and what you and my mother did to him." Izzy spat the words at him in her rage.

"Isabelle!" her mother exclaimed.

"Leave it, Margeurite. It's not a problem. After six hundred years, I've had worse insults than that, believe me," Pieter stated, trying to calm the situation down. He looked across at Izzy once more and calmly asked her, "So what do you know so far?"

"I know all the family secrets about your past and how old you are. I know you've been fighting the vampires for over six hundred years. I know you and my mother had an affair, that my father found out and that now he's dead because of the two of you," Izzy said, maintaining her anger.

"That's not fair, Isabelle. I never said we had an affair. I said we crossed a line," Margeurite replied defensively.

"I've had two days to think over what you told me, Mother, and it's what you didn't say that hit me the most, so you are hiding something. If you don't have anything to hide, then why have you waited two days to meet up and tell me the truth about what went on? The pair of you has obviously been talking behind my back, trying to get your story straight. That's the real reason for the delay and why you're both here to tell me the same lies, isn't it?" Izzy rambled on, almost at the point of rage.

Margeurite was about to say something again when Pieter raised his palm toward her once more, to interject and stop her.

He said, "Okay, Izzy, I understand where you are coming from, and how you could have misinterpreted things, the way they have played out, so I'll explain it all for you, then you'll understand. Firstly, the reason it has taken two days to get together for this meeting is because I've just returned from a trip to Hong Kong."

"Need a new iPad, did you?" Izzy said sarcastically.

"No, actually, I went to visit a guy called Charles or Charlie Wu, as he's known. You may have heard of him. He was Grace Tam's fiancé. He was also the guy who sold her into slavery, thinking she would be some rich Arabs plaything for the rest of her natural life. Instead, she was sold to an operator who supplies the Boston vampires with girls to be fed on."

Immediately after Pieter mentioned Grace, Izzy changed her attitude. Instead of glaring at him accusingly, her features softened and she dropped her head slightly to look down at her hands, which were now clasped together on the table-top. Margeurite sensed the change in her daughter's attitude and reached across to hold her daughter's hand to comfort her.

"What did you do to him?" Izzy asked in a slightly more subdued manner.

"I disposed of him, his lackey, his two bodyguards, and anyone else I came into contact through him, but not before I gathered enough intelligence on the operation they used, to be able to infiltrate it and bring it down."

There was a pause for a few moments; no one said anything.

Then Pieter shifted in his chair and started to explain what had happened with Izzy's father. "I had re-established closer links with your family a few generations earlier and got to know your father very well as he grew up. Not only was he a good businessman, but he was also a fiercely determined man in all that he did. When he lost his first wife to another man, it affected him very badly. Jean-Paul was of the opinion that Claudette had gone out looking for a lover on purpose, and then ran off when she'd found a suitable partner.

"Unfortunately, there are always two sides to an argument, and Claudette was simply lonely, stuck at home as she was while Jean-Paul travelled around on business and on secret hunter operations. He never told his first wife about his secret business of hunting vampires, and she thought his long, unexplained absences were liaisons with other women. In their final year together, Claudette almost left him twice, but he never noticed how unhappy and lonely she was. When she met a rich investment banker who had lost his own wife to cancer three years earlier, she simply clicked with someone equally as lonely. Your father turned very nasty for a while there, planning his revenge on the couple and trying to ruin her new man financially. All he achieved, however, was to push them closer together, causing the banker to retire early and live off his very substantial investments.

"Your mother came to Jean-Paul's attention some three or four years later. She was a very young and beautiful prize that your father wanted the moment he saw her. She wasn't just a society girl from a good family like Claudette; she was a successful businesswoman in her own right, and she matched your father in many ways, not least in her determination to get the job or the deal done. Jean-Paul chased your mother incessantly, showering her with expensive gifts, taking her out to all the new shows and social events. However, I think I'm right in saying your mother initially had reservations about entering into a relationship with Jean-Paul because of his drinking." Pieter paused a few moments to look across at Margeurite, who nodded her agreement at his outlining of the story. "Your mother may be quite a stubborn lady when she has to be, but I'm sure it's something she learned from your father when he took her under his wing, brought her on board with his own company, and mentored her. For her part, your mother got his drinking under control and made him a much more pleasant person to deal with. He was still as ruthless a businessman as ever, but now, he did it with a smile and a gift or two rather than with threats and intimidation. Your parents were seen as an idyllic couple, very much in love and very much in tune with each other. Your father made up for his mistakes in his first marriage and took my advice to bring your mother into his confidence on everything, including his work with the hunter organization, and eventually, he revealed my secrets to her as well.

"Margeurite took to military training like a proverbial duck to water, as the saying goes, and suddenly, this attractive, slim, and petite businesswoman was happily shooting crossbows and guns alike. In fact, as I recall, she was also pretty mean with a flamethrower and it was only the weight of the fuel tank that prevented her from using that weapon in an actual attack."

"You went on actual field missions?" Izzy said, looking shocked at the news of her mother's prowess.

"Yes, dear, I was a hunter, which, as you are well aware, meant we all went into battle together," her mother replied.

"Wow! I never knew. I thought you just did some of the training for show, but never actually did anything," said Izzy.

"Your mother was a well-respected hunter with a high sniper rating as well as being an expert in unarmed combat, as I recall," said Pieter. "In fact, it was her design that they manufactured into the current hunter ammunition. She had the idea of a softer outer shell that would split or splinter upon impact, with a dense core that would continue to penetrate. That gave the hunters a better chance of damaging the heart of the vampire they were shooting at and therefore immobilizing it. It's a shame that the bullets would never be accepted under the Geneva Convention, as technically, it's designed as an illegal 'dum-dum' bullet. Otherwise, you'd have become millionaires as arms dealers. Of course, if events should ever turn to an all-out war with the vampires, your family would be well positioned to quite literally make a killing."

"Okay, I get it, my mom became GI Jane. So what went wrong?" Izzy interrupted.

"Well, to be honest with you, Izzy…you did," Pieter said, holding her eye contact.

"What do you mean I did? What did I do?" Izzy demanded, raising her voice again.

"It's not what you did, Izzy," Pieter answered. "It's what changed after you were born. You see, once your mother fell pregnant with you, she suddenly changed from being this 'gung ho,' take-no-prisoners battler of the boardroom and battlefield, to a stay-at-home mother who devoted her life to looking after and protecting you. She no longer wanted to spend her time practicing shooting, fighting, or running over assault courses. She tried to encourage your father to settle down into more of an administrative role, too. Unfortunately, your father, being older, saw this as a challenge to his male virility, and so, instead of easing back to spend more time with you and your mother, he pushed himself more, trying to prove his worth. It's easy to look back on now and see the signs, but at the time, none of us did.

"He was getting old and slowing down, but simply wouldn't admit it to anyone, least of all to himself. As he began to spend more time away from home, he started drinking again, but this time, he hid it from those around him until it became a real problem. On one of his routine medicals, they picked up that he had cirrhosis of the liver due to his drinking. This led to a more thorough examination, where it was discovered that he was also suffering from advanced prostate cancer, which had metastasized to his bones in several locations. Again, he kept all of this information a secret from your mother, and knowing he faced a very uncertain time ahead, he threw himself into his work to secure yours and your mother's future.

"Your mother and father had initially fallen in love very quickly and your father had proposed while they were staying as guests at the chateau in the south of France. With the chateau holding so many special memories for them both, your father had eventually purchased the property and the surrounding winery as a surprise for your mother. From then on, every summer was spent there, enjoying the peace, quiet, and warm weather. It was also where I met up with your mother and father each year to bring them up to date on what I had been up to and to share intelligence on the vampire threat. The previous year, I'd been chasing vampires through both America and the Far East, mainly following old colonial links through Singapore and Hong Kong.

"Your father had only spent one weekend with us the whole of that holiday, which was the summer of 1985, just before your sixth birthday. Because of this, the three of us spent a great deal of time together without your father around. You were very bright and inquisitive, always asking me questions about this and that and my travels around the world. It was during this time we spent together that you took to calling me the 'Sunny Man' due to my pale skin when compared to your much darker, suntanned complexion, brought on by your virtually living in the pool during the day."

"I remember some of that time. Wasn't there a dog there somewhere?" Izzy chipped in.

"Yes, there was. It was a big German shepherd, as I recall," Margeurite confirmed.

"Her name was Bronny," Pieter told them. "The lady next door had gone out and brought the dog as a puppy without ever discussing such a thing with her partner. The dog had then wrecked all the landscaping the guy had done on their garden and pool surround, and that had signaled the start of the final deterioration in their relationship. The poor thing had been left at home alone a lot, as it was the guy's daughter who used to play with it the most. So when he and his daughter were asked to move out as the relationship ended, the dog had found a way through the fence to come and play with Izzy instead."

"I can remember how happy you were swimming from one side to the other, Isabelle, and how you laughed out loud as the dog chased around the pool, barking at you until you splashed water at her," Margeurite said, laughing at the memory.

"Yeah, and I can remember how happy you were when you found out the woman next door hadn't even bothered to toilet train the dog and it happily squatted down anywhere it pleased, leaving you the mess to clean up," Izzy said, warming to the conversation.

"Thank you for reminding me," Margeurite said with obvious disgust.

Pieter paused for a few moments, letting the pleasant and not so pleasant, but still funny, memories float around in the minds of the two women. Knowing as he did that the next phase of his recollection would soon put a "damper" on their collective mood, he wanted them to enjoy the memories a little longer.

Then Pieter began telling the story of that fateful evening...

Chapter Forty One

Family

The story began as they were returning home after a session of drinks with a few of the local neighbors. The evening had been going well, until the woman next door had become a little bit too merry on her red wine and started moaning about the situation she'd got herself into with her ex. As Margeurite was one of the few people to bother to hear the other side of the story from the guy concerned, she knew he'd ended the relationship when it was clear that the woman was never going to accept his daughter, and had abused her during their time together. Anyway, rather than listen to anymore of her drunken self-pity, they had made their excuses and left, saying that they had to get Isabelle to bed.

Isabelle had been experiencing problems sleeping in the summer heat and was always getting out of bed and asking for a glass of water to cool down. Pieter was always up late, reading by the moonlight on the verandah, so Isabelle always came out to ask him for the drink. On this occasion, Margeurite had fallen asleep in the hammock next to Pieter's chair, as the wine they had consumed at the neighbors' took its toll on her. About an hour after she had been put to bed, Isabelle came out complaining about the heat and laid down on Pieter's lap, only to fall asleep against his cooler body temperature.

The line Margeurite said they had crossed was when they started to act like a family in her husband's absence, as unknown to them, Jean-Paul was heading down toward the chateau with a vampire trussed up in the boot of his car that very night. He arrived without warning at about three o'clock in the morning. He knew Pieter's habits well enough that he would be occupying his usual place, reading out on the verandah, underneath the grape vines. As he'd raced around to see Pieter and get his help transferring the vampire from the boot of his car, down to the cellars, he wasn't expecting to see both his wife lying asleep next to him or his daughter curled up in his arms.

The hunter group he controlled had captured the inexperienced, youngling vampire who had been feeding on backpacker tourists in Paris about a week earlier. Rather than slay the vampire after a brief bout of questioning, as was usual, Jean-Paul had decided to bring her with him, down to the chateau. Pieter had always presumed Jean-Paul had wanted to question her more. Maybe he thought Pieter could get more information out of her, or the two of them would be able to fool her into thinking Pieter was a senior vampire and force her to reveal more about her own clan, or at least the vampire who had sired her. Pieter was never really sure, as the reasons were never discussed between them.

Pieter carefully lifted Isabelle off his lap and laid her down in the hammock next to her mother, then proceeded to join Jean-Paul in the front driveway. They took the vampire down into the cellars together and secured her in place. Jean-Paul had obviously thought about what he was going to do to some extent, as he had bought the chains and equipment he required to keep the vampire held in captivity with him in the car. Luckily, the chateau lent itself perfectly to the cause with the many cellar rooms available underneath the main house.

Jean-Paul then instructed Pieter not to disturb either Margeurite or Isabelle, as he claimed he was tired from the long journey down from his office in Paris. He said he would catch up with them in the morning, after some much-needed rest. So Pieter returned to his chair and continued to read, with Margeurite and Isabelle sleeping peacefully next to him. The last thing Pieter heard from Jean-Paul that night was the distant "clinking" sound of him replacing the stopper in the brandy decanter before he ascended the stairs on the east wing. Pieter thought nothing of this act, as Jean-Paul's breath had given off no trace of any alcohol upon his arrival.

The next morning, as Isabelle awoke, Pieter sent her up to her father's room, telling her there was a surprise waiting for her there. She immediately guessed that her father was home again, and ran off as quickly as she could to find him. However, when she reached his room and failed to find him there, she went searching for him, racing down the west staircase on the opposite side of the house. Pieter had failed to hear Jean-Paul go down that side of the house some time during the early hours of the morning and had not heard any sort of commotion to alert him as to what had occurred.

In her excitement to find her father, Isabelle had gone all the way down to the cellars, thinking he was playing hide and seek with her. As she ran around from one room to the next, calling out for him excitedly, Pieter had mistaken the level of the house she was calling from. He'd known Jean-Paul's room was at the far end of the west wing and knew that was the direction the calls had come from. The vampire girl chained at the neck was also aware of the little voice calling out in each room, and although somewhat inexperienced, she planned an escape for herself.

Reaching over, the vampire grabbed Jean-Paul's lifeless body and heaved him up to a standing position with his back toward the door. She quickly wrapped his arms over her shoulders and hugged him close, as if they were embracing each other. As she saw the door handle start to depress from the outside, she began to talk in gentle tones.

"But of course I will. There's nothing I'd like more than to meet your wife and daughter."

Isabelle was completely fooled by the scene in front of her. Being so small, and with the angle the vampire held her dead father, she couldn't see the collar and chain around her neck, securing her to the back wall. All she saw was the back of her father as he appeared to be hugging and chatting to some lady friend. Isabelle ran up to him excitedly, wrapping her arms around his legs to surprise him.

"Got you, Papa," she squealed.

"No, actually, I got you, little 'un," the vampire stated coldly as she dropped Jean-Paul's lifeless body to the floor and grabbed Isabelle by one arm roughly.

Isabelle screamed in shock at being grabbed so suddenly, and then kept screaming even more as she caught sight of her father's pale face and the blank stare of his eyes. Pieter reacted immediately. Where he'd mistaken her location before as he heard her moving around at the other end of the house, this time, the echo of the empty cellar room left him in no doubt where she was.

"Jean-Paul came home early this morning and brought a vampire with him that we locked in the cellar. That's where Izzy's scream just came from," Pieter shouted as he ran past Margeurite, who was just coming back out to the verandah after making herself a cup of coffee.

As he ran down the stone steps, Pieter heard Margeurite's coffee cup smash on the floor as she, too, quite literally dropped everything to assist. Pieter sprinted up the long corridor as fast as he could and burst through the three-quarter open doorway to the cellar room. The door smashed against the wall noisily as he did so. The vampire was hugging Isabelle with the young girls back close to and protecting her own chest. One arm was held tightly around her infant waist while the other hand was holding her by the throat, seemingly ready to rip the soft flesh apart.

"That's close enough, 'fanks,' mate," she said seriously.

Pieter stopped in his tracks and raised his hands in a show of submission to her demand.

"Now, if you don't 'wont' this little cherub of yours to get 'er 'froat' ripped out, you better slide them keys to this 'ere collar over to me pretty quick smart," the vampire instructed.

"That's not a French accent, young lady; that's more 'South London innit' loike… Are you over here on holiday?" Pieter asked, trying to play for more time while he worked out how he was going to get Isabelle safely out of her grasp. He could see no other option but to give her the keys and remove Isabelle from immediate danger, as the vampire would need both her hands to be able to undo the padlock using the key. Just before he threw them across to her, however, he twisted the key he knew was the one on the bunch the vampire required to unlock her restraints. It wasn't much of a twist, just a little one, but hopefully large enough to cause the vampire a complication in her use of the key to open the lock. Pieter hoped he would then be able to use the distraction to get Isabelle free from her clutches. He was just about to make his move when Margeurite came running into the room. Pieter had been aware of her slowly and almost silently creeping down the corridor behind him, but for some reason, she now chose to reveal herself and came running into the room.

Upon seeing her daughter, Margeurite started to run forward toward her.

The vampire pulled Isabelle back in close to her body as a human shield and placed her hand around the young girl's throat once more.

"Don't hurt my baby, please, don't hurt my baby," Margeurite cried as she suddenly halted, adopting the same stance as Pieter had earlier with her hands up, displaying her empty palms to the creature holding her daughter.

"Back up, lady, get back wiv' yer' 'usband and the nipper'll be awright," the vampire instructed in her South London accent.

Margeurite did as she was told, bringing her hands up to her mouth as if to stifle a cry. The vampire, judging that there was enough space between them all, pushed Izzy to the ground in front of her and placed one of her feet on her back to stop her from crawling away to safety.

"You just stay there little 'un, while I get this 'fing' off me neck," said the vampire as she kept a close eye on both Pieter and Margeurite.

It was then that Pieter noticed the automatic pistol sticking out of the waistband at the back of Margeurite's three-quarter length denim jeans. Suddenly, he realized what Margeurite had planned; she had run into the room in front of him so she could pass him the concealed weapon with which to deal with the vampire. He figured she had already cocked the weapon and removed the safety catch, so all he had to do was withdraw it, aim, and fire it into the vampire's chest once Isabelle was clear of the target. The moment the vampire took her eyes off them to start working on the lock, Pieter acted. His right hand darted forward and wrapped around the pistol grip as he withdrew it from Margeurite's waistband. Leveling it and aiming it in an instant, he fired off two shots in quick succession. Both bullets hit their target in the middle of the vampire's chest and she crumpled to the ground, immobilized.

Izzy had screamed, putting both her hands up to cover her ears and protect her delicate hearing from the loud, cracking noise. Within a couple of seconds, Margeurite had scooped her up into her arms and was taking her out of the cellar room as quickly as she could. Pieter quickly checked Jean-Paul's body for a pulse, but he already knew just from the pallor of his skin that his friend was dead. Pieter then spent about an hour hacking the young vampire's head off and then chopping the body up into small enough parts that could be burnt on the brazier he set up at one end of the estate.

When he returned to the main house some time later, Isabelle was still inconsolable, and he suggested a trip into town, to the local doctor and chemist, for a sedative would be in order. Margeurite agreed, but didn't want to leave her daughter or drag her out of the house in such a state. So it was agreed that Pieter would go into town and get the prescription from the family doctor, then go to the pharmacy and return home as soon as he could. With Jean-Paul's car blocking the main garage, Pieter waived at the winery manager as he was about to jump into his own car. After a quick chat with the man, he confirmed that he was going into town and would be able to give Pieter a lift.

About half an hour after Pieter had left the house, Isabelle began to settle down, and shortly after, both she and her mother fell asleep together on the big, four-poster bed. After about an hour or so of fitful sleep, Margeurite felt a cool hand on her left shoulder. The hand slowly traced a line down her upper arm and then came back up again. Margeurite smiled in her half asleep, half awake state. She didn't want to wake up, but knew she should at the insistence of Pieter's cool hand. Then the hand slowly slid back down again, but this time, it angled more toward her front and caressed the side of her breast.

"Pieter!" Margeurite exclaimed angrily in hushed tones as she shrugged her shoulder.

Then the hand suddenly grabbed her upper arm and swung her over and onto her back roughly. Within a moment, she was pinned to the bed with the full weight of her dead husband covering her. Izzy screamed again as she awoke to the horrible scene beside her. Jean-Paul slapped her across the face with his left hand, intending only to shut her up, but instead sending her sprawling across to the other side of the room, unconscious.

"Isabelle!" Margeurite screamed as she saw her daughter being hit and then flying off to lie crumpled and motionless on the floor.

Jean-Paul grabbed her by the chin and twisted her head to look at him. "Don't be worrying about her, my dear. Worry about yourself. Initially, I thought about turning you, too, so we could be together forever, but now I think my hunger has gotten the better of me and…well, maybe we should just do lunch," he menacingly as he opened his mouth and bared his fangs at her.

Margeurite tried to slap and punch his face in an effort to gain some leverage to get out from under him, but it was no use. He was both too strong and too well positioned on top of her. Then Jean-Paul started to rip at her clothes, as she continued to try to struggle against him, to little or no avail.

"Ha, you treacherous bitch, you liked the cool hands stroking up and down your arm when you thought it was your half-vampire lover, didn't you? Now it's your vampire husband, you aren't so keen, are you, bitch?! *Are you?!*" Jean-Paul shouted angrily into her face.

Margeurite ceased to struggle as Jean-Paul grabbed her, placing each of his hands on the sides of her face as he leaned forward to look directly into her eyes. As she was forced to look up at him, she saw the crimson eyes blazing back at her and noticed the protruding canine teeth extending down from his top dentition.

"I'm going to feed on you until you die looking into my eyes. Then I'm going to turn our daughter into a vampire, just like me, and the two of us will live forever while you rot away in your grave, you adulterous cow," he said, sneering into her face.

She shot both of her hands toward his face and slammed her thumbs forcefully into the inside corner of each of his eyes. Then she dragged them both outward, scratching the nails across the eye surface. Jean-Paul screamed in anger and rage, releasing his hold on her face and twisted his body over to his right to escape the pain. Margeurite seized her opportunity and twisted her body below him to throw him off to the side. Jean-Paul fell off the bed to the floor, momentarily dazed. Margeurite rolled to her right and scrambled off the other side of the bed. Quickly, she started looking for a weapon to use, but there was only a stool by her dressing table, which she picked up, ready to use to fend off his next attack.

"You fucking whore! You think your little scratches will hold me back? I'm a vampire now. I can almost see already, and in a moment, my eyes will be healed and then you will be mine," Jean-Paul hissed at her.

Seeing her off to his left, on the other side of the bed, Jean-Paul leapt up onto the mattress and skipped forward to land on the floor in front of her. Margeurite swung her arms in a horizontal circle from right to left, hoping to hit him and topple him sideways. Jean-Paul anticipated the movement and caught the stool with one hand. Twisting the stool in his grip, he loosened her hold on it and simply tossed it aside. Then springing forward, he caught her off guard with his speed and grabbed Margeurite's wrist. Immediately, Margeurite swung her right fist toward his face, but Jean-Paul caught it in mid-flight. Holding her by both a wrist and around her clenched fist, Jean-Paul knew exactly what move she would attempt to extricate herself with next, and just as she began to change her stance to put all of her weight on her left foot and bring her right knee up to his crotch, he squeezed. He exerted all the pressure he could with his right hand, crushing the two bones in her left forearm. Margeurite yelped in pain and sank to her knees on the floor.

"That's more like it. On your knees and beg for my forgiveness," Jean-Paul said gleefully, knowing he now had her subdued and at his mercy.

Margeurite began to sob from both the pain and hopelessness of her situation.

Jean-Paul sank down on his knees in front of her and pulled her right hand up to his mouth. She could do nothing but watch as he smiled wickedly at her, his crimson eyes seeming to shine brightly now. He licked her wrist, a long, slow, lingering movement of his tongue, leaving a trail of saliva glistening on the surface of her skin. Then he peeled his lips back and opened his mouth to fully reveal his fangs.

Just then, Margeurite suddenly straightened herself up and spoke to him with no small amount of venom. "You are a stupid, jealous fool, Jean-Paul. Go to hell.

.　.　.

Pieter was just about to get in the car with the vineyard manager when he spotted his neighbor coming out of the vet opposite. Knowing it was out of the manager's way to return him back to the chateau, he decided to ask her if she was going back home, and if so, could he catch a lift with her. Luckily, she was taking her dog, Bronny, back home after the latest checkup with the vet. Unfortunately, a few months earlier, she'd accidentally run over the dog, damaging her nose and face, which had required surgery. During the journey back, Pieter made a comment about veterinary bills being expensive, and the neighbor had joked that she'd conned the money out of her new boyfriend by crying poor again.

Pieter had picked up on the "again" part of that comment, but said nothing more about it, due to the fact she was sitting there reeking of the sweat and perspiration of yet another man upon her and it was not her latest boyfriend. Pieter had previously seen her car parked at a local out-of-the-way and discreet guest house called Le Gilston Retreat, as he'd travelled along the seldom used backroads to the chateau. He had a habit of using a different route in all of his journeys back to the estate, for security reasons, and her car was easily identifiable with its big black bull bar on the front, of the silver four wheel drive. Later that same evening when socializing with the neigbours, the then boyfriend had confirmed that he believed she was away on a business trip. With his acute vampire senses Pieter had often picked up the woman was lying in her everyday conversations with friends at social gatherings, especially when talking about her ex sending her broke and stealing all her money. She made up stories about the ex being the one to initiate expensive renovation projects on her house, and even though all her friends knew her to be both determined and single minded, they chose to believe her lies. Pieter never felt it was his job to tip off the old or the new boyfriend that he knew she was lying. She was, he felt, heading down her own path of self-destruction, and nothing he said would have convinced either guy as to what was really going on. More importantly, how could he explain such a thing, without revealing he was part vampire and had special senses that had detected the lies.

As soon as they were close enough to the chateau for her to drop him off, he asked her to pull over, saying the exercise of the walk back through the vineyard would be good for him. The real reason for wanting out of the vehicle was that he'd picked up another more subtle scent on the woman, it was the unmistakable smell of a cancer growing inside her. He knew what she was like, and how she had treated others around her, so he felt no compunction to hint at her getting a check-up. In her own way she was a vampire of sorts, taking what she could from others around her without a care for the consequences. He was happy to see the back of her, as she drove away.

Where Pieter had been glad for the lift, he was even more grateful that the journey had been a short one, he disliked spending time with such false people. Besides, in the social situations that he had attended, he had always found her ex-partner to be a likeable and honest fellow, who Pieter felt certainly deserved much better than her.

It only took him two to three minutes of brisk walking through the estate before he stepped onto the verandah. He quietly walked into the east wing of the house, not wanting to disturb the girls if Margeurite had managed to calm Izzy down enough to get her to sleep. He was glad to be out of the sun and into the cooler shade of the house. Then just as he was about to sort out the sedative he'd purchased in town, he smelled it, and the hairs on the back of his neck stood up. The scent was unmistakable, the deathly smell of a newly sired vampire. Pieter knew there was nothing quite like the smell; it was a weird combination of rotting human flesh and developing vampire flesh. There was only one thing that made that awful smell go away, and that was feeding. Once newly sired vampires fed for the first time, their recuperative powers start to work in full and the rotting human smell was cast off. Right now, the smell was so strong that it was almost burning at his more sensitive nostrils.

Suddenly, he heard a scream; it was from Isabelle. He judged that it came from up in the direction of the room he'd left her and her mother in. Pieter quickly removed his shoes, but kept his socks on, so his feet wouldn't clatter, or slap on the floor, and give his movements away. Then he sped as quickly as he could along the corridor, to the crossed swords and the shield on display there. He silently removed one of the swords, and then bounded up the stairs toward the room he suspected would be where they were gathered. As he crept silently along the corridor, he picked up on the conversation between the vampire that had been Jean-Paul and Margeurite. He heard the hatred in Jean-Paul's voice and the threats of how he intended to turn Isabelle.

Now he knew he had to be careful and move as silently as possible, or Jean-Paul would be sure to attack Margeurite and kill her before he had a chance to act. He heard the struggle on the bed as he reached the halfway point along the upper corridor. Then he heard Jean-Paul twist the stool out of Margeurite's grasp and throw it away as he reached the three-quarter point. Just as he reached the open door, he heard the two bones in Margeurite's forearm, the radius and the ulna, snap under the pressure exerted by Jean-Paul's grip.

Pieter slowly entered the room behind Jean-Paul as the new vampire knelt down in front of his wife and began to lick at her wrist, in an attempt to further extend his pleasure and her torment. As Jean-Paul drew back his lips and bared his fangs, ready to bite deeply into his wife's wrist, she calmly looked up into his face once more. Just then, his newly acquired vampire senses kicked in to warn him—someone in the room suddenly smelled like a German shepherd dog.

Jean-Paul hardly heard his wife spit out her reply to him as he turned to look behind. No sooner had Margeurite said her final goodbye of "Go to hell," than Pieter swung the sword across Jean-Paul's neck and severed his head from his body. There was no great spray of blood, just a kneeling, upright body that seemed to topple sideways in slow motion as the head bounced a couple of times on the polished wooden floor and came to lie by the side of the wardrobe in the corner of the room. The eyes stared off blankly into the distance, and for the second time in the last twenty-four hours, Jean-Paul Lancar died.

Margeurite quickly ran over to her daughter, struggling to pick her up and cradle her with her broken forearm. Pieter dropped the sword and hurried to assist her. Luckily, Isabelle soon recovered consciousness and was only a little concussed.

"After a brief discussion on what to do, your mother and I decided to set fire to the chateau and make your father's death look like an accident. Once that was done, the two of you stayed in a local hotel for a few days and then returned to Paris, where your mother dealt with your father's affairs and sold all the businesses. With my help, she then relocated the two of you over to America, where you grew up to become the woman you are today," Pieter concluded.

"Initially, we stayed close to our hunter friends who had relocated to the United States, but eventually, I managed to break away from them and tried to give you a normal life," Margeurite added.

"And then, being the stubborn, foolish, little madam that I am, I rekindled all those contacts through college and got roped into being a hunter, too," Izzy said with a sigh.

"I never wanted the life of a hunter for you, Isabelle. I wanted to protect you from all the horror, pain, and misery that come with anything to do with vampires," Margeurite said as the tears began to build up in her eyes.

"I know, Mother, I know," Izzy said, reaching across to embrace her mother.

"Pieter, I never thanked you enough for being there for us, either. Can you ever forgive me for ignoring you for all of these years and having nothing to do with you?" Margeurite asked.

"I never blamed you for wanting out of the situation you were in, and I actually admired you for trying to protect Izzy from it all. So you don't have to apologize for anything Margeurite," Pieter said softly.

"But you've been alone for so long. I knew how much your time with us meant to you. We were the only ones to give you a family to be a part of, and we took it away from you," said Margeurite.

"Like you always say, though, I'm part vampire and people always die around vampires, so I understood your reasons."

Izzy pushed back her chair and broke away from her mother as she stood up. She pulled an automatic pistol out of her pocket and looked at it for a moment, and then at Pieter.

Margeurite was frozen in her chair and powerless to act; Pieter just stood still, watching her.

"I came here to get some answers and I fully intended to put some bullets into you to get those answers. Now, after what I've heard and piecing the bits of my memory together, I know that you are not the bad guy here, and I owe you every bit as much as my mother." Izzy placed the gun on the table. She then walked over to Pieter. As the tears started to form in her eyes once more, she opened up her arms then wrapped them around his body, as he wrapped his arms around her to returned her embrace. As Izzy pulled herself in toward him, she squeezed him tightly.

Margeurite pushed back her own chair and quickly joined them, spreading her arms around both of them as Pieter's arms also embraced them both for a group hug. Pieter had to be careful not to break their ribs with the sudden wave of emotion he was feeling, and as both women shed copious amounts of tears, he attempted to hide the fact that his eyes were leaking a little, too. He now felt that he had a family to be close to again, and with it, a link to the real world once more. While these joyful emotions of belonging were a very welcome feeling for him to be experiencing again, he couldn't help, but think about his past and how every time he got involved with a human family, someone always ended up dying. Maybe this time, with all that he had learned over the last six hundred years, he would be able to protect them and keep them all safe. Maybe.

Book One

Epilogue

A yellow New York taxi pulled up at the main entrance to a large house and a powerfully built man, seemingly in his late thirties or early forties, climbed out of the back. The driver rushed around and struggled to remove the man's large suitcase and smaller briefcase from the car trunk. The man was well dressed in an expensive suit and was wearing dark aviator-style sunglasses. He paid the taxi driver, who was of scruffy, Middle Eastern appearance, in cash with a large tip included. The driver happily got back into the taxi and drove off, smiling broadly. The man then casually and easily lifted both his suitcase and briefcase, and turned to walk into the building.

Upon entering the building, the man placed his bags down beside the entrance and walked along the main corridor, unchallenged by the many men and women moving around, seemingly busy with their jobs of preparing for some kind of meeting. Another man of similar appearance, stood in the middle of a large hall, being set out with row upon row of chairs, but no tables. This second man had his back to the main entrance to the hall, and was busy directing those around him in a stern, commanding voice.

"Ah, Thomas, how goes the preparations for tomorrow's meeting?" the powerfully built man asked as he entered the hall and removed his sunglasses. His voice boomed out and all present stopped to turn and look at him.

The man called Thomas, recognizing the voice, immediately turned around. "Lord Dimitri!" he exclaimed. "My apologies, my lord. I was not informed that you had arrived, or I would have come to meet you myself," Chancellor Thomas said quickly, scampering toward the man and bowing deeply in front of his vampire master.

All the others present immediately adopted an equally reverent bow toward the man identified as their lord and master. They remained in this position, awaiting leave to return to their tasks at hand. All were well versed in the etiquette required to greet the third oldest vampire in the known world.

"No matter, Thomas. I thought I'd surprise you and check up on how all the preparations are coming along," Lord Dimitri said as he looked around at the grand hall.

"Well, as you can see, my lord, the hall is set up and ready for the council meeting," Thomas replied proudly.

"Indeed it is. Please have your staff continue," Lord Dimitri acknowledged, instructing Thomas to have his work party return to their other preparations.

Chancellor Thomas simply clapped his hands twice as he looked around the room, and all present returned to making themselves look as busy as they could. None dared to look at Lord Dimitri, for as one of the three remaining ruling vampire lords, his word was law and to upset him would have the most dire of consequences.

"The teams of young-lings have been trained in the etiquette required to serve all the vampire lords and senior council members, and there are sufficient numbers of them to be able to clear the room for the festivities after the meeting within ten minutes," Chancellor Thomas explained.

"Ten minutes, you say," Lord Dimitri pointed out as he raised an eyebrow in Thomas's direction.

"Yes, my lord. Our best rehearsal time is seven minutes and twenty-three seconds, but I thought it prudent to add a minute or two, as one or two of the senior council members may get in the way of the staff and so delay them momentarily," Chancellor Thomas responded.

"Yes, I think that is wise, considering the fact that the lords and ladies of Europe and Asia will no doubt continue to look down on our American clan as being the underlings, and not worthy of a position in the council," Lord Dimitri confirmed.

"You expect trouble, my lord?"

"No, nothing so brazen and open, Thomas. There will be minor insults to our clan and such like, but the other two lords will have briefed all their attending council members to be on their best behavior. The last thing the other two want is to accidently start another clan war, not while we are having problems with the hunters. No, they will use this meeting as an opportunity to view my position here in America and gauge the strength I have in numbers, and then once the hunters are dealt with and are no longer a threat, then they will make their move against me."

"Would it not be better to act against them now, my lord, while they are all gathered here together?"

"Indeed it would, Thomas, but with all three vampire rulers giving their word that no harm shall fall upon any vampire attending this meeting and extending their protection for a period of one week to either side of the meeting, I would be stupid to choose to act now, as to do so would unite the whole vampire world against me. No, the time is not yet right to take such overt action. Now is the time to move the pieces around the chessboard and position ourselves to take advantage of any future developments or actions against us."

"I bow to your superior wisdom in such matters, my lord," Thomas affirmed with another slight nod of his head.

"Now, enough of such matters, Thomas. Take me through the buffet arrangements," Lord Dimitri instructed, changing the subject.

"Ah! Now here is where I hope I can truly satisfy my lord's curiosity and provide something appropriately special. Please come this way, my lord," Thomas stated enthusiastically, indicating the direction he wished to take his vampire master.

Just outside the hall and back down the corridor toward the main entrance, there was a large side room on the right. The two men entered and Thomas explained the workings of the room. There were eight tables in the room; four were positioned on each side of the room. All of them had a set of foot stocks at one end and could be tilted up to almost vertical with the stocks at the upper end. Each table was fitted with a motor, which could be set to cause the tabletop to vibrate at different levels of intensity. Thomas took great delight in explaining the workings of the system he had personally devised to Lord Dimitri.

The captive humans were held in the cells down below this very room and could be accessed by the stairwell at the far end of the room. The cellar below not only included the eight cells set apart for the eight different blood groups but also included a large furnace for the destruction of the human corpse once drained. The human was simply dragged up to the room with their hands secured behind their back. They would then be laid out on the table and the feet were secured in the foot stocks. A large gauge cannula would then be inserted into each of the human's carotid arteries by direct puncture. The cannula was then secured in position and connecting tubing attached to collect the outflow of blood. The blood was directed to a warmer system before being deposited into the thermal flasks that kept it at the correct temperature before the young-ling servant waiters took it out to distribute among the guests. To improve the blood flow during draining, the table would be tilted to maximize venous blood return to the heart by gravity, and this could be further improved with the table vibration system, causing involuntary muscle contraction, which would again assist venous return to the heart.

The young-lings being used as waiters and waitresses were all completely familiar with the setup and how everything was to work on the night. They were also in no doubt about what would happen to them should they mix up the blood groupings and contaminate the thermal urns they were to use to distribute the blood. Dimitri had been most impressed with the design Thomas had implemented, and congratulated him on his organizational skills, as well as his ingenuity. Thomas further confirmed that should any of the guests prefer to take a more personal approach in the selection and procurement of their nutritional needs, then he had several more senior younglings who were trained to assist the council members and guide them through the selection process in the cellar below. Furthermore, the rooms lining the opposite side of the corridor were set up to contain small booths for the senior council members' use for feeding purposes. The vampires who had accepted Lord Dimitri's hospitality and were staying in the rooms above the great hall were to be given the opportunity to select their humans, who would then be made available to them when they were required. Those who had chosen to find their own accommodation were obviously responsible for their own dining arrangements outside of the meeting.

As he concluded the tour of the draining room, Thomas asked Lord Dimitri, "Would you care to select from the refreshments available now, my lord, and at the same time make your choice for tomorrow night?"

"Thank you, Thomas. But, no, I have more pressing matters to attend to. I'm sure you have plenty of the type of stock I prefer stored away down in the cellar, so I'll sort something out tomorrow as I require it. Thank you for the offer, though. And once again, I congratulate you on your organization. I look forward to showing those snotty 'mainlanders' how we young Americans do things our way."

"I feel any failure to impress will be borne solely from their bigotry toward us and not from lack of effort on our part, my lord," Thomas interjected.

"Agreed, Thomas. Now, I must take my leave, I have other matters to attend to before tomorrow. I take it you have a car and driver available for me, and can have my bag there taken to my room?"

"Indeed I do, my lord. And I will ensure your bag is unpacked, and your clothing and robe are prepared for the meeting."

Thomas then signaled to two other pale-looking men to attend to him and instructed one to bring the car to the front and to take Lord Dimitri where he required, remaining at his disposal. The other, he gave instructions toward taking Lord Dimitri's bag to the room prepared for him. Thomas then quickly informed Dimitri that his own personal valet would take care of the unpacking and the preparations ready for Lord Dimitri's return and the council meeting the following day. Once everything was organized and the staff had departed to carry out their appointed tasks, Lord Dimitri turned and spoke to the chancellor in more hushed tones.

"One other thing, Thomas…" Dimitri said.

"Yes, my lord?" Thomas answered attentively.

"I will require the use of your office for a private meeting after the main council meeting. Attending will be myself, Lord Vladimir, Lady Guinilla, and one other, who, I'm led to believe, will be the head of the Scarlatti family," Dimitri replied, holding eye contact with Chancellor Thomas.

"A Scarlatti! Here in America? For what purpose, and what does this mean?" Thomas said in shocked tones.

"I know not, Thomas, but I'm sure we'll find out tomorrow. Make the arrangements, will you?" Dimitri added dismissively as he walked back up the main corridor, replaced his sunglasses, and stepped out into the daylight.

"Yes, my lord. As you wish," Chancellor Thomas replied, still shocked at what Dimitri told him. He then almost ran up the stairs to the next level and burst into his own office, where one of his subordinates sat reading. "Jasper, I need you to organize something for me tomorrow after the meeting."

"What is it you require, master?" the subordinate asked.

"There will be a second meeting to be held here in my office with the three vampire lords and one of the cursed Scarlattis." Thomas almost spat the last name out.

"Who are the Scarlattis?" Jasper questioned.

"The Scarlattis, my young protégé, are the only family of vampires in existence—the only Sicilian family of vampires in existence, to be more correct."

"So what are they, some kind of vampire mafia?" Jasper asked jokingly.

Thomas stopped staring off into space and turned to stare directly into the eyes of the very young-looking vampire next to him.

The Scarlattis were the only Sicilians, ever allowed to be sired. It was always thought that with their family honor code, the Sicilians and their mafia organization would be too dangerous to be brought into the vampire clans for fear of them taking one over and the whole thing getting out of hand. The Scarlattis have only one function within the vampire clans—they are raised to become vampires, but before they can become one, they are first trained to be assassins. They are, to put it into its most basic terms, the executioners or the hit men of the vampire world, and one of them is coming here tomorrow.

. . .

This story will be continued in **The Unsired: Vampire Lords.**

For more information regarding the author, Lee Duke, The Unsired series, and other writing projects (both completed and at the planning stage), please go to…

theunsired.com